PROMIS

Charlotte Moore grew up in Sussex and now lives there with her husband and their two sons. She has a degree in English from Oxford University and in Art History from London University and until recently taught at Westminster School. She now reviews in *The Times*, and the *Spectator* and has contributed articles to a number of publications including the *Independent on Sunday* and the *Daily Telegraph*, in addition to writing fiction. *Promises Past* is her first novel.

'Charlotte Moore's descriptions of the countryside in an idyllic summer are so evocative one can almost smell the flowers. Her portrayal of a close-knit community, with its love and illicit desires played out against a rural background has a Shakespearean quality to it which adds to the enchantment . . . Promises Past is a talented first novel of great promise.'

Titia Sutherland

For Min

PROMISES PAST

Charlotte Moore

ARROW

First published in Arrow in 1995

1 3 5 7 9 10 8 6 4 2

This edition published in 1995 by Arrow,
Random House UK Limited,
20 Vauxhall Bridge Road, London SW1V 2SA

Random House Australia (Pty) Limited
20 Alfred Street, Milsons Point, Sydney,
New South Wales 2061, Australia

Random House New Zealand Limited
18 Poland Road, Glenfield
Auckland 10, New Zealand

Random House South Africa (Pty) Limited
PO Box 337, Bergvlei, South Africa

Random House UK Limited Reg. No. 954009

Papers used by Random House UK Limited are natural, recyclable products
made from wood grown in sustainable forests. The manufacturing processes
conform to the environmental regulations of the country of origin.

ISBN 0 09 955341 4

Typeset by Deltatype Ltd, Ellesmere Port, Wirral
Printed and bound in Great Britain by
Cox & Wyman Ltd, Reading Berks

ACKNOWLEDGEMENTS

Many thanks are due to Sarah Molloy, my literary agent; to Mary Loring, my editor; to Elspeth Sinclair for copy-editing and for her initial encouragement; to Delia Bettger for looking after my children; and above all to my husband Min for his unfailing help and support.

Know that Love is careless child
    And forgets promise past;
He is blind, he is deaf when he list
    And in faith never fast

Sir Walter Ralegh

CHAPTER ONE

It was the last Saturday before Christmas. All over South London tempers were frayed. Butchers had muddled their orders, toy shops had sold out of the right kind of batteries, traffic stood nose to tail all the way along the arterial road that runs through Clapham and Balham. Huge teenagers sauntered in and out of the traffic, treating the road as an outsize playground; log-jammed cars posed no threat. The sky was thick and grey, the wind was keen. In the markets, vendors' fingers, raw and swollen, protruded from their black mittens like dirty cocktail sausages; on the commons older children tangled their kites in trees whilst toddlers, immobilised in snow suits and gloves and wellingtons, howled with frustration and cold and boredom. From overhead came the rescuing cry of wild geese flying in formation.

Adrian Stanhope, stuck in the traffic on the edge of his particular common, heard the cry, and wondered idly if the geese should be doing that at this time of year. He couldn't remember. He had once been a keen member of the Young Ornithologists' Club, but that was a long time ago, and now he was anxious to get back home to put his cratefuls of champagne on ice. The Stanhopes didn't often drink champagne, but tonight they were holding a party, a combined Christmas and house-cooling party. Immediately before Christmas they were moving to the country, and Adrian was going to become a commuter.

Adrian had lowered his window because the car had got so steamed up inside. The rawness of the air was like a slap in the face; almost pleasurable at first, but soon the cold began to hurt. Perhaps Sarah had been right; she had wanted mulled wine. He had stuck out for champagne, saying it would be less trouble. He never really liked the way bits of stick and peel and things kept bumping against your lips when you drank mulled wine. Sarah had said that champagne would actually be just as much trouble, because they'd have to fill a bath with ice to chill it. And now it looked as though he'd be so late back she'd be right – it wouldn't chill in time. Oh well. Thank goodness she'd submitted to the dictates of common sense and let caterers organise the food.

A rap on the windscreen broke Adrian's reverie. He started when he saw the two black boys, about fifteen years old, gesticulating at him. They wore hooded sweatshirts but no coats or jackets; they must have been freezing but they didn't show it. They obviously wanted to say something to him. Was he about to be mugged? That really would be ironic, to be mugged for the first time only days before abandoning South London for ever. Adrian hesitated. They looked harmless enough. Where was his bloody Christmas spirit, anyway? He lowered his window again.

'Merry Christmas, mister,' said one of the boys. 'Want your windscreen washed? We'll do it for fifty p.'

'Sure, go ahead.' Fifty pence! It was amazing that anyone would still do anything for fifty pence. The operation took about fifteen seconds. Adrian handed the smaller boy a pound coin, and said, 'Keep the change. Merry Christmas.'

The boys grinned and made some kind of valedictory gesture. The traffic had begun to move a little. Adrian lurched forward, feeling slightly proud of himself.

Back at 12 Norfolk Road, tension was running high. Sarah Stanhope had had to break off from decorating the knocked-through living-and-dining room because Thomas needed to be fed. She didn't really like doing it in front of the caterers, but she didn't want to go upstairs because then she wouldn't be able to keep an eye on what they were doing. Her milk supply was always poor in the late afternoon, and Thomas clearly wasn't impressed. He kept throwing his head back to howl, and each time her wet nipple was exposed to the gaze of whichever of the three slim blonde girls happened to be bustling past with a covered tray at that moment. Sarah wondered, vaguely, why such stunning creatures wanted a job like this. Sorting out other people's parties seemed like hard and unrewarding work. Perhaps mopping up the spare men at posh functions was the perk. Well, they wouldn't have much fun tonight, poor things, she thought. Most of Sarah and Adrian's friends were very firmly encoupled.

Overhead Sarah could hear her two older children, Hannah and Gabriel, thundering – really *thundering* – up and down. She knew what they were doing; jumping from the furniture at ever more daring heights. They would start with the toy-chest then graduate to the chest of drawers, then hurl themselves off the top bunk onto a pile of duvets. At some point Gabriel, who was only just three, would be bound to miss the duvets, and then he would certainly wail and want his Mummy. Sarah's sister Nicola was supposed to be supervising them, but her idea of adequate supervision was to lie in a deep, scented bath with the door slightly ajar and yell an unheeded command at them every so often. Nicola was still in her twenties, and had no children. What she did have was an amazing new job in New York, working for a glossy magazine, starting in the New Year. Sarah hoped that her farewell-to-London party wasn't going to turn into Nicola's send off, but she was pretty sure it would.

Sarah sighed, and buttoned up her cardigan. Thomas wasn't getting anywhere with this feed; she'd have to give him a supplementary bottle. Perhaps she should have weaned him in time for Christmas and the move, but people said that four months was best for a baby's health, and he wasn't quite four months. She took a bottle of formula – luckily she'd made a couple in advance – from the fridge and put it in the bottle-warmer. She'd carried on breast-feeding the other two until they were at least six months; there had been no reason not to, since she was at home all day. For the same reason she had never hired any help, except for one disastrous *au pair* soon after Gabriel's birth. They could probably have afforded it, but it seemed wrong, when she wasn't working.

Consequently all her activities, even the most mundane, had been subject to frequent interruption for the past six years, and this evening was no exception. All day she had been trying to finish these blasted decorations, and now time was running out. She was hanging – or attempting to hang – swags of greenery, intertwined with real and artificial fruit and flowers, all orange, green and white, round the living room walls. She had made the garlands herself, late last night; she enjoyed that sort of thing. A bunch of mistletoe, brought from the greengrocer's at disproportionate expense, hung over the archway between the living and dining areas, where the door had been before they knocked it through. She couldn't decide whether to leave it up or not. Perhaps mistletoe was a little cringe-making.

'Sorry.' 'Excuse me.' 'Ooops!' Sarah, standing in her own

kitchen jiggling Thomas and waiting for the bottle to warm up, was obviously in the way. The three caterers were smiling, but in a glassy-eyed way. They kept putting hot or damp things down on polished wooden furniture. Sarah had already mentioned it, but they seemed to have forgotten. Should she make a fuss, or ignore it and put it out of mind? She decided on the line of least resistance and went upstairs with the wailing Thomas and the warm bottle. She mentally transferred her irritation with the caterers to her husband; what could have kept Adrian so long? At this rate the champagne would be lukewarm by the time people started to arrive.

She settled herself on her bed with Thomas, and was immediately and predictably leapt on by Hannah and Gabriel. Hannah, who was nearly six, was usually quite a calm, almost retiring child, but the combined excitements of Christmas, the party, moving house, and the glamorous presence of Aunt Nicky, had wound her up like a top. As for Gabriel, it never took much to get him going. Their faces were streaked with something – it looked more like make-up than felt tip pen. If it was Nicky's make-up, serve her right, thought Sarah uncharitably. 'Hannah, what has happened to your face?' she asked.

'Aunt Nicky did it. Gaby is a tiger-tiger-burning-bright, and I'm a Tabitha Twitchit. Mummy, can I stay up for the party a bit? Just a bit, Mummee ...'

'Don't whine, Han. If you are as good as gold about having your bath and getting into your nightie, then you can stay up for half an hour, but you've got to be angelic – I mean it.'

'Can Gaby stay up too?'

'Gaby can stay up if he's going to be a little angel.'

'Boys don't be angels,' said Gabriel. 'Boys be shepherds, and anyway I am Jophes.' He was referring to a recent triumph in the kindergarten nativity play. Sarah had been amazed at the casting, and sure enough her little 'Joseph' had fidgeted throughout, but he had managed to sing 'Away in a Manger' quite nicely.

Nicola appeared in the doorway, one towel tucked in under her armpits, another wrapped around her wet hair. She made a face at the children. 'Sorry,' she said in response to Sarah's reproachful look, 'but I had to have a bath. Anyway, they've had a lot of fun.'

They heard the front door open. Adrian was back, with the

champagne. 'I'm sorry, my love,' he called up the stairs, 'the traffic's appalling.'

Everybody seemed to be apologising to her, thought Sarah, but nobody really meant it. 'OK,' she called back, 'can you shove it into the ice and then get the children ready? I've got to finish those decorations and get changed.'

The story of my life, she reflected, glowering at her sister's retreating back. There would be no time for a bath now.

A couple of hours later, Sarah's spirits had lifted. The decorations had worked. 'Cor! Looks like Harrods Food Hall!' Nicola had said, but she meant it as a compliment. Sarah had bought a new dress just for the occasion – crinkly velvet, midnight blue with a dropped waist – and it felt just right. The generous cut hid the post-Thomas bulges that she hadn't really tackled yet; the colour set off the milkiness of her skin and made her hair look fairer. The house was full of delicious smells – Adrian had been right to insist on caterers – and the guests had arrived thick and fast. Sarah felt a pleasant anticipatory glow.

Kate Stringer, heavily pregnant, orange juice in hand, stood talking to her husband, Ollie. Kate was an old friend from Sarah's publishing days. Sarah moved in on them, embracing them with enthusiasm.

'Sarah, I can't believe you're really leaving London,' Kate exclaimed, 'what do you think you'll miss most?'

Sarah had asked herself this question several times and had failed to find a satisfactory answer. She replied glibly, 'Oh, friends, definitely. I don't think we'll miss London itself at all. The traffic and everything ... It took Adrian nearly an hour to get back from the wine shop today, which must be all of a mile and a half away.'

Ollie said, 'I know what I'd miss. Cinema and theatre. We go a lot.'

'Oh, but Ollie, you haven't got children. Just you wait!' Sarah, smiling, patted Kate's extended abdomen, taut under a black linen shift. 'In a couple of months you won't know what's hit you. I shouldn't think Adrian and I have been to the cinema more than half a dozen times since Hannah was born. That's six years.'

Ollie made a face. 'Sounds grim.'

'There's always videos,' said Kate a little uncertainly.

'Not the same at all,' said her husband. 'No atmosphere.'

'Of course you can still go out,' Sarah put in hastily. 'I suppose it's more that we don't get round to it. Organising a babysitter just takes that bit more effort. Talking of videos,' she went on, 'do you know Pingu, the little penguin? Well, he's a sort of Plasticine puppet. Adrian's secretary lent us a Pingu video and the children adored it so we kept it for ages. She doesn't have children so we assumed she didn't need it. Then one day she plaintively asked Adrian if she could have it back – turns out she and her boyfriend used to sit and watch it almost every night, they thought it so sweet.'

Kate and Ollie laughed. Sarah felt a twinge of guilt the minute she had told the little story. It was snobby and bitchy, wasn't it? One of the caterers appeared with a plate of prunes wrapped in bacon. 'Devils on horseback! Superb!' said a fruity voice behind Sarah's shoulder. It was Rupert, an old college friend of Adrian's, who had done extremely well for himself in the Eighties' property boom. They didn't really have much in common with him and would perhaps have drifted apart if he hadn't been in pursuit of Sarah's sister, on and off, for some time.

'Hello, Rupe. I didn't know you'd arrived.' Sarah kissed him on both cheeks. 'Do you know Kate and Ollie?' Nods and smiles were exchanged, but the Stringers, arty types as Rupert would have called them, were deterred by his pink-striped, tailor-made shirt and florid cheeks, and edged away to join a nearby group who were talking about Canary Wharf.

'So, Sarah, this is it,' said Rupert. 'The Big One. How do you feel about leaving the smoke?'

'Very positive,' said Sarah. She could never quite think what to say to Rupert.

'And Nicky's off as well?'

'Don't let her hear you calling her that. It's officially Nicola now.'

'Thanks for the tip.' Rupert winked. 'You'll miss her, won't you? You sisters are very close.'

Are we? thought Sarah. Aloud she said, 'It'll give us a good excuse to visit the States. But, Rupert, you haven't got a drink.'

Adrian had got rather stuck with his back to the Christmas tree, fenced in by three youngish women who Sarah had met through

NCT classes. The situation was slightly farcical, he thought. There was no common ground between them, really, except that they had all become parents in the last few years, and they all lived in the same postal district. And that, of course, was soon to change. They were talking about the new huge Sainsburys that was about to open. This would not have enthralled Adrian at any time, and since he had only two more days in the area he found the conversation wholly redundant. When the doorbell rang he sprang to answer it with relief.

By half past nine the place was packed. Women's lipstick had worn off; beads of sweat were appearing on men's foreheads. The champagne, which in Adrian's opinion was cool enough, though only just, was proving to be more appropriate than mulled wine. The caterers were doing very well indeed, slithering in and out of the knots of people without wobbling or spilling or losing their wide, white smiles. Devils on horseback had given way to more substantial snacks; skewers of chicken to be dipped into satay sauce; spicy meatballs with yogurt and mint; deep-fried mushrooms in crisp batter; hot pastry rolls that turned out to contain not pink pasty sausage but large and flavoursome prawns. People were chomping and slurping and licking their fingers; Sarah noticed with amusement that Libby Johnston, who was very greedy but thought no one noticed, was pursuing a tray of particularly delectable miniature anchovy pizzas as it made its way around the edge of the room. And here was a late arrival, Andrew Malone, one of the partners at the firm of solicitors Adrian worked for, coming to embrace her and, doubtless, to ask whether she'd miss London.

'Well, Sarah, we'll miss you, but the question is, whether you'll miss us?' His voice had a peculiar quality, somewhere between a boom and a honk. Sarah had never been able to bear him; she wasn't quite sure why. It could have been because he always assumed a proprietory attitude towards Adrian, implying 'we men understand each other,' or it could have been because of the little flecks of white spittle that collected at the corners of his mouth whenever he spoke.

'You won't miss Adrian,' said Sarah, stating the obvious rather tartly, 'you'll still be seeing him every day, of course.'

'It won't be the same, though,' said Andrew with a theatrically lugubrious air. 'It's hard enough getting him to stay for a drink after work as it is; he always wants to dash home for baby's bathtime or something or other. With a train to catch as well it'll be impossible. Mind you don't turn him into a hermit.'

'He wouldn't mind being a hermit actually,' said Sarah. 'He's more that way inclined than I am.'

Andrew was unabashed. 'Oh, by the way, Nina sends her apologies. Can't make it. We were both in working this morning on this Lloyds case, and she thought she'd better carry on.'

Nina was another partner in the firm. It was hard to believe that a stylish and successful woman like her could be having an affair with a tubby bore like Andrew, but the possibility had crossed Sarah's mind; they seemed to spend a lot of time together. Sarah had asked Adrian but he seemed to have no opinion. As a gossip he had always been an absolute dead loss.

Andrew was hailed by another acquaintance, and Sarah slipped away. She wormed her way upstairs on the pretext of checking on the children – if they were crying it would never be heard above this din – but also to give herself a few minutes off.

Gently she pushed open the door of Hannah and Gabriel's room. In the orangey twilight created by the glow of the street lamps filtering through the gaps in the curtains she could see two small humps, one on each bunk. She tiptoed nearer. Hannah's face still bore traces of her Tabitha Twitchit stripes. Gabriel's thumb hovered near his half-opened mouth. She stood there for a while, motionless, soothed by their quiet breathing. You can forgive children a lot when they're asleep, she thought, laying a finger lightly on each peachy cheek.

No sound from Thomas, either, in his narrow little box room. How marvellous it would be in their new house, with lots of space! In London one was forced to inhabit spaces unworthy even of the average mop and bucket and call them bedrooms. How much saner their new life would be, with fresh air and no traffic and proper, dark, silent nights.

She went into her own bedroom where coats were piled on the bed and flicked at her thick hair with a comb and reapplied her lipstick. It was an old Rimmel one, Perfect Plum or something silly like that. She never seemed to get round to buying new make-up. Her sister's bag was lying on the dressing table too, and she couldn't resist inspecting it. The amazing thing about Nicola's make-up was that everything matched. It was quite austere in a way – one eyeshadow, one foundation, one blusher, one mascara, one lip gloss, one powder compact – no fussy extras, but all were in identical, expensive-looking containers; deep blue edged with gold. And it was all clean. Sarah's things always seemed to be smeary and dusty, but Nicola's gleamed.

When Sarah decided to rejoin the party she paused on the landing; from here she could see about a third of what was going on. Nicola stood in the middle, slim, animated, swaying slightly in her simple, short, close-fitting charcoal-coloured dress. Her back and arms were bare; she wore a diamanté choker and matching earrings, but no other jewellery. Her straight fair hair, finer and closer to golden than Sarah's, swung to her shoulders; every so often she would flick it back from her face and laugh. She was talking to ghastly Andrew now, but she showed no signs of boredom or irritation. Nicola never talked to women at parties.

Everything seemed to be going just right. Sarah let her gaze rove over the room which, in theory, contained almost everyone in the world she was most fond of. But in actuality, how many did she care about? She asked herself the question so many others had asked her; what or who would she miss?

Nerissa Gracey was talking to Adrian, making him laugh. Nerissa was good fun, pretty, bright, very open, but they knew her because she was married to Adrian's old school friend Hugh. She didn't quite feel like one of Sarah's own friends. The NCT trio were still close to the Christmas tree in the corner; they didn't look very different from how they looked by day, pushing buggies on the common. They were still wearing bright bobble jumpers, though as a concession to festivity they had put on sheer black tights and low-heeled black court shoes instead of woolly leggings and flat pumps. They were now talking to Felicity Rix, who was probably Sarah's oldest friend. She and Felicity had sat next to each other at Assembly on the first day at their secondary school when they were eleven, and had remained friends ever since. Her oldest friend – and therefore in a sense her closest. There was so much water under the bridge. But Felicity, who had never married, sometimes seemed almost pitiable to Sarah. She had become so cautious. She had quite a good job, in the civil service, and was an active member of many worthy organisations, but she had collapsed in on herself, somehow. As Sarah looked at her, dumpy and bespectacled, trying to look interested in anecdotes about other people's children when she had none of her own, she felt a rush of affectionate sympathy. She must go and rescue Fliss. But feeling fond of and sorry for someone wasn't the same as feeling really close to them.

Felicity – Sarah had often reflected how increasingly unsuitable that name seemed for its owner – had never mastered the art of extricating herself from moribund party conversations and she was grateful to be rescued. As usual, her mind was running on practical concerns. 'What I don't understand,' she said to Sarah, 'is why you chose to move just before Christmas. I mean, surely –'

Sarah made a face. 'Good question,' she said. 'The dictates of Diana, that's why.'

Felicity had heard plenty about Sarah's difficult mother-in-law over the years. She sighed in sympathy and drained her orange juice. 'Let me guess – she wasn't well enough to have you for Christmas this year, but couldn't possibly contemplate coming to London –'

'You've got it. Christmas in London isn't really Christmas, is it?' said Sarah sarcastically.

'So instead you're going to have a really festive time unpacking boxes and sorting out the plumbing.'

'Plumbing?'

'Whenever people move house the plumbing always goes wrong. Or the heating.'

'Or both. Oh God! Treats in store.'

'Adrian should have put his foot down,' Felicity continued. 'Seriously, Sarah, it's awfully unfair on you. I'd offer to come and help but …'

'Oh no, no,' Sarah put in hastily. Felicity, so efficient in the office, was absolutely clueless about domesticity. 'No, don't worry. Come and visit us when we're settled and I've stopped being grumpy with Ade. It'll be great when it's all sorted out – use us as your weekend retreat.' She felt herself grabbed round the waist and spun round to see someone she really did almost love.

Louise was thin and Jewish and never stopped talking; she had read languages at the same university as Sarah, and had made friends with her, borrowing change for the telephone by the pigeonholes in their first week. She had changed so little in the last twelve or thirteen years; she now wore her black hair in a bun, instead of streaming down her back but she still loved clanky jewellery and outrageous shoes which made her long thin legs even more flamingo-like. Giving birth to two thin dark children had made no difference whatsoever to her angular figure, and had if anything increased her amazing energy. Felicity, who found Louise daunting, faded quietly away in search of more orange juice. Louise pulled Sarah aside to whisper amusingly catty remarks about those guests about whom Sarah felt most ambivalent; she always hit the target. Yes, Sarah would miss her, but the trouble was that everybody loved Louise. Her social circle was large, but her extended Jewish family was larger, and if she belonged to anyone, it was to them.

'So when are you going to come and see us, Lou?'

'As soon as possible – you won't be able to get rid of me. I can't wait for all that fresh air. We'll have huge cooked breakfasts and go for hearty walks. I'll buy some boots, you know, with laces, and sheepskin round the top. They've got them in Russell and Bromley.'

'Hmm. We're going to be living in a town, you know, although it's quite a small one.'

'Well, I'll come and help you make cakes for the WI or man the bric-a-brac stall at the local fête or something. It'll be a laugh.'

'You're such a townie, Louise, I don't think you can draw breath outside London. You find it quite difficult leaving Hampstead. Admit it, south of the river's a foreign country to you.'

'True, I always do feel like I'm going backpacking for a month whenever I cross the river. But that's fun! You've got to invite me as soon as you've unpacked. I'll bring the kids and we can shut them all out into the massive garden you're going to have, and then we can lock the door and get on with our cake baking. They can sort each other out.'

'It'll be January. But the principle's excellent. You're first on my list, OK?'

By midnight the party had thinned out a little. Several people had taken the mistletoe as an excuse to kiss Nicola. Pink-shirted, pink-cheeked Rupert was among them, but since she was leaving the country so soon it seemed pointless to waste much energy, and he had now resorted to chatting to the caterers in the kitchen. They had handed round hot mince pies and grapes frosted with sugar and were now allowing themselves a little relaxation and their first drink of the evening. Rupert, who was tipsy, couldn't decide which one to home in on; the truth was, he couldn't really tell them apart.

The NCT women had long since departed, they had to relieve their babysitters at a sensible hour. Felicity, too, had gone, just because she didn't like late nights. Kate Stringer, who couldn't drink much because of being pregnant, had stopped enjoying herself an hour ago and was quietly agitating to go, but Ollie was sitting on the floor with an actor and an architect and they were all hooting with laughter. Sarah, noticing the problem, sat Kate in an armchair and went off to make her a cup of tea. Adrian was going round with a bin bag, stuffing debris into it. Sarah wished he wouldn't; it looked so obviously as if he'd had enough. But he had had enough – easily. Adrian didn't really like parties.

The tail end of parties was actually the bit Sarah liked best, when the noise level had dropped, you had cleared the earlier hurdles of banal opening remarks, and you could actually talk to people in that weary, disjointed but cosy way, as she was doing with Kate, both of them clutching mugs of tea. Kate was worried about the birth – not really about the birth itself, she was quite good about pain (Sarah smiled inwardly, but didn't say anything), but about the effect the birth would have on her relationship with Ollie. She wasn't sure if Ollie was really ready for parenthood; sometimes she thought he resented the baby already. Sarah said don't worry, no one's ever ready for parenthood; of course it would put pressure on their relationship but that was only temporary and in many ways it would strengthen their marriage and bring them closer. As she said this, Sarah glanced at Adrian and his irritating bin bag. He looked thin and tense; he'd lost a lot of hair in the last year or so. An image flashed into her mind, of a party they'd been to in the early months of their relationship, about ten years before. She remembered what she'd been wearing; a diaphanous white muslin dress with hundreds of tiny pleats, gathered softly at the waist.

Adrian hadn't been able to stop touching her, had hardly left her side, and she'd loved it. She saw them, together, leaning against a wall drinking from the same glass, talking to other people but never moving apart. She realised with a shock that this evening they'd hardly exchanged a glance. She mentioned none of this to Kate.

Most people were sitting on the floor by now. The carpet was in a terrible state but the joy of moving house was that it really didn't matter – the new owners would probably rip everything out and start again. That's what people did in London. The atmosphere was gentle and mirthful. Louise was talking to Nicola – on a sofa, as Nicola's dress was too short to allow her to sit on the floor. Trust Louise, the only female who could persuade Nicola to talk for more than a few seconds. Sarah was listening to what Kate was saying to her, but she could pick up quite a bit of Louise's conversation too; she had a deep, indiscreet, almost horsy voice.

'... but do you really think family doesn't matter, Nicky? I think, when you come down to it, that's all there is.'

'Family's fine,' Nicola replied, 'but they're not really ... progressing, are they? I mean Mum and Sarah and Adrian and the kids – they're background. They're comfortable, and I'm glad they're there, but they're not ... I can't explain it ... they're not what's happening to me. My career is what's happening to me right now.'

'But Sarah's your sister. She loves you. Won't you miss her?'

'Louise, you won't tell Sarah this, will you? But no, I won't miss her. I quite want to get away.'

'But she will miss you, won't she?'

Nicola gave Louise a blue, blank stare, of a kind she was famous for. 'Oh, yeah – of course she will.'

Andrew Malone, who had been on a personal mission to make sure that no bottle was left standing, clapped his hands and suggested some party games. Mercifully, the doorbell rang. A fleet of minicabs, telephoned for earlier, had arrived. Nearly everybody took their leave, with many hugs and kisses and promises to stay in touch. Andrew, who had arrived by car, was obviously incapable of driving back, and for a few terrible moments Sarah thought he was going to have to stay the night.

Louise, who for all her Londonness was very sensitive, took

charge; she and Jack were driving and no, Fulham wouldn't be out of their way. They steered Andrew away from Nicola, who was recoiling from his embraces, and propelled him towards their Saab.

Nicola, who was staying the night, said, 'It was a great party. Let's clear up in the morning, Ade.' She gave Sarah a brilliant, candid smile. 'How do you feel, Sal?'

Sarah could hardly look at her sister, let alone reply. What Nicola had said to Louise had soured the evening for her. Why should this be? It was only what she'd always assumed. Why should hearing a truth spoken make it so much worse?

'I'm incredibly tired,' said Sarah. 'Nicola's right, darling. We can finish this in the morning.'

In the event it was Adrian who did all the tidying himself, while Sarah lay in bed, exhausted but sleepless. He hated to think of Hannah and Gabriel wandering down in the early morning and stepping on a splinter of broken glass or chewing a cigarette end. He filled three black sacks, tied them neatly, and put them out on the front doorstep. Then he made himself a cup of tea and a sandwich – he'd been so busy being a host that he'd missed most of the caterers' offerings. He switched the dishwasher on, pleased at the tiny saving being made by using it so late at night. At last he joined Sarah, who, though too tired to take her make-up off, was sitting up in bed reading.

'What did people talk to you about?' she asked as he undressed. His legs looked very thin and white beneath his shirt tails.

'About how awful commuting would be, mainly. What about you?'

'About what I'd miss. Whether I'd miss them.'

'And will you?'

'I don't think so. I'll miss Louise.'

Adrian slipped into bed. He put his arm around her, briefly. 'It went well, didn't it?'

'Oh yes, it went well.'

'Goodnight, Sal.'

'Goodnight.'

Adrian rolled over, pulling his share of the duvet tightly round his bony shoulders. Sarah closed her eyes, but sleep was elusive. She thought of her sister in the spare room bed, how she would be stretching her long limbs luxuriously, her sleek head full of gratifying visions of fame and fortune in New York. It wasn't that she envied Nicky, but ... Sarah stroked her sagging stomach and thought of the next few days, of cardboard boxes and removal men and living on tins and takeaways and the sound of her own weary, nagging voice. Oh well. It would be different when they got to Barcombe. Once they were all installed things would be different. She'd do the house up with loving care; it was a pretty house, and she meant to do it justice. And she'd do herself justice too. Lose weight, get fit, make new friends. You had more time out of London, as well as more peace and fresh air. And time was freedom. Wasn't it?

CHAPTER TWO

On a soft rainy afternoon, two girls lay on a single bed, sharing a glossy magazine and a packet of Cheddars. One was small and slight, with long, thin hair hanging over her face; the bare feet protruding from her baggy black jeans were bony and narrow. The other was larger, with thick, curly, almost black hair. She had small pudgy hands and nibbled fingernails, and at least a dozen thin bangles on each wrist, which jangled every time she turned a page. The larger girl reached for another biscuit.

'These are brilliant if you spread cream cheese on them but it has to be really thick.'

'Mm. Give us another.' The slender girl pointed to a picture in the magazine. 'She looked better before.' The article featured the transformation of drab readers into pouting starlets, courtesy of the magazine.

'No she didn't. She had terrible skin.'

'Well, that won't have gone away. They've just plastered her in make-up. Anyway that suit looks stupid on her.'

'Yes, it's a bit … eighties. How old is she? Twenty-five? My God, she looks older than that. How come your mum looks so young, Elinor?'

The smaller girl rolled over and off the bed. She picked up a hand mirror and scrutinised her chin for blackheads. 'Well, she is quite young. She was only nineteen when she had me.'

'So that makes her thirty-six now? Ten years younger than my mum, but mine looks about a hundred. Do you share her clothes and stuff?'

'Not really. My mum's clothes are pretty gross … just sort of embarrassing.'

'She's got a brilliant figure.' The plump girl sighed. 'I'm definitely starting the F Plan diet tomorrow. Meanwhile, may as well finish these.' She took the last two Cheddars. 'You know,' she continued, 'if your mum's only thirty-six, she could have another baby. Or two.'

'Oh no she couldn't,' Elinor retorted quickly, and then paused, startled at the speed of her reaction. 'I mean she could in theory, but she hasn't got a man. And I don't think she'd want one.'

'Want what? A baby or a man?'

'Either ... both.'

'She must want a man, everyone does.'

'Just because you're desperate, Laura. No, Mum's fine with just me.'

'But she must have had boyfriends?' pursued Laura. 'Or had affairs with married men, or something?'

'Well she has had a few boyfriends, but not serious ones. She likes her space, that's what she says.'

'A baby wouldn't take up much space and she could have one of those ... she had you on her own, didn't she?'

'Yes, but that was a mistake, and it was a long time ago. What are you asking all these questions for anyway?'

'Your mum interests me, that's all. I think you're so lucky. And she lets you smoke at home.'

'But I don't want to smoke.'

'I know – wasted on you. I, however, do want to smoke – now. Yes, OK, I'll open the window.' Laura lit a Marlboro, opened the wardrobe door, and stood in front of the mirror, hands on hips, legs apart. 'Drop dead sexy, hey?'

'Drop dead of lung cancer, more like. I can't think why you want to smoke. It's against the national trend.'

Laura flicked ash out of the window. 'No, my sweet. You are wrong. The numbers of young women aged fourteen to twenty-two who smoke are *rising* and I do not intend to miss out because a) it winds my mum up, b) it makes me look cool and sexy and c) it might stop me eating so much. OK?'

'a) You wind your mum up just by existing, b) you didn't look cool and sexy when Sam Newton offered you one and you put the wrong end in your mouth, and c) you have just effortlessly consumed three quarters of a packet of Cheddars. OK?'

Laura laughed and shrugged good-temperedly. 'Give me a chance, I'm still practising. Watch how I stub this one out, very cool. I can hear your mum coming in – let's go and say hello.'

' All right – but don't mention babies.'

In the kitchen below, Hilary Nightingale reached for the kettle in that automatic way engendered of a damp afternoon and a car full of carrier bags from Safeway. She had pulled off her boots and was flexing her toes – another automatic response. From this, and from the muscled curves of her legs and straightness of her back one could guess that she had once been a dancer. She wore tight black leggings and a huge cotton jumper the colour of cinnamon; one thick woolly sock was moss green, the other grey. Her face lit up as the girls entered the room.

'Hello, you two. Want some coffee? Or tea? Laura, do you like this herbal stuff?'

'No thanks, Mrs Nightingale, it tastes like lawnmower clippings. Can I have a coffee? Shall I get your shopping in from the car?'

'Now there's a really well brought up girl. Yes, please do – on condition you call me Hilary. I never was Mrs Nightingale, you know.'

'Laura's only offering so she can see what you got at Safeway's. She is *obsessed* with food. She once bought a carton of double cream and drank it all straight off.'

Laura, unperturbed at her friend's interjection, corrected her. 'Not once – several times. Actually Mrs ... Hilary, I was just wondering if by any entirely brilliant chance you happened to have bought any of those ginger and chocolate-chip cookies that my dear mother refuses to buy on the grounds that they are ruinously expensive, though how she can say that when she has just paid for a brand new kitchen is beyond me.'

'Well, Laura,' Hilary replied, 'I must be clairvoyant because in Safeway I was overcome by a sudden overwhelming force directing me towards those selfsame cookies, and I bought two packets. And if your mother's just paid for a new kitchen I'm not surprised she's feeling broke.'

The two girls started to unload the car, and Hilary watched them through the misty window, smiling indulgently. She was sure that Laura's blooming carnality and fearless manner was a good influence on Elinor, who tended to be reserved and censorious, self-controlled to a fault. Her daughter was without doubt the centre of her life, and yet how different they were, Hilary thought. Where her own instincts led her to intervene, to communicate, Elinor's led her to observe, to judge, to withdraw.

It took Elinor and Laura three trips to empty the car. 'Brilliant! I won't have to do that again for another month.' As Hilary unloaded the carrier bags, Laura noticed that she bent from the knees, not from the waist.

'Mum, you've gone mad!' exclaimed Elinor, discovering two tubs of expensive ice-cream. 'Praline *and* raspberry sorbet! What's all this about?'

'A celebration – I've got a commission. I'm going to decorate a nursery for a solicitor's family. They live on Maiden's Hill, by the windmill. It's a lovely house and she seemed nice, gave me more or less a free rein.'

'A nursery, how sweet,' said Laura. 'Won't it make you feel broody?' She cast a sly, sidelong glance at Elinor.

Hilary laughed. 'I doubt it, though I must admit the baby is rather a poppet – the fat fair variety. You know, looks like he's got rubber bands round his arms and legs. There was a beautiful little boy, too, like a gypsy child, he was screaming his head off most of the time because his mother didn't want him to play outside with bare feet. That reminded me of what a pain the whole business can be.'

'Mum! Was I ever a pain?'

'No, my darling, of course not – you were a model child.' Hilary winked at Laura. 'Now if you will excuse me I'm going to put my feet up for half an hour. Shopping always wears me out.'

The rented cottage in which Hilary and Elinor lived was at the end of a long bumpy track, almost impassable in the worst of winter. It belonged to a neighbouring farmer, who had let it to Hilary for a pittance on the grounds that she would do a little cleaning and cooking for him. Since his wife had died he'd let things go a bit, he didn't mind admitting. So on two mornings a week Hilary tidied the kitchen, loaded the washing machine, ran a Hoover over the never-used sitting room, and prepared a beef stew and a heavy fruitcake, or perhaps a small gammon joint and an apple pie, that would last Mr Pitchford for a couple of days; such things kept nicely on the cool slate shelves of his old fashioned larder, even in hot weather. The rest of Hilary's week was spent painting and decorating – ornamenting bathrooms and bedrooms with stylised plants, fruit, birds and fish if she could get the custom; if she could not she would strip wallpaper and sand wooden floors, anything to earn a living. She also knitted jerseys for sale in a Barcombe craft shop; tiny Fair Isle cardigans for toddlers, with brown leather buttons, vast fishermen's sweaters with intricate textures, jolly jumpers for plump mums, all created with a certain originality and eye for detail that vindicated their high price tags.

Petts End Cottage was very small, and Hilary with her artist's eye sometimes regretted the lack of clear light and vaulting space, but the tiny deepset windows and the misty green light that filtered through them had an almost subaqueous charm. The cottage was set against a bank; the back windows looked out on nothing but a rising green expanse. When Hilary had first set eyes on it she had thought of hobbits. Only a few yards further up the track was Petts Wood, and both Hilary and Elinor felt that the proximity of bluebells, young badgers scuffling at dusk, the eerie interchange of owls, and swathes of luxuriant blackberries in autumn made up for the many deficiencies of the little house.

As Hilary lay on her bed on this misty afternoon, hands cradling the mug of camomile tea, a slow, secret smile crept over her face. She had more to celebrate than the commission to paint the Stanhopes' nursery, welcome though that was. She had been asked out to dinner – and for once by a man in whom she really felt interested. So far, things had worked out as they should do in theory but so rarely did in practice; her closest friends in the area had invited her to dinner specifically to meet a neighbour, the novelist Joe Coventry. She had liked him enormously, he had seemed attracted to her, but they had failed to exchange telephone numbers. Then this very afternoon she had bumped into him at Safeway. They had chatted eagerly, and naturally.

'Isn't it amazing,' she had said, gesturing to all the supermarket shelves, 'all this stuff. Who buys it? I mean, who does buy tins of marrowfat peas and packets of custard powder?' Joe Coventry had laughed, and gestured to his trolley. 'Now you know. So glad to enlighten you.' There lay two tins of marrowfat peas and – well, not custard powder, but a packet of instant whip, butterscotch flavour. 'Oh dear, I'm terribly sorry,' said Hilary, but she was laughing, and she could see he didn't mind a bit. 'Tell you what,' he had said. 'Come for dinner tomorrow night. And in order to avoid the instant whip, I'd better take you out somewhere decent.

Shall I call for you at half past seven? Where do you live exactly?' For once Hilary had felt no need to evade or stall the request. 'Yes, thanks, that would lovely,' she had said, tearing her shopping list in half to scribble down directions.

And now the only snag was how to tell Elinor, who was always so put out by any evidence that her mother was still a youngish woman. The wind set the unopened buds of the clematis tapping against Hilary's bedroom window pane in a kind of pattern of restlessness. Hilary sprang up, and went to run a bath. She could always think more clearly in the bath. Funny how she, the independent, adventurous Hilary Nightingale, was a little afraid of her palefaced teenage daughter.

CHAPTER THREE

'Bewitched! I'm bewitched!'

Sarah Stanhope, who was wiping the lower rungs of the high chair with a damp J cloth, straightened her back and stared at the three-year-old Gabriel. Where on earth had he picked up that word? And what connection did that word have with the activity he was currently engaged in, making a tottering tower of brown bread crusts on an upturned red plastic beaker? Sarah smiled vaguely at her son, hooked a lump of hair behind her ear, and resumed her wiping.

'BewitchedbewitchedbewitchedbeWITCHED!' The words were taking on a rhythm, almost a tune. 'Bing bong, the witch is dead, the wicked witch is DEAD!' On the last word the beaker was flung into the air. It sailed into the playpen in a graceful arc; the crusts lay scattered on the floor like pinecones.

'Gabriel, that's very naughty, I've told you lots of times ...' but Sarah's voice was heavy and her admonition tailed off wearily. It was so hard, so hard to be effectual and consistent; her reproofs and punishments had long since lost their sting. But did it matter? She gathered the crusts and set them aside to go on the bird table later. Gabriel had already leapt down from his chair and was flailing on the kitchen floor. 'I do headover heels, Mummy watch me.'

Sarah glanced at the clock. Half past five. Another hour and a half before Adrian returned. Too early to start their baths, really. She opened the back door; it was a mid-April evening, mild enough for them to play out of doors for another half hour.

'Come on, you.' She heaved the baby out of his playpen where he had been sucking on the hurled beaker. If he had been her first baby, she reflected, she would never have let him drink from so unsterile an object.

'Come on, Gabriel. Outside.'

Gabriel darted into the garden, squatted on the path, and scooped the gravel into a pile. Sarah knew what would happen next and made a conscious decision to turn a blind eye. Family harmony seemed more important than hygiene at that moment. Sure enough, the small boy filled his mouth with stones and spat them out neatly one by one into an empty flower pot.

Sarah looked away, sitting on the low parapet wall, jiggling Thomas on her knee. He had a fistful of her hair in one hand; with the other he investigated her nose and mouth. The effort of concentration made him dribble. Sarah sighed. Today was their wedding anniversary. It didn't feel like one. The soft evening air, the nodding daffodils almost over now, the papery bridal cherry blossom – nothing seemed to raise her spirits. A shivery little wind parted the uncut lawn into silver waves. Sarah rose suddenly. 'Bath time, boys. In we go.' Gabriel ignored her; he was now arranging his stones in descending order of size along the top of the little wall, murmuring their colours as he did so. 'Brown one, white one, grey one, 'nother brown one.' Sarah called his name. 'Gabriel, come on Gaby,' but in this mood it was impossible to reach him; it was almost as if he were in a trance.

The doorbell rang, distantly, and Sarah jumped. She had almost forgotten; Hannah was being delivered back from Brownies by a neighbour. She felt a little stab of guilt about how easy she found it to forget about Hannah; how difficult she found it, by contrast, to switch off from Gabriel. She was terribly afraid that their looks had something to do with it. Hannah's straight, light brown hair hung in orderly lines round her pale, plump, rather anxious little face. Her eyes were deep-set, grey, a little too close together; her teeth – still a full set of milk teeth at six years old – had always seemed crowded in her small mouth. Hannah was not ugly, not even plain, really, but she was not physically memorable; superficially she seemed interchangeable with at least half a dozen of her classmates. Gabriel, though – Gabriel was different. Even when he was a small baby strangers had stopped her in the street to comment on his looks. 'What an enchanting child!' 'Just look at those eyelashes.' 'I don't think I've ever seen such an engaging little chap.' And now he was a three-and-a-half-year-old imp, a leaping, dancing, singing flame of a child, with thick dark curls glossy as fallen conkers, wide brown eyes with wickedly pointed corners, sturdy, slender limbs that turned brown at the first hint of sun, and tiny, evenly-spaced white teeth between his curvy mulberry lips. Too much of Sarah's admiration went to Gabriel,

23

she knew; too much of her anxiety too. Even this move, from a busy South London suburb to the small market town of Barcombe, had been made in large part for Gabriel's benefit, to allow him more scope for his eccentricities, more space to spread the gossamer wings that in imagination Sarah saw sprouting from his shoulders.

But now here was Hannah at the door with Mrs Crump from down the road, and Sarah's rush of guilt gave way to the real if low-key love she felt for her first born. 'Hello, my darling. Did you make that at Brownies? How lovely. Is it a kite? Thanks so much, Mrs Crump. Would you like a cup of tea, or something stronger? Are you sure? Oh well, thank you again – yes, same time next week would be lovely. Goodbye – Hannah, say bye bye and thank you.' As the door closed Hannah said, just in time, 'Bye bye, thank you. It's a kite for Daddy. It can really fly. Do I have to have a bath?'

An hour later, Sarah kicked off her scuffed suede loafers and stretched herself out on the sofa in the living room, irritated by the sight of three cardboard boxes in the corner of the room, still unpacked since the move. The children were all in bed – plump Thomas, creature of habit, always fell asleep the minute he was placed in his cot, clasping the satiny edge of his cot blanket between his fingers and with one cheek resting against the soft toy badger his grandmother had given him when he was born. Hannah and Gabriel shared a room; they were not asleep. Sarah could hear, faintly, Hannah teaching her brother a song she had learned at Brownies – '*Sing* HosHannah! *Sing* HosHannah! *Sing* Hoshanna!' she heard him warble, amid much merriment.

Why, Sarah asked herself, should she be feeling so flat? Her happy, healthy children were stowed safely away upstairs; her loyal, bright, sensible husband was on his way home. Here she was, lying in comfort in the pretty house that they had chosen together and had been lucky enough to be able to afford. This was her new life. And yet here she was, on her wedding anniversary with Adrian due any minute, sprawled unromantically in grubby leggings and sweatshirt, staring indiscriminately at the television and hogging the whole sofa. She sat up. She had to snap out of it. Though Adrian had shown no sign of remembering their anniversary, that didn't mean that she shouldn't make an effort. She glanced at her watch – five past seven; he was already a little late. It would only take her a couple of minutes to change. She hurried upstairs, peeling off the grey sweatshirt as she went.

How about wearing a dress for a change? The weather was getting milder; it really was time to get rid of the dark woolly garments, all more or less shapeless, in which she had huddled throughout the winter. She rummaged in the back of the wardrobe, pulling out clothes she hadn't looked at since Thomas' birth. Since long before that, in fact – since early pregnancy. Here was a smart navy skirt and top, polka-dotted with white. She had worn that to Nerissa and Hugh's wedding and had felt good in it. Hardly the thing for a relaxed evening at home, but never mind. She tried it on. The skirt didn't even begin to do up, and the buttons at the front of the blouse strained slightly, showing little glimpses of flesh. She threw them on the bed and tried again. And again. Nothing worked. Sarah felt her chest tightening, she felt heavy with disappointment. Might as well give them to Oxfam, she thought, pulling on a floral maternity skirt with an elasticated waist and a white jumper which, though dull, was at least clean.

She brushed her hair with her head upside down to make it fluff out, then hovered over a light pink lipstick. She so rarely wore make-up, especially since leaving London. Would Adrian be flattered, or would he interpret it as some kind of pressure or hint? Better leave it. Anyway, where was Adrian? It was half past seven. Sarah decided she couldn't wait any longer for that drink.

As she stood in the kitchen chopping salad ingredients and sipping at a generous gin and tonic, Sarah felt irritation turn to hot anger. He might have rung if he was going to be late; anyway, it obviously meant he had forgotten the anniversary. Their seventh. The seven-year itch. Did that phrase mean anything? Was this what the seven year itch felt like? Was she even capable of feeling it, or had small children and loneliness blunted her sensibilities to the point where she could feel little more than annoyance and boredom? Perhaps Adrian had the itch – perhaps he was late because he was seeing a woman? Why hadn't she thought of that before – and if he was, how much would she mind? Once the idea had entered her mind, it didn't take long for an elaborate fantasy to develop. The woman was one of the partners in Adrian's firm of solicitors – Nina, the one with long legs, no children, and a huge disposable income. Nina belonged to an expensive health club – perhaps Adrian had popped in there with her after work. They might be touching toes in the Jacuzzi, sharing shower gel, diving in the deep jade-green pool and catching each other under the water. Sarah, chopping mushrooms, sliced a tiny flap of skin from the tip of her thumb. The blood spoiled the row of velvety white slices. With her injured thumb in her mouth, Sarah scooped up the mushrooms with her other hand and tossed them into the bin.

And suddenly here was Adrian, carrying a stiff, shiny carrier bag with string handles in addition to the usual briefcase. 'Sorry I'm late, my love – I've been shopping.' Sarah admitted inwardly he didn't look as if he'd been anywhere near a Jacuzzi, and the fantasy fled to the deep recesses of her mind.

Adrian was smiling rather coyly. He encircled her waist, but then stepped back before kissing her. 'What's happened?' He pointed to the five or six drops of blood hanging on the front of her fluffy white jumper.

'Oh shit! It's handwash only, don't touch me. It'll smudge and soak in.' She tore off a piece of kitchen roll and held its edge against each drop, to absorb as much as possible.

Adrian watched the procedure with a look of impatience. 'Can I touch you now?' he asked, as she crumpled the bloodstained paper and threw it into the bin. 'It is a special day, after all.' So he had remembered. They embraced, and Sarah became more aware of the carrier bag he was still holding.

'So what's this, then?'

'A little anniversary present. Do you want to see?' From between sheets of tissue paper Adrian drew out some improbable underwear, all black. A basque, lace, with dozens of tiny hooks; a pair of briefs, silky, with a lace leaf-shaped panel at the front. A couple of pairs of stockings. Stockings! Sarah, remembering her earlier struggles with zips and hooks, felt painfully the inappropriateness of the present. She knew she must say the right thing, but felt herself incapable of doing so.

'Well?' Adrian's smile grated on her nerves.

'It ... must have cost you a fortune.'

Adrian looked proud. 'That doesn't matter, try them on.'

Sarah realised how very, very much she did not want to try

them on. She said sharply, 'They're tiny. I'll never get into them. Anyway, this isn't a present for me, it's a present for you.'

Adrian swept the soft black mass back into the carrier bag and left the room. Over his shoulder he said as he went, 'It was meant to be a present for us.'

Sarah shrugged, and searched for a plaster for her throbbing thumb. As she resumed her chopping she felt her throat tighten; hot tears prickled at the back of her eyes. Why couldn't she have managed to be gracious, today of all days?

When Hilary Nightingale cycled to the Stanhopes' house on Maiden's Hill that Saturday morning she was singing aloud, so great was her energy and confidence. Dinner with Joe Coventry the night before had been all she had hoped; conversation about art, books, gardens, animals, children, all unforced and natural, with no detectable pressure of any kind. He had driven her home, and she had not asked him in. If Elinor had not been there, would she have? Lucky, perhaps, that the decision was made for her. Elinor was waiting up for her, uncharacteristically watching television. The conversation between herself and her daughter was perhaps a little strained – but Hilary quickly put that out of her mind, and instead reminded herself that she and Joe had arranged to meet the following Wednesday, to see a silly film showing at Dinsford – a Hollywood blockbuster of the kind that it would be no fun to see on one's own, or with a hyper-critical teenage daughter. The sun was out, so was the cherry blossom; the breeze in her face was like clear water washing over her. Life was good – but perhaps she'd better stop singing before the Stanhopes heard her. She didn't want them to think her odd.

She parked the bike in the Stanhopes' porch – she rarely bothered to lock it. She unhooked her bundle of measuring and drawing equipment, rang the doorbell and stepped back to look at the house. In the sunshine it looked even prettier than it had on the previous Thursday; square, flat-fronted, red brick, like an old fashioned dolls' house, perhaps early nineteenth century; large friendly-looking windows with deep, cushioned window-seats inside and long cream shutters. The porch was a later addition – a regrettable one, since it obscured the elegant solidity of the front door and its oval fanlight. Still, creepers rampaged attractively over it, and the piles of firewood stacked beneath its low wooden seats made it seem homely. Wellington boots were ranged under one of the seats; the smallest pair had feet shaped like frogs' faces. Hilary smiled.

At that moment Sarah Stanhope opened the door, looking flustered. 'So sorry to have kept you waiting – the baby just fell off the sofa and cut his lip. No, he's fine, really. Do come in.' Thomas, on his mother's hip, stopped bawling to scrutinise the smiling, colourful woman on his doorstep. He stared particularly at the large painted wooden beads round her neck, then shot out a fat hand to grab them.

'Thomas likes your beads. So do I,' said Sarah, steering him away from them and leading Hilary into the living room.

'Thanks. I made them.'

'Really? They're lovely. Do sit down. My husband's taken Hannah and Gabriel to the sea front at Dinsford so we can have a bit of peace.'

Hilary took some rolls of paper from her workbag and spread them out in front of Sarah. 'Here are some sketches I've done for the nursery. What do you think?'

Sarah settled Thomas on the carpet in front of a basket of toys. 'There you go, Thomas, there's your squeaky rabbit.' She turned to the drawings, and beamed with delight at the leaping frieze of nursery characters. 'How wonderful. Humpty Dumpty – and the dish who ran away with the spoon. And who's that? Old Mother Hubbard? This is fantastic – and you've worked so quickly.'

'Oh, these are only outlines. That's the easy bit. If you like them I could start measuring up now.'

Sarah installed Hilary in the baby's room and left her to get on. She had moved the cot into the master bedroom; there it would stay while Hilary's work was in progress. Another barrier between herself and Adrian; sharing a bedroom with an eight-month-old didn't make for intimacy or romance. Adrian had suggested putting him in the spare bedroom, but she had objected on the feeble grounds that they'd only have to move him again if anybody came to stay. She knew that in reality she wanted this barrier – she wanted to create a distance. Part of her longed for Adrian to assert himself, to insist that the cot went in the spare room, to claim the bedroom as his prime territory. It irked her that

28

he submitted meekly. But then again it would have irked her to be overruled.

She had meant to use this time as a chance to concentrate on Thomas, to play with him constructively and without interruptions. But as she listlessly piled bricks into a tower for him to knock down she found herself thinking about Hilary and the vibrant picture she had made as she stood on the doorstep with her twisty auburn hair and her amber lipstick, her home-made beads and her outsize green sweater. She had opened the windows because of the sunshine; she had heard Hilary singing as she cycled up the hill, singing that peculiar song from – was it – South Pacific? 'Happy talking talking happy talk, talk about things you'd like to do.' Hilary had stopped singing as she approached the house. Sarah hoped that her house wasn't one that automatically stopped people from singing.

She felt a strong desire to find out more about this woman and what made her sing. It was a little early for Thomas' nap, but she'd risk putting him up anyway and offer Hilary coffee as a pretext for conversation. Thomas snuggled down obediently; as long as he had Badger and Blanket he was really quite happy.

Sarah tapped on the nursery door and opened it gingerly in case Hilary and the stepladder were just beyond it. They were. 'Would you like a cup of coffee?' Sarah asked, looking up at Hilary's midriff.

'I'd love one. I think I should carry on working, but do come up and keep me company.'

Sarah, encouraged by the easy friendliness of Hilary's manner, quickly fetched two mugs of coffee and the biscuit tin. 'How long have you lived in this area?' she asked, settling herself on the floor.

'Not for long – only since last July. We used to live in Bristol, and I used to dance for a small company. I taught dance as well, a bit. Then I decided I was just too old for it, and I fancied living in the country again – I was brought up in the country, and town life never really suited me. An old friend of mine knew of this cottage to let, so I came and had a look, and stayed.'

'And who is we?'

'We?'

'You said, we used to live in Bristol. I didn't realise you were married.' Sarah looked at Hilary's ring finger which was bare.

'Oh no – I've never been married. I live with Elinor, my daughter. She's just seventeen. She started at the Abbey School last September. She's always been educated in the state system, but then her grandparents, who've never shown much interest in her, suddenly offered to pay her school fees for the sixth form years, so I thought why not, let's give it a go. And I must admit she's doing well there. Are you going to educate your children privately?'

'Oh yes – we already are, Hannah's at the Abbey Juniors in fact. We're lucky that we've got the choice. Adrian's mother said she'd help us with the fees, if necessary – I don't think the idea of her flesh and blood at a state school appeals to her, though I must say I wouldn't mind. Adrian went to board himself, when he was seven – not that we'd do that to our boys ...' Sarah held the biscuit tin up to Hilary. She couldn't help wondering what the prim headmistress of the Abbey School thought about Elinor's illegitimacy, though she admired Hilary's obvious lack of concern about it. But how odd that such a lively and attractive woman had never married. Sarah's interest in her deepened. She was glad their daughters were at the same school. Perhaps they could be friends – though how dull she must seem to Hilary, how dull and conventional.

'And what about you, Sarah? You moved here quite recently too, didn't you?'

'Yes – only last Christmas. We used to live in South London, but it just didn't seem to be the right place to bring children up. You know, crime, and dogmess, and spending hours in the car stuck in traffic jams ferrying them about the place. They love it here, they didn't mind moving at all. The commuting's a bit of a bore for Adrian, but he can work on the train.'

'And why did you chose Barcombe?'

'Mainly because Adrian's mother lives here. It's a good thing for the children to see a lot of their grandmother, I suppose, though I must admit I find it a bit of a strain. She's not very well, you see, and of course Adrian's working all the time so it's always me who has to help out. Sometimes it just seems to be one more thing to tie me down.'

Hilary glanced at her swiftly. 'Do you feel tied down?'

Sarah coloured slightly. Here she was being disloyal to Adrian in front of a virtual stranger. She really must get a grip on herself.

She tried to think of a satisfactory answer to Hilary's question, but at that moment the front door opened and the sound of children's voices filled the hall. 'Mumm-ee! Where are you? I found the mermaid's purse.' That was Hannah. Gabriel was singing, as usual. 'Happy Birthday to you, Happy Birthday to you. Happy *Birthday*, dear seaside, Happy Birthday to you.'

'I'd better go and sort them out. I'll see you later.' A few moments later Hilary could hear Sarah reprimanding Adrian for not having remembered the children's wellingtons. Their feet, it seemed, were wet. Hilary smiled ruefully to herself, and then thought about Joe Coventry's eyes as she sketched the outline of the Man in the Moon.

CHAPTER FOUR

After his exuberant return from the seaside, Gabriel Stanhope's spirits went into a rapid decline. He refused his sandpit, would not sit on his tricycle, petulantly pushed away *Ant and Bee and the Rainbow*, and pressed himself against his mother's legs, sucking his thumb and twiddling a lock of hair just above his ear. Sarah, who was trying to bake a cake for her mother-in-law's visit the next day, was irritated. He might be ill, she supposed – but when he was ill he was usually sick first, and there was no sign of that. Adrian was reading the paper in the kitchen, to keep Sarah company. His presence added to her irritation. She would rather have been alone.

'Can't you play with him, or something? He's really in the way.' Her voice sounded much snappier than she meant it to.

Adrian put down the *Independent* and held out his hand to his son. 'Come on, Gaby. Shall we get the Play Doh out?'

The boy shook his head and whimpered.

'I don't think he's well, Sarah. His eyes look funny to me.'

Sarah shook flour through the sieve too vigorously; some fell to the floor like a little flurry of snow. 'Damn. No, he's fine. He just didn't eat enough lunch and his blood sugar's low. Mind out, Gabriel, Mummy's got to get the brush to sweep this up.'

'Let's give him something to eat now.'

'What – and ruin his appetite for supper? That's just a vicious circle. The reason he picked at his lunch was because of that ice-cream you gave him in Dinsford.'

'Oh, come on, you can't go to the seaside and not have an ice cream. Anyway he dropped most of it. I'm going to give him a biscuit now. Anything to stop this moaning.'

Sarah said, 'Do what you like,' in a tone which suggested the opposite. Adrian found a chocolate finger and held it out to his son, but Gabriel again shook his head and clung closer.

'He must be ill, if he won't eat a chocolate finger. How about giving him Calpol?'

'I tell you, Adrian, he's not ill, he's just in a mood. If he had earache or something he'd be screaming. Why don't you plonk him down in front of the video, then at least he'll be out of my way.'

Gabriel dozed in front of *Thomas the Tank Engine*, but his spirits did not improve, and by bedtime Sarah acknowledged that he might be getting a cold. She felt guilty for her earlier harshness, and kissed him tenderly as she tucked him up. He fell into a deep, heavy-breathing sleep immediately.

Hannah was sitting bolt upright reading *Gobbolino the Witch's Cat*. She had a precocious appetite for books, and had now learnt to read without speaking the words aloud. Her lips still moved, though, and her face revealed every emotion the author had meant her to feel; fear, amusement, surprise, flitted in turn across her little features. With her light hair neatly brushed, wearing a pink smocked nightie, she was a charming sight. It seemed a shame to turn the light out.

'Hannah, as a special treat, because it's Saturday night, would you like to read one more chapter? Gabriel's fast asleep, I don't think the light will disturb him.'

When Hannah was delighted she clapped her hands, in the way that children are supposed to in old-fashioned storybooks. It was one of her most endearing characteristics, and she did it now. 'Oh thank you, lovely, lovely Mummy.'

As Sarah went downstairs, soothed by the charm of her children, she made a resolution to apologise to Adrian for her earlier ill-temper, or at least to admit he had been right about Gabriel's illness. But the minute she entered the living room he switched off the television, stood up, and said, 'Right, I'm going.'

She was startled. Adrian never said things like that. Her heart jumped. Surely he couldn't be going to leave her.

'Out for a drink with Henry. Don't you remember? He rang last night.'

She did remember now. Henry was someone she had never met. Adrian had got to know him on the commuter train; he lived in the middle of Barcombe, and worked in London, in advertising. Having this last baby had simply destroyed her memory; time was when it would have been impossible for her to forget a detail like that.

'Of course. All right. But what about supper?'

'I'll eat at the pub. See you later.' He left without a kiss, without a smile.

Sarah wandered into the kitchen, took a lump of cheese from the fridge, and began to slice it, absently eating each slice as it fell from the knife. That departure had shaken her. Was she sailing too close to the wind, with her grumpiness, her touchiness, her endless fault-finding? Adrian was not the type to walk out on a wife and three children – but some men did do that. You read about them in magazines. Wives who had led comfortable existences found themselves wrangling about alimony and visiting rights, scouring charity shops for clothes and worrying about affording winter shoes. Could she do without Adrian financially? Could she do without him emotionally?

If it weren't for the money, being alone might be quite fun. Thinking her own thoughts, choosing her own friends, making all the decisions about the children. Taking her own lovers perhaps – and then getting rid of them when she'd had enough. She thought of Hilary Nightingale, her bicycle and her ready smile and her home-made beads. Everything about her suggested completeness and contentment. How many married women generated that kind of energy? If she were on her own she could be like Hilary – vibrant and thin.

Sarah looked down at the chopping board and found she'd eaten all the cheese that she had been going to make into a Welsh rarebit for her solitary supper. What would Hilary eat, she wondered. Something cheap and healthy, but exotic – cracked wheat salad perhaps, or something with chick peas in it. Sarah scanned her cupboards and fridge. Nothing suitable – but here was half an avocado, its cut side slightly blackened and shrunken. That would have to do. She would mash it with garlic and lemon juice, and make herself a little guacamole. That's what Hilary would do – she wouldn't just scoop out the flesh with a spoon, without even bothering to take the sticky label off the outside skin.

Sarah cut a lemon in half. As so often these days, she was surprised at her own train of thought. This fantasy about being alone was a load of nonsense – it wasn't Adrian who made her fat, and dull, and tired. Or was it?

The evening was unusually quiet. Maiden's Hill was never

busy, but for some time now not a single car had passed. Sarah remembered that Hannah's light was still on, but there was no murmur or rustle from the room. She opened the back door and stood leaning against the lintel, inhaling the night air – such luxury to do this, after the winter months. It was not yet quite dark; a tiny fingernail moon rose in a velvety violet sky.

A scream tore through the silence, followed by another and another. Sarah's bones melted; she was unable to move. Then she heard little feet pattering and Hannah's voice calling, 'Mummy! Mummy! Gabriel's making a noise.' A wave of giddiness washed over her and she sprang into action, bounding up the stairs and lifting the stiff, arched body of her son from his bed. His eyes were screwed shut, his open mouth was a rigid square. The sounds he was making were unlike any she had heard before – high, piercing, like a malfunctioning machine.

Hannah had her hands over her ears and was dancing about in the middle of the room. 'Oh Mummy, make him stop, make him stop.'

'Calm down, my love, I'm trying my best. Come on, Gaby, Gaby, Mummy's here, Mummy's here.' His body was burning hot, his pyjamas damp with sweat. She carried him into her bedroom and stripped him on her bed. He stopped screaming, but began to shiver and whimper instead. Thomas stirred in his cot, but mercifully didn't wake.

Sarah covered Gabriel with her counterpane and reached for the telephone. In a moment of efficiency she had Sellotaped the doctor's out-of-surgery-hours number to the bedside table on which the phone stood. She expected to hear the kind, reliable voice of their GP, Dr Maxwell, a sensible middle aged woman who was particularly good with children. Instead she heard a deep male voice give his name as a statement.

'Pierre Prescott.'

Dr Prescott, one of the other doctors in the practice. She had never seen him but she remembered his name from the brass plate by the surgery door.

'I'm sorry to bother you on a Saturday night, Doctor, but ...' She described Gabriel's condition.

'I'll be right over. Don't give him anything until I come.' Dr Prescott took details of how to find the house and rang off.

He was there unbelievably quickly. Gabriel had stopped shaking and had fallen into the inert unconsciousness that at bedtime Sarah had mistaken for peaceful sleep. He did not respond to the doctor's prodding. Hannah had crept into the bedroom despite Sarah's efforts to confine her to her own bed, and stood staring at the doctor with one finger in her mouth, her other arm wrapped firmly around her mother's waist. In his cot, Thomas slumbered on.

Dr Prescott finished his investigations and straightened up. He looked directly at Sarah. 'I'm taking this very seriously, Mrs Stanhope, because there has been a case of meningitis in the neighbourhood. However, the chances are that it's nothing more than a nasty bug. I'm saying this because I can see that you're an intelligent woman who will not be thrown into a panic at the mention of the word meningitis.'

Sarah nodded. Her heart had jolted painfully when he had used that word, but his last words made her determined not to show it. She stroked the top of Hannah's head. 'So what do we do?'

'Admit him to hospital at once. You should go with him of course.' He glanced at Hannah. 'Is there anyone on hand to babysit?' He looked around the bedroom as if checking for evidence of a stable matrimonial state, and seemed to find it in the paisley dressing-gown hanging on the back of the door. 'Your husband?'

Sarah realised with chagrin that she hadn't even asked Adrian which pub he was going to. She said grimly, 'My husband is out for the evening. I'll have to take the children with me. Hannah, go and get dressed. We're going in the car.' She indicated the sleeping Thomas. 'I'll leave that one till the last minute.'

'Good God! There's a third.' Dr Prescott's dark face broke into a grin. 'I hadn't noticed. Does he always sleep this well?'

Despite her anxiety Sarah laughed, affectionately patting the well-padded bottom in its fleecy sleep-suit. She made efforts to get him to lie on his side, but Thomas often ended up, face buried in his badger, sleeping on his knees with his bottom in the air.

'I'll ring the hospital to let them know we're coming.' The doctor noticed Sarah's expression of enquiry at his use of the first person plural. 'Oh yes, I'll drive you there. Are your car seats here?'

'Yes, Adrian walked to the pub. Oh Doctor, that would be so kind …' Her voice wobbled. She turned away and busied herself with reclothing Gabriel in his pyjamas. Dr Prescott picked up the telephone.

'I warn you, he may start screaming again at any minute. Be prepared.' For the first time, Sarah noticed the personal detritus surrounding him. On the telephone table were a packet of contraceptive pills, a dirty coffee mug with an apple core in it, a half-written letter to an old schoolfriend in Australia and the novel she was reading – a Margaret Drabble. Laundry, including underwear, was bundled at the foot of the bed, waiting to be put away. Thank goodness it was clean. Adrian's side of the bed was so much neater – nothing on his table but an alarm clock, set for 6:30, and a copy of *The Economist*. Sarah wondered which of these details the doctor had noticed.

A few minutes later, after Dr Prescott had given Gabriel a shot of penicillin, they were all in the doctor's car, he having pointed out that Adrian would need theirs in order to join them. In the same calm, masterful way he had ordered Sarah to write Adrian a note explaining the situation. She hadn't thought of it. What clues must he be picking up about the state of their marriage? None, probably – after all, it would be of no interest to him. Gabriel's continuing inertia allowed her to absorb some information about Dr Prescott. There were no child seats in his car, and no evidence of children either. There was, however, a dog grille. The interior was tidy; cassettes were neatly packed into a case, maps were tucked away into the glove compartment. To allow the child seats in, Sarah had to sit in the back, beltless, between her two sons. From time to time she caught a glimpse of Dr Prescott's eyes in the rear view mirror. They were large, widely spaced and very, very dark. The fanning lines at the corners made Sarah guess his age as about thirty-six.

Beside her, Gabriel moaned. Sarah cradled his hot, dangling little hand. She had astonished herself. Her precious son – how often had she chastised herself for finding him the most precious of her children? – was possibly seriously ill, and she was finding time to dwell on the possessions, the habits, the physical appearance of a stranger. Worse, she had been considering – even worrying about – how she would appear in his eyes. If Doctor Maxwell had been on duty she wouldn't have given the objects on the bedside table a second thought.

Gabriel did not have meningitis. He was kept in hospital for two nights for tests and observation; his high temperature continued, the glands in his neck felt like marbles, and he ate nothing and refused all drink until Hannah intelligently suggested Coca-Cola, which he was normally forbidden. Sarah stayed with him all the time, of course; when Adrian turned up at midnight on the Saturday he had expected to take Hannah and Thomas home with him, but they looked so comfortable sleeping in the Family Room that Sister said, 'Why disturb them?' and they stayed. Hannah, indeed, loved the hospital so much, and was so impeccably well-behaved, that she was allowed to stay for the whole of Sunday too. She was fascinated by everything from the beds which cranked up and down to the perfectly-rounded scoops of mashed potato, and as Gabriel refused it she was allowed his portion of ice-cream and tinned fruit salad. The beauty of the radiantly white ice-cream as a backdrop to the glowing red cherries and warm orange cubes of – peach perhaps? – seemed to strike her forcibly. In between meals she sat so still, observing without speaking, that one of the nurses remarked that she was 'just like a little doll'. Sarah, noting the smug expression creeping over her daughter's face, knew that this remark would be treasured and acted up to.

Adrian, alone with baby Thomas, took Monday off work. He had always been a conscientious father, but had tended increasingly to concentrate on the elder child; he had been deeply involved with Hannah as a baby, to the point where she had often favoured him above Sarah. He had shared his wife's anxiety about, though not her rapport with, Gabriel, and, he now realised, had taken his youngest's quiet good nature so much for granted that he hardly knew him. As he struggled with the poppers on Thomas' babygro that evening he remembered with affectionate nostalgia the early months of Hannah's life, the satisfaction at getting her to finish a mushed-up meal, the thrill of amazement at seeing her hold her own rusk or swipe accurately at a mobile, the almost pleasurable tedium of re-stacking plastic beakers or wiping the sticky covers of picture books. He thought wistfully, too, of the way he and Sarah had marvelled at her together. They'd recorded her progress in minute detail in a baby book, and had sometimes almost fallen out over the privilege of changing her nappy. In those days parenthood had brought them closer together; now it seemed to be nudging them apart. Was it just because they were, with three children, outnumbered? He almost hoped the hospital would keep Gabriel another day; this half-purposeful pottering was a welcome change from earning money.

On Monday, however, Gabriel was discharged at teatime. Despite a continuing high temperature any specific pain seemed to have disappeared, and it was no longer possible to confine him to bed. He whizzed up and down the ward on a toy tractor, singing 'Daisy, Daisy, give me your answer do' at surprising volume. When the doctor gave him a final examination and pronounced him fit to leave the relief was general. 'Keep him as quiet as possible,' Sarah was told, 'and don't worry about the eating – just make sure he has plenty to drink. Your GP will visit you tomorrow.'

Adrian had made a special effort to welcome her home. The place looked neat and tidy, and he'd ordered a take-away Chinese meal, and stocked the fridge with little bottles of her favourite German lager. He'd made Hannah's bed up in the spare room, in case Gabriel's nights continued to be restless. Thomas, in his high chair when they reached home, crowed and waved his spoon in welcome. Sarah hugged her husband, with more warmth than she'd felt for months. And when he told her that she'd been strong and brave and that he felt proud of her, she loved it. She did still care what he thought.

Sarah knew that it would be Dr Maxwell who called to visit Gabriel the next day, so when she saw the stout, iron-haired woman standing on her doorstep she felt only the tiniest pang of disappointment. And as the week wore on and Gabriel's health improved, so too did the state of her marriage. She found a renewed feeling of contentment in this, the last week of the school holidays; sewing on Hannah's nametapes, sorting out Thomas' outgrown clothes for Oxfam (there was definitely not going to be a fourth baby), reading mountains of stories to the convalescent Gabriel, all seemed pleasant and valuable, and she was pleased to find that a combination of anxiety and unpalatable hospital food had made her lose a couple of pounds. Heartened, she made a new resolution to take snacks from the fruitbowl, not from the biscuit tin, and kept it. Each evening, she looked forward to Adrian's return they talked over dinner, and watched a couple of videos that they'd been meaning to hire for ages.

Adrian's mother, whose Sunday teatime visit had necessarily been cancelled, came on Thursday instead, bearing gifts for the ex-invalid. Sarah found the inevitable inappropriateness of the presents less irritating than usual. This time there was a straw donkey wearing a flowery hat. Panniers were attached to his sides by long pins; once Sarah had removed these he was quite acceptable. Gabriel showed little interest in him, but Hannah said he was sweet, and filled the panniers with the daisies that had just begun to appear on the lawn. There was also a packet of felt tip pens, of the kind that made apparently indelible marks on clothing and furniture; Sarah let Gabriel scribble with them while his grandmother was there, but resolved to replace them with a less harmful make the next day. He leaned on the kitchen table, drawing huge swirling circles with the purple pen – 'Gaby is drawring a funderstorm.' How did he know about thunder? It must be from some story or other – she couldn't think of a real storm since last year.

'Have you got any Minadex for him, dear? I always gave Adrian Minadex.' The elder Mrs Stanhope pinched her grandson's arm with investigative, not malicious, intent. 'He's still very thin.'

'He'll pick up soon. His appetite's come back.' Sarah put a plate of fruit scones on the table, just out of reach of the whirling purple pen. She resolved to have hers without butter. She had, over the years, made it a matter of principle not to take any of her mother-in-law's frequently-offered advice. 'Put porridge in his bottle – that'll make him sleep.' 'If you give him a dummy he'll never learn to talk.' 'Toothpaste will give him a tummy ache – just give him a piece of apple to chew.' The suggestions had nearly all been directed at Gabriel; Hannah and Thomas more nearly matched Diana Stanhope's idea of well-brought-up children.

She was not an old woman – a veil of mystery was thrown over her age, but she couldn't have been much above sixty – and yet she carried with her this curious flavour of another era. She condemned breast feeding ('quite unnecessary') and recommended the manufacture of something called 'oat jelly'; she deplored all-in-one suits for infants ('stunts the growth') and had even knitted some misshapen woolly leggings in an early burst of enthusiasm for the arrival of her first grandchild. She was tiny, almost worryingly thin, but dedicated to the promotion of weight gain in others as a prerequisite for good health. Her house and garden, three miles the other side of Barcombe, were immaculate, and she never arrived at the house on Maiden's Hill without tugging a tuft of groundsel from the front path or running a finger over the sideboard in the dining room to check for dust. Such actions were too automatic to be construed as criticisms, and when her morale was high, as it was now, Sarah felt perfectly able to rise above them.

Now she sat in the kitchen approving the scones ('very light – most digestible') but looking askance at the tea, which contained a number of floating 'strangers'. ('Have you mislaid your tea-strainer, dear?'). Hannah sat next to her, shyly stroking the silky fringes of the deep-red shawl Mrs Stanhope flung dramatically about her frail person almost regardless of the weather. Hannah admired her grandmother immensely, especially the neatness of her small black shoes that buttoned on one side and the pleasing snap that her stiff round handbag made when opened or shut. But her habit of wearing hats, which made her amusing to Thomas, was slightly intimidating to the little girl; it was not wholly disassociated from the idea of witches. Gabriel usually ignored her, as he ignored most people. Sometimes he would cry, as if frightened, on her arrival; even more occasionally he would rush at her and hug her so hard that she almost tottered.

'I have brought something for you, my dear,' she said now, opening the snapping handbag to Hannah's delight. She brought out a small brown envelope and handed it to Sarah. Inside was a black and white photograph; a tiny fair-haired boy holding a dressed monkey. Clearly, it had been taken by a photographer at some seaside resort.

'It's Adrian!' Sarah was pleased. She had seen few pictures of her husband as a child; the Stanhopes had not possessed a camera. The little boy's intense expression of nervous excitement was charming. 'Isn't he like Gabriel?' she exclaimed. 'I've never noticed it before – but the expression, the smile, don't you think?'

Mrs Stanhope took the photograph back to examine it more closely. 'A little like,' she admitted, 'but of course in character they differ very greatly. Here you are, Sarah, it's yours to keep.'

Sarah thanked her, and propped it up on a high shelf, out of the reach of sticky fingers. She was very much drawn to the little image and its glimpse of a vanished life. She looked forward to contemplating it later. The child's expression reminded her, not only of Gabriel, but of the Adrian she had once known. When they had first met there had been a quality of intensity, an almost neurotic vibrancy about him, that seemed to have disappeared completely now, eroded by routines of working and travelling, eating and sleeping. To what extent was that erosion her fault?

'Grandma,' said Hannah suddenly, as if voicing her mother's thoughts, 'what was Daddy like when he was a little boy?'

'A very good little boy, my darling. He set his own place at the table from when he was four years old, and helped to clear it away afterwards. He loved animals, and looked after them beautifully.'

'What animals did he have, Grandma?' Hannah knew the answer but loved to hear it again.

'He had a number of guinea pigs, and a little ginger cat. It was a brave little cat. Once, when it was no more than a kitten, it fought a huge brown rat. They fought all over the kitchen, and Custard finally won. The rat died standing up – leaning back against the kitchen cupboard like a wounded soldier. We found it like that when we came down to breakfast the next morning. Meanwhile Custard crept up to your father's room and lay on his pink eiderdown, bleeding heavily. Little Adrian woke up and fetched warm water and bathed poor Custard's wounds. In a few days he was quite, quite better. And we forgave poor Custard for ruining the eiderdown because he had been so brave.'

'What's an eiderdown, Mummy? I forgot.'

'A bit like a duvet, darling.'

'And why was he called Custard, Grandma?'

'Because of his colour – a very pale ginger, almost yellow. He had big green eyes like gooseberries. A most edible-looking cat.'

'And did Daddy have any more pets?'

'Yes, we had a Jack Russell terrier called Horatio, after Nelson. He was a faithful little dog. When your grandfather died Horatio pined and pined, and wandered about looking for him. He was killed on the road shortly afterwards; we think he was trying to find your grandfather, following one of his favourite walks.'

'Grandma, were you very sad when Grandfather died?'

Diana Stanhope paused and sipped her tea before replying, 'No, my dear, not very sad. You see, I had your father to keep me company.'

'So didn't you pine and pine?'

'No, I did not pine and pine. That was left to Horatio.'

'Mummy, would you be sad if Daddy died?'

'Oh yes! Of course I would, Hannah!'

'Even though you've got me and Gabriel and Thomas and Percy to keep you company?' (Percy was a goldfish.)

'Yes, because I'd still miss Daddy. What a gloomy conversation, Hannah.' Sarah busied herself with refilling the tea pot. She turned her head away from the teatable, but not before she caught a glimpse of her mother-in-law's small sharp eyes fixing her with a look that could only be described as quizzical.

CHAPTER FIVE

It was unusually warm for April. By the time term had begun again for Hannah and Gabriel the fruit trees had almost finished blossoming and the front garden path was flanked with noisy tulips; hot scarlet, pink like nail varnish, striped yellow and red like flags. Sarah loved the way they threw open their hearts to the sun, proudly revealing their intricate centres – which someone had told her were a kind of parking system for bees – and then, at evening, closed up, smartly, but a little less tightly with each passing day. Between them were puffs of forget-me-nots, a few sugar-pink ones amongst all that baby blue. The previous owners of the house had been imaginative gardeners. The front garden had a boxy, dolly mixture charm, like an illustration from a children's book. At the back things were looser. A clematis shook its dusty blue bells amongst the dark green fronds of another climber; Sarah thought it would turn out to be a jasmine, but she wasn't sure. Violets, fading already, grew between the paving stones; campanulas and aubretia tumbled over the parapet wall. It was exciting to see all their predecessor's plants appearing, but Sarah resolved to find out more about gardening for herself. She wanted to make the place her own.

On the whole, these warm spring days, her heart was high. Her weight loss continued, steadily and relatively effortlessly. To celebrate and encourage this change she arranged a babysitter for Thomas, booked an appointment at the hairdresser's, and set out to spend a significant sum of money on herself first. There were only two boutiques in Barcombe, but as time was short she did not go further afield; it would be a good discipline to force herself to choose at least one item from each shop.

The first shop, on the High Street, was faintly depressing. Everything was nearly nice, but not quite. Crisp cotton blouses turned out to be mixed with polyester; colourful scarves proved on close inspection to be not silky smooth, but slimy to the touch. A pale denim dress caught her eye, but its buttons were made of ugly plastic. Every item seemed to be trying and failing to imitate something better. She reminded herself of her vow to choose something, and found a skirt to try on; it was an acceptable stone colour, and it was long and slim-fitting – a shape that was newly fashionable.

Alas, the skirt, rather than proving the amount of weight already lost, merely seemed to advertise how much was still left to be shed. It clung to Sarah's bottom and thighs, meticulously revealing every undulation, then in its narrowness bound her ankles together so that she could hardly hobble. Stripping it off, she decided she was too old to be a fashion victim. She bought a couple of pairs of tights in honour of her vow, and left.

The second shop was in a little precinct which had been created out of a cluster of disused Victorian warehouses. Here was Barcombe's only expensive restaurant, with its discreet bottle-green sign and its menu, hand-written daily in French. Here, too, was a children's shop full of smocked frocks and sailor suits; the kind of clothes Sarah never bought for her own children, but very occasionally bought as presents for the children of her friends. Bright, wooden toys with astonishing price tags were scattered artfully amongst the clothes; in the window pranced a dappled wooden rocking horse, far too smart for any child to ride.

This precinct, with its combination of high prices, genuine quality, and a kind of smug tweeness, had always annoyed Sarah, but her failure in the High Street shop had made it all the more imperative that she should find something to buy here; she was determined not to waste all that good babysitting time. She examined the display in the window of the boutique. Instead of the usual female dummies the clothes were hung on flat wooden cut-outs. The predominant colours were apricot and mauve, by no means her favourites, but subtly and harmoniously interlinked here. She pushed open the door.

Cushiony piles of gently-folded sweaters caught her attention immediately. The colours were glorious; sage green, tomato, ivory, and a kind of muted indigo very similar to the lovely clematis rioting over the back garden wall. The price was far more than she would usually pay for a sweater, but never mind. She pulled an indigo one out from the pile and shook it out. It was made of a blend of cotton and silk; it had an interesting nubbly texture and an unusual scooped neckline. She asked to try it on.

The light in the changing room was soft and flattering, very different from the merciless neon strip that had made her complexion look positively corrugated in the first shop. This light, like candlelight, gave her cheekbones and shadowy temples; the blue of the sweater intensified the somewhat indeterminate blue-grey of her eyes. Her neck and upper chest rose, moulded and creamy white, above its rounded, slightly scalloped edge. Yes, definitely, she must have this one.

She left the shop wearing it, with the old checked shirt she had been wearing stuffed into the smart rope-handled carrier bag. No time for more browsing; she was due at the hairdresser's. Anyway, that one purchase was so perfect it would be foolish to push her luck any further.

The hairdresser's was just opposite. She hadn't had a cut for months and months; probably not since before Christmas. Her thick, tawny hair showed no signs of grey yet, though it wouldn't show up as much as on a darker person. When neglected, as now, it became heavy with a kind of halo of frizz. The hairdresser held up handfuls and let them fall, her face a study in disapproval.

'Ever thought of highlights?' she asked. Her own hair was dyed red, short, with lots of little curls at the front and cut sharply, almost shaved, to a point at the back of her neck. She was young and thin; her skinny legs were made to look even frailer by the clumpy black platform shoes she wore. Sarah found her quite frightening.

'No, I've never used any colour at all. Do you think I should?'

'Well, yeah, it would give it a bit of a lift. Think about it, and give me a ring; you got my card. For now, I'll just give you a bit of a layered bob, OK?'

Sarah submitted and was led over to the washbasins feeling both indulged and subtly humiliated. The experience of having her hair washed and cut involved a kind of sensual focus that she both enjoyed and hated. She wasn't sure she wouldn't rather be at the dentist; at least there the emotions were uncomplicated. A little water trickled down her neck; she tucked the towel more closely in to protect the new sweater. The shampooist giggled and said sorry. Her giggle seemed to be an occupational hazard. 'Got any holiday plans?' she asked. 'No? Me neither.' Giggle. 'Can't afford it.' Giggle. 'D'you work round here?' Sarah disclosed her housewifely status. 'Aw, that's nice.' More giggling.

Sarah knew she would be regarded as snobbish, but she didn't want to talk. She wanted to indulge in a daydream which had been forming somewhere at the back of her mind, but which she hadn't quite dared to develop yet. She knew it featured Dr Prescott – in fact it starred Dr Prescott. The trouble was she couldn't get rid of the logistics. How could she write Adrian and the children out of the script without taking their misery into account? If she were a less plodding, literal-minded person she would be able to blot them out entirely for the duration of the fantasy, she thought, but her life was too firmly rooted in reality to allow that. Death, divorce, deceit – the necessity of one of these would keep popping up in her mind like a no entry sign.

Nonetheless she asked for a magazine while her hair was being cut and held it open more or less at random while she perfected a mental picture of Dr Prescott – Pierre Prescott. The French forename suggested an interesting family history, a small, discreet apartment on the Rive Gauche, sunlight on the balcony and the rustle of plane trees. Or perhaps a villa by the Mediterranean – balmy air, baskets of bursting figs, lizards darting into cracks. The alliterative Ps of his name were pleasing – definite, decisive, like his face, with its square-cut jaw and strongly-marked eyebrows. Sarah smiled, suddenly aware of the corniness of the fantasy. A dark Frenchman with a cleft chin? Positively Mills and Boon. She glanced at her magazine and realised that for at least twenty minutes she had had it open at an article about male impotence. Doubtless the stylist had drawn her own conclusions about Sarah's apparent absorption in this subject. Deciding to re-enter the real world and lay the silly daydreaming to rest, she smiled at the young woman's reflection in the mirror. 'Have you worked here long?' she asked.

The finished cut was a good one. Sarah's hair now swung rather than fell. It ended just below her ears. This and the low neckline of her new jumper made her neck look more than usually long and slender. She tipped the girl generously and stepped out into the sunny precinct full of confidence, with three-quarters of an hour left before she needed to relieve Thomas' babysitter. She could sit in the smart little café, opposite, eat a civilised, if early, lunch and watch the world go by. She stood looking into the café window, considering its menu.

'Well. Hello!' Somebody tapped her on the arm. 'Mrs Stanhope, isn't it? How's your little boy? I rang the hospital, I gathered it turned out to be a false alarm – but is he quite over it?' Amazingly, it was Dr Prescott, in jeans, laden with shopping. His jaw wasn't quite as chiselled as she'd remembered it, but his smile was friendlier. She answered his enquiries as coolly as she could, but her heart was racing. The feeling was closer to guilt than pleasure.

'I was just stopping here for a cup of coffee,' he said. 'Why don't you join me?'

And why not? He directed her to a very public window-seat, as if to emphasise that there was nothing illicit in the encounter. The café was smart and impersonal. The furniture was bent chrome and matt black wood; three deep purple irises sprang from a square glass vase in the centre of the table. Sarah focused on the precise detail of their leaping yellow tongues in order to calm her mind.

He ordered two cappuccinos, without asking whether she wanted one. He chatted naturally and easily, arranging large amber sugar crystals in a straight line on the tabletop, absently but fastidiously, with the handle of his spoon. She learnt that he'd taken a few days' holiday, that he was shopping for a long weekend he was spending with friends; it was somebody's birthday, he was looking for presents. 'Doesn't your wife buy things like that?' said Sarah, surprised. 'I thought that was one of the proven gender differences – that men were incapable of buying presents and greeting cards.'

Pierre laughed. 'My wife's working. I'm going on my own. And no, I usually deal with that side of life. I enjoy shopping, and I'm good at it – so I'm an exception to your rule.'

Sarah wanted to find out more about his wife, but didn't want to seem to interrogate him. She started to cast about for a neutral topic of conversation, but there was no need. Pierre talked with a woman's ease, though more decisively than most women. After half an hour she knew a lot about his tastes and preferences – for the sun, for the sea, architecture, photography; if he hadn't been a doctor he'd have been a photographer, he said. His preferred subjects were people; people were the most interesting thing in the world. She had an exceptionally beautiful little son; would she allow him to take pictures of him one day? And of her other two children, of course. 'Oh that would be lovely – we could do it for my husband's birthday present,' said Sarah instinctively, and then wished she hadn't.

'Talking of children, I have to go,' she said, opening her handbag. 'The babysitter's got to leave at half past.' She pulled out a couple of coins. 'Will that be enough?' she asked, gruffly.

'Don't be ridiculous.' He passed them back to her. 'And now, excuse me.' He leaned over, and with a quick, firm action dabbed at her chin with a paper napkin. 'Only a little foam, from the coffee. It looked rather beguiling.' He laughed. 'It was good to talk to you. We'll meet again soon.' As she stumbled to the door, catching her carrier bag on the corner of a table, he swivelled round in his chair, and added, 'Oh and by the way, that blue suits you. Goodbye.'

'But don't you want to know who your father is?' asked Laura. The girls were sitting cross-legged on Elinor's bed, searching each other's hair for split ends. 'Jesus, if it was me I wouldn't shut up about it until I'd *made* her tell me.'

'I bet you wouldn't.' Elinor's tone was ironic. Laura ignored it.

'I mean, when I was – I don't know – about twelve I suppose,' she continued, 'I used to fantasise that Mum and Dad weren't my real parents, that I was the missing heiress to a huge estate in Cornwall or something –'

'Why Cornwall?'

'Why not? I'd been reading what's her name –'

'Daphne du Maurier?'

'Yeah, that kind of thing. And there was something on telly – never mind. It was all a load of crap, obviously.'

'Well, you're the spitting image of your mother.'

'Yes, unfortunately. That's what everyone says. And I've got the same birthmark as my dad – look –' Laura tugged down her T-shirt to reveal a brown mark, almost star-shaped, on her plump white shoulder. 'He's got one too, in exactly the same place. Weird, isn't it?'

'I think it's rather pretty.' Elinor touched the mark lightly. 'Like a tattoo. I wouldn't mind a tattoo, but I'd never have the nerve.'

'I used to think I wanted one, but then I read somewhere that Paula Yates really regretted hers, and that put me off.'

'Who's Paula Yates?'

'You know, that stupid blonde woman. God, you don't know anything, do you? But you're very good at side-tracking.'

'What do you mean?'

'I want to get back to your father. It's really interesting. Why don't you ask?'

'I used to ask, but Mum said she'd tell me when I was older.'

'Well, you are older.'

'Yes, but at the moment I don't particularly want to know.'

'I don't believe it. If you won't ask her, I will.'

'Laura, you wouldn't!' Elinor sprang off the bed. 'Say you wouldn't, Laura, please.'

Laura was taken aback by the panic in her friend's voice. 'No, no, Ells, of course I wouldn't. Only joking. Come on, sit back down.' She pulled at Elinor's sleeve. 'I won't talk about it if it really pisses you off. But you've got to admit it's interesting.'

Elinor resumed her perch. 'The thing is,' she said at length, resuming her monkey-like investigation of Laura's hair, 'that it's always been just Mum and me. And I never wanted anyone else to get in the way. I used to be even jealous of her friends, like Cl – Mrs P. I was so afraid of – I don't know what.'

'But just knowing about your father wouldn't mean your mum would – you know – get him back, or anything.' Laura's voice was gentle.

'I suppose not,' said Elinor, 'but it was like a superstition to me. If I knew his name then it would make him real, and I didn't want him to be real.'

'But you said you used to ask –'

'Yeah, I did at one time. I read something about diseases that run in the family and I had this thing about inheriting a disease from my father, because I was really small for my age, even though Mum was tall, and I thought I was going to be a midget or something –'

'Not very likely that your ma would have gone to bed with a midget,' put in Laura, laughing.

'Well you never know, she might if she felt sorry for him. She's weird. I mean the one she's seeing now – the one I saw out of the window – he's so gross. He's got a round belly – like this.' Elinor's hands described a balloon shape.

'Oi!' retorted Laura, patting her own ample stomach.

'Sorry, Lor, but it's different on a girl.'

'I thought you said she wasn't really going out with him,' said Laura.

'Well she isn't, he just took her out to dinner. But you never know what she'll do if she feels sorry for someone.'

'He sounds interesting, though. He's a writer, isn't he? It doesn't really matter what they look like.'

'Why not?'

'Well, people don't have to look at them much. They can just stay indoors and write. But anyway, you grew.'

'Grew? Oh yes.' Elinor laughed. 'Yes, I stopped thinking I was a midget. And I stopped asking about my father.'

'And now you want me to stop asking, right? OK – on one condition. Can I make myself a toasted sandwich on that dinky little machine of yours? Cheese and tomato, preferably, but almost anything will do.'

Claudia Prescott sat in a corner of the staff room, reading the paper. She held it up in front of her face, but that didn't deter Raymond Spanner from addressing her.

'Claudia!' he exclaimed heartily, sinking into the armchair next to her with an 'oof', 'How's the play going?'

Raymond Spanner taught geography and had had a hair extension. His presence was unwelcome, but there was really no harm in him, and it must be tough, living with a name like that. Claudia folded the paper with deft, neat movements.

'Fine, thank you. Most of the girls have begun to learn their lines, and I'm due to meet the art department to talk about the set after school.'

'Who's your star?'

'Caroline Crouch is Orlando, and Caroline Marston is the Duke. Laura Taylor is Rosalind; she's the one I'm most worried about, but I think she'll manage.'

'Well, I'm not *au fait* with the play myself, but if you ask my

51

opinion, Laura Taylor is a bit of a handful. In more than one sense, if you'll forgive me.' He chuckled meaningfully. Leonie Spencer, one of Claudia's colleagues in the English department, glanced up from her marking at this point and gave Claudia a sympathetic glance.

'I find Laura tractable enough. I'm just not sure she has enough sensitivity for the part,' Claudia replied.

'Sensitivity! No, Abbey girls aren't well known for that. She is a big girl, is Laura. Perhaps you could get her to lose a pound or two before the big night. It's not till the end of term, is it? Bags of time.'

Claudia smiled thinly but said nothing.

'And what about yourself, Claudia? You never put on an ounce. What's your secret?' Raymond continued.

'Metabolism, I expect. Now if you will excuse me, Raymond, I must make a telephone call before the end of break.' Claudia rose, and smoothed out the crinkles in her straight navy blue skirt. Leonie Spencer accompanied her into the inner room. 'You haven't really got to make a phone call, have you?' she asked.

'I need to let Pierre know I'll be late back. But it could have waited till lunch break. I just felt I'd had enough of Raymond Spanner on the subject of the female form.'

'I always feel as if I've heard enough of Raymond on any subject, before he's even opened his mouth. What I don't understand is how you haven't scared him off yet. You terrify most people.'

'That's you myth making again, Leonie. Anyway, Ray's a brave man.'

'He must be, to wear that wig.'

'It's not a wig.'

'The girls think it is, they say you can see the edge of it just above his ears.'

'Really, Leonie! Gossiping with the girls about Mr Spanner! They are welcome to scrutinise his ears if they choose, but the idea makes me feel faintly bilious. Anyway, I've got some photocopying to do for 4N. Coming?'

The photocopier was in a little room of its own, leading off the staff-room. It was the most private room in the school, more private than the Ladies, which was haunted by Veronique, the French assistant constantly adjusting her make-up, and by Doris, the indefatigably cheerful cleaner. The photocopying room had a thick door, and the drone of the machine muffled their voices. Claudia had no particular confidence to impart – she never did, really – but she guessed from Leonie's eagerness to follow her that the younger woman had something particular to say. Claudia squashed the lid of the photocopier down on an open poetry book, and waited.

'What are you copying?'

'Oh just a couple of war poems for 4N. Their GCSE theme is Conflict. How imaginative.'

'I'm doing the other one – the Life Cycle or whatever. Though I am getting a bit sick of all those nature poems – Heaney, Hughes et cetera.'

'Life Cycle? Those poems always seem to be about death. Dead farm animals, usually.'

'Well, they're about both. Anyway, guess what?' Leonie's mouth twitched.

'I think I know, but I don't want to say, in case I'm wrong.'

'Go on – you're right.'

'Well then – you're pregnant.'

'Yes! But how did you guess?'

'Because you've stopped drinking coffee and your brain's already started to go soft. But seriously, Leonie, that's marvellous news.' Claudia patted her friend awkwardly on the arm, and turned to the photocopier, which had finished its run. She doubted the adequacy of her response. 'When's it due?' she asked, with face averted.

'December. So it's early days. The due date is actually Christmas Eve. Handy, eh?'

'Well, at least you won't have to stay with John's parents this year.'

'No, but they'll come to us. His mother's already said she'll come and bloody help.'

'You'll have to get used to that, my dear – the family really starts weaving its web once babies appear on the scene. That's something I've been fortunate enough to escape.'

Leonie glanced sharply at Claudia, as if suddenly realising that the news might not be entirely welcome in some quarters. 'Claudia, you are pleased aren't you?'

'Of course I'm pleased. Now I've just got time to ring Pierre before the end of break. He's going away for the weekend without me, and I probably won't see him before he goes, because I'm having a meeting with the art department. So come on – I must hurry.' She turned and looked Leonie full in the face. 'Leonie, I really am pleased. And I think it'll be a very lucky little baby.'

Leonie's little round face flushed pink with pleasure. 'Thank-you,' she said, and kissed Claudia quickly.

Claudia stiffened involuntarily, but she managed a half smile. As she crossed the school's Victorian Gothic quadrangle with a pile of exercise books clasped to her chest she wondered how many of her female friends were still childless, and found she could think of none. Those members of 4N who had omitted to hand their prep in that morning soon found themselves regretting it.

CHAPTER SIX

'That was Henry,' said Adrian, putting down the telephone one Sunday morning. 'He wants me to go and try out the new squash courts with him. Do you know where my racquet is?'

'What, now? You're going to play squash now?'

'If that's all right with you.' Adrian's tone implied that there was no reason why it shouldn't be.

Sarah squashed her automatic impulse to object, and succeeded only in part.

'OK, fine. But you said you'd take Hannah and Gabriel to the rec, remember –'

'I'll do that after lunch. I'll only be gone an hour or so.' Adrian ruffled Sarah's hair, smiling. 'I thought you liked getting me out of the house.'

'Don't be daft.' Sarah moved away. 'Your racquet's probably in the cupboard under the stairs, in one of those cardboard boxes. You haven't played since we moved, have you? Don't overdo it, Ade, will you?'

'I'm sure Henry will marmalise me, but I'd like to get a bit fit again.'

Once the door had closed behind her husband, Sarah allowed her fantasy full rein. Ages ago she had read an article in a women's magazine about a bigamist who had maintained two separate establishments, with neither family knowing about the existence of the other until after his suicide. He had always told wife number one that he was going to play squash; after his death she had opened his sports bag to find it full of equipment in perfect, unused condition.

Sarah listened at the door of the children's room; Gabriel and Hannah were playing harmoniously with their farm animals. She slipped into her own bedroom and opened the wardrobe door, taking care not to jangle the hangers because Thomas was deep in his usual late-morning nap. She delved into all the pockets of Adrian's four work suits. There wasn't much to go on. A few receipts. A clean handkerchief. A circular letter beginning 'Dear Beer Lover'. The tiny wrappings, neatly folded, of a few Tunes, from a recent cold.

She turned to his black leather briefcase, propped against his bedside table. It was funny, she'd never once looked in this before. She'd always assumed, in so far as she'd given the matter any thought, that its contents would be completely uninteresting. And they were. There were several legal documents, a bank statement, a Barclaycard bill. Behind these she glimpsed the back cover of a magazine – the kind of magazine about property and restaurants in London that is handed out free at railway stations. The sort of thing Adrian would accept absent-mindedly and never look at again. She replaced it exactly as she found it.

There was one small side pocket that she'd nearly overlooked. Its contents were more promising. An old envelope, with a telephone number written on it – a local number. She carefully copied it out onto a scrap of paper and put it in the drawer of her dressing table, right at the back. She would ring it one day. Then she looked inside the envelope. Her heart thumped as she saw the shiny edges of a photograph. Here at last was a real clue.

She drew it out, her hand trembling, and looked down on an image of her former self. There she was, leaning against a lump of rock, smiling, windblown, tanned. She was wearing a white sundress – what had happened to that dress? – made of broderie anglaise, drawn in at the waist by an Indian scarf, saffron-coloured, printed in scarlet with ohm symbols and little suns. They had chosen it together in Portobello market. She remembered everything about the picture. Adrian had taken it in Calabria, on the first holiday they had had together. She was smiling at him because he'd been doing an impersonation of a fussy portrait photographer. He was good at impersonations – or used to be. She remembered the salty wind, the vibrating turquoise sky, the greasy salami and squeaky bread they'd shared for their lunch that day. The scent of wild thyme; the way wasps had pursued them so that they'd had to eat their picnic on the run. The olive grove they'd found for their siesta. Her head pillowed on Adrian's chest.

'Mummy!' Hannah, standing at the door, adopted her most grown-up tone. 'I think it's almost certainly time for juice and biscuits. Gabriel thinks so too.'

'Hush, darling, you'll wake Thomas.'

Sarah thrust the photograph back into its place and snapped the briefcase shut. 'OK, go downstairs and we'll have elevenses.' She busied herself with beakers and Garibaldi biscuits, trying not to analyse her feelings which seemed to be surprisingly close to disappointment. But there was still the telephone number.

Elinor Nightingale and Laura Taylor had spent their break in a kind of plywood cubicle at the edge of the school grounds. Sacks of garden refuse were dumped here; they made reasonably comfortable seats. The only other attraction of the place was that it was possible to smoke in peace. Most of the girls favoured the lavatories for this purpose, but Laura said she didn't want to smoke in a crowd until she got really good at it, and in any case about once a term the teachers would lose patience and organise what Laura termed 'a massive bust'. The garden hut was preferable; Mickey, the gardener and handyman, was known to smoke in there, so no member of staff seeing smoke drifting out from above the swing doors would bother to investigate. Mickey himself encouraged the girls, and had an unspoken sub-letting arrangement; any break-time smoker left one cigarette for him on a little wooden ledge on the wall. Propped on the same ledge was Mickey's calendar of Penthouse pin-ups. Elinor said she thought the combination of the cigarettes and the calendar was politically highly unsound, but Laura said she liked the 'girlies' and found them an inspiration. She couldn't quite explain why. 'It's – well, men are so easily pleased, aren't they? It's kind of sweet.' Mickey himself, with his self-imposed semi-military khaki garb and maroon beret, his gappy grin, and his unguessable age, was regarded as 'kind of sweet' by most of the girls, and a little sinister by most of the staff.

'I wish I wasn't in this bloody play,' said Laura on this particular occasion. 'We're going to be rehearsing virtually every night and Mrs Prescott's going to be taking it really seriously. She starts each session off with a discussion of the scene we're doing and it's a bit like an extra English lesson. Except it's not really a discussion because its only Mrs P and Caroline Crouch talking. Oh and Kelly Thacker, but she just says really moronic things.'

'I didn't know Kelly Thacker was in it. Who's she playing? I didn't know she could act.'

'She can't. She's Audrey, the country wench. One of the country wenches. Katie Burrell is the other one. I wish you were in it, it would be a lot more fun.'

'I can't act.'

'So, you'd have a lot in common with the rest of us. And Mrs P likes you, so she'd be in a better mood. She hates me.'

'She doesn't hate you. If she hated you she wouldn't have given you the best part. And she only likes me because my mother's friendly with her.'

'I keep forgetting that. Tell me again – why they're friends?'

'Oh they've known each other for years – before I was born, I think. Maybe they were at school together, even. We didn't see much of her, though, until we moved here; we used to stay with them about once a year or something. And once we went on holiday with them, to France. They're why we moved here, really.'

'Isn't it weird being taught by your mum's friend? Especially when it's Mrs P?'

'What do you mean, especially when it's Mrs P?'

'Well, you know what she's like, I mean she's so … strict. When you were on holiday, did she wear a bikini, or what?'

'It wasn't that kind of holiday. It was inland. I can't remember that much about it. Mrs P was reading a lot. She wore shorts, I think. She's got good legs.'

'Maybe she has, but you never think of her as having good legs – you never think of her as having legs at all. It's like I read somewhere that someone said Mrs Thatcher had good legs, but it's just kind of … irrelevant. It's hard to imagine her and your mother being friends. Your mother's so lively. I mean, until you came, no one even knew that Mrs P's name was Claudia.'

'She's different out of school. I expect they all are.'

'I bet Mr Spanner's the same, wherever he goes. Mrs P's husband's nice, isn't he? The doctor.'

Elinor paused. 'I didn't like him much.'

'Didn't? You still see them, don't you?'

'I mean I didn't like him much on that holiday. We do still see them, but we usually see her, on her own. He's very busy.'

'Why didn't you like him?'

'You *do* ask a lot of questions, don't you? I don't know why. He was ... ingratiating. Hurry up and finish that fag. There's the three-minute bell.'

Laura ground out the cigarette end with her toe, and popped a Polo mint into her mouth. 'What've you got next? I've got geography. I'm going to have to ask Spanner for an essay extension, which isn't going to be easy. *He* doesn't like me either.' Laura placed a cigarette on the ledge, and the two girls left the hut.

Claudia Prescott's meeting ended earlier than she expected, so she was home in time to say goodbye to her husband. The Prescotts lived in a modern brick bungalow. This fact was of some surprise to their newer acquaintances, who seemed to associate Pierre with something more traditionally tasteful, and Claudia with something just plain old-fashioned. The bungalow had in fact been designed by the two of them together, five or six years earlier. Its great glory was its situation, on a wooded incline just outside Barcombe, buffered against winds by well-grown timber on three sides but with a panoramic view of the town opening out unexpectedly on the fourth. They had spent a fair bit of money on landscaping the garden, which dropped down in three terraces to a large ornamental pond. The garden still looked a little raw. It was Pierre's province, mainly, and he liked to surround each shrub with a thickly strewn circle of woodchips or, in some cases, gravel. He didn't like plants to overlap; they punctuated the view but did not unify it. Pierre was not much interested in flowers, so Claudia had decided to create a herbaceous border along the front of the house, but her interest in it was sporadic, and even now, in late April, it looked under-stocked. She had tied the dying daffodils into strangulated knots; somehow these caught the eye more than the primulas and auriculas at their feet.

The Abbey School was at the opposite end of Barcombe from High House, so Claudia drove to and from work. She had her own car, a second-hand, but well-maintained, Fiesta; it pleased her immensely not to have to share her husband's car. She parked it now, on the neat gravel sweep in front of the house – she could see that Pierre's Peugeot was in the garage. The circumstance caused her a mild throb of annoyance; Pierre would be leaving soon anyway, and could easily have left his car out so that she could have put hers away for the night. As it was she'd have to move it later. Through the bedroom window she could see him moving about, packing.

She did not call to him when she entered the house but greeted with an absent-minded pat the dim-looking Bassett hound that pushed its smooth flank against her legs in welcome. She picked up a handful of letters and scanned them quickly. Nothing of immediate interest. She hung her blazer on a hanger in the hall and adjusted an arrangement of dried leaves and flowers on the windowsill. It was looking a little dusty. Time to throw it out, really. Pierre opened the bedroom door. 'Hello, my dear. Cup of tea?'

'Thank you.' They went back into the kitchen.

'You're back early.'

'I know. Marcia Bond was very accommodating about the set. When are you leaving?'

'How charming.'

'I'm sorry. I didn't mean it to sound like that. I just wondered.'

'OK. About half past six, I think. They're expecting me for dinner.'

'It'll take about two hours, won't it?'

'Oh no, nothing like. Not with that new road bridge. Shouldn't be much more than an hour.'

He pulled the teabag out of her mug and flipped it into the bin, leaving brown splashes all over the swing top. He knew she hated him doing that.

'What's all this?' she asked, indicating the smart carrier bags leaning against the cooker by pointing her toe at them.

'Shopping.'

'I can see that.'

'Just a few things for the Smiths. It's Fiona's birthday, you know.'

'Oh yes. I suppose I'd better sign a card. Did you get one?'

'Don't sound *too* enthusiastic, will you?'

'You know I don't like Fiona much.'

'I don't know why you can't be more tolerant. She's a very delightful person, just different from you.'

'She's delightful *because* she's different from me.'

'Claudia, are you trying to pick a fight?'

'I thought *you* were. This tea's disgusting.'

'Don't drink it then.'

'I won't.' She tipped it down the sink, and ran the cold tap.

There was a silence. Pierre cast about for something neutral to say. 'Any news from school?' he asked.

'Not really. Oh yes; Leonie's pregnant.'

'Good for her.' He turned. 'I must finish my packing.'

Claudia gazed out of the window, biting her lips, with folded arms. Pierre glanced at her. 'Does it upset you?' he said, awkwardly.

She said, without turning round, 'Of course.'

'I'm sorry,' he said, and put an arm round her shoulders. She waited a few seconds before shrugging it off.

Some time after Pierre had gone, Claudia reached for the telephone. She didn't need to look up the number she dialled. 'Hilary? Hello, it's me.'

'Hello, my duck. On your own?'

'Yes.'

'Want to come over?'

'If that's all right.'

'Of course it's all right. Come for supper.'

'Can I bring anything?'

'Yes, something to drink. I've got nothing. Plenty to eat, though. See you soon.'

Claudia had a pile of marking to do, but decided it could wait till another day. She was bored and lonely and annoyed, and Hilary Nightingale was the only person who could cheer her up. She opened the garden door to let the dog out; it waddled into the middle of the lawn to do its business. Pierre always rushed straight out with a little plastic scoop; Claudia decided not to bother. 'For the next few days,' she told the lugubrious animal, 'you crap wherever you choose.'

Having redirected it to its basket and blanket by the front door – it was supposed to be a guard dog, after all – Claudia put the burglar alarm on and double-locked the house. Dusk was falling; though she had to put her headlights on it was marvellous that some daylight yet remained. The sky was pinky violet, like the inside of a rare sea shell; against it the twigs with their tufts of new leaves formed a fragile net. The evening star hung over the hushed valley; it looked like a dab of luminous paint. As Claudia drove around the sharp bends in the lane, a little too fast, each time, she felt her spirits rise.

The windows of Hilary's kitchen were all steamed up, and when the front door was opened a warm gust from some fragrant, herbal dish wafted out. Claudia admired the way Hilary never subsisted on the dismal, scrappy meals so many women regarded as adequate when they had no man to feed. A thick brown earthenware casserole stood on top of the Rayburn, its lid off. Having embraced her friend, Hilary returned to it, stirred in a trickle of something like molasses, put the lid back on and slid it back into the oven.

'What's in that? It smells gorgeous.'

'Beans, mainly. I've made some soda bread, but it looks a bit flat.'

'I like it flat. Well, I expect I do. I've never had it.' Both women laughed. 'Look, here's your booze. Let's open it right away.'

'Rioja! How fantastic. I love it – tastes of earth and acorns. Or rather, it tastes of what earth and acorns ought to taste of.'

'Hilary, you're burbling. Where's the corkscrew? How many glasses shall I get out?' Claudia moved about the kitchen almost as familiarly as if it were her own.

'Two. Ellie's out at Filmsoc. She'll be back before much longer, I should think, unless she goes round to her friend's house.'

'Don't you worry about her being out so late?'

'Late? Half past seven? No, I don't worry – she's on her bike. I always feel safe on my bike, so I assume she does too.'

'But Hilary, feeling safe isn't the same as being safe.'

'Isn't it?' Hilary fixed Claudia with a candid gaze. She had large green eyes – not hazel, but distinctly, purely green. 'Sometimes I think it is, actually.' She poured the wine. 'I love that glugging sound. So Pierre's gone, has he? Where's he off to this time? I've forgotten.'

'To a house party, at Simon and Fiona Smith's place. In Essex, almost Cambridgeshire.'

'Is she the one you don't like?'

'There's several I don't like.'

'I mean, is she the one who talks about pelmets?'

'Yes, and "placements". She has little cards on the table with the names on, even when it's just four of you.'

'What's their house like?'

'Absurd. Probably quite nice once, but they've exposed every bloody beam. And they have dozens of ludicrous dogs.'

'You're a fine one to talk about ludicrous dogs, Claudia.'

'True, but remember we had Jaques thrust upon us, as it were. I would never choose to own a dog. And Fiona Smith's have long white fur which she's always brushing, but they dribble brown saliva down it. They look like disgusting old men with nicotine stains on their beards.'

'It's remarkable that she's still called plain Smith.'

'I bet she won't be for much longer. Last time I saw her she was toying with the idea of incorporating Fanshaw, her mother's maiden name.'

'But not her own maiden name?'

'No, that would be too much like an American feminist writer – first name, own name, husband's name. Anyway I think hers was Sudd.'

'I've never asked you, Claudia. Why didn't you keep your own name?'

'I didn't even consider it. I'm not ashamed of being married, you know.'

'I'm not suggesting you are. I just can't imagine changing mine, that's all.'

'Maybe if I'd had a beautiful name like Nightingale I would have kept it. But Pierre wouldn't have been too happy. We're both quite old-fashioned in some ways, I suppose.'

'Do you think Pierre's glad you haven't gone to this house party?'

'I expect so. I tend to show him up – the dashing doctor and his frumpy wife.' Claudia changed her voice to imitate that of a village gossip. ' "That handsome Dr Prescott. He's really thrown himself away, poor chap." "Still, they do say she's brainy." "Well, well – Be good, sweet maid, and let who will be clever." ' Her agitation was obvious. She ran the tip of her finger round and round the rim of her wineglass. 'Look, I'm trying to make it squeak.'

Hilary put a hand on her friend's shoulder. 'Claud, I've never heard anyone say that, or anything remotely like that.'

63

'You haven't been here long, my dear. It's what they think, anyway. Don't worry, I don't care. I know my worth. And Pierre's not that dashing in private, unless you count dashing after poor old Jacques with that pooper scooper. I wish he'd just allow that dog to crap in peace.'

Hilary laughed and moved to answer the ringing telephone. 'Hello? Oh, hi, darling. No that's fine. Of course. Do you need anything? You'll borrow Laura's. OK. See you tomorrow. Bye.'

'Elinor?'

'Yes. She wants to stay the night with her friend, Laura.'

'Laura Taylor? She's my Rosalind, unfortunately.'

'Why do you say that? She's a super girl.'

'Maybe, but she's got as much finesse as a cement mixer. Shall I lay next door?'

The cottage kitchen was too small to eat in comfortably, even for two. Claudia carried plates and cutlery into the living-and-dining room. The table was occupied by a huge display of spring flowers. Creamy, strong-scented narcissi, pale pink tulips, irises, white freesias, fanned out from a glass vase shaped like a giant goblet. The air was thick with their scent. 'My God! Hil, where did these come from?'

Hilary was out of sight, bending over the casserole. If her face was red it could be attributable to the heat and effort of cooking. She replied, as casually as possible, 'Where did what come from?'

'These bloody flowers, of course. Own up. You didn't send them to yourself.'

'No, I did not. They came from someone you know, actually.'

'Not Joe Coventry? Don't tell me that bit of matchmaking paid off!'

'Well, put it this way – he sent the flowers.'

'He must be extremely keen. He's not given to theatrical gestures.'

'I don't know – he's a writer. Creative people are a bit funny – I should know.'

'Yes, but Joe is cautiously creative. Writing novels is not a flamboyant thing to do. Not like directing plays, or something.'

'Would you describe yourself as flamboyant, Claudia?'

'Me? No, of course not. Anything but.'

'Well, you're directing a play at the moment, aren't you?'

64

'I am directing Barcombe Abbey Girls' School Summer Shakespeare production – this year, *As You Like It*. As usual I have been roped into doing it. Hardly flamboyant.'

'I bet they didn't have to rope very hard. You know you enjoy it.'

'Hmm. Yes and no. I certainly don't want to sit by and see Shakespeare despoiled by any of my colleagues.'

'I think there's more in it for you than you allow. Anyway, a creative act is a creative act, whether it's the Abbey play or the RSC. Or whether it's a jumper with sheep on the front for Barcombe Craft Fair, or a novel about angst in the English middle classes.'

'Joe's novels aren't about angst in the middle classes. Haven't you read any?'

'No, I don't have time to read.'

'Even books written by your lover?'

'He's not my lover. I've only met him three times. Four, if you count your dinner party. What are his books about, then? Tell me, so I don't have to read them.'

'Oh they're always about some obscure historical event – seen obliquely, via changing viewpoints, et cetera, et cetera. You know the sort of thing I mean – slavery, or corruption in the Belgian Congo in the nineteenth century, or the Fenians, or something.'

'You certainly are no saleswoman, Claudia. They sound ghastly.'

'They're not, actually. They're a bit mannered, and too overtly philosophical – men's books, really. Still, at least he's having a go. But look – stop evading. Do you like him? Is this a Meaningful Relationship?'

Hilary ladled out generous portion of stew for herself and Claudia. Three of Joe Coventry's novels, newly purchased, were piled on her bedside table – hardback editions, too. But there was no reason why she should tell Claudia everything.

'As I said, I've only seen him on his own three times. Three and a half – I bumped into him at Safeway, if I'm to be scrupulously honest. He's nice, I get on with him. But the flowers are a bit over the top.'

'A poor answer. Still evading. Never mind, I'll let you off the hook. Can I have some more of that bread, please? I do like it flat. What does Elinor think of Joe?'

'Nothing.'

'Nothing? Aren't you going to tell her about him?'

'I know better than that. She hates it when I try to confide in her. She hasn't met him, and she hasn't said anything.'

'Presumably she's noticed the flowers?'

'She has studiously ignored them, so far.'

'Hard to do, since they take up most of the space in this room. She must be upset.'

'Probably. She's never been happy about my past liaisons; in fact she's usually been the one who's sent them packing.'

'You shouldn't pay so much attention to what she thinks.'

'How can I not pay attention? One's child is the most important thing in one's life. Oh God, I'm sorry, Claud. I didn't mean to be tactless.'

Claudia rose and cleared the plates with abrupt, jerky movements. 'When one is tactless one doesn't mean to be, almost by definition.'

'No, but I really am sorry. I really am.'

'It's all right, Hil. I don't usually count you as having children in the annoying sense, since yours is so old and there's only one of it. By the way, I think she's very bright.'

'Who, Ellie?'

'Yes. I mean *really* bright. I've just marked her essay on the significance of place in *Jane Eyre*; absolutely excellent. She was the only one who got the point, out of the whole fourteen of them.'

'She loved that book. When she'd finished reading it she turned back to the first page and read it all over again. She read the introduction and the footnotes – everything.'

'Has she ever considered entering for Oxford or Cambridge, to read English?'

'Here, have some fruit – no proper pud, I'm afraid. Do you really think she's that good?'

'She could be.'

'We've never discussed it. When she was at the comprehensive in Bristol that kind of thing just wasn't an issue. I'd love her to have a go. Shall I mention it? Or will you?'

'You decide – she's your child.'

'Yes, but I'm scared of her and you're not. You do it. I'll put the kettle on. Is that wine finished?'

'There's a drop left. You have it – I'm driving. How's business?'

'Good. I told you about this commission for a nursery from a family on Maiden's Hill? That's quite fun. Nice woman – a bit bored and lonely, I think. You'd like her.'

'Oh no, Hilary, not another one of your lame ducks. I know you – you're trying to find friends for some pudgy dull housewife. No thanks.'

Hilary smiled. 'Well, I do feel sorry for her. She moved here quite recently and doesn't know anyone in the area. Her husband's a commuter – a solicitor, in the city. All she's got to do all day is ferry the children to and from school and Hoover the living room carpet.'

'If she's married to a solicitor she could pay someone to do that. I've got no sympathy. Why doesn't she get out and do something?'

'Well, the baby's only a few months old.'

'Ugh! That's no excuse. How many children did you say?'

'Three. They're very sweet, I must say.'

'All the more reason for my not wanting to meet her. Kettle's boiled. I'll make it.'

Claudia left at about eleven. She hadn't mentioned her feelings about Leonie's pregnancy, and hadn't needed to. Being with Hilary often provoked envy, and occasionally real pain, but it was exhilarating and warming too. She drove home full of buoyancy, and was pleased, checking the answerphone on her return, to find that Pierre had called while she was out.

Almost the minute Claudia left, Hilary's telephone rang again. 'Hilary? It's Joe. I just rang to say goodnight.'

Hilary's heart thumped. 'That was kind of you.' She paused, and then said hurriedly, 'You can come round and say it in person if you like. Elinor's out for the night.' She put the receiver down without listening to Joe's reply. There, she'd done it now. Rash, perhaps, but she liked to call the tune. She ran upstairs to brush her teeth and hide the novels. Five miles away, deep in the countryside, Joe Coventry's key was already in the ignition.

CHAPTER SEVEN

Over the weekend the glorious weather came to an abrupt end. Saturday was dominated by a small, enclosing rain. Confined to barracks, the Stanhope family grew fractious. Videos and stories soon palled, but to launch an expedition seemed too much effort for Sarah. The elation she had felt on her shopping expedition had ebbed away to a grey, flat feeling; the next meal seemed the only thing to look forward to. Adrian was affectionate and cheerful, undismayed by the weather. To Sarah he seemed irritatingly insensitive. Monday was the first May Bank Holiday; the thought of another two full days with him in this crowded house was almost too much to bear.

'Why didn't we arrange something this weekend?' she asked, thinking aloud. 'We could have had someone to stay, particularly as it's Bank Holiday.'

'I did suggest having Ollie and Kate down, but you said you couldn't face all the cooking,' Adrian reminded her mildly.

'You always have to be right, don't you?'

Adrian was hurt. 'Well, it's true. Anyway, I like being at home with just us. It's a treat for me.'

'We could invite someone over for tomorrow lunch, I suppose. Someone local. What about the famous Henry? I've never even met him.'

'Tomorrow lunch? Mother's coming, isn't she? I don't think it would be an ideal social mix.'

'Well what about Monday? Henry won't be working, will he, on Bank Holiday.'

'It's rather short notice.'

'Don't be so cautious. Either he can come or he can't.'

'He might think it was odd.'

'I don't mind whether he thinks it's odd or not. I'm bored and I'd like to meet him.'

'I'd rather do it properly, some other time. Get some other people in as well, maybe.'

'You're just making excuses because you don't want me to meet him.'

'Don't be daft. I'll certainly invite him round, I'll just give him a bit more notice. Should we take the kids to the seaside this afternoon since you're so bored?'

'What, and walk on the beach in this weather? No thanks.'

'We could go on the pier. Or take them to the swimming pool.'

'Gabriel's still not strong enough. Come on, Gaby, Hannah, do you want to help Mummy do some cooking? We could make pastry shapes. Adrian, put Thomas in his cot, will you? It must be time for his nap by now.'

'All right,' said Adrian, 'but there's no need to snap my head off.' He shouldered Thomas and marched off, his holiday humour now cold and flat.

It had occurred to Sarah before now that Henry did not exist, except as a cover for some affair of Adrian's. She had no evidence for this except for the fact that she had never met him, but this conversation did nothing to dispel her doubts. It would be unlike Adrian to do something as audacious as invent a whole character – maybe Henry did exist as a friendly acquaintance on the commuter train, but the evenings Adrian had ostensibly spent with him in the pub had quite possibly been falsehoods. If that was the case, though, Adrian's mistress would be someone local – which put the kybosh on her theory about Nina the leggy solicitor. Nina definitely lived in West London, in a huge open-plan penthouse flat, with thick white – white – carpets and large splashy abstract paintings on the interestingly-angled walls. Sarah had felt subtly humiliated at a drinks party there once. Frankly, it was unlikely to be Nina, anyway. She was exceptionally good-looking and successful, and really did seem to be up to something with dreadful Andrew Malone, who, though obviously inferior to Adrian in every other way, was higher up the pecking order than him. No, it was probably a fellow commuter – a secretary, perhaps. A local girl with a frizzy perm and a short denim skirt. How to find out? Did she want to find out? She hadn't tried that telephone number yet.

'Mumm-ee!' A little hand had been tugging at hers for some time. 'Mummy, pay attention. You said we could do cooking.'

'I'm sorry, Hannah. I was daydreaming. Put your pinny on and we'll do cooking.'

'What's daydreaming?'

'When you make up stories in your head. Can you fetch Gabriel's pinny too, please?'

Hannah nodded, satisfied. She knew all about making up stories in her head. So did Gabriel, probably, though it was so hard to tell with him. He was lying on the kitchen floor describing circles in the air with a small plastic zebra, singing to the theme tune of *Neighbours* – 'Zebras! Every baby needs good zebras!'

'Gabriel, my love, you're bonkers,' said Sarah tenderly, scooping him up. 'Let's put your pinny on and do something constructive for once, shall we?'

Adrian was marvellous on Sunday morning. He brought Sarah the paper – extracting only the sports pages for himself – and a large mug of tea, and ordered her to stay in bed while he got the children dressed and breakfasted. The marital bedroom was directly above the kitchen; Sarah heard Hannah say, 'Oh Daddy, I wish you did our breakfast every day', and guessed correctly that Adrian had let them have golden syrup on their cereal, but she was able to smile indulgently as she leafed through the review section. The fine misty drizzle outside the window which had dampened Sarah's spirits so much the day before made the piled up pillows and duvet seem even more cocoon-like. Contentment was easy enough, thought Sarah. You just had to keep reminding yourself that you were happy.

Her mind ran on late spring Sundays in South London. The children skipping down the street as other people's music drifted out of the newly opened windows. A romp on the common, fresh and vigorous in early May, not a bit like its tired, dusty late-summer self. The weeping willows casting their blurry emerald veils over the ponds; children's boats, vibrating triangles of pure colour dotting the water's surface. Brunch in the child-friendly wine bar on the corner, where they supplied you with wax crayons so that you could scribble on the paper tablecloths. They'd meet friends as often as not. Smoked salmon and scrambled eggs in a sunshiny mound; Buck's Fizz and black coffee. Sarah let the paper slip from her fingers. She wished they'd invited the Stringers for the weekend. She'd never even seen their baby. The fact that she'd only vetoed the idea of inviting them because it was Adrian's suggestion aggravated her like a mouth ulcer. Adrian came in with a plate of toast. 'You look as if you're a million miles away,' he said, fondly. 'What were you thinking about?'

'Sundays in London.'

'What about them?'

'Oh, our walks on the common, and meeting people in Parson's – that sort of thing. I was missing it, vaguely.'

'Which bit were you missing? The dogshit on the buggy wheels?'

'Hey, don't shatter my illusions!' Sarah sat up and bit into the toast. 'I hope you haven't left Thomas alone in the high chair.'

'No, he's in the playpen. I'll go back down in a moment. Shall I take them to that ghastly place, give you a chance to cook lunch in peace?'

Sarah knew which ghastly place he meant. Hannah and Gabriel often begged to be taken to Jungle Jim's, an indoor play area on the front at Dinsford, full of nets and climbing frames and squashy slides rising out of a sea of multi-coloured plastic balls. The nose-curling smell of stale urine and the noise of about a hundred children enjoying themselves made Sarah's head swim. She'd turned Jungle Jim's into a Daddy-only treat. She assented to Adrian's suggestion with delight. A couple of child-free hours in which to prepare Sunday lunch for her mother-in-law seemed like a real treat.

She watched Diana slicing her lamb into tiny slivers and thought, I knew I should have left out the garlic. Her gaze travelled round the table. Hannah had pushed her meat to one side and was picking gloomily at her vegetables. Gabriel was eating nothing but the outsides of the roast potatoes. She'd puréed a little of everything for Thomas; the result looked like runny putty. He'd applied it to himself with enthusiasm – Sarah could see it drying crustily as far up as his eyebrows – but little, if any, had made its way into his mouth. Even Adrian had a reproachful you-know-I-don't-like-cauliflower look on his face. Sarah looked at the remains of the fragrant leg of spring lamb, the crispy golden roast potatoes, the three different kinds of vegetables, chosen for their contrasting colours, and felt her temper rising.

'Eat your meat, Hannah,' she snapped.

Hannah pulled a face. 'It's got blood in it,' she said. 'And white bits.'

'It's supposed to be pink like that. And the white bits are fat. You can cut them off.'

'Can I cut off the pink bits too?'

'No, because then there won't be anything left.'

'There will. There's a grey bit here. I'll eat that.' Hannah inserted a piece of meat the size of a cornflake into her mouth. 'There!' she said. 'Finished.'

'Hannah,' said Sarah, a warning note in her voice, 'I said eat your meat.'

Hannah's eyes filled with tears.

'Is it a French idea, Sarah,' put in Diana, 'to serve lamb so underdone?'

Sarah did not reply. 'Adrian,' she said, 'get Hannah to eat it, will you?'

Adrian looked defiant. 'I don't see why,' he said, 'you haven't given Gabriel any.'

Hannah snuffled, and gave her father a small complicit smile.

'Gabriel is only three,' said Sarah, as if explaining something to someone of subnormal intelligence, 'and Hannah is six. When Gabriel is six he will have to eat his meat too, whatever colour it is.'

Her hectoring tone decided Adrian. He picked up Hannah's plate. 'She's eaten some,' he said, and carried it into the kitchen.

'Did Daddy have to eat his meat when he was six, Grandma?' asked Hannah, emboldened by triumph.

Diana placed her knife and fork neatly together. 'It was never an issue, dear. Your father always ate whatever he was given. Except cauliflower, of course.'

Of course, thought Sarah. She crashed the remaining plates together and took them through to the kitchen.

'You might support me in front of your mother,' she hissed at Adrian. 'It's the least you can do.'

His face was rigid. 'You didn't have to make such an issue of it,' he muttered. 'Poor old Han.'

Sarah seethed. She carried a cheese board and side plates into the dining room. 'Just fruit and cheese to follow, I'm afraid,' she said brightly. 'And fromage frais for the children. Adrian, would you make coffee please?'

'I see you need grape scissors,' said Diana, hovering over the fruitbowl. 'I'll bring you my spare pair, next time I come. It'll be no trouble.'

'It's not fair,' said Hannah. 'You gave Gaby the strawberry one, and now there's only apricot left. And you *know* I don't like apricot.'

'Hannah,' said Adrian perfunctorily, 'don't be rude to your mother.'

'She did it on purpose,' wailed Hannah.

Sarah felt her mother-in-law's gaze upon her. She gritted her teeth.

The change in the weather affected Pierre Prescott, too. The house party at the Smiths' was a disappointment. The other guests were loud, hearty types, and Fiona Smith had put on a considerable amount of weight. Her bottom seemed positively to have collapsed. The weekend revolved round meals at which too much was eaten and drunk. Between times people snoozed, or read the papers; evenings were spent in trivial banter and mirthless party games. Pierre found it hard to remember why he had come.

His telephone conversations with Claudia irked him, too. Several times she was out; he felt there was something faintly degrading about leaving messages on his own answerphone. When at last he got hold of her, she answered briefly and impatiently. She obviously didn't miss him, he told himself.

He left earlier than any other guest, straight after breakfast on the Monday, pleading heavy traffic. The weather was lifting a little; still chill and grey, but at least it had stopped raining. As he neared Barcombe he realised that he still had the best part of the day with which to do what he pleased; Claudia was at work, as the Abbey School chose to ignore the May Day holiday, to the great annoyance of most of its customers. No need to go home straight away, particularly. As his car reached the top of Maiden's Hill he spotted a flat-fronted rosy brick house, and pulled in on impulse. He had offered to take photographs for that nice solicitor's wife. Why not pay her a visit now?

Sarah and Adrian were on their knees, wrestling with a flatpack bookcase they'd ordered from a London store. Both hated DIY, and had already delayed tackling it for several weeks, but now, with Adrian on holiday and the two older children at school there was no excuse not to have a go. Thomas had been installed in the playpen with mountains of squeaky, rattly toys and a rusk to suck. Sarah's mouth was full of rawlplugs when the doorbell rang. She spat them out into the palm of her hand. 'Who on earth's that? Must be a Jehovah's witness.'

'I'll see them off,' said Adrian.

'No, I'll go – you'll only get involved in some argument.' She was on her feet.

'Oh! Dr Prescott! Is – is everything all right?' In her nervous confusion Sarah felt primarily the atavistic fear of the doctor at the door.

Pierre grinned. 'That's really for *you* to tell *me*. How is the little lad? But I haven't really come here with my medical hat on, if you'll excuse the ghastly phrase. May I come in?'

'Of course. Dr Prescott, this is my husband, Adrian.' Adrian had emerged from the living room. The two men shook hands, and both said, 'We've met,' at the identical moment. 'Oh yes, at the hospital. How silly of me,' said Sarah. Pierre, seeing that she was transfixed like a rabbit in a car's headlights, took charge.

'I bumped into your wife the other day in Barcombe. I don't expect she mentioned it,' he said affably to Adrian. 'And I wondered whether you'd allow me to take some photographs of your exceptionally lovely-looking children. Photography is my passion and I'm trying to build up a portfolio; might be useful in the event of the increasingly likely total collapse of the NHS. I expect Sarah's forgotten all about it, but I was passing by anyway so I thought I'd call in on the off chance.'

'No, no, I hadn't forgotten. I told you about it, Adrian, didn't I? The day I had my haircut. Or maybe I didn't – no I didn't, because I was thinking of having the photos done as a birthday surprise for you.' Sarah was talking very much faster than usual. With her whole being she wished that she was wearing anything other than a holey grey jersey of Adrian's and last year's espadrilles.

'And now I've spoilt the surprise, I'm *so* sorry.' Pierre's voice was a kind of throaty purr. 'But you see, I forgot to ask for your telephone number, so I had to drop in.'

Adrian had been called back into the living room by the sound of Thomas throwing something hard against a glass-fronted cabinet, so he heard this exchange without registering his wife's furious blushes or the doctor's soothing smile. He rejoined them in the hall, saying, 'I'd be delighted to have their photographs taken. We've been meaning to do that for some time. Have you time to stay for a cup of coffee now? We've only one child here, and that's the plainest of the lot, but perhaps we could arrange another time.'

'I'll make the coffee,' said Sarah, darting into the kitchen. She flung open the back door, in the hope the air would cool her burning face. A silver plated meat cover hung on a hook at the side of the dresser; she scrutinised her reflection, shaking out her hair and running a finger tip over each eyebrow. The distortion of the rounded surface made her nose look huge. Her shoes were by the back door – she could change out of her espadrilles. But then he'd notice, and would know she'd made a little effort for him. She could just go into the living room and kick her espadrilles off – inside them, her feet were bare, and she had pretty feet. Adrian would probably pick up on that, though, and see it as uncharacteristic. Better just to leave the wretched things on.

When she went in with the coffee Adrian and Pierre were conversing with apparent ease and animation, amidst the half-constructed bookcase. Perhaps her encounter with him in the café had meant nothing, after all; perhaps he was as friendly to every passing acquaintance, male or female. 'Did you know Dr Prescott's wife teaches at the Abbey School, Sarah?' Adrian remarked. 'Perhaps she'll get to teach Hannah one day, if we stick around this area for long enough.'

'Oh but I hope you will stick around,' said Pierre emphatically. 'It's a lovely area, really, though perhaps you find it dull after London?'

'Not really; it's just that most of our friends still live in London, and Sarah gets a little lonely, don't you, Sal?'

'It's just a question of picking up a few contacts in the neighbourhood. Come and have a drink with us sometime. Claudia would be very pleased.'

Sarah managed to say 'thank you.' To avoid looking at Pierre she swooped down on Thomas, who had started to grizzle out of boredom. 'Are you sure you want to photograph this object? He's awfully slimy.' Her tone was passably jaunty.

'Love to, love to. Let's fix a time. When the other two are here, of course. I'm only sorry I haven't got any examples of my work on me, but as I say, I was just passing by.'

They made a tentative arrangement for the following Saturday afternoon; Pierre said he'd have to confirm it with his wife. 'I'll ring you,' he said, looking at Sarah. 'I'll take your number now if I may.' As Adrian tore a piece off the telephone message pad to give him, Pierre caught Sarah's eye and winked.

When he had gone, Adrian said, 'He seemed a nice fellow. Bit of a smoothie, but quite interesting. You were saying we never invite anyone over; let's have him. And his wife – she's Head of Department, you know. Sounds like he's very proud of her.'

'No,' said Sarah, 'let's not. Let's invite Henry.'

'Why not both? Perhaps together – they might get on. Why did you say no? Don't you like the doctor?'

'Not much,' said Sarah, 'though he was very good when Gabriel was ill. But … Oh Adrian, let's not invite them … Not yet.' She put her arms round her husband, who stroked her hair. 'Why not, Funny Features?' he said gently, smiling.

'I don't know. I … just can't be bothered I suppose.' She hugged Adrian quite hard, to kill off the memory of the wink. But later, when she was alone, she thought of it, and shivered.

Pierre Prescott decided to go straight home. He'd take Jaques for a walk, and make things comfortable for Claudia so she would be pleased when she got back. He could do with a little revival of conjugal affection. He wondered why he'd winked at that girl. She had looked rather frumpy today, and he'd almost decided to call it off. But there had been something so vulnerable about her little bare ankles, showing just above those grimy espadrilles! Well, he'd done it now. He'd winked, and he'd have to follow that through.

The Friday afternoon of that wet weekend, Elinor Nightingale came home early. Her French teacher was ill, so the last two lessons of the day had been cancelled. In theory the girls were supposed to work in the library at such a time, but in practice nobody checked. Elinor, who had spent the previous night at Laura's house, was keen to get home and see her mother. Somehow she hadn't seen much of her over the last couple of weeks. It would be good to have a proper chat again.

Cycling home in the chilly drizzle might have been trying — she didn't have her cagoule with her as the day before had been so glorious — but Elinor didn't mind. She rather liked the feeling of the fine spray in her face, the tiny droplets clinging to her hair like dew on a cobweb. Elinor, having lived in Bristol for several years, was surprised to discover how much she liked being in the country. Her new classmates assumed it would be otherwise, and kept asking her if she missed 'the Night Life'. When, at first, she told them that Bristol night life had more or less passed her by, they had said 'Oh' and looked disapproving, so now she embroidered her past a little. Yearning for the city seemed as much a symptom of other people's adolescence as greasy hair and spots; in this as in so many other things Elinor found herself alone. Even to Laura, her newfound best friend, she had to pretend a lot; honesty didn't get you very far at school. One had to run with the hare and hunt with the hounds, at least to some extent.

She turned into the track that led up to Petts End Cottage. You couldn't cycle all the way up, it was so steep and rutted. The gaps between the trees were filmy with bluebells; she'd get Mum to come out later for a damp little ramble and pick loads and loads for the house. Their honey scent wasn't as powerful when the sun was in, but you could still catch it if you were careful and didn't sniff too hard.

The door of the cottage was locked, but her mother's bicycle was there, and so was the car. Strange — or perhaps she'd already gone out for the bluebell walk herself. Elinor let herself in.

'Mum!' she called, although she could feel that the house was empty. She slung her schoolbag into a corner of the kitchen, alongside the vegetable rack, and went upstairs.

Her mother's bedroom door was open. Elinor went in, vaguely looking for a clue to Hilary's whereabouts. The room seemed less orderly than usual, somehow; the bed was made, but the clothes Hilary had worn the day before lay in a tangle on the floor. Odd — Mum was famously neat. The room felt different, smelt different. What was it? Then Elinor saw something that made her jump.

On her mother's side of the bed was a dirty coffee cup. Fine – it was one of her few sluttish habits, to take drinks to bed and leave the cups lying around. But on the other side – the side never used, except as a place to spread the Sunday newspapers – on the floor by the other side was another, identical cup. Identical, except that a used teaspoon lay on the saucer. Hilary never took sugar.

Her head swam. So it was true. Her mother was sleeping with that man who had taken her out to dinner and driven her back that time. He had obviously sent those flowers that Mum had said nothing about – that enormous bunch, which Elinor hadn't commented on because she didn't want to see her mother looking pink and pleased. How long had she known him, for Christ's sake? She couldn't have seen him more than two or three times; was it really necessary for her to jump into bed with a virtual stranger? Or perhaps she'd been seeing him for ages, in secret. Perhaps every time Elinor was out of the house she'd summon him over. Well, Elinor wouldn't be spending the night away again, that was certain.

She closed the door as quickly and quietly as she could, making sure the latch fell into place, and tiptoed downstairs, even though there was no one in the house. She opened the living room door, and the odour of flowers rushed out at her. With quick, deliberate movements she took an old newspaper from the basket by the fire, unfolded it, took the flowers from their vase, and wrapped them in the paper, folding it like a parcel so that not a petal was visible. She placed the bundle carefully, almost tenderly, in the dustbin, emptied the vase, washed it, dried it, and put it away. Then she sat on a stool in the kitchen feeling as guilty and exhilarated as a murderer, wondering what to do next.

She was on the verge of rescuing the package and restoring the flowers when her mother came in by the back door, scraping the mud off her wellingtons on the sharp edge of the doorstep. She was singing to herself, as usual – a hymn, oddly. 'Praise God from whom all blessings flow, Praise him all creatures here below.' Elinor felt her throat tighten.

'Hello, my darling,' Hilary called out when her boots were off. 'How's my very favourite daughter?'

Her tone seemed false to Elinor, who just replied, 'Hi.'

'You're back early, Ells. You all right?'

'Of course I am. Madame Lebrun was away, that's all.'

'OK, don't snap. It's lovely to see you.' Hilary dropped a kiss on the top of her daughter's smooth, dark head.

'Where have you been, Mum? I came back early just to see you. I could've stayed at school and got some work done.'

'Well, I'm sorry, honey, but I didn't expect you back before half past four. I've been helping Mr Pitchford out; he's poorly. I helped his lad round up the sheep – quite fun, really – and then I got some tea sorted out for him. Poor old boy, he's awfully lonely I think.'

'You always think people are awfully lonely.'

'Well, a lot of them are. I'm sorry to say.'

'And when you think someone's lonely you start talking like them.'

'Talking like them? What do you mean?'

'You just said Mr Pitchford was "poorly", and that you'd been helping his "lad". Both those words belong in Mr Pitchford's vocabulary, not yours.'

Hilary stared at her daughter, and laughed. 'Claudia was right.'

'Right about what?'

'She said you were very bright. You are.'

'When were you talking to her about me?'

'Last night. She came round for supper, when you were out. What are you looking so pleased about? Didn't you know she thought that?'

Elinor breathed a long sigh, and tried to suppress the twitching at the corners of her mouth. That coffee cup was Mrs P's! They most likely went to Mum's room to gossip and look at clothes, just like she and Laura did. She got off her stool and encircled her mother's waist, pressing her face against her chest as if she were a much younger child. She was a head shorter than her mother; they weren't sure whether she had finished growing or not.

'Mum. Tell me what else she said.'

Hilary stroked her hair. 'She wondered if you'd considered trying for Oxford or Cambridge.'

'Me? Wow!'

Hilary smiled at the idea that anyone who said 'Wow!' like that could be remotely ready to think about going to university, but she kept her thoughts to herself. 'Well? Have you considered it, Ellie?'

Elinor pulled away and busied herself with her schoolbag. 'It's silly. I'm not good enough.'

'Claudia said your *Jane Eyre* essay was far and away the best.'

'Yes, but the others are thick. No, I don't mean that – but I'm the only one who liked the book.'

'Well, that shows you're good at English.'

'Just liking something doesn't mean you're good at it.'

'It does, if you like it in the right way.'

Elinor stuffed her games kit into the washing machine and threw a few sweet wrappers and scraps of paper into the bin. Her school bag now contained only her homework. She shouldered it, and left the kitchen.

'Where are you going?' Hilary asked.

'To my room. I'm going to think about it,' she called back. 'Will you come for a bluebell walk with me in about half an hour?'

'Of course. See you then.'

Elinor lay on her bed allowing pleasing daydreams of academic success to run through her head. She heard her mother pottering about in the kitchen; comforting little domestic sounds of rummaging, chopping, splashing. Then she heard the living room door. Elinor was on her feet in seconds. The flowers! How could she have forgotten them?

She heard Hilary open the door, and pause on the threshold. She braced herself for the cry of surprise but none came. Elinor stood stock still, listening as hard as she could. Hilary closed the door, went out to the dustbin, lifted the lid. Elinor tiptoed out to the corridor; you could see the dustbin from the corridor window. Hardly breathing, she pressed herself into the corner, just peeping out. She saw her mother lift the package and peel back a corner of the paper as if she were lifting a shawl off a sleeping baby's face. As Hilary re-entered the house, Elinor scuttled back to her room and lay down on the bed again.

Half an hour later Hilary called up the stairs, 'Do you still want to go for that walk?'

'Oh – no thanks, Mum. I'm working.'

That wasn't true. What was true in this house any more? If that man hadn't stayed the night, he surely had sent the flowers – so it was only a matter of time before he did spend the night. Unless she could do something to stop it. Her mother might be about to make a terrible mistake; it was up to her, Elinor, to find out more. She allowed her guilty feeling about the flowers to be subsumed in a surge of anger against the unknown intruder.

At about eight o'clock Hilary called brightly, 'Supper!' She had laid it out on two small trays – yellow omelettes flecked with herbs, a colourful salad with red and green peppers and chunks of avocado, a few toasted almonds sprinkled on top. The tumblers contained only tap water, but with ice cubes in it. A blue checked napkin was neatly folded on each tray. Mum was always so careful about details.

'I thought we'd eat in front of the telly,' said Hilary. 'Friday night's good for telly now.'

The flowers were not in the living room, and Hilary still had said nothing about them. Perhaps she'd put them back in the dustbin after all. Elinor decided she really must say something.

'Those flowers gave me a headache,' she said gruffly. 'That's why I chucked them out.'

'I thought it might be that,' said Hilary sweetly, pressing the channel changer, 'so I've put them in my bedroom. Look, it's that police thing you liked.'

Elinor hadn't liked it that much, but she decided to watch it to avoid conversation. Why did her mother always have to be so bloody perfect?

Joe Coventry leaned back in his chair and stretched his arms high above his head. He yawned hugely. On the desk in front of him lay the usual muddle of spiral-bound notebooks, dirty mugs and malfunctioning Biros. From time to time he had read articles in the Sunday papers about professional writers. They always claimed that their working day began at six with a cup of herbal tea, and that absolute order and discipline were essential to nurturing the creative talent. Joe could never quite believe it. It was six years now since he had given up his post as a university lecturer to become a full time novelist; six years since he'd bought himself an in-tray and some box files for admin, and these items still lay somewhere in the corner of his study, thick with dust. He scratched his beard ruefully and picked up one of the pens. He was making no progress on his latest book, and his agent and editor were becoming agitated, in as tactful a manner as possible. Laying the pen down again he shuffled together the last few pages he had written. He always wrote longhand first. The very shapes of the words made suggestions to him that typeface could never emulate.

Joe's cottage stood on a river bank. From his study window he could see gnats dancing above the rushing water and dragonflies, airborne turquoise matchsticks, zigzagging across its surface. He could also see two ancient deckchairs and a rug, sodden from last night's rain, parked forlornly on the hillocky grass. An empty wine bottle lay nearby; a frilly orange slug crawled across it. The remains of a boozy lunch-time rendezvous with Hilary two days earlier. He'd forgotten to bring the things in. Of course he had! It had been hot then, and when it's hot you can never imagine that one day it won't be. It was the same as being with Hilary. When he was with her, basking in her sunshine, he could not imagine or remember what it felt like to be anywhere else.

He let the sheets of paper fall from his hand. There was no way he could work that morning. Love was a sickness. Suffering acute attacks in your teens and early twenties didn't seem to provide immunisation. He might as well humour himself, he decided. He leaned his elbows on the windowsill and stared at the deckchairs. There she had sat. There she would sit again.

The telephone rang, and Joe's heart fizzed like sherbet. But it was only his editor, trying to say something about entering for a literary prize. Joe paid her the kind of attention the seasoned traveller gives to the air hostess explaining the emergency procedure before the plane takes off. His replies didn't fit the questions being asked.

'Joe, are you drunk?' asked his editor at last.

'You could say that.'

'I'll ring another time then, shall I?'

'Please. I'm sorry, Pat.' Joe replaced the receiver.

In her London office, Patricia Hale turned to her secretary. 'Joe Coventry's out of his brain at eleven o'clock on a Thursday morning. I don't believe he's doing any work at all.'

'It must be love,' said the secretary. It was, in her case.

'Love? He's about forty-five and quite plump.'

The secretary shrugged. 'There's someone for everyone,' she replied philosophically.

In Sussex, the lapsed novelist stood up. He wanted to fill her house with flowers, but she had said, no more flowers, it upsets Elinor. He wanted to write her a poem, but his efforts read like the insides of greetings cards. Love had reduced his mind to a mush. He decided to walk along the river's edge. Two hours to go until she finished work! The time had to be whittled away somehow. He hauled his battered corduroy jacket off the back of the chair; a tiny glint on the lapel caught his eye. A single long, twisty, coppery hair was trapped there. He drew it off, holding it reverently between his thick forefinger and thumb. 'Like gold to airy thinness beat,' he said aloud. Then he coiled it with tender care, sealed it inside an envelope, and slipped it into his inside pocket.

CHAPTER EIGHT

Mid May, and the countryside was heaving with colour and life. The brick and tile houses of the old market town arranged themselves in a broken circle around the dove grey abbey and formed a stiller, redder interlude in the clamour of greens and yellows that vibrated across the countryside for miles around. This was an agricultural landscape, and everything was on a human scale; neat fields, a clear, acid green at the moment, were bordered by small woods, trembling with new leaves, now lemon and silver. By July these woods would be solid, heavy blocks, but now in May they were still in a state almost of liquidity. From a car one glimpsed a blur of bluebells in every clearing; the May-blossom in the hedgerows looked like fallen washing. In the midst of this delicacy the buttery fields of yellow rape jumped out, hot, almost barbarous.

For Hilary and Joe Coventry, the burgeoning woods and fields became their territory, their private domain. On week days, when Elinor was at school and Hilary had finished at Sarah's or Mr Pitchford's they took picnics and roamed for miles. They sat on the banks of streams amongst twisting roots, or drove to the sea and dared each other to swim, or lay on grassy banks and held hands and stared up at the pattern of the leaves against the sky. They ate Brie and chunks of brown bread and garlicky pâté; they drank rough red wine from the neck of the bottle.

Joe read poetry to her; there always seemed to be a couple of books in the pocket of his baggy jacket, or in the canvas bag for carrying the wine, or lying on the floor of his car. Once, as they lay, his head in her lap, beneath a row of limes on the edge of a little orchard that was certainly private property, Joe said, 'This is perfect, isn't it? There's no greater freedom than this.' Hilary stopped threading violets into his wiry hair, and said, 'There's no such thing as freedom. But this is a good approximation.'

Joe sat up. 'I want,' he said, 'to take you somewhere far away and very, very lonely. Somewhere where I can have you entirely to myself.'

Hilary smiled, and shook her head.

'For just one week? A Hebridean island with seals and sea-birds for company?'

'Joe, you know I can't.'

'I'm talking about one tiny little week, for Christ's sake.'

'There's nothing I'd like more. But I can't, so don't push me.' She glanced at her watch. 'Half an hour left. Don't let's spoil it by talking about things we can't have.'

'Just one bloody week ...'

'Not yet, Joe. Not yet.'

For Claudia the season was an irritation as well as a delight. Driving to school in the morning she would glimpse flashes of enticing colour; from her kitchen window she watched the whole Maytime drama unfold. But she was always so terribly busy, or so it seemed. The GCSE class were completing their course-work; her upper sixth, gripped by A-level panic, clamoured for extra lessons at every available moment. It was absurd to be talking about *Tess of the D'Urbervilles* and the heroine's connection with the landscape in a stuffy class-room to a group of girls whose slouched backs were resolutely turned to the windows, but that, it seemed, was what was required of her. And the play took up so much of her time that it was usually down to Pierre to escort Jaques on his slow ambles through the moist woodlands and fragrant meadows. Claudia was aware that the best of the year was passing her by, as was any opportunity of getting her marriage back on a decent footing, and the awareness made her short tempered.

For Sarah, too, this first spring out of London was not without frustrations. Rural, or semi-rural, life did not present the unalloyed freedom she had naïvely envisaged. She longed to explore properly, to tramp for hours with no particular aim in mind, to listen to birdsong and learn the names of the wild flowers. But roaming through fields and woods was difficult with a heavy nine-month-old; hardly possible, indeed, unless it was a weekend and Adrian took him in the backpack. And if it was an expedition of this nature, Hannah and Gabriel had to come too, which was hardly conducive to a sense of freedom and oneness with nature. What Sarah really wanted was to be alone, completely alone with her increasingly elaborate daydreams. At dusk she would wander in the garden bare-armed and barefooted to drink in the thick purple smell of lilacs and touch the heads of elder-flowers, creamy and knobbly like old-fashioned dinner plates, improbably heavy on their slender stalks. She would lean back on the children's swing and gaze up at the opening stars. Moths and bats floated by on secret errands; in the flower beds, the colours of day drained away leaving the flowers – the stocks and sweet Williams and Canterbury bells – with their second, ghostly identity. A cat would scuffle in the bushes; the voices of half-grown lambs and their mothers, from a farm a quarter of a mile away, filled the valley with a sound like a distant sea. And then she'd hear the front door swing open and there would be Adrian, ready for his supper and so irritatingly unaware.

The decorations for Thomas' nursery were coming along beautifully. Hilary usually spent two mornings a week on them, and Sarah was considering inviting her to do something to the bathroom when she'd finished. Sarah had got into the habit of sitting and talking to Hilary while she worked; Hilary said no, it didn't distract her in the least, in fact it helped her concentrate. Working freelance as she did could be lonely; she said she missed the interaction of the dance teaching she used to do, and of course in Bristol she'd had a lot more friends, having lived there for several years. Sarah was so entranced by Hilary's looks, skill and ease of manner that it took her several sessions to believe any kind of friendship could develop that wasn't mainly one-sided; at last, however, the warm interest that the older woman took in her home and her children convinced Sarah that she could indeed be an object of curiosity and affection.

'You must meet my friend Claudia Prescott,' said Hilary one day when the two of them had been discussing the Abbey School. 'She's head of English in the senior school. She's my oldest friend – it was because of her that we moved to this area, really.'

'Claudia Prescott? You mean the doctor's wife?'

'Yes – have you met her? I think I told you about her before.'

'You mentioned your friend, but you didn't say her name, at

least I don't think you did.' Sarah could feel herself start to gabble. She paused, and put her head out of the door, ostensibly to listen for Thomas, who had been put down for his nap. 'No – fast asleep. I haven't met her, but I've met Dr Prescott. He was the one who came round that time Gabriel was ill.'

Hilary looked at Sarah very hard, and said, 'What did you think of him?' Sarah couldn't help but colour slightly under such unexpected scrutiny. Was Hilary a mind reader? Or was she just highly interested in other people's reactions to her friend's husband – perhaps, indeed, her friend in his own right?

'He seemed very … good. A good doctor. He was very helpful about Gaby,' she replied, lamely but fairly coherently.

'Mm, yes. He is a good doctor. I think. I go to Dr Bray in Three Oaks, myself – it's a different catchment area, or whatever you call it. But I must introduce you to Claudia. She's a marvellous person. Quite difficult to get to know, but well worth it. I'll invite you both round, for supper or something. Would Adrian mind you going out without him?'

'Goodness no, I shouldn't think so. Not that I often do, though I used to a bit when we lived in London. Adrian could babysit – it would be fine.' Sarah felt, suddenly, that it would be immensely important to meet Pierre's wife. She wondered why Hilary had not suggested inviting the Prescotts and herself and Adrian as two couples, but her unvoiced question was soon answered.

'My cottage isn't big enough to feed six comfortably; even if Elinor went out it would still be a squash. In any case you'd get to know Claudia better if you saw her on her own. She can be quite prickly, but don't let it put you off. She's got a heart of gold.'

Sarah swallowed, and said, 'Dr Prescott came round to take photographs of the children last Saturday.' Hilary was at the top of the stepladder, and her back was turned. It was hard to gauge her reaction, but Sarah was almost sure she saw her give a little jump.

'Did he now? And how did that come about? Could you pass me that rag, Sarah, would you mind? I need to clean this brush.'

'Oh, we'd been meaning to get photos done of them for ages, and when he said he was an amateur it seemed like a good idea.'

'Were they good? I should think your children would be very photogenic.'

'That's what he said. I haven't seen them yet; he said he'd bring them round next week some time. Does he – do they – have any children?'

'No. They can't.'

'I thought not. How sad.'

'It is, very. I think it's eating Claudia up inside. Though she's frightfully keen on her career and everything. Have you considered going back to work, Sarah?' Hilary felt she had been straying into a dangerous area with the mention of her friend's infertility and changed the subject. It was not something Claudia herself was ever willing to discuss.

'I haven't really got any work to go back to,' said Sarah, also relieved that the conversation was back onto a less loaded topic. 'Before Hannah was born I worked in publishing, I specialised in books in translation. I read modern languages at univerity. But I gave it up to have babies. I've done nothing since.'

'I don't call this nothing,' Hilary waved her brush with an expansive gesture, to imply the house, the garden, the children, the husband – the whole fabric of responsibilities.

'No, but – it feels like nothing. No, that's wrong. It feels like a lot, but not especially to do with me. I mean, look, I can't even decorate my own nursery.' Sarah laughed, a little hollowly.

'Don't be daft, why should a publisher decorate a nursery?'

'I'm not a publisher any more, I haven't been one for nearly seven years. It's funny, when we were in London I never missed work, but now –'

'What about the children? They are very much to do with you, aren't they?'

'It doesn't always feel like that. Sometimes I'm overwhelmed by their – otherness.'

Hilary climbed down from the stepladder; she had finished one wall, and now stepped back to scrutinise her work. 'I know what you mean. Elinor is part of me, very much, but increasingly I feel she doesn't belong to me. She's far brighter than I am, for one thing. But you could go back to work, couldn't you?'

'It wouldn't be easy. We couldn't have two of us commuting, so I couldn't go back to my old job, or anything like it. I've always vaguely thought I'd like to run my own business. But I'm not complaining, really. I have a good life.' Sarah, too, looked at the frieze. A tangle of nursery characters painted in intense but muted colours, chalky and soft, tumbled along the space between the ceiling and the dado rail. Hilary, as she got to know the family, had altered the design to incorporate portraits of them. Thomas' plump face beamed from his cradle 'on the tree top', Hannah was an anxious Bo-Peep in a sky-blue bonnet, and Gabriel, as Wee Willie Winkie, darted by with a glowing lantern in his hand. Hilary had suggested putting him in pyjamas instead of in a white nightgown, but Hannah had said, with a gravity that had made them smile, 'I think Gaby would prefer to wear a dress,' and Gabriel himself had confirmed this by appearing in his mother's nightdress and high-heeled black suede court shoes – her only smart shoes. 'Now Gaby is a mummy – a naughty mummy,' he had said.

'It's brilliant,' said Sarah, 'I love it. It's so clever. I don't believe Elinor can be brighter than you.'

'Oh but she is. I'm not a bit academic.'

'Is she more like her father?' Sarah surprised herself with her own audacity. For the first time since she'd known her, she saw Hilary's face harden.

'I don't know. I don't know her father.' She was wrapping her brushes in a roll of cloth.

Sarah felt awkward and afraid. 'Sorry,' she said, 'I shouldn't have asked.'

Hilary stood up, and smiled at her. 'Oh that's all right. You weren't to know. But it's a closed chapter.' She turned to the frieze again. 'I'm glad you like it. I'm quite pleased, I must admit.'

'I can't wait for the children to see it.'

'I'll start on the other wall on Friday, OK? And I must get you round to meet Claudia. Which day is best for you?'

When Hilary had gone Sarah wandered round the living room, fiddling. She meant to give it a thorough going over, but she couldn't get started. She was trying to piece together the things she'd heard about Claudia Prescott, to build up a kind of emotional photofit. What had Hilary said? 'Marvellous.' 'Prickly.' 'A heart of gold.' 'My oldest friend.' And childless – barren. Poor Pierre. No wonder he wanted to take pictures of other people's children.

The photo session had been a great success. Pierre had charmed the children so that he could do anything he wanted with them – even Gabriel, who normally shunned strangers, had been at his beck and call. Pierre had pulled faces, made funny noises, tickled them – he was a very physical person, Sarah realised. Unlike Adrian – and unlike herself, really. Though perhaps she didn't fully know herself. All sorts of ambitions and desires had been pushing their way up recently, like mushrooms shouldering their way through compost.

She had misled Hilary when she had said that Pierre would bring the pictures round 'next week some time.' He had told her he'd bring them as soon as they were developed; on the doorstep, out of Adrian's hearing, he had said, 'When can I ring you?' And she had said, 'Tuesday, at twelve o'clock.' Because she knew she'd be alone then. And today was Tuesday and it was five to twelve now.

The telephone rang, like a firework exploding in the night sky. She forced herself to count three rings before she picked it up.

'Mrs Stanhope? It's the Abbey School here. I've a message from kindergarten to say Gabriel's been sick, and Mrs Meadows doesn't think he should stay for lunch.'

'That's fine,' Sarah said wearily. 'I'll be along to pick him up right away.' She replaced the receiver. She would have to wake Thomas and drive to school immediately. If Pierre did ring, she wouldn't know. What a fool she was. She had no business with this kind of intrigue. Her function was to look after her little boy, who had been sick at school. Poor little chap.

On her way up the stairs to fetch Thomas, the telephone rang again. She darted back into the living room. 'Yes?'

'Sarah, it's Pierre.' That deep, chocolatey voice.

'Oh, hi.' Her own voice sounded squeaky, like a schoolgirl's.

'The results have come through and I'm quite pleased with them.' Sarah realised that he was ringing from the surgery and talking in a kind of code. 'When would be a convenient moment to discuss them?'

'Whenever would suit you.'

'Early one evening, perhaps? Say six o'clock tomorrow?'

'Absolutely fine. I'll be with the children, of course. Will you come here?'

'Surely.' He put the receiver down.

Six o'clock. One hour before Adrian got back. Rush hour at home, too, with the children having their baths. How did anyone *manage* to have an extramarital affair? Still, as she bundled the sleepily protesting Thomas into his car seat, her heart was singing.

Pierre turned up at six on the dot. Sarah, determined not to look as if she was waiting for him, had the children half undressed for their bath. The day had been warm, and she was able to wear a pink and white print dress, gathered at the waist and buttoned down the front, that she knew suited her, even though it was a few years old. The full skirt concealed her rounded stomach and broad hips, the pink made her fair complexion glow. She left the top button undone, and this time, her small feet with their short, neat toes were bare.

She greeted him breezily. 'Do come upstairs, if you can bear to. I can't leave them, I'm afraid. Let's grab a drink on the way – is white wine all right?'

'Marvellous, thank you. I'd love to see them having their bath – if they'll let me.'

'Oh no problem. They love you.' Sarah put as much warmth into her voice as she dared. The children did not let her down. They greeted Pierre with cries of delight. Hannah, who was taking off her T-shirt, was not quite old enough to be embarrassed by nakedness. Gabriel, who was already in the bath, tried to turn a somersault and had to be discouraged. Thomas had tipped up the laundry basket and was pulling out all the dirty clothes; he crowed at Pierre and held out a sock, in salute. Sarah quickly righted the basket and stuffed the clothes back in, while Pierre held her glass of wine as well as his own. When he handed it back to her, their fingers touched.

Pierre entered into the spirit of bathtime completely. It was hairwash night; he moulded their stiff, soapy hair into shapes, a queen's crown for Hannah, a unicorn's horn for Gabriel, a curly drake's tail for Thomas who had only a few blond wisps as yet. He played 'Row, row, row your boat' on the floor with each of them once they were dry and read *Where the Wild Things Are* to Gabriel while Sarah manipulated Thomas into his babygro. He listened when Hannah recited a poem about a hedgehog that she'd learnt at school, and then taught her a limerick which to her joy was very, very faintly rude. Sarah, her face mobilised by smiles, watched with delight and sympathy; what a terrible shame he would never be a father. What a sacrifice he made in sticking with Claudia despite everything; so many men would have simply abandoned her and started again with someone young and fertile.

The children, exhausted after a day of bouncing in the sunshine, were all in bed by a quarter to seven. Sarah joined Pierre in the kitchen. He had already gone down to refill their glasses. 'Good,' she said briskly. 'Now let's have a look at those photographs.'

Pierre swung round suddenly and said, 'Sarah.' He put his hands to either side of her face and kissed her swiftly. Then he held her face away from him, put his head on one side like a craftsman assessing his handiwork, and said her name again, softly, twice.

She said, 'He'll be back soon.' He let her go, and picked up the packets of photographs he'd left on the kitchen table. He turned to her with a searching, yearning look that made her head reel. 'Then we'll go and sit in the living room and pretend we're looking at these,' he said.

Saturday morning. Elinor sat up, checked her clock, then rolled herself up in her duvet once more, happy in the fresh remembrance that there was no school that day.

She wondered, idly, what she would do with the day. Laura, during a French lesson, had pushed her a note saying 'What's your ideal day? Tell me yours and I'll tell you mine.' They had spent the rest of the lesson composing their fantasies. Laura's had involved food and a tropical island and a rock star who Elinor had thought was dead, but who was obviously still pretty active according to Laura's account. Elinor, whose instinct was always to conceal herself, wrote something about winning a prize for her brilliant novel, at the bottom of which Laura had written 'BORING. What about SEX?' So Elinor had added a P.S. about a tall slim poet with black curls and a wide-brimmed velvet hat. Laura had added 'OK. But is he RICH?' Then the lesson had come to an end. And now here she was with an empty day in front of her and she didn't really want to get out of bed.

She listened to the sounds her mother was making as she bathed and dressed and made breakfast. There was lots of humming, and a certain amount of outright singing. Mum was in a good mood –

but then, she usually was. She was singing 'The Foggy Foggy Dew'. Elinor remembered how she'd loved that song as a child, but had been puzzled by the story. Why did the bachelor's son remind him of the fair young maid? But the need to be kept safe and warm, to be kept from the foggy foggy dew, that had made sense to her infant self. Hilary's voice brought back the dark cosiness of the big bed, the scent of warm skin and the tickle of hair, the banishment of night terrors. Elinor remembered, once, in their first flat in Bristol – the first flat she remembered, anyway – how she'd woken convinced that a poor starving Ethiopian child was scratching at her window pane, begging to come in in a half comprehensible language. She remembered the rising tide of pity and terror, the knowledge that she should open the window, and the certainty that even if she didn't the child would force its way in and crawl, angular, like an injured bat, on her bedroom floor. She had run to her mother's room and jumped into her arms – and seen the dark bulk of a man rise up like a sea-monster beside her. 'Don't be frightened, darling, it's only Angus,' her mother had said, but she had fled, back to her own bed and the scraping at the window. Her mother had followed, murmuring consolation, but even now, at least ten years later, the memory made her wince.

Angus. She hadn't thought about him for years. Of course, in daylight she'd known him perfectly well; an amiable Scotsman with an open-topped car who'd taught her how to play chess. What had happened to him? She thought about the other men who had featured in her mother's life – there weren't very many of them, really. She didn't think she could recall any before Angus. After him there had been the Michaels – first Michael with a Labrador, who lived in the country. Elinor had quite liked him. At any rate, she'd liked his dog. Then there had been Michael the dancer, who had cold blue eyes and a head that was virtually shaven. Elinor remembered saying to him, 'You're not as tall as the other Michael,' and she remembered not really understanding the uneasy laughter which followed.

And then, not so very long ago – four years, perhaps – there had been Sunil. Sunil was a school teacher, but he didn't look like one. Elinor could visualise quite clearly the soft, dusky skin round his eyes, his long, straight, silky eyelashes, his slim brown fingers that were as elegant as a woman's. It occurred to her now that Sunil had been quite important. Certainly, she remembered covering her ears to shut out the sound of her mother's sobs when it all came to an end. Hilary had sat on her bed and tried to confide in her; she had started to say something about Sunil's religion and how this made things impossible; but Elinor hadn't wanted to know. She had fidgeted and fiddled with the rag doll that even at that late stage had been her bedtime companion, and had interrupted her mother to ask if they could go to see some film or other at the weekend. Even at the time, she had known she was being childish; she'd known, too, that childish was what she wanted to be.

It was soon after Sunil that they'd been on holiday with the Prescotts. To France, to a rented house near a wide, flat river. Elinor couldn't remember the name of the area. It was surprising how little she remembered about the whole holiday, in fact, seeing as she'd been quite old at the time – about thirteen.

She remembered Mrs P reading a lot – on a garden seat in the shade of a large plum tree, on one of the uncomfortable folding kitchen chairs that left red stripes imprinted on your bare legs, and on the river bank after their picnic lunches while her mother and Pierre went for walks and she, Elinor, made patterns out of the stones or picked at her sunburnt toes or read one of the historical romances she had then been so fond of. She remembered Mrs P's awful white sun-hat and her thin, pale, elegant legs, but she couldn't remember anything she'd said, or anywhere they'd gone except to that river bank. Oh, and to get ice-creams in the village. Pierre used to drive Elinor down to the village in the car they'd hired that had no seat belts. There had been a huge poster on a hoarding by the side of the road showing a blonde in a red bikini advertising something like low-fat yoghurt. Elinor had asked Pierre to translate the slogan, and he had explained that it was some kind of pun about vital statistics. 'What are your vital statistics, Elinor?' he'd asked, with a little laugh that she didn't quite like.

She had shared a bedroom with her mother. Despite the mosquito mesh on the window the room always seemed to be full of insects. She quite liked watching the daddy-long-legs making their progress round the whitewashed ceiling, like moonwalkers with their high weightless steps, but her current irrational fear had been scorpions, and even though Pierre had assured her that there were none in that region she had worried endlessly that one might crawl up the wall and drop onto her bed in the middle of the night. One night the fear had woken her; she thought she'd heard a scuffling sound and she'd called 'Mum! Put the light on.' There had been no reply, and eventually she'd plucked up the courage to reach for the light herself. That was when she'd found that her mother's bed was empty.

Hilary stopped singing and tapped on Elinor's door. 'It's half past ten,' she said. 'Can you really be still asleep?'

Elinor feigned a sleepy grunt. Hilary opened the door.

'I need to go into town to choose some paints,' she said. 'Do you want to come? I can wait, if you do.'

Elinor yawned and stretched. 'Oh, no thanks, Mum. I'm still really tired for some reason.'

'OK, darling. I'll see you later.'

Elinor pulled the duvet right over her head. She would need at least the rest of the morning to come to terms with the fact, which she should have realised years ago, that her adored mother was the kind of woman who slept with other people's husbands.

CHAPTER NINE

'Sarah!' Adrian, prone in a hot bath, heard his wife passing on the stairs. 'Sarah, bring us a drink.'

Sarah stuck her head round the bathroom door. Wallowing in the bath with a drink was one of Adrian's few sybaritic habits, but it was one he rarely indulged. These days he often took a shower, which he disliked, just to save the time.

'What would you like? Scotch?'

'Mm. Please. Bring one for you, too.'

She returned, but with only one glass.

'Stay and talk, Sal,' said Adrian. 'I've missed you.'

He had been working exceptionally hard over the last week, and had been coming home only to sleep for six hours and put on a clean shirt. Now the important case was resolved and the pressure had slackened.

Sarah perched herself on the edge of the bath. She remembered briefly their shared baths in the early days. They'd take drinks and plates of toast and balance them on the bathrack and wash each other's hair and tickle each other's toes. That had been in their first flat, a rented basement in Stockwell.

'Do you remember the fungus on the bathroom wall in Douglas Road?' asked Adrian, as if reading her thoughts. 'That black frilly stuff? And Hugh said we should try cooking it?'

Sarah smiled. 'Remember when the net curtains froze to the windowpanes? My God!'

She looked down at Adrian's body, long and pale under the water. He hadn't changed much in ten years. A softening at the waist, a clearing on the top of the head, a couple of vertical furrows between his eyebrows – that was all. Nothing had changed radically, but something had been ... diluted. She glanced at the ceiling. 'This room needs redecorating,' she said. 'Look at that peeling patch.'

'I'll take your word for it.' Without his glasses, the ceiling was a steamy blur. Adrian sat up. 'Will you scratch my back? Right in the middle. It's driving me mad.'

Sarah complied reluctantly. Since Pierre's kiss, touching any part of Adrian had been extraordinarily difficult. 'Shall I ask Hilary Nightingale to do it then?'

'Do what?' Adrian, grunting with pleasure, was paying little attention.

'Redecorate, of course. When she's finished the nursery.' The idea of retaining Hilary in the house for several more weeks was a very attractive one to Sarah.

'By all means. Up a bit. Ah, that's great.'

'Hilary asked me to supper, actually.'

'Just you?' Adrian sounded a little put out.

'Yes – to meet Claudia Prescott. The d–doctor's wife.' Sarah stumbled over the word. 'It's to be a girly evening. Hilary says her cottage is too small for two couples.'

'Perhaps she doesn't like inviting other people's husbands because she hasn't got one of her own.'

This remark annoyed Sarah, and she stopped scratching. 'I doubt it. She likes being on her own. Anyway, I think she's seeing someone.'

Adrian chuckled. 'If I wasn't in a good mood because of finishing the British Gas job, I'd point out how contradictory you're being. But I'm glad she's asked you. I'm worried that you haven't made more friends in Barcombe.'

Sarah stood up. 'Don't be patronising.'

'I'm not. Sit down, Sal.' He took her hand, and pulled it. She complied. 'But I am worried about you. Admit it – you must be lonely.'

'Not at all. It's just such a relief to be out of London.' The last thing Sarah wanted at this time was for Adrian to worry about how she spent her time. That way, he might start to notice things. 'I love the garden, and everything. I'm not bored.'

'But you can't talk to flowers. At least, I hope you don't.'

'I've got lots of people to talk to. The mothers at the school and ... and your mother, and Mrs Crump –' Adrian pulled a face by way of interruption – 'and Hilary too. So you'll babysit if I say yes?'

'Of course. I want you to get to know Claudia whatsit. She sounds like an intelligent woman.'

'I'm not particularly interested in her,' said Sarah, with face averted, 'but I do like Hilary Nightingale.'

'Good. I'm glad she's invited you. You're too bright to be spending all your time chatting to the Mrs Crumps of this world.' Adrian scrambled to his feet. Sarah moved to the door to be out of the range of the shower of water drops. Adrian always shook himself like a dog when he was wet.

'Are you being snobby?' she asked, handing him a towel.

'You know I'm not.'

'OK, I didn't mean it. I'd better go and start supper.'

'I was hoping you'd massage my shoulders. They're in knots after all those late nights.'

Sarah hesitated briefly, but retreated. 'That fish won't keep. If I give you a massage now, I'll be too tired to cook later.' She vanished before Adrian had time to take issue with her sense of priorities.

'Hilary? It's me.'

'I hoped it was.'

'I only rang to hear your voice. And to procrastinate.'

'Writer's block playing you up again?'

' 'Fraid so. And it's all your fault.'

'Funny. It has the opposite effect on me.'

'What does?'

'Oh, you know … being with you. It energises me.'

'But the point is, my lovely, that I'm not with you. Alas.'

'No, but I mean, even when you're not there. I can think of you and it makes me do things.'

'What sort of things?'

'Well, I'm knitting like a mad thing. I've got the phone clamped to my ear and I'm clacking away with the needles. Can't you hear?'

'Sort of. Is there such a thing as knitter's block?'

'No, but there's knitter's elbow.'

'When am I going to see you, Hilary? I want to take you out to dinner again. Remember that place Pierre was talking about, at Quayles Green? Tomorrow night?'

'Yes please! What's tomorrow? Oh – I'm sorry, Joe. It's parents' evening at Ellie's school.'

'The day after, then.'

'Thursday? No, I couldn't. Ellie and I always watch that Dickens serial together.'

'You can't go out because you want to watch television? Are you serious?'

'It's not that I particularly want to watch television. It's just — there are certain things I do with Ellie, and it wouldn't be fair to stop doing them.'

'I see.'

'You don't sound as though you see.'

'Well, I'm trying to see.'

There was a pause.

'Joe, don't go away.'

'I haven't.'

'I could do Friday evening. I think. If Ellie —'

'If Ellie what?'

'No. OK. If Ellie nothing. We'll do Friday.'

'I'll pick you up at seven. Oh and Hilary? I've just remembered why I rang.'

'Yes?'

'To tell you that I love you.'

'Oh Joe!'

'Which I haven't said to anyone else since the last time flares were in fashion.'

Hilary telephoned Claudia to arrange a date. Claudia grumbled and said she was busy with rehearsals, but Hilary said firmly, 'All the more reason why you should do something different. Give yourself a break. She's really nice, I promise you. Come straight on from school and chat to me while I cook if you like.'

Adrian was quite content with the prospect of a quiet evening in front of the television. Sarah, after thinking about what she would wear all day, decided to go for understatement. She chose a pastelly floral skirt and a sleeveless white blouse — she quite liked her rounded upper arms, and the evening was warm. She looked mumsy, she knew, but that was all to the good. She didn't want Claudia to pick up any warning notes. She settled the children down for the night, loaded the washing machine, put a pre-prepared Marks and Spencer's fisherman's pie in the oven for

Adrian, set the timer, left the kitchen door open so that he would hear it ping, issued a few instructions as to what to do if the children woke (they almost never did), ran upstairs to apply some last-minute lipstick, ran into the downstairs lavatory to rub it off again, in case it made Adrian needlessly suspicious, popped back into the living room where Adrian, whiskey in hand, was watching the Channel 4 news, planted a kiss on his bald patch, told him not to wait up for her, and left. As she got into the car she realised that it had been a very long time since she had driven anywhere entirely on her own.

She had not been to Petts End Cottage before, but found it easily, because it was exactly as she had imagined. As the Volvo bumped up the rutted track she found the thought of meeting Claudia made her almost dizzy. What she dreaded most was liking her, because then how could she carry on? But when Pierre had kissed her last week she hadn't felt she had any choice about carrying on in any case. She had picked up a bunch of thick pink cabbage roses for Hilary, most of them still in bud. The latest jolt scattered them over the front seat and the floor.

Claudia had arrived some time before. She had come straight from school and was still wearing the clothes she'd worn all day, a longish black pleated skirt and a round-necked cream cotton sweater, totally unadorned. Her concession to the time of year was that she wore no tights; her thin legs rose pale from her well-polished navy pumps. Her fine, straight hair, nearly black, was pulled back from her face and fastened with a straight gold-coloured clip. This, and her wedding ring, provided the only hint of colour. Sarah was glad she had wiped her lipstick off.

Beside Claudia, Hilary glowed, or shone. She wore cut-off denim shorts; her long legs were already quite brown. Her smooth shins shone, her even teeth gleamed, her nails, though not painted, were polished, and her green eyes sparkled as she received Sarah's regathered roses and pressed them to her face. Her coppery hair wriggled in points like a blaze of light round her head; silver spiral earrings jostled against her cheeks. Her shirt was a kind of thick silk, deep pimento red; she had tied it up under her breasts to reveal a couple of inches of enviably flat midriff. Her feet, of course, were bare – long and bony, with high arches. Sarah would have thought she looked like a Christmas tree, except that there was nothing fussy or overloaded about her. She had the same effect on people that Christmas trees had; a kind of cheering excitement, a promise, when she turned on them the blaze of her personality.

'They really are gorgeous,' Hilary said, jiggling the rose buds so that they settled into a pewter bowl. How amazing, Sarah thought, that she had instantly selected a vessel that complemented so perfectly their short spreading bushiness and the density of their deep pure colour.

'They're from my garden. It's looking wonderful,' said Sarah. She turned to Claudia. 'I can say that because I've hardly put a thing into it yet. Are flowers important to you?' What an uncharacteristic remark for me to make, she thought. It must be the effect Hilary has on me.

Claudia looked surprised. 'Not particularly,' she said, unsmiling. 'It's odd, but I find it hard to remember their names.'

'But you don't have to name something to like it,' put in Hilary.

'I think you do, actually. Or I do. Until something's named it's not real to me. I suppose that's because words are my business.'

'You're an English teacher aren't you?' asked Sarah. 'I'm a linguist.' She saw Hilary give a tiny approving smile at this assertion, and carried on, 'So I think I know what you mean about names – words – defining things for you. When I named my children …' Oh God, she thought, I've put my foot in it again. She can't have any. How could I have forgotten? She'll think I did it on purpose.

It seemed less awkward to carry on. 'Um … naming the children helped to settle their characters for me. We couldn't decide what to call Thomas for ages – I wanted to call him Max – and it was several weeks before we made up our minds. I must admit I didn't get a sense of his character for a long time, not like with the other two. Isn't that a terrible thing to say?' She finished brightly, casting a slightly desperate look at Hilary.

'One excellent thing about having Elinor on my own,' said Hilary, pulling glasses out of a high cupboard, 'is that I could make all my own decisions about that sort of thing. I thought Elinor sounded romantic and Arthurian. Talk of the devil, here she is. Hello, my love, want a drink?'

Elinor had been upstairs, dozing. It was tiring, keeping herself awake each night to see whether her mother got any late-night telephone calls. 'Were you talking about me?' she asked, a little grumpily. 'I heard my name.'

'It was your name we were talking about. By the way, this is Sarah Stanhope, the nursery lady.'

'Oh hello,' said Elinor, turning round. 'I didn't see you there. Mum says your baby's really sweet.'

They all do it, thought Claudia, even the young ones. They just can't help it, it seems. And I just can't help minding.

Sarah beamed. 'Well, yes, he is, most of the time. You must come and see him one day.'

'Sarah, if you ever want a babysitter …' put in Hilary, 'Ellie's got quite a lot of experience.'

Elinor frowned. Did Mum have to make it quite so obvious that she'd like to get rid of her some evenings? Well, she wasn't buying it. 'Mum, I've got too much work,' she said in a childish whine.

'You can't work all the time, love.'

'I don't work all the time. I'm off to Laura's now, as a matter of fact. No thanks, I don't want a drink.'

'Goodbye then, darling,' Hilary called after her, but when her daughter had gone she sighed and shrugged her shoulders. 'I don't know what's gone wrong lately, but she flies off the handle at any tiny thing.' She turned to Sarah and smiled ruefully. 'Treats in store for you.'

'Did somebody mention a drink?' Claudia remarked. 'I've nearly finished these bloody peanuts.'

'Oh, I'm sorry. I got distracted. What would you like, Sarah? Red, white, or I think there are a few beers in the fridge. Shall we sit outside? I think it's still warm enough.'

Elinor cycled away from the cottage as fast as she could, letting the pedals take the force of her aggression. Being a vigilante was tedious, lonely, and probably pointless, since she was at school all day and therefore had no control over her mother's actions. She had come home early one afternoon, pretending to have a headache, but had found Hilary sitting on her own in the garden finishing off a patchwork cushion for a forthcoming craft fair, and the tender solicitousness with which her mother received her had added to the guilty confusion. What exactly was she looking for, anyway? Hilary had made no secret of her evenings out with Joe

Coventry. There had been three such evenings since the incident with the flowers, two meals in restaurants and one amateur opera – Gilbert and Sullivan – in Dinsford. They'd come back early from that one – they'd only gone because Joe knew someone in the chorus, but his friend had been ill on that particular night, and neither of them really liked that kind of thing. He'd come into the cottage for a coffee, and that was the only time Elinor had met him properly. She thought him hideous – fattish, and bearded, and possessed of an execrable dress sense – but she'd had to admit he had been pleasant, even funny. He'd stayed for about half an hour, and then he'd gone, pecking Hilary on one cheek and shaking Elinor's hand with perfect propriety. And her furtive, shameful raids on her mother's bedroom had yielded little in the way of evidence. She'd found several of his novels to be sure, but that wasn't surprising; if she had a friend who wrote novels, she'd want to read them too. There'd been nothing else – no notes, no more flowers.

When she thought it through like this, it all seemed perfectly acceptable. Mum wasn't hiding anything from her, and why shouldn't she have an interesting new friend? Mum, as Laura was always reminding her, was very good-looking for her age, and Joe wasn't; they weren't likely to become lovers. So why did Elinor feel these surges of hot anger? Why did she only dare go out on an evening like this, when she felt sure that her mother wouldn't be going anywhere, hedged in as she was by a couple of women? And she knew that even tonight her own enjoyment would be marred by her circular, sterile, hurtful imaginings.

She'd made up her mind to confide in Laura tonight. Laura seemed increasingly disappointed at Elinor's frequent refusals to go anywhere and do anything, and her stock excuses – too much work, not enough cash – were wearing very thin. Laura was loyal, but she wanted to have fun; Elinor knew that if she couldn't provide any fun, Laura would be driven to look elsewhere. And she'd hate to lose Laura's friendship. She loved Laura in the way one might love an exuberant, rather mischievous puppy; she felt affectionate, indulgent and very slightly superior towards her. Elinor didn't imagine that Laura would be able to help her. She knew what she'd say – why not let your mum have a bit of fun, she deserves it, she's still young, et cetera, et cetera – and she knew she didn't want to listen to it, but she owed it to Laura to tell her what was going on. That was what friendship was all about. As she turned into the short, immaculately gravelled drive that led to Laura's house, she was rehearsing in her mind the possible ways of initiating the subject of Joe Coventry.

Laura, her parents, her two younger brothers and her red setter lived in an ugly, warm, comfortable house that had been built in the 1970s. In an attempt to fit in with what was considered to be the local vernacular, the house had been built of red brick and was tile-hung to half way down. The tiles were brownish, like raw liver, and made of some durable substance which meant they hadn't weathered in the least. There was a pitched roof, and two chimneys, even though there were no fireplaces inside. The front of the house was edged by a fleet of minicabs, representing one of Gordon Taylor's many successful business enterprises; through a brick archway could be glimpsed a garden, not large, dominated by a turquoise swimming pool. By the side of the pool were several painted barrels containing white alyssum, dark blue lobelias and, sticking proudly up from the centre of each, a geranium the colour of skin when a scab has just fallen off, or so Elinor thought.

As she dismounted from her bicycle, Elinor looked up at her friend's bedroom window. Sure enough, there was Laura, grinning and waving. The round curly head disappeared and a moment later Laura opened the front door, before Elinor had a chance to sound the chimes.

'Shh!' she said melodramatically, pulling Elinor into the house. 'Creep upstairs. They mustn't know you're here.'

'Why not?'

'Don't talk, whisper. Because if they see you they'll want to talk to you, and we haven't got a moment to waste.'

'We've got all evening. I don't have to be back till eleven.'

'Eleven! That's ridiculously early. But quick, come upstairs, not a sound, not a sound.'

It was easy to walk quietly in this house, where every inch of the floor was covered in a beige carpet so thick that it stood up in little crests and ridges. Once in her bedroom, Laura put on some music and turned up the volume. 'What's this?' asked Elinor.

'Nirvana. But it doesn't matter. We are Going *Out*.'

'Where? What's the big mystery?'

Laura was rummaging in the chaos of one of the drawers of what her mother would have called a vanity unit. 'Oh shit, where is it?'

'What?'

'Eyeliner. Oh, here.' She drew a wobbly black line underneath one eye, then rubbed it off with a tissue. 'I can never get this right.'

'Laura, would you please tell me what's going on?'

'No I won't, because if I tell you you won't want to go. So all you need to know is that we're going out. I've got to look good, but you don't need to if you don't want to.' Laura cast a doubtful look at her friend's jeans and droopy grey cardigan. 'But you can borrow my crushed velvet top if you want.'

'No thank you,' said Elinor, 'your boobs are about fifty sizes bigger than mine and it would look extremely silly. But listen, if I wouldn't want to go if I knew, then I might just refuse to come in the first place.'

'No you won't, because curiosity will overpower you. And you won't want to let me down. I know the workings of the human heart.'

'But if you think I won't let you down I'd go anyway, whether I wanted to or not. So tell me.'

'No. Because if I told you, you'd waste heaps of time arguing about why we shouldn't go, and we'd be late, because you'd agree in the end. This is all part of a time and motion study. You see, I'm ready, and we're hardly going to be late at all. Do you want to brush your teeth?'

Back at Petts End Cottage, the three women sat in a row on the grassy bank. Or rather, Claudia sat, straight-backed, thin arms clasped round her knees; Hilary, in the middle, lay stretched out, propped up on one elbow, and Sarah, inclining towards Hilary, sat with her legs tucked under her. It was by no means dark, barely dusk, but already the sounds of night were beginning. 'It's amazing here,' said Sarah, sipping her glass of golden wine. 'You can't hear the road at all. We could be anywhere.'

'I know,' said Hilary, 'I love it. It's bliss, to live where the next door wood is louder than anything else. The young badgers fighting make an incredible racket. I was quite frightened before I knew what it was.'

There was a pause. Hilary glanced at Claudia, hoping that she'd make some kind of effort, but the small pale face with its Egyptian profile was set in an abstracted stare. She pulled the bottle out of its terracotta cooler. 'More wine, Claud?'

'Thank you. It's very nice.' But nothing more.

Sarah could hardly look at Claudia. The shadow of the unmentioned Pierre loomed over them, darkening that perfect, scented evening. For the white tobacco plants that grew by Hilary's back door were bewitching the air with their dizzying fragrance.

Abruptly, Claudia turned her head. 'I think you've met my husband,' she said.

In an instinctive movement Sarah put her hand to her face. She ran her fingers through her hair, and as she did so her long-stemmed wine glass toppled over on the bumpy grass. 'Oh, I'm sorry,' she said. 'Could I have a little more, please, Hilary?' It gave her a minute of breathing space, and a reason, albeit slight, for the pinkness she felt sure must be spreading over her face. 'Yes, yes, I have,' she said. 'He came over when my son was terribly ill. He was so kind – drove us to the hospital. And now he's taken the most marvellous pictures of the children …' She ambled to a stop. Hilary was watching her, steadily, even anxiously. Sarah furrowed the grass with her fingers. Claudia's reaction was impossible to gauge.

'Has he invited you to his party?' she asked.

'No, actually he hasn't. I hardly know him – I wouldn't expect –'

'That doesn't usually stop him – he's very gregarious. He's always issuing invitations to people he hardly knows. I'm sorry, that sounds awfully ungracious. Would you like to come? Bring your husband – and children too, if you like – it's at lunch-time. Saturday week. It's his birthday. Are you coming, Hil?'

'Of course! How could I forget Pierre's birthday?'

Claudia smiled. She said to Sarah in a more confiding tone, 'You see Pierre's a baby, really, and he always insists on making a big fuss of his birthday. Hilary's known us for years, and she's been in on dozens of these faintly silly celebrations.'

'It can't be dozens!' objected Hilary.

'Well, a dozen, at least. A baker's dozen. But really, do come. Pierre would be pleased.'

Laura and Elinor walked briskly out of the house. Laura paused to put her head round the living room door. 'Bye, Mum. Just going to Ellie's. Got to dash.' They cycled to the centre of Barcombe, and then, on Laura's instructions, chained their bikes to the churchyard railings. 'They're less likely to be nicked on hallowed soil,' said Laura. 'And now for stage one of our magical mystery tour. We're going to get the bus to Dinsford.'

'We could cycle to Dinsford.'

'Are you kidding? It's six miles. I haven't begun my fitness programme yet. Anyway, we might not be in a fit state to cycle back again.'

'Laura, it's Monday night.'

'So? It's only double geography first thing tomorrow. I always sleep through that anyway.'

'I've got maths, actually.'

'Well, you don't need to get drunk. You never do.'

For some reason Elinor was nettled. 'I do get drunk.'

'I've never seen you.'

'You're never in a fit state to notice.'

Laura laughed. 'Too true. A pint of shandy and I'm anyone's.'

'Make that a half.'

'Piss off, I'm not that bad.' They were giggling when the bus arrived, and the journey passed merrily. When I'm with Laura, Elinor thought, I get the confidence to behave like a normal teenager, mindless and daft. I like it.

The bus stopped at the war memorial in the centre of Dinsford, a fair-sized seaside town with an incurably seedy atmosphere. 'Here we are,' said Laura, nudging Elinor. 'And here they are.'

'Who?'

'Kelly Thacker's brother and his mates. Over there, by the memorial. I told you I fancied him. Remember?'

'Yes, but I didn't think you were going to do anything about it. How did you know he'd be here? Is he expecting us?'

'Kelly set it up, sort of. She told him she'd meet him here with some of her posse.'

'So why didn't she come with us?'

'Because she wanted to go out with Carl, that one with the tattoos who works at the garage in Westling Road, and her mother would go spare if she knew, so she told them she's going out with her brother, and I'm going to tell him that she's not coming because she's working. What a tangled web we weave.'

'So we don't tell him about what's-his-face at the garage either?'

'Certainly not. He'd go even sparer. They're all snobs, the Thackers.'

'But he'll realise when he gets home?'

'He doesn't live with Kelly. The parents split, and they got one each. Baz lives with his dad and he's allowed to do what he likes. But shut up now, he's seen us.'

Baz, who wore a black leather jacket and a pony tail, was indeed looking in their direction. He had quite a few spots, Elinor noticed, but quite nice eyes. He narrowed them at Laura now, and let his mouth hang open in a shape that corresponded to a smile.

'Doan' I know you?'

'Yeah, I'm Laura. I saw you at the Horse and Groom last Saturday. Kelly's not coming. She told me to tell you.'

To Elinor, Laura's manner seemed pathetically eager. Despite the eyeliner, she looked like a sweet girl on a Sunday outing, with her round pink cheeks and dimples. Elinor could not believe that Baz would ask them to spend the evening with him and his friends, three or four of whom were, like Baz, propped up against the war memorial.

'Oh. Right.' That was all Baz said.

Laura wrested a packet of Marlboro from the top pocket of her denim jacket. She placed a cigarette between her teeth. 'Gorra light?' she asked.

'Sure.' Baz flicked at a lighter, his features contorted in what Elinor suddenly realised was an effort to suppress a triumphant smile. 'You girls going anywhere?'

'No,' said Laura, dragging on the cigarette. 'This is Ellie, by the way.'

'Hi, Ellie. We wuz just going down to the beach. Wanna come?'

Elinor had been quite wrong. Baz stood up, and picked up an

Oddbins carrier bag and crash helmet. His friends, similarly equipped, shuffled along behind him. Elinor cast a look of panic at Laura, who took her arm. Elinor thought, it's a beautiful evening. I can always just look at the sea.

At about eleven, Sarah left the cottage. She wasn't sure whether she had enjoyed the evening or not. They had gone indoors but Hilary had left the garden door open, so that moths and flower scents and, eventually, moonlight had spilled into the little living room as they ate. Hilary had cooked sole and mange-touts and tiny new potatoes – simple, and utterly delicious. Then strawberries – the first Sarah had had that year. Instead of sugar and cream, Hilary had soaked them in red wine with a little black pepper. 'A trick I learnt in Italy once. Sounds disgusting, but it works.' And it did work. They ate them out of clear glass bowls, wielding silver spoons with long slender handles. 'Heirlooms – just about the only ones I've got,' said Hilary when Sarah admired them.

They had drunk coffee out of small dark green mugs decorated with splashes of orange. Hilary had made the mugs, of course. Sarah had sat on the shabby, comfortable, little sofa; Claudia, opposite, had sat fully upright on a rush-seated, ladderbacked chair. Hilary had sat crosslegged on the floor, leaning against the sofa. Sarah, looking at Claudia's bony legs winding round each other, wondered if she ever relaxed. Conversation was brisk, not intimate. Claudia described with vivacity her rehearsals for *As You Like It*; Hilary had recounted anecdotes about various theatrical and musical performances with which she had been involved, all more or less disastrous. Sarah asked polite questions and listened to the replies with interest. Everything was pleasant, but nothing seemed to develop. By eleven, Sarah, feeling she knew little more about Claudia than she had at the beginning of the evening, took her leave, and Hilary did not attempt to detain her. Claudia reiterated her invitation to Pierre's birthday party. It's obvious she suspects nothing, thought Sarah, though she felt once more the faint pressure of Hilary's scrutiny as she accepted the invitation, and wrote down the details of time and place.

In the car, she tried to make sense of Pierre and Claudia's relationship, and failed. Claudia seemed different from him in every way – sharper, dryer, older. She seemed closed where he was open, cerebral where he was sensual. Her appearance, too, was surprising. Her strong-featured face could perhaps be described as handsome, Sarah conceded, but with her angular body, her scraped-back hair, her large-framed glasses, she was hardly a match for his undeniable good looks. When she thought of Claudia's bony barrenness, Sarah's heart ached for Pierre.

As soon as Sarah had gone, Hilary said to Claudia, 'I'm worried. Ellie's not back yet; it's most unlike her.'

'It's only just gone eleven. Should you be worrying yet? You told me off last time I suggested you should worry.'

'It's Monday night. She hardly ever stays up late on a weekday. She's normally so bloody sensible, it's almost unnatural.'

'I'd take it as a good sign. She could do with branching out a bit.'

Hilary glanced at Claudia, who had tucked herself into a corner of the sofa Sarah had vacated. 'You're a fine one to talk.'

'What do you mean?'

'You're the most self-controlled person I know.'

Claudia swirled the dregs of her coffee and stared into the depths of her mug. 'But I'm not seventeen. I've done my bit of living.'

'Claud! How can you say that? You sound as if you're drawing your pension.'

'Oh, I'm not complaining, but in emotional terms life's bound to be pretty uneventful for a woman in her late thirties who can't have children.'

'Is the glass half full or is it half empty? For you, it's always half empty.'

'Hil, don't preach. I'm perfectly all right. But marriage is not an – ongoing story, d'you know what I mean? It's a question of doing time.'

'That's a terrible thing to say. If that's how you feel you shouldn't be married. At least with no children, you're a free agent.'

'No, I'm not. I took some vows, and I meant them. I'll never leave Pierre. I love him, as it happens, even though … but what about Ellie? It's half past now. Did she go out with Laura? You could ring the Taylors.'

Hilary knew when it was pointless to pursue a conversation

further. 'I could. But I don't want Ellie to think I'm nannying her. She's too dependent on me as it is – she hardly leaves the house these days.'

'That's because you're seeing Joe Coventry.'

Hilary flushed. 'Don't be ridiculous. She can't mind that much. I've been out with people before.'

'But this is different. This is serious, isn't it?'

'It might be. How did you know?'

'Because you never talk about him. It's something so brilliant you can't even bear to shed daylight on it in case it all crumbles away. You're holding your breath, in a manner of speaking. Am I right or am I right?'

'You're right.' Hilary stood up, and leaned her forehead against the mantelpiece. 'You're right. It *is* special – or it could be. But Ellie doesn't know that. She's only met him once.'

'She can sense it. You're not all that sphinxlike, old thing. So she's trying to cling on to you. After all, you're all she's got.'

'But as you say, she's seventeen. Surely –'

'I'm not saying it's how things should be, I'm just saying it's the way they are.'

Hilary turned round. 'Claud, has she said anything to you, at school?'

Claudia laughed shortly. 'I don't talk to Elinor. Or at least I do, but only about Victorian novels. Do you want me to ring the Taylors? Then I can play the bossy schoolmarm and take any stick there is to be taken.'

Hilary shook her head. 'No, I'll do it. She really is late.' But as she moved to the telephone it started to ring.

'Oh, hello, er …' (Mrs Taylor could never decide what to call Hilary, so she normally just said 'er') 'Maureen Taylor here. So sorry to ring at this time, but we wondered if Laura was still with you?'

'With *me*? I thought Elinor was with you.'

A pause. 'So – she's not with you then?'

'I'm afraid not. Should we worry, do you think? I've no idea where they are.'

A note of cold annoyance sounded in Maureen Taylor's voice. 'Well really, I did think … I had naturally assumed they would be under your care.'

'Mrs Taylor, there's no point in getting annoyed with me about it. There's obviously been some misunderstanding.'

'Misunderstanding? There's been some barefaced lying, if you ask me. I shall call the police. They could be in all kinds of trouble.'

'Don't you think we should wait just a little longer before we call the police? It's not midnight yet, and –'

'You do as you please, Mrs, er – but for myself I shall certainly call the police. Goodbye.'

Hilary put the telephone down, and smiled ruefully. 'I know what she's thinking. Single parent family – flighty artsy mother – can't keep her daughter under control.' She shrugged. 'Maybe she's right.'

'Don't be daft,' said Claudia. 'If either of those two is out of control, it's Laura. I bet they've just gone off somewhere with some boys.'

'Ellie doesn't know any boys.'

'Well, it's about time she did. Do you want me to stay with you until she gets back?'

'Thanks, but I'll be fine. You need to rest or you won't be able to face the next rehearsal. I'm not that worried. Not much harm can come to them if they're together.'

'Are you sure? Because I'm quite happy to –'

'No, really, Claud. Look, I'll ring you if I get really worried, OK?'

As the door closed behind Claudia, Hilary realised she had not asked her what she thought of Sarah, and neither had Claudia volunteered a single remark. That's quite odd, she thought. Presumably she didn't think much of her, but didn't want to say so for fear of hurting my feelings. But why would she have such a low opinion? Sarah had been so pleasant, and livelier than usual too. It was possible, of course, that Pierre ... no, he couldn't have done, not already. Sarah was bound to fancy him – everybody did, at first – but that didn't mean ... but you never knew with Pierre.

The night was still amazingly warm. Hilary threw on a cardigan and sat on the wooden bench by the front door. She left the door ajar in case the telephone rang. She took a piece of tapestry with her but it was too dark to sew, despite the lemony moon that was almost full. She sat there in the noisy night, thinking of her two friends in danger and watching anxiously for the return of her daughter.

On the twilit beach at Dinsford conversation was sporadic. The amorphous mass of denim and black leather, as it had seemed to Elinor, settled down and turned itself into four individuals, or five, counting Baz. There was Slash, who was tall and spindly with lank colourless hair; he said very little indeed, but seemed to have a system of wordless communication with Piggy, the shortest and plumpest of the group. Piggy had a round face with a bumpy texture, like orange peel. His eyes were very small indeed. He drank the most, and had a knife, and he kept cutting little notches in the breakwater against which they leant. He was relatively talkative, but Elinor found him more intimidating than Slash; she never knew whether he was trying to be funny or not. The other two were a little more comprehensible. Charlie was smiley and noticeably handsome. He made several remarks that were intended to charm. 'What's a gorgeous girl like you doing hanging around with a loser like Baz?' he asked Laura at one point. Laura had merely simpered in reply, but Baz, to Elinor's surprise, had chuckled and done nothing to dispel the idea that he and Laura were hanging around together. Charlie didn't say much to Elinor, but he smiled at her once or twice, encouragingly and a little pityingly. Elinor appreciated his effort and wished she could think of something – anything – to say to him.

The last member of the group was Clicker. He had dark red hair and terrible skin; he blushed whenever he said anything and Elinor knew he was making a real effort. As time wore on and it became obvious she was unable to join in any conversation, even in the most rudimentary fashion, about rock music and motor bikes, he actually broke the unacknowledged but powerfully sensed taboos and asked her what A-level subjects she was doing. 'Oh yeah. Maths. I'm doing maths,' he said. Elinor couldn't conceal her surprise.

'You're doing A-levels too? But I thought –'

'You thought what?'

'She thought you were thick as shit, Clicker,' called out Piggy. Everyone laughed.

'No, no, I thought you were ... older,' Elinor faltered. Her voice sounded gratingly pure in the still evening air.

'I'm eighteen,' said Clicker. 'Got my exams in a couple of weeks. We all have, 'cept Slash. Wanna tinny?'

He broke a can of Heineken lager off a six pack, and pulled back the ring before handing it to Elinor. She wanted to ask Slash why he wasn't doing A-levels, but his hooded eyes and pasty expressionless face were off-putting.

They all drank steadily, and occasionally threw stones into the sea. Elinor, who had eaten nothing that evening, found her stomach rebelling against the sour, gassy liquid. Whenever she dared she tipped a little out of her can onto the pebbles, where it heaved and bubbled with a quiet hiss before subsiding out of sight. Not smoking was a problem, too, not for the first time in her life. To give herself something to do she started absently plaiting the fringe of a leather jacket lying discarded close to her. By the time she realised it was Clicker's it seemed more awkward to stop than go on.

The moon hung low over the water, looking near enough to touch. The night was very still, but pools of light broke and reformed like oil on the surface of the sea. The beach was deserted now, except for a derelict old man with a dog on a string. Piggy threw a stone; the dog jumped and yelped, even though it had not been hit. The old man cursed them; Piggy cursed him back, with a low-key backing from Slash.

'What d'you do that for?' demanded Charlie. 'Leave that poor old geezer alone.'

'That's the Cat Man,' said Slash, unexpectedly. 'Everyone curses him. You got to.'

'Why's he called the Cat Man?' asked Laura. 'He's got a dog.'

'He eats cats, that's why,' said Piggy, shortly.

Laura squealed in amused disgust. 'You're kidding!'

'No, he does. He catches cats and roasts 'em. The pigs are always on at him, but they can't stop him.'

Laura appealed to Baz. 'They're taking the piss.'

'No, it's true,' said Baz. 'Piggy's telling the truth for once. No shit.'

Charlie said, 'Let's make a fire.'

'And roast moggies on it? No thanks.'

But the idea was generally accepted. The boys gathered driftwood and garbage from the fringe of dirty sand that lay between the shingle and the sea's edge. Laura and Elinor were left to crumple up a copy of the *Dinsford Argus* into balls.

'That's my paper,' Slash had objected, but Baz told him it was tough shit.

Laura edged closer to Elinor. 'You OK?' she whispered.

'Yes, but what time is it? Mum will be worried.'

'It's only half nine. Don't be pathetic.'

'I'm starving.'

Laura felt in her pocket. 'Here, have a Rollo.'

'Are Rollos part of the F Plan diet then?'

'It's been discredited. Anyway, anyone who loves me has got to love me the way I am. Big is beautiful.'

'I've been telling you that for months.'

'Shut up. You're skinny, so what you think doesn't count. What do you think of Baz?'

'Um ... quite nice.'

'Quite nice. What's that supposed to mean?'

'Shh, they're coming back.'

Charlie, whose idea it had been, took charge of the construction of the fire, waiving offers of assistance. He did a good job. Despite the dampness of the materials, they caught quickly. Elinor had always been fascinated by fires, and this one was particularly beautiful: the flotsam and jetsam they were burning held scraps of metal and paint and plastic, and every now and then a swirl of pure sapphire or emerald or amethyst would rise up amidst the steadier orange flames. Elinor knelt, hands clasped between her knees, staring into the heart of the fire; she shuffled back a little as the heat intensified. Charlie yelled at the others to keep on bringing fuel, and Laura joined them, holding her arms out for Baz to fill. Elinor was left alone.

The fuel-gatherers wandered further along the shore, drifting apart, filling the carrier bags that had contained the beer and using their jackets as improvised sacks. Elinor gazed after them; seen through the pall of heat above the bonfire, their black silhouettes seemed to jump and twist like shadow puppets. She saw Baz lunge at Laura, pick her up, and make as if to throw her into the sea. Laura's shrieks of laughter seemed very far away. The smoke was beginning to make Elinor's eyes water. She pulled down her cardigan sleeves and rubbed them.

A body flumped down beside her, and a voice said, 'You OK?' It was Clicker. He sounded concerned. She looked at him. By moonlight his eyes appeared larger, his cheeks hollower. She could hardly see his acne at all.

'I'm fine – it's just the smoke.' She smiled weakly at him, and to her amazement he put his arms round her. The realisation that he was going to kiss her made her head spin. Before she could decide what to do his mouth had descended on hers. It was like having a damp bar towel clamped over her face. Their teeth clashed slightly. Just when she thought she was going to pull away in order to breathe, Clicker pulled back, looked at her, and said, 'Emma. You know, I think you're really nice.' And then the bar towel descended again. Elinor closed her eyes. The embrace came to an abrupt end a few seconds later when a handful of sand and tiny stones rained down on her back. They were aimed at Clicker, but Piggy in his drunkenness was not a good shot. 'Clicker, you old goat, break it up.'

'Fuck off,' said Clicker. He pulled away from Elinor, grinning sheepishly, but kept an arm round her shoulders. The others had returned and were throwing their spoils onto the dying fire, which suddenly revived. Piggy unscrewed the top of a bottle of vodka, swigged from it and passed it on. Slash licked the edges of cigarette papers and stuck them together. He then split a cigarette lengthwise, tipped out the tobacco onto the papers, held a small black lump of something under the flame of a lighter, scraped off a little and crumbled it evenly along the flattened roll of tobacco. Elinor knew what he was doing although she'd never seen it done before. I've led a sheltered life, she said to herself. She watched intently as Slash lit the twisted ends of his construction and dragged on it. He coughed a couple of times and then got into his stride. Elinor had no idea what to expect – would it make Slash sing, vomit, think he was a bird? It appeared to do none of these things. After a few more drags he passed it to Charlie, who was on his left. Elinor realised that, as she was to the left of Charlie, she would be the next recipient. She looked at Laura for guidance, but Laura was fiddling with the front of Baz' jacket and giggling. She and Baz now seemed to be an established couple; Elinor could see she would get no more support from that quarter.

Charlie had already drawn on the joint several times; it was only a matter of seconds before he handed it to Elinor. She panicked, turned to Clicker and began to kiss him, frantically.

By midnight the Taylors and Hilary Nightingale had engaged in a couple more tense telephone conversations, and Hilary had agreed, reluctantly, that the police should be notified. Claudia had also rung, and had offered to return and keep her company, but Hilary had insisted she was fine on her own. Hilary turned on all the lights in the cottage to make it look welcoming for Elinor when she did return. Telling herself she was silly, she undressed and made herself ready for bed; telling herself she was irresponsible, she dressed again, in warmer, more practical clothing, perched herself on the stool by the telephone and tried to read. She realised, suddenly, overwhelmingly, that what she really wanted to do was ring Joe Coventry. She also realised she knew his telephone number by heart. Giving herself a shake, she told herself to fill in the time usefully, and started to clean out the fridge.

The supply of driftwood was soon used up; the vodka bottle was empty. Three or four joints had been passed round; Elinor had managed to avoid all of them, through a series of apparently passionate embraces with Clicker. It did cross her mind that Clicker had also therefore missed out and that he might resent this, but if this was the case he didn't let it show. His kisses had become more adept and less disgusting. By the time the party staggered to its feet, Elinor felt that they were getting somewhere.

Laura, who had partaken freely of everything on offer, lurched off in the direction of the waterline and was sick. Baz seemed undeterred; indeed it seemed to bring out some latent chivalric instinct. He made her wear his jacket and guided her solicitously across the beach. Elinor had no idea what the time was but was pretty sure they had missed the last bus; she and Laura would have to take a taxi and get their parents to pay at the other end. Clicker kept his arm round her all the way back to the war memorial. She wondered if he was her boyfriend now; could he be said to be her boyfriend if he thought she was called Emma? And she didn't know what he was called, either. He couldn't have been christened Clicker.

The motorbikes were parked next to the war memorial. 'Here,' said Clicker, handing her his crash helmet, 'I'll take you home.'

'Oh, we'll get a taxi, thanks,' said Elinor quickly. Her voice sounded like the Queen's, she thought. 'Laura —' she called, but to her dismay, Laura, wearing Baz' helmet, was already up on his bike, clasping her arms round Baz' waist. Elinor could see she had no choice. Instinctively she clutched at Clicker's arm. 'I've never done this before,' she whispered, her voice faltering.

'S'alright. I'll take care of you.' Clicker's voice was gentle. She was on the bike, clinging to Clicker, feeling wholly exposed. As the bikes roared away through the night she felt as if she and Clicker were astride a meteorite, alone, hurtling through space. She suddenly realised that she loved it.

A straight A-road led from Dinsford to Barcombe, but Baz led the way and took a more circuitous route through narrow, empty country lanes. There was too much noise for Elinor to ask questions, but she assumed the detour was because Baz liked going round corners fast. At every corner both bikes leaned over at such an angle that Elinor couldn't see why they didn't fall over. The hedges, the ditches, the sky and the stars, all felt very, very near, but the feeling was thrilling, not frightening. She imagined falling, but only as a slow roll through the air. The noise, and the speed, and the wind rushing through her thin clothes, were mesmerising.

Ahead, a dark shape — perhaps a log, or a cardboard box — loomed in the middle of the lane. As if in a dream she saw the bike bearing Baz and Laura hit it, and she saw the dark shapes of their bodies flung doll-like through the air. Clicker swerved, and they ground to a halt just beyond the scene of the accident. Baz was already on his feet, but Laura was not.

Elinor staggered in Laura's direction. She was chilled to the marrow, and the tight grip she had kept on Clicker and the bike had made her body stiff and unmanageable. Laura, on the edge of a field, was propping herself up on one elbow, but her left leg was bent double under her. It occurred to Elinor that the fact that the field they'd been passing was neither hedged nor fenced was an incredible piece of luck. Baz' trousers were ripped and he was badly grazed, but despite the absence of a crash helmet he had got off lightly.

Laura was fumbling at the strap of her helmet. Elinor took it off for her, and knelt behind her so that Laura could use her as a pillow. 'I can't walk,' said Laura, quite cheerfully. 'You'll have to carry me.' She shifted a little, and then fell back onto Elinor. 'Oh shit,' she said, and her eyes fell shut.

Laura's leg was broken; the seriousness of the injury made her punishment less severe than it might otherwise have been. She was made to write a letter to the police, apologising for wasting their valuable time; she was also ordered to apologise to Hilary for 'leading her daughter astray'. Maureen Taylor constructed a verbose treatise on the subject for her daughter to copy out. Laura complied, but on the back of the envelope she managed to write 'Dear Hilary, I was coerced into doing this. Come and visit me please, Luv, L.' She was pleased with the word 'coerced', and gave her letter to the nurse to post. Her allowance was stopped for a month, but then, as she later pointed out to Elinor, she had nothing to spend it on in hospital and she'd never had so much free chocolate in her life. In theory she was banned from further contact with Baz, but in truth Baz was conspicuous only by his absence. Laura didn't seem to care, claiming that he had bad breath. Hospital was boring, but it was well worth a few weeks' tedium, she maintained, to get out of exams and her part in the play. There was no way she could be Rosalind now.

CHAPTER TEN

Claudia Prescott was in a quandary. She'd always scorned the notion of understudies, saying they were more trouble than they were worth, but she really couldn't have Laura clomping through the Forest of Arden in a plaster cast. There were only a few days to go before the Whitsun half-term. Anybody joining the cast at this late stage would have to do a lot of work on their part over the break, especially when the part was that of Rosalind. 'I really think I'll have to cancel the whole thing,' Claudia said to Leonie Spencer in the staff room, the day after the accident.

Leonie shook her head. 'You can't, the art department have made all those lovely trees.'

'They could use them for the Christmas panto or something. Rosalind is more important than trees.'

'Only just. I thought the play was all about the healing powers of Nature. "Sermons in stones, books in the running brooks," and so on – isn't that the one?'

'As far as I'm concerned it's far more to do with the herd instinct, and with the healing powers of sex.'

'I don't remember any sex in it.'

'Well, marriage. Sex sanctioned by society. Glorified even.'

'Hmm. I seem to remember that trees loomed fairly large. Or are they just phallic symbols?'

'Don't be facetious. It's irrelevant in any case, because it's going to be simply impossible to replace Laura at this late stage.'

'That seems a bit feeble,' said Leonie, leafing through the staff room copy of the *Times Literary Supplement*.

'Unless you'd do it,' said Claudia.

Leonie put down the paper. 'You must be joking.'

'No I'm not – I'm desperate. You look young enough. It might even be fun.'

'But I'm pregnant.'

'It doesn't show. And even if it did by then that wouldn't be wholly inappropriate – you could be a kind of emblem.'

'Ta very much. I don't know if I fancy being an emblem. Why don't you do it yourself?'

'I look too old – don't bother to contradict me – and I'm too shy. I never could act. But I want you to take me seriously. You could do it. Will you?'

Leonie thought for a moment, sipping the herbal tea she had taken to drinking since becoming pregnant. 'In some ways I'd quite like to,' she said at last, 'but one problem is, I get evening sickness. I throw up between five and six, regular as clockwork. Isn't that when your rehearsals are?'

'All right,' said Claudia, 'I submit. That is a fairly insurmountable problem. We can't have everyone slipping in pools of vomit – they might break a few more legs. Bloody Laura Taylor – trust her to do something daft like that.'

The newspaper on Claudia's other side rustled, and was lowered. Behind it sat Jonquil Trowbridge, the classics mistress, who had an irritating habit of being right about everything. 'Elinor Nightingale was involved in the incident too, one gathers,' offered Jonquil in her implausible clipped pre-war BBC accent. 'You've always been something of a supporter of hers, Claudia.'

'But Elinor didn't break her leg, and she isn't in my play, so it doesn't matter,' snapped Claudia.

'Hardly a rational response.' Jonquil made a sound halfway between a sniff and a giggle, and raised her newspaper once more.

'Elinor Nightingale! She's the obvious choice,' cried Leonie.

'She wouldn't want to,' said Claudia. 'Laura tried to persuade her to audition in the first place, but she flatly refused. I've already thought of her.'

'She might rise to the occasion. She's quite a responsible child – I think she's even got some sort of rudimentary sense of duty.'

'A precious commodity in the prevailing moral climate,' came Jonquil's voice. The *Daily Telegraph* was still up, so Claudia and Leonie could exchange a grimace.

'She's certainly the only one who's intelligent enough to do the part at such short notice,' said Claudia. 'I'll think about it. I've got a free period before lunch, so I'll go swimming. I always have my best ideas when I'm swimming.'

Sarah Stanhope often used the Barcombe Leisure Pool. She loved water, and had introduced all three children to it as early as possible, and all three had taken to it in their different ways. Hannah swam, solemnly and proficiently, in straight lines, avoiding splashers, across and across, still using her water-wings though she could probably have managed without them. She didn't exactly enjoy swimming, she had confided to her father one day, but she thought it would be useful to learn in case of being in a shipwreck. When Adrian had told her that he didn't like it much, either, but only did it because it kept him fit, she seemed relieved, but pulled his head down to her level and whispered in his ear, 'But we mustn't let Mummy know.' Sarah's enthusiasm had been more effectively communicated to her two sons. Gabriel was a little water rat. He would run round the edge of the pool, teeth chattering, dark hair sticking to his scalp revealing pointed fawn-like ears, skinny goose-bumped legs trembling, and then with a tremendous cry of 'here he COMES!' he would take a running jump and plunge into the water, submerging himself completely. He would have jumped in as confidently from any height, Sarah thought. Baby Thomas was a tremendous splasher, but his favourite part of all was sitting over the little hole, where the water spurted out, in the shallowest part – the Barcombe children's pool shelved gently, like a real beach – slapping his fat little hands over the unstoppable jet of water. On this Tuesday morning, the day after her visit to Hilary's cottage, Sarah had taken Thomas along, as she often did when Hannah and Gabriel were at school. She was a strong swimmer, and could manage to get a certain amount of exercise thrashing up and down the pool holding Thomas under one arm.

She had finished now, and had dried the pair of them, and was rewarding herself with a cup of hot chocolate while Thomas, clad only in a nappy and a stripy T-shirt, munched on a biscuit at her feet. She always enjoyed this part, idly watching the swimmers from the cafeteria area, feeling her muscles warmed from the exercise, thinking her own thoughts. She had been watching a slim young woman in a plain black costume with admiration as she dived from the top board and completed length after length apparently effortlessly, and was thinking about how marvellous it would be to go swimming unencumbered with children and use the adult pool again, when the young woman hauled herself out of the water and strode off in the direction of the changing rooms, and Sarah saw, despite the white rubber hat and the goggles, that this slender girlish creature was Claudia Prescott.

Sarah drew back a little and held out another biscuit to Thomas, to give herself a pretext for not saying hello, but kept one eye on Claudia. Her body seemed so much younger than her face. When clothed, she looked bony and awkward; in her sleek black costume she looked natural, almost graceful. Her pale skin was smooth – no stretch marks, no cellulite, no spots. Her neck was long, her back was straight, her gait was easy and confident. Why, Sarah wondered, did she conceal so much potential beneath her school-mistressy manner and dowdy clothes? What perversity was it in her? Sarah had been pleased with the sight of her own body in the changing room mirror as she dried herself, and had been congratulating herself on her continuing weight loss – hence, ironically, the reward of the hot chocolate. Now the sight of Claudia made her feel like an elephant seal.

Claudia had not seen Sarah. She looked preoccupied. She reached the door of the changing room and disappeared. Sarah's attention was caught by the conversation of the two old ladies – members, presumably, of Barcombe's Young at Heart Fitness Club, which performed gentle exercises to a modified disco beat in the shallow pool every Tuesday morning.

They, too, had spotted and recognised Claudia. 'I do think it's a shame,' said one, trying to unwrap a portion of butter from its foil with trembling fingers. 'Such a lovely man. He'd make a wonderful father. Oh bother this fiddly thing – I can't seem to make head or tail of it.'

'Here, Joyce, let me have a go.' Her companion took the tiny pat of butter and folded back the paper slowly but systematically.

'He was lovely to me when I had that pneumonia that time. Ooh, if I was twenty years younger ...' Both women cackled, their wobbly chins working.

If you were twenty years younger, thought Sarah, amused, you'd still be in your fifties, and would probably not stand much of a chance with Pierre. If indeed you would have done at any point in your life. It was hard to imagine away that folded skin, yellow and mauve, that sparse wiry hair, those liver-spotted hands, and detect any vestige of physical attractiveness.

'They do say,' continued Joyce, pressing the butter onto her scone in a vain attempt to make it stick, 'they do say she's refused treatment. They can do all sorts of things these days, but it seems she's too proud.'

'And her a doctor's wife,' replied her companion. 'It's a wonder she's kept him. Husbands don't hang about these days, not like they used to. And she's a bundle of skin and bone.'

'Just like Princess Diana,' put in Joyce, and they both fell to muttering, 'too thin – oh, far too thin,' as they ate their scones.

Sarah realised that the conversation was unlikely to return to the absorbing topic of the Prescotts' childlessness, and in any case Thomas was becoming restless. She unfolded the pushchair, strapped him in, hung the changing bag over the handlebars, and made her way out into the bright sunshine.

Blinking in the car park, she saw Claudia again, this time unavoidably close. She was wearing almost exactly the same clothes as she had worn the night before, Sarah noticed, only the cream top had been exchanged for one in a kind of oatmeal colour. Her hair was still damp but was neatly confined in its gold clip. She must have dressed with remarkable speed, but her appearance was cool and composed. Her face still wore a look of intense preoccupation. 'Er – hi!' said Sarah, nervously.

Claudia stared at her for a moment as if unable to register her presence, and then said, with a faint smile, 'Hello.'

'It was nice to meet you last night,' said Sarah. 'I'd heard so much about you, from Hilary.' The moment she had said it she realised it struck the wrong note, as if she were monopolising Hilary's friendship.

Claudia looked straight at her. 'And of course, you'd met my husband,' she said.

'Of course,' said Sarah. It was hardly possible that she wasn't blushing. 'Been swimming?' she asked feebly.

'Yes. I have to get back to school now – I can only just fit a swim into a gap in my timetable.'

'I'm driving to the school,' said Sarah, boldly, 'to pick up Gabriel. Would you like a lift?'

Claudia hesitated before replying. 'No thank you, I like to walk. But thank you for asking.' Her manner was ungracious.

Well, sod you, thought Sarah, but aloud she said breezily, 'It's a

lovely day for a walk. Goodbye. Thomas, wave bye bye, bye bye.'
Claudia seemed disinclined to wait for Thomas' one party trick.
Raising her hand briefly she turned and strode off.

As she installed Thomas in the Volvo and heaved the collapsible
pushchair into the boot, Sarah was fuming at Claudia's unfriendli-
ness. But going over the little incident in bed that night while
Adrian breathed evenly beside her she asked herself what right she
had to be angry. She was, after all, on the brink of committing
adultery with Claudia's husband – the woman didn't exactly owe
her any favours. Oh Pierre, she thought, vaguely but with aching
poignancy, if only. If only. If only.

It didn't occur to Claudia that it was rude to refuse Sarah's offer of a
lift. She never liked getting into a car with somebody else's baby in
it – there was something insufferably smug about the way they
were strapped in to those neat padded seats – but more important
than that was her preference for her own company. A solitary walk
to school through the dazzling sunshine would set her in order for
the rest of the day; five or ten minutes of social chat in Sarah's car
would destroy her equilibrium. She walked quickly, enjoying the
sensation of swinging her limbs in the warm air – walking in the
sun was not unlike swimming, she decided – and by the time she
reached the huge wooden gates that filled the arched entrance to
the abbey she had decided to put pressure on Elinor to accept the
part of Rosalind. She'd got quite a long way with *As You Like It*;
the rest of the cast would be terribly disappointed if it was
scrapped. Content with this motive, she didn't trouble to examine
other feelings – that being busy with the play gave her less time to
worry about Pierre, or about her widowed mother, who had
suffered from a string of ailments that didn't seem to be responding
to treatment, and who had sounded uncharacteristically gloomy
on the telephone over the last two or three weeks.

Elinor was not in school that day. Apparently she hadn't
reached home until three in the morning, and had presumably
stayed up considerably later than that, giving an account of her
dramatic evening to her mother. It was quite possible that she
would stay at home on Wednesday also; that left only Thursday
and Friday of school time for Claudia to approach, persuade and

prepare her for the role. Claudia decided to behave unprofession-
ally, and get Hilary to use her influence with her daughter. It
would be a distraction for Elinor, stop her dwelling on Laura's
injury, Claudia told herself. Now that she had decided that the
play must be saved, it seemed to assume a significance that it had
never had before when things were going smoothly.

Elinor spent that Tuesday curled under her duvet with her curtains
closed. For company she had a packet of chocolate biscuits and *The
Mill On The Floss*; the biscuits gradually disappeared but she didn't
get beyond page fifteen. This wasn't George Eliot's fault. Elinor's
mind was spinning. Her mother assumed she was asleep – Elinor
knew this because Hilary had tiptoed up and stood in the doorway
a couple of times, but Elinor hadn't stirred and she'd gone away
again. Elinor just lay and watched the dust motes glitter in a shaft of
sunlight that slanted through where the curtains didn't quite meet,
and images from the night before turned and tumbled and made
no sense, just like those twirling random motes. One idea alone
came through clearly – that Elinor cared less about Laura's
accident than she cared about her own encounter with Clicker –
and she wasn't even sure that she liked Clicker very much. I never
realised before, thought Elinor, what an incredibly self-centred
person I am.

She didn't know whether she wanted to see Clicker again. It
would be hard for him to find her – they hadn't even got each
other's names right, let alone exchanged any concrete information
like addresses or telephone numbers. He knew where she went to
school – she was sure of that, because she remembered every single
one of the simple and banal remarks they had exchanged with
ringing clarity – but she hadn't asked him where he went, though
she assumed it was the local sixth form college. When she thought
of his skin, and their teeth clashing, and him getting her name
wrong, she cringed, and thought how much easier it would be
never to set eyes on him again, but when she thought of the way
he had kept his arm round her even when the others teased him,
and how he had found a telephone box and called an ambulance
after draping his jacket over Laura to keep her warm, the sense of
unfinished business became strong and she longed for a significant

word or touch. They had been through something important together; it couldn't just be ignored.

For the hundredth time, Elinor chastised herself for dwelling on Clicker, whom she had known for a few short hours, and failing to think about Laura, who had been her loyal friend for – well, for months. She remembered, dimly, how one of her intentions when she set out for Laura's house had been to confide her fears about her mother, and Joe Coventry; how distant that all seemed now. Let her mother get on with whatever she wanted; Elinor had her own life to lead.

At midday she decided to have a bath, and moved to the door where her lilac-sprigged cotton dressing gown hung. How childish this garment looked – and she had once thought it so pretty! As she lifted the latch she heard the telephone ring, and stepped noiselessly out on the landing to eavesdrop – it might be the headmistress (punishment was a possibility, though not a very alarming one) or the hospital, reporting on Laura's condition. It couldn't possibly be Clicker. Could it?

'Hello – oh Joe! Oh God, it's good to hear from you.' There was a sob caught somewhere in Hilary's voice. 'Yes, she's all right. She's asleep now. Thank you for listening to me last night. I was so, so worried ...' A pause; Joe was obviously making a suggestion of some kind. Then Hilary's voice again: 'I don't know. I don't think you'd better. It might upset her. Yes I know, but she might wake. Maybe tomorrow afternoon ... oh but Joe, I'd really *love* to see you.' Elinor let the latch fall as softly as she could and crept back to bed. She closed her eyes, but fuzzy blotches of colour, purple, green and orange, swam in front of her closed lids and made her feel sick. Her mother – her strong, proud, independent mother – had been grovelling over the telephone to that man, acting weak and helpless just because she, Elinor, had had a night out. The anger wasn't distant after all. She pulled her pillow over her head, clenched her fists, and made a futile effort not to cry.

She must have slept in spite of herself, because the next thing she knew the quality of the light had changed and she was aware of a presence in the room. The shaft of sunshine and the dancing motes had gone. Her mother was standing by her bed holding a wooden tray decorated with painted flowers and fruit.

Elinor associated the tray with the comfort of childhood

illnesses and had always been particularly fond of it. Seeing her open eyes, Hilary smiled and set it down on the floor next to the bed, pushing aside the fallen copy of the *Mill on the Floss*. On the tray were a tiny fat tea pot, turquoise with a gold rim, a matching milkjug, hot water jug, cup and saucer, a plate of hot buttered toast, an embroidered linen napkin, and a round-bellied glass vase in which lolled three of Elinor's favourite roses. They rambled along the fence on either side of the garden gate, and were yellow; pale lemon with a heart of golden stamens when fully open, darker, almost bronze, when in tight pointed bud. Elinor's heart ached, but all she said was, 'Thanks, Mum.'

'How are you feeling?' asked Hilary. 'You've been asleep all day. I rang the hospital and Laura's fine – chatting a lot and eating heartily, they said, so I knew they got the right person. And Claudia rang; she's very worried about *As You Like It*, because of course Laura can't be Rosalind now. She'd love you to do it. She says you're the only one bright enough to take it on at this short notice. I said I didn't think you'd be interested because you've never fancied acting ... was I right?'

'I'll think about it,' replied Elinor, biting into the toast. 'I don't want to talk about it now. I think I'll get up when I've finished this. Can I visit Laura?'

'Of course you can, as far as I'm concerned. And I don't see how Maureen Taylor can stop you, really.'

'I meant will the hospital let me in?'

Hilary smiled. 'I should think so. You don't look so very sinister. Not today, though – they said they were trying to keep her quiet. Some chance!'

'What time is it?'

'Half past five. Do you mind if I pop in on Mr Pitchford? I told him I couldn't go and clean for him earlier because of you, but I think I ought to check that the old boy's got something to eat.'

'OK. Though he managed to survive before we moved into the cottage.'

'Only just. He was in a bit of a state, actually, when we arrived.'

'Oh Mum! Your name should be Florence Nightingale, not Hilary. I want to have a bath. Will the water be hot yet?'

'Should be – I turned it on early.'

Elinor never ceased to be amazed at her mother's capacity for thinking of everything. She sipped her tea, propped against her pillows. As Hilary left the room she said, 'Mum, were there any other phone calls?'

'I don't think so, darling. See you later.' Hilary hadn't turned her head.

After their lukewarm encounter in the car park of the leisure complex, Sarah didn't expect the invitation to Pierre's birthday party to be renewed. She assumed that Claudia, like most wives, exercised the ultimate control over the guest list – though she remembered her conversation with Pierre over that fateful cup of coffee, when he had been shopping for birthday presents for friends. When, therefore, at the end of that week, a convention-ally-worded card arrived to say that Pierre and Claudia requested the presence of their company, Sarah was surprised and excited. The event might be painful but it could not fail to be interesting.

She propped the invitation up against the gilt carriage clock in the living room – a wedding present she had never particularly liked. Adrian, on the contrary, admired it and took a pleasure in winding it up every evening just before bed; this was when he spotted the card.

'You didn't tell me about this,' he said, picking it up.

'Oh no. Sorry, I forgot. That arrived this morning.' Sarah, who was mending Hannah's blue gingham school dress, kept her eyes on what she was doing.

'He's spelt my name wrong,' said Adrian.

'Has he?' Sarah hadn't noticed. 'How can you mis-spell Adrian?'

'A–drain. Perhaps it's a joke.'

'I doubt it. Probably she wrote it.'

'She's less likely to spell it wrong than he is, she's an English teacher.'

'True.' Sarah rose and took the card from her husband. Sure enough, in big, ornate handwriting was written 'Sarah, Adrain and family.' A drain. Had Pierre done that deliberately?

'Do you want to go?' she asked, resuming her sewing.

'Oh yes. Nice fellow, I thought. Nice of him to include the kids.'

'Mm.' Sarah remained vague. She bit off a thread. 'There! Finished. I'm done in – I'm going to bed. Coming?'

'I think I'll watch *Newsnight*,' said Adrian, pouring himself a whiskey. 'See you later.'

'OK.' Sarah brushed her cheek against his and put her sewing bag neatly away in the chest of drawers. She hummed a tune as she climbed the stairs, but her heart thumped painfully. Adrain. She felt angry with Pierre for writing it, but even angrier with herself for acknowledging the description. She brushed her teeth hard, and spat forcefully into the basin. 'Oh God,' she said aloud, her words muffled by the swishing water, 'please make something happen soon.'

CHAPTER ELEVEN

Claudia placed two large jars of mayonnaise carefully in a corner of the trolley where they wouldn't squash the bread. There was already a thick substratum of frozen chicken portions, like permafrost in the tundra. Now she needed mango chutney, which surely must live somewhere near the mayonnaise. Or perhaps it belonged with Herbs and Spices? She wheeled in that direction. No chutney, but what about curry powder? She had some at home, but she probably hadn't used it for a year or so. She didn't think it went off ... Deciding that chutney must be classed as jam, she pushed away from the spice racks, consulting her list as she did so. Easy-cook white rice, tinned pineapple, frozen sweetcorn ... the green salad ingredients she would buy nearer the time, but meanwhile she would cook large amounts of coronation chicken and freeze it for Pierre's birthday party. The recipe was one she had cut out of a magazine a few years ago, when she had gone through a short-lived Domestic Bliss phase, sewing things and polishing things and even making marmalade. That was when she still thought they could have a baby.

Coronation chicken, rice salad, green salad, and strawberries and cream to follow. Plus of course a birthday cake, which she'd ordered from the baker in Barcombe High Street. Even at the height of Domestic Bliss she hadn't felt up to fancy icing.

Better get a couple of ready-made quiches for the vegetarians – there were bound to be a few. The guest list was written in the same spiral bound notebook as the shopping list. She ran her eye over it ... Leonie and John were veggies, so were Viv and Geoffrey Payne ... Sarah and Adrian? Who? Oh of course, Hilary's new friend. She had that slightly plump, slightly pale look some vegetarians had, but she'd certainly eaten fish at Hilary's.

She'd invited Sarah to please Hilary, and rather regretted it; it spelled the beginning of a tenuous and probably fruitless acquaintance, as they'd be certain to ask herself and Pierre back to something or other – she was that type. It would take several such meetings before the tacit conclusion was reached that they didn't have an awful lot in common. They would be bringing their children, of course, damn it. Claudia hurled a giant pack of crisps into the trolley with considerable force.

Pierre had been quite keen to invite them – nonchalantly insistent. It was possible he fancied Sarah; with Pierre, that was a perennial possibility. She wasn't what Claudia considered to be his type – Pierre usually favoured a degree of glamour and artifice, but his tastes were quite catholic, and Sarah was fecund.

How many of the other women on the list were flames of Pierre's, guttering or otherwise? Claudia gave a grim little smile. People would be surprised if they knew how little she minded, now. She'd worked at it, the not minding. She'd have to work harder at not minding about the babies either; she was a mature and rational woman, and yet she never bought toothpaste at the supermarket because it was next to the nappy section, which she *had* to avoid.

As she lined up at the check-out, she recited a poem inside her head, to act as a baby barrier. It didn't matter what the poem was, as long as it was easy and rhythmical; John Masefield's 'Cargoes' was a good one. To Claudia it was the equivalent of one of those tools the Japanese used to push commuters into their jam-packed trains. The poem helped to shove babies, nappies, babywipes, woolly bootees, smiling mums, and dinky little jars of fruit purée into a lockable compartment of her brain. There they would stay until someone or something came along with the key and out would tumble the whole sticky, smiley, pastel-tinted cascade. What she needed, thought Claudia, was to be sole possessor of that key.

The poem worked a treat today. It was the first Saturday of half-term, the sun shone, Elinor Nightingale had agreed to take Laura's part in the play, and she was shopping for Pierre's party well ahead of time. Claudia liked to feel in control of the various elements of her life, like a falconer in touch with his hawks even when they were out of sight. Her mother, who had been bedevilled by illness for several months now, sounded much better and was coming to stay for a few days. She had insisted on managing the journey alone: this must be a good sign. Claudia was to meet her from the station in half an hour.

In the Stanhope household that Saturday morning, the telephone rang, neatly bisecting a small but wearisome argument Sarah and Adrian were having about whether you should wash old tins out before you took them to be recycled. Adrian had discovered that morning that Sarah left them dirty, and had made an insufferable speech about unhygienic and antisocial habits; Sarah had snapped that as Adrian never dealt with such matters his opinion was of no interest. The telephone's shrill cry prevented the otherwise inevitable escalation of the discussion into mutual airing of often-rehearsed grievances. Sarah leapt to answer it as she often did these days, in case it was Pierre. It wasn't.

'Oh, brilliant! How are you?' Sarah's voice was full of genuine warmth. Adrian mouthed 'Who is it?', and Sarah mouthed something back but in such a way that Adrian couldn't understand her.

The caller was Louise Feldman, Sarah's old college friend. She was proposing to spend some of half-term with the Stanhopes, together with her two young children. Jack, her husband, was very busy, but Louise had a few days' holiday owing to her and she'd been meaning to visit Sarah for ages. Sarah was delighted.

'And you remember Leah and Jacob, don't you, darling?' she said, hugging Hannah. 'Won't it be lovely to see them again?'

Hannah had always found thin, dark Leah, almost exactly her age, rather daunting, but she was suggestible and her mother's mood was infectious. 'We could have a midnight feast,' she offered.

'Where on earth did you hear about midnight feasts?' asked Adrian, laughing. Hannah looked cross.

'You told me, Daddy. You told me you had them at your school.'

'Told, Han, not telled. Did I? I'd forgotten.'

Sarah saw that Adrian's comments had nettled Hannah. It must be awfully tiring to be as sensitive as a six-year-old, she thought. To restore good humour, she said, 'Yes, you can have a midnight feast with Leah. What would you like to eat for it?'

Hannah said, 'Twiglets. What would you like for your feast, Gaby?'

Gabriel was turning somersaults on the sofa cushions, which he had ranged on the floor. He stopped, and said, 'One piece of chocolate cake, one ice-cream cone, one pickle, one slice of Swiss cheese, one slice of salami, one piece of cherry pie, one cupcake and one slice of watermelon.' He then resumed his acrobatics.

Adrian looked at Sarah and said, 'My God!'

'Daddy, don't swear.'

'Sorry, Han. I don't think "My God" is a proper swear though.'

'Miss Colenut says it's the worst swear.'

'Does she, indeed? But Gabriel, if you eat all that for your feast you'll go pop.'

'Gaby's only saying that because it's in his caterpillar book. He doesn't know what he wants to eat, really.'

'Yes he does,' said Gaby.

'What, then?'

'One nice green leaf, and after that he felt much better.'

'I've got to get out of this madhouse,' said Adrian, grinning. 'I'm going to the seaside. Anyone want to come?'

We really are just a normal happy family, thought Sarah as she rummaged in the hall chest for buckets and spades. Louise's call had buoyed her up. Life felt rich.

'Do you have to do that, Mum? I can't read while you're doing that.' Elinor, lying face down on the grassy bank beside the cottage, sounded peevish.

Hilary straightened her back, and gave a tuft of groundsel a little shake to get rid of the soil on its roots before throwing it onto the pile of weeds that lay on the bumpy brick path, wilting in the afternoon sun.

'I could state the obvious,' she replied calmly.

'Which is?'

'That you can read anywhere, but I can only weed in the garden.'

'Oh Mum. Don't try to be reasonable. You don't have to weed now, you could go and knit or something.'

'All right. Mind if I knit out here?'

Elinor shrugged. 'Do what you like.' She returned to her book. Hilary smiled to herself a little ruefully. She knew that her presence, whatever she was doing, would be an irritant to Elinor, but she couldn't allow herself to be at her daughter's beck and call.

She fetched a deck-chair and some knitting and placed herself by the back door, in the sun.

Minutes passed. The click of the knitting needles, the tiny grunts Hilary unconsciously made to mark the end of each row, grated terribly on Elinor's nerves. She turned the pages of *As You Like It* without absorbing anything. At last she could bear it no longer.

'Aren't you worried about skin cancer?' she burst out. Her voice sounded harder than she meant.

'Me? No, not particularly.'

'Of course it's you.'

'I'm sorry?'

'You said "Me" – well obviously – oh never mind.'

Another pause. The clicking continued, steadily, rhythmically. In another mood Elinor would have been soothed by the way it mingled with the hum of bees and the soft swish of leaves from the wood. But today it was unbearable. Annoyed by her own pettiness, Elinor slammed her book shut and stood up. Hilary raised her eyes from her task. 'Where are you going?'

'Indoors.'

'Oh, why?'

'I can't stand it.'

'Stand what?'

'Your breathing, since you ask.'

Hilary laughed, and the note of genuine amusement was a fresh source of aggravation.

'I apologise for breathing.'

'Oh for God's sake, Mum, you know what I mean.'

'I'm not sure that I do.' Hilary laid her knitting aside. 'Ellie, sit down. Let's have a talk.'

Elinor flumped down onto the grass as gracelessly as she could, but at least she stayed. Bending over a clover head and pulling out the slender purple tubes, she muttered, 'What about?'

'Well, perhaps you'd tell me why you're so angry with me.'

'I'm not, it's just you were breathing like that and I couldn't concentrate.'

'I don't mean just now, I mean in general. Either you avoid me, or you snap at me. I can't put a foot right.'

Elinor glanced sideways at her mother from beneath lowered

lashes. Hilary was wearing an old cotton sundress, cornflower blue but faded now, with a grass stain on the skirt and one white daisy-shaped button missing from the bodice. Her honey-coloured limbs arranged themselves with ease over the stripy deck-chair, her hair spiralled out from beneath a wide-brimmed straw hat. Elinor wished she could paint. She could make a picture to show her mother how deeply she loved her, she thought, though she could never do it in words. But love her she did, from the saggy bits just beginning to show on her neck down to her dirty bare feet with their long monkey toes.

'I'm not angry. I'm under pressure because of the play, that's all.'

'Ellie, I don't think that's true.'

'It's a big deal, learning the part, and –'

'I know it's a big deal, but something's been wrong for longer than you've had the part. Can't you tell me, Ells? You can't shock me, you know.'

Unfortunately not, thought Elinor, but you can shock *me*. Aloud she said, 'There's nothing to say, Mum. I'm all right. Really.' The clover head was finished with. Elinor threw it aside.

Hilary took a deep breath. 'All right. Well, there's something I want to tell *you*. I think you should know that – I've met – well you know about him –'

'I know, I know, you're seeing that man. What'shisname, with a beard. That's not a secret.' Elinor made as if to leave.

'Elinor, I love him.'

Elinor felt her scalp crawl. She allowed herself a glimpse of her mother's face; the mingled expression of triumph, relief and embarrassment was repugnant to her. She pulled down a strand of hair and fiddled with the ends. 'So?' she said.

'It's important, darling. I haven't felt like this about anyone since … for a long time. I've got to tell you, we shouldn't have any secrets from each other.' Hilary knelt beside her daughter and put her arms round the thin shoulders. 'Oh darling, aren't you glad I'm happy?'

Elinor wrenched herself free, and stood up. 'I think you're disgusting, if you really want to know.' She walked to the front of the cottage, mounted her bicycle and rode away down the rutted track before she could see that her mother, who had remained kneeling motionless on the grass, had buried her face in her hands.

CHAPTER TWELVE

'But what do you actually do all day?' Louise jabbed her half-smoked cigarette onto a saucer, making it buckle. She and Sarah sat opposite each other at Sarah's kitchen table. The French windows were wide open so that they could keep an eye on their children playing in the sandpit.

'Well … you know,' said Sarah. 'You know. What anyone does.'

'I don't know, actually. I'm out at work, or I'm ferrying Leah and Jacob around to their endless activities, or I'm trying to get ready to go out to dinner with some of Jack's clients, or I'm dashing to late night shopping at Brent Cross. But presumably you don't have to dash anywhere. I mean, do you just clean the house and stuff?'

Sarah could see that Louise, who for all her air of scattiness was fanatically house proud, was surveying the kitchen for evidence of any such activity, and finding precious little. The bin was so full that the lid wouldn't fit back on properly, the work surfaces needed wiping, and under the vegetable rack a little whirlpool of papery garlic and onion skins had accumulated, along with a shrivelled mushroom and a blackened carrot.

'Does it look like it?' she replied. 'I don't know what I do, really, but the time just seems to go. I take the kids to school, take Thomas shopping, cook a bit, clean a bit, collect the kids … that's it, really.'

'Don't you go mad with boredom? I mean, in London at least you used to see friends quite a bit.'

Sarah was too familiar with the directness of Louise's approach to be offended.

'Not mad with it, but weighed down by it sometimes. But I couldn't cope with what you do, Lou. Don't you worry you'll wear yourself out?'

'Maybe, but at least I'll go out with a bang. If I stayed at home all day I'd be like a mouldy battery eating away at itself in a drawer.'

'Do I seem like a mouldy battery to you?' asked Sarah, smiling.

'Well yes, a bit, if the truth be known. I mean, it's really pretty here and the kids are blooming, but I can't help thinking there's not a lot in it for you. JACOB! Leave Gaby's spade ALONE!'

'You just think of anywhere outside London as a kind of rural theme park, don't you?' said Sarah. 'You're quite happy to pay your money and spend an afternoon playing around in it, but then you pack up and go and you don't really believe it exists once you've gone. But actually, Barcombe's a real place, with real people in it.'

Louise looked doubtful. 'Do you know any of them?'

'A few. There's a really nice woman who did the frieze in Thomas' room. She's going to start on the bathroom next. You'd like her – anyone would.'

'Anyone else?' Louise helped herself to another flapjack. If she hadn't been so fond of her, Sarah would have been maddened by the way Louise ate exactly what she wanted and never gained an ounce.

Sarah hesitated for a moment before replying, 'On Sunday, we're going to a birthday party for the local GP. His wife's a teacher at Han's school, in the senior part. He's the one who took those photos of the children. I told you.'

Louise's antennae quivered. 'They are lovely pictures. Get him to take some of you.'

'Me? Why? I never have my photo taken.'

'Maybe you should. Adrian would like it.'

Sarah fetched the chopping board and a sharp knife and set them down on the table with a little thump. 'I don't think he would, particularly. But it's an idea. I'd better do something about lunch. Do your two eat spaghetti bolognese?'

'They love it. The poor things are a bit deprived, most days, because their nanny's a vegetarian and she cooks for them. How's Nicola getting on in New York? Have you heard?'

'Not for a while. As you might imagine, she's not the world's best correspondent. We get the occasional post card, and the even more occasional telephone call.'

'Does your mother fare any better?'

'A little. Last time I spoke to Mum she said she thought Nicky wasn't as happy as she had been, probably because the novelty had worn off. And she's manless. She claims there are no single men in New York.'

'Except gays, I suppose.'

'Not even those any more, because everyone's dying of AIDS. Nicky says people still talk about it incessantly. Seems a million miles away to me.' Sarah paused in her chopping to gaze at the scene in the garden. The efforts of the two girls to build a sand palace for their Barbie dolls were frustrated by Jacob and Gabriel who claimed to be 'digging to Australia'. This seemed to entail emptying nearly all the sand out of the moulded plastic pit onto the paved patio. Sarah remonstrated with them briefly, but hardly needed to bother; Leah and Hannah were bored with sand and had decided to undress the dolls and cover them with leaves.

'Blimey!' said Louise. 'If Nicola can't find a man, then there must be an acute shortage. When's she coming back?'

'I don't know – she muttered about taking a week off in the summer, and it's nearly summer now. The Americans hardly take any holiday, you know. She gets about ten days a year.'

'I know. They're ridiculous, the Americans. Shall I make a salad?'

Louise had a knack of making herself completely at home wherever she happened to be. She moved round Sarah's kitchen collecting everything she needed as if she'd known it all her life, instead of only having arrived the evening before. Watching her friend make the salad, Sarah realised that Louise's way of doing things hadn't altered a bit since the days when they had shared a flat in their final year at college. It gave her a great sense of calm.

After lunch they went shopping, at Louise's instigation. Sarah knew that it was pointless to mention that Barcombe shops had little to offer compared to what Louise was used to in London; she knew that until she had investigated whatever shops there were, Louise felt disorientated. She remembered a far-off holiday when they had taken a tiny damp cottage on the Welsh border, just the two of them, and how Louise had wandered down to the little post office in the village every morning to stare mournfully at the packets of cornflour and faded greeting cards on offer. She reminded Louise of this as they meandered through Barcombe's one shopping precinct. 'Oh God, I remember that holiday!' Louise exclaimed. 'I'd just split up with David – remember the moustache? – and you'd just met Adrian. You talked about him all the time.'

'Did I? How tactless of me. Gaby, hold onto the pushchair, there's a good boy.'

'I can't make the same accusation now.'

'What do you mean?'

'You seem to be acting as if Adrian doesn't exist.'

For the first time, Sarah resented Louise's bluntness. 'Don't say things like that – the children will pick it up,' she snapped.

'Hardly,' said Louise, indicating Hannah, Leah and Jacob, whose noses were pressed to the window of the expensive children's shop several yards ahead. Gabriel, having ignored his mother's injunction to hold onto the pushchair, was gazing through the grid at the coins in the bottom of the brick wishing well that stood in the centre of the precinct. He pointed into the well and muttered to himself, dead to the adult world.

Louise looked hard at Sarah and said, 'Well?' Sarah knew she would not be let off the hook. 'What … what makes you think that?' she asked, weakly.

'I've been here for nearly twenty-four hours now,' Louise replied, 'and you haven't talked about Adrian at all. And last night at supper you made it quite plain he was *de trop*. He was quite upset when he went to bed. Didn't he say anything?'

'He was asleep before I went upstairs. I don't think he was upset.'

'He was. He went very quiet – that's his way, isn't it? And when I suggested this morning that he'd like you to have your photograph taken, you were very dismissive. Sarah, don't tell me it's not my business, because your whole life's my business, and mine's yours. I've watched you and Adrian together for years and years, and it's never been like this, not even when you were depressed after Gaby was born. So much tension in your house – it's crackling with it.'

Thomas, strapped into his pushchair, began to fidget, and Sarah jiggled him to and fro as she spoke. 'I didn't realise it was so obvious,' she said, looking away.

'What's happened? Is there anyone else?'

'Maybe … I've sometimes wondered if Adrian …' Sarah was appalled to find her voice choking with tears.

'I'm sorry.' Louise laid a hand on Sarah's arm. 'I haven't exactly picked my moment, have I? We'll talk later, when we can get rid of the kids. And now I'm going to buy you a present. I never got you anything for your birthday.'

Louise rounded up the children and herded them and the protesting Sarah into the clothes shop where Sarah had bought the violet-blue sweater only a few weeks before. With the speed and skill of the professional shopper she selected a couple of items and paid for them before the little boys created too much havoc or Sarah could object too forcefully against the extravagance. She chose a silver Celtic cross on a black thong for Sarah and a baggy tangerine-coloured T-shirt for herself, then steered the whole group out again. 'And now,' she said, 'where could we buy some ice cream?'

Sarah half looked forward to, half dreaded, her talk with Louise. She couldn't imagine that it could take place that day; after the ice-creams it was time to go home to begin the tea, bath and bed routine and then Adrian would be back and they could hardly discuss him when he was in the house, even if he did retire early again. The children, excited by each other's company, cavorted endlessly, and no one was remotely ready for bed by the time Adrian got back. He seemed ebullient – Sarah heard him whistling as he walked up the garden path – and, having kissed everyone, he turned to Sarah and said, 'You go and put your feet up for a while. Lou and I will dispatch this lot. I'm going out for a drink with Henry after supper, by the way, so you two can have a good talk.'

Oh the irony, thought Sarah as she lay on the living room sofa with the newspaper, half-listening to the sounds of mayhem upstairs. Why is he putting on his ideal husband act – for Louise's benefit, or because he's going to meet his mistress later on? Both, probably. He'll want to impress Louise because he thinks she'll tell me how lucky I am, so I won't notice what he's up to. Well, she's sharper than he takes her for.

Discarding the unread paper she got up and wandered to the window. On the window seat lay the packet of photographs Pierre had taken of the children. She must have gone through them scores of times, but now she did so again. They were marvellous. Only someone with special sensitivity could have captured their different characters so perfectly; Thomas' sunny imperturbability, Hannah's cautious but sweet-natured engagement with the world, Gabriel's glorious, maddening absorption in – what? One never quite knew. She pulled out the picture that she liked best of all; oddly, it was a back view of Gabriel, standing in the kitchen doorway gazing out into the sunlit garden. He was holding his hands behind his back; you could just see that he was clutching a scrap of turquoise ribbon, something he had treasured ever since it had arrived adorning a chocolate egg at Easter. The dark whorls of his double crown, the aching vulnerability of the nape of his neck, the mood of complete concentration somehow conveyed by the set of his shoulders … his otherness, which she had sensed so strongly from the first day of his life, was expressed in every detail. For the second time that day Sarah felt the suffused and painful warmth of rising tears. Her tenderness for her little son was mingled with a tenderness for the man who had somehow tapped a vein of love and loss in her. Let Adrian do what he wanted with his bit of skirt tonight. It didn't seem to matter a bit.

Adrian maintained his jaunty air throughout supper, after which, declining coffee, he took himself off. 'See you later,' he called as he closed the front door. 'Be good!'

Louise hardly waited for the click of the Yale lock before rounding on Sarah. She leaned her elbows on the table, propping her face between her long, thin hands, amidst the debris of fruit and cheese. 'So,' she said, 'what's going wrong?'

Sarah sliced off the runny edge of the Brie and ate it before replying. She had made up her mind to keep Pierre out of it. Adrian and his affair must be her decoy.

'Well,' she said slowly, 'where do you think he's gone tonight?'

'Sarah!' Louise sat bolt upright. 'You don't mean it! You don't think he's gone to see … someone.'

Sarah shrugged and said nothing.

'But he's gone to see his friend. What's his name? Henry. What makes you think –? Who is Henry anyway? What's he like?'

'I don't know,' Sarah replied. 'I've never been allowed to meet him. I don't even know if he exists.'

It was Louise's turn to remain silent. She plucked grapes absently from the large bunch spilling over the fruit bowl and arranged them in a circle round the base of her empty wine glass.

Sarah said, 'It all adds up. I've asked to meet this man time and again and Adrian's always been evasive. And he's been late back from work sometimes, claiming he went for a quick drink with colleagues. Well, he never used to do that – or hardly ever. And we've had the baby sleeping in our room for ages, and even though his nursery's finished now Adrian's made no attempt to get me to move him back.'

'Well, why haven't you moved him back?'

Sarah was stumped. 'I just … I suppose I just haven't got round to it.'

Louise fixed her with her small, bright eyes, 'That's pretty feeble,' she said. 'Look, I know Adrian really well. I know you better of course, but I do know Ade. And he is not capable, in my opinion, of inventing a whole human being in order to deceive you. He really isn't.'

'You mean he's not imaginative enough?'

'No. I mean he's not wicked enough.'

'That's an old-fashioned word.'

'I chose it carefully. Lots of men have affairs and regret them and it doesn't have to mean a lot, but to exploit your trust and make a fool of you to that extent – he couldn't do it.'

'Don't you think he's capable of infidelity?'

'I didn't say that. He may be – most men are, though Adrian strikes me as less likely to than most. But I don't think he's doing it now.'

'You think most men … Has Jack ever?'

'Yes. Oh God yes. All those business trips … the girls are laid on for them. And I hate it, but I get over it. I'd be stupid not to.'

'Oh Lou – you never told me.'

'No need. I'm strong, I can cope.'

'But,' said Sarah, almost crossly, 'you said my business was your business, and now I find you haven't even told me –'

Louise smiled ruefully. 'I know, I know. You feel cheated, because you didn't know that about me. But the thing is, I understand the nature of my marriage, so it wouldn't really help to tell.'

'And I don't understand mine? Is that it?'

'I'm afraid that's what I think.'

Sarah stood up and began to clear the plates with jerky, angry movements. 'I think you've got a bloody nerve,' she said.

Louise twisted each of her several chunky rings in turn. 'I'm sorry, Sal. I've really cocked this one up. I just wanted to do something, because I know you're unhappy, but all I've managed to do is make out that I'm superior to you, which I'm not, and never will be.'

Sarah set down the pile of plates she was carrying. The sight of her friend's thin shoulders, slightly hunched, was so exactly as it always had been that she was moved. Louise was only here for a couple of days. Why waste it?

'Oh well,' she said, 'let's have some more wine. Do you like this sweet stuff – Muscat? Nicky brought a load back from France last year. It's brilliant.' As she set a glass down on the table Louise encircled her waist and squeezed it. Sarah patted her friend's shoulder. 'So, convince me I'm mad. Prove that this Henry character does exist.'

'Well, that bit about Thomas being in your room. Why don't you move him out, and see what happens?'

'Mmm. Perhaps. And Henry?'

'As for staying for a drink after work – it's hardly aberrant behaviour, you know. The poor man's got to have some life of his own.'

'OK. But Henry?'

'Perhaps he doesn't want you to meet Henry because –' Louise's sentence was cut short by the sound of a key in the lock. They sprang apart, almost guiltily. 'But it's not even ten o'clock!' murmured Sarah.

'Hello there!' Adrian called, ushering in a tall, fair-haired, almost absurdly good-looking young man. 'You two are looking fairly conspiratorial, I must say. Anyway, here's Henry. He's been wanting to meet you for ages.'

'It was good to meet Sarah at last,' said Henry to Adrian on the train next morning. 'And her friend's a laugh too.'

'Louise? Oh, Louise is a hoot. I'm glad she's come. It'll cheer Sarah up a bit.'

'Does she need cheering?'

'Well – you know how it is. Moving to a new place, not

knowing many people, stuck with the kids all day. I worry about her sometimes.'

Henry looked thoughtful. 'Emma couldn't stick it,' he said. 'It was her idea in the first place, to move out of London. She was nuts on the house, spent a fortune doing it up. We used to spend every bloody weekend trawling antique shops. And then she just threw it all in and disappeared.'

'And where is she now?'

'I haven't a clue. Last time I heard from her was a post card from Sydney. A post card! Not even a letter – and we were as good as married. We'd started to plan the wedding – the works.'

'That's incredible,' said Adrian. He was frowning with anxiety. 'You don't really think that living in Barcombe could be the whole reason –'

Henry laughed. 'Oh no. God no. There were lots of things wrong between us. Looking back, moving out of London, buying the house and everything – it was all just diversion tactics. We thought that if we bought the perfect lifestyle we'd have the perfect relationship. Emma had the sense to see the fallacy before I did.' He shrugged. 'To an outsider like me your set-up with Sarah looks pretty perfect. But I suppose you never can tell.'

'It is pretty perfect,' replied Adrian, 'Or would be, if ... I just wish Sarah had a bit more to – well, to interest her I suppose. She used to be a lot more outgoing and – I don't know the right word. Energetic. That will do.'

'Having three kids is enough to drain anyone's energy.'

'Sure, but it's not just that. We're not comunicating much at the moment. I'm tired when I get back from work, and Sarah never seems to want to talk. God, I sound like I'm writing a letter to an agony aunt. Sorry.'

'She should get a job,' said Henry. 'It's work that keeps me sane.'

Adrian thought about it. 'But Thomas is still a baby – if she worked as well she'd be even more exhausted. And we'd have to employ someone –'

'You can afford it,' said Henry. 'Oh well, just a thought. Pretty heavy conversation for this time of the morning. Fancy a game of squash later this week? Thursday?'

'I'll check with Sarah, but yes, in theory, great.'

The train was approaching Tarton Spa. By unspoken agreement Henry and Adrian conversed every morning until this point in the journey, then read or worked until they reached London. Henry unfolded his newspaper. 'You check with Sarah,' he said, and winked at Adrian. 'Sometimes I think I'm well out of it.'

CHAPTER THIRTEEN

Naomi Randall pressed her cheek against the window of the railway carriage. The sight of all that rolling greenness was almost dizzying after the long expanses of hospital white and the muted pastels of her own small suburban flat, which was just about all she had had to look at for weeks and weeks now. What a pity the window was so dirty. The grime on the glass was so thick, it was almost as if she had to peer round the corner of a dingy screen to glimpse the glorious unfolding early summer landscape. The jolting of the train caused ripples of pain to echo through her shoulder, but she was learning to live with pain. It was a part of her now, and always would be, always that is, until they gave up on her, and filled her up with morphine to wash it all away.

How long would that be? The doctors were maddeningly vague. They didn't seem to understand how much it mattered to her, that she wanted to know for certain whether she would ever see the first of June again, because if she knew she wouldn't then she would wallow in it, saturate herself inside and out with the colours and the sounds and the warmth ... If she knew, then she could somehow summon up a final great burst of energy before going into that goodnight, but if her life was to be spared a few more years, then she could afford to relax and fritter and muddle through in the way that most people did.

The train drew up at a little country station. Woodgate. Only two more stops before Barcombe, where Claudia, her only daughter, would be waiting for her. She never could quite think of Claudia as her only child, because of that tiny blue-faced seven months' boy who had struggled with life for a few hours, just long enough for her to hold him in her arms and name him Peter. Claudia had come before Peter. She had been given a rubber doll in anticipation of the new arrival, and even now Naomi would shudder if she chanced to remember the awfulness of watching the little girl bathe and dress and feed her toy, in unconscious imitation of the sacred routines that her mother was rehearsing time and time again in her imagination, but was never in actuality to perform again. Claudia was thirty-seven now. Naomi, always humbled by her daughter's cleverness, had never dared to ask, but the tense set of Claudia's mouth and the surreptitious and incongruous affection she showed to the unresponsive dog Jaques surely revealed that, like most women, she longed for a child.

Naomi's knowledge of medical science was sketchy, but she had always assumed that Claudia had inherited some mysterious problem from her side of the family. She was an only child herself (mind you, that was fashionable in the 1920s) and had waited for five years before Claudia had come along. And then after the loss of the little son, she and Harold had tried and tried, so much so that if she were honest with herself marital relations had become nothing more than a means to an end, an end never fulfilled. They had not sought help, of course – one didn't, in those days – but she had always hoped that the fact that Claudia had married a doctor would mean that things got sorted out for her. But they hadn't. Not yet.

And now time was running out for Claudia, and for Naomi too, as the web of pain spun itself throughout her seventy-year-old body. She put her hand up to the place where her left breast had been and ran her fingers lightly over the cleverly moulded pad, in a habitual gesture that looked as if she were simply smoothing her blouse. She had decided that on this visit she would be bold, and probe Claudia – gently, of course – about the whole baby business, Claudia was so proud – too proud, sometimes, to look a problem squarely in the face.

The train reached Barcombe station and juddered to a halt. Naomi thrust her arm through the window and fumbled with the fastening – why couldn't one open these doors from the inside? She did hope that the guard would remember to hand down the suitcase; one advantage of her illness was that she had fewer qualms about asking for help. A friendly hand relieved hers of the stiff door handle – here was that nice guard, helping her down from the train, holding her suitcase in his other hand. People weren't nearly as bad as they were made out to be. And there, striding to meet her through the patchwork of strong sunlight and deep shade was Claudia, looking too thin, but pleased and vigorous.

Claudia kissed her mother with unaccustomed warmth. She

had been so encouraged by Naomi's decision to make the journey alone that she found herself ill-prepared for the alteration in the older woman's appearance. Her mother looked tiny. Her hair had been carefully tinted and set, but it was easy to see how much thinner she was, and her dark eyes were like black holes in her small monkey face. Claudia initiated a stream of chat to mask her reaction. It wasn't until she had installed her mother in the car that she noticed her swollen ankles. Naomi followed her daughter's glance. 'I've had to get special shoes,' she said, 'but don't worry, dear, it's not as painful as you might imagine.'

Claudia's throat tightened – 'Well, you're here for a good rest. You can stay as long as you like, Mother. You know that, don't you.'

'That's very kind, dear, but I don't want to impose. I shall go back after Pierre's party. I couldn't think what to get him; he always seems to have everything. So I got him some gardening gloves.'

'That's excellent, he gets through them very fast.'

'How is he?'

'Fine. Busy. He's on call today so he may not be there when we get back.'

'Poor Pierre. I hope you see enough of each other?'

'Plenty,' said Claudia, rather grimly. What did her mother mean by that remark?

The car lurched into the drive. 'I always think you take corners rather fast,' Naomi ventured.

'I'm sorry. I know I'm an impatient driver. But I've never had an accident, as you know.'

'Don't tempt Fate, dear. Could you help me with this seat belt? I don't quite see how it … ah, that's it.'

Claudia took her mother's arm and helped her from the car. It was the first time she'd ever felt the need to do that. Pierre, she noticed, was out. She guided her mother into the living room and placed her in a soft chair by the large picture window. Next to the chair was a glass-topped coffee table on which lay a couple of books of photographs – portraits, wildlife – and the newspaper.

'I'll get you a cup of tea, and then we'll have lunch in about half an hour. All right?'

'Lovely, dear. It's marvellous to be waited on.'

Claudia busied herself in the kitchen. Jaques shuffled in and pushed himself against her legs. This usually meant that he wanted to relieve himself. He rarely made contact with humans unless to express a specific need. Hilary said he was a Low Responder. I'm a Low Responder too, thought Claudia as she opened the door for Jaques. My mother might be dying and I'm going to find it impossible to mention any such possibility. She'll stay here for a week and we'll engage in only the most superficial chat.

She put the tea pot on a little metal tray with a strainer and a hot water jug; her mother liked things done properly though she rarely complained if they were not. She heard the soft swish of the newspaper sliding from Naomi's knees onto the floor as she entered the room, and was surprised to see that her mother made no attempt to retrieve it. As Claudia set the tea tray down on the coffee table Naomi said, 'I'm sorry to have to ask you, dear, but could you pick the paper up for me? This chair's so lovely and soft, that it's difficult for me to get out.'

'I'm sorry, I wasn't thinking.' Claudia folded the paper and placed it in her mother's lap. She thought about the last time she had seen her mother, in the Easter holidays. She and Pierre had driven up one Sunday; when they arrived Naomi had been perched on a stepladder hanging up a flypaper. Now she couldn't even get out of a chair.

'Oh, the *Guardian*!' Naomi commented.

'Yes we've finally abandoned *The Times*. It's no better than the tabloids now.' Claudia poured the tea.

'I've switched, too – back to the *Daily Mail*.'

'Mother!'

'I find it much easier to handle. And I must admit there's a lot to read in it.'

'But … I thought I'd trained you out of it.' Claudia's tone was teasing as well as reproving.

'I'm sorry, dear. Perhaps you can't teach an old dog new tricks. I do find these broadsheets tire the arms so.'

'I'll see to the lunch.' Claudia retreated into the kitchen.

'Anything I can do, dear?'

'Not a thing. Just relax. Ah, here comes Pierre.'

That night Mrs Randall retired early, exhausted by the journey, and Claudia quickly followed suit. A long night's sleep would be a great help, she thought, in preparation for the strains of the week ahead. She told Pierre not to hurry to bed; 'I'm going to try to get off to sleep early.'

But switching off the light at a quarter to ten didn't work, and when Pierre came in a good hour and a half later Claudia was sitting in the chair by the window, gazing out at the moonlit garden. Pierre started. 'I thought you were asleep.'

Claudia shook her head. The moon, almost full but with one fuzzy edge, hung huge and peach-coloured just above the witchy silhouettes of the two large yew trees at the end of their garden.

Pierre came and stood behind her chair. 'What an amazing night,' he murmured. 'I've never seen the moon look like that before. It's almost orange. Is that an omen, do you think?'

'Pierre,' said Claudia, keeping her gaze averted, 'how do you think Mother is?' Her hands were clasping the curved arms of the upright easy chair.

'Not good,' he said, 'not good. I think we must prepare ourselves, Claudie.'

It felt like years since he'd called her that. Her shoulders heaved.

All at once, his arms were round her. 'Claudie, Claudie, poor little one.' His mouth was pressed against her hair. 'I'm here, don't worry, it'll be all right.'

How can it be? she thought, but she choked down the urge to say it. Instead she allowed him to lift her out of the chair and carry her to the bed, where she lay curled up, knees nearly touching her chin. Pierre cradled her until her sobs subsided and she was able to feign sleep.

'And how is Hilary?' Naomi Randall asked, twisting off the green starry leaves of a strawberry. She had insisted on helping with the preparation of lunch, so Claudia had given her the least taxing task she could think of. Even so, she noted with a pang, her mother's touch was no longer sure. Some of the strawberries were leaking juice, where Naomi had gripped them too hard, while others retained fragments of their leaves and stalks.

'Hilary's extremely well,' replied Claudia, scrubbing new potatoes. 'There's a new man on the scene – a friend of ours, actually, Joe Coventry.'

'Didn't you tell me about him, dear? Isn't he an artist?'

'A writer. A novelist. He's doing pretty well – he was runner-up for quite a big prize last year, and they're making one of his books into a TV series.'

'How exciting. Let me know when it comes on, won't you, dear? You know I never manage to watch the right things. So this man is interested in Hilary, is he? Is he right for her, do you think?'

Claudia paused, potato in hand, staring out of the window. Between herself and the brilliant June landscape, the patches of woods and fields glowing almost with the clarity and intensity of stained glass, there interposed a vision of Hilary, talking about Joe, brimming with the kind of excitement that craves notice and privacy at one and the same time. Claudia had never yet seen Joe and Hilary together, not since that initial dinner party, but – 'Yes,' she said slowly, 'I think he's absolutely right for her. And I've never thought that about any of her other men, you know.'

'It is surprising, isn't it,' mused Naomi, 'that she never has remarried. She's such a treasure, after all.'

'Mum,' said Claudia crossly, 'how could she remarry? You know perfectly well she was never married in the first place.'

'Well, dear, you know what I mean. One would have thought she would have found a replacement for Elinor's father.'

Claudia felt quite angry. Why did women like her mother make these assumptions about the overwhelming significance of men? She said, quite rudely, 'Elinor's father didn't need replacing. Elinor's father was utterly insignificant. Hilary and Elinor have been quite all right on their own.'

Naomi stole a glance at her daughter and kept silent for a while. She could tell by the set of Claudia's shoulders that she had irritated her, though she didn't fully understand why. She had finished hulling the strawberries. Meticulously she scooped up all the debris and put it back in the little blue punnets. 'Is there anything else I can do, dear?' she asked at last.

Her humility smote Claudia's heart. She had made a promise to herself that she would get through the whole week without speaking sharply to her mother; she had already broken her resolve several times. She rinsed the potatoes and joined Naomi at the kitchen table. 'No, absolutely not,' she said. 'I'll put the fish under the grill in a moment; everything else is done.'

Naomi recognised her softened conciliatory tone, and returned to a subject that had always interested her. 'I don't think,' she said, mildly but firmly, 'that Elinor's father could have been so very insignificant.'

'What makes you say that?'

'Well, presumably he must be significant to Elinor. I know she doesn't see him, but she must wonder. After all, half of her belongs to him.'

'I think Hilary has always tried to forget about that. She's always behaved as though Ellie is utterly and totally her own.'

Naomi said, 'Fond though I am of Hilary, I do think that's asking for trouble.'

Claudia didn't ask why. She knew why, and she'd often thought the same herself. Hilary had tried to make her influence over her daughter too absolute, with the result that any show of difference in Elinor unnerved her. She was scared, now, of Elinor's academic competence, Claudia suspected – scared as well as genuinely delighted. But she replied, 'I'm not sure that Ellie's father ever even knew of her existence. He was ... married, you see, and Hil was very young.'

'I assumed it was something like that.' Naomi had no intention of prying any further into that particular area. 'But I still find it odd that he had no ... successor, if you like, since "replacement" won't do.'

'Well he did.'

'Oh, I know she's had men friends, but none of them seem to stick.'

'There was one.' Claudia wiped the table and put the potatoes on to boil. 'I think there was one that really mattered. Sunil, he was called.'

'What kind of a name is that?'

'Malaysian, I think. He was very beautiful. I met him when I went to stay with Hilary in Bristol, just after she'd moved from her flat into a little terraced house. I thought the move might mean she was getting ready to live with him, and I think she thought so too. Certainly she was making everything very homely.'

'She's always been such a natural homemaker.'

'Yes, but this time it was even more than usual. And he was

spending a lot of time round there – his shoes were lying about in the hall, that sort of thing.'

'I can't remember, dear. Why did it end?'

'I never was exactly sure, but I think it was to do with his family, and their religion. Her already having a child – that was definitely a problem. Anyway, Hil was desperately cut up about it. We asked her to go to France with us soon after, to cheer her up, and she wasn't really herself at all.'

'I was always glad you didn't marry a foreigner, Claudia. It must be very difficult.'

Claudia laughed. 'But I did!'

'Oh, only half. And I don't count French as foreign.'

'It still makes a difference,' said Claudia. There was an edge to her voice. She burrowed in the fridge, looking for the fish, discouraging further conversation. She had raised a memory from the French holiday that she had always striven to suppress – a memory of Pierre's knuckles, running fleetingly over Hilary's shoulder, and Hilary, almost imperceptibly, arching to meet his caress. No, Hilary had certainly not been herself on that particular holiday.

CHAPTER FOURTEEN

Pierre was banished from the house on the morning of his birthday party. The day was breezy, and cooler than it had been for some time, but with pockets of sunshine and scudding clouds. He took Jaques and his camera and set off in search of a relatively unpopulous stretch of coastline. At ten o'clock Hilary turned up to give Claudia a hand with the food.

Hilary had offered to mastermind the whole operation, in fact, though she was not surprised when her offer was rejected. She considered Claudia's cooking to be virtually inedible, though of course she'd never said so, but she understood Claudia's desire to produce the meal herself and resolved to be content with small, furtive adjustments of seasoning and presentation.

Hilary arrived looking glorious. Joe Coventry was coming to the party, of course, and she knew she wouldn't have time to change later, so she'd done everything in advance except her make-up – and that would be minimal. She had gathered her hair into a topknot, to be out of the way of the cooking, so her graceful neck was more in evidence than usual. She wore a voluminous dress of dove grey which fell into soft pleats below the low waist line; it was nearly ankle length. On her long brown feet she wore Roman sandals; two huge wooden bangles, painted a dull gilt, hung on one wrist, and a gold necklace made of close, flattened links followed the contours of her delicate collar-bones. Her earrings were plain discs, of the same muted gold. That was all. 'If anybody else wore that dress,' said Claudia, ushering her into the kitchen, 'they would look like a nun in a bin-liner. But you look like Titania. Lucky cow.'

Hilary laughed, and pulled a huge wraparound apron from her bag. 'Come on, let's get our pinnies on. I'm ready for action.'

'I've done the chicken already,' said Claudia, 'but I've hardly started on the rest.' Large platters of coronation chicken were ranged in rows on the work surfaces, pale humps shouldering through sickly yellow sauce. 'What else are you doing?' Hilary asked, feeling that she knew the answer.

'Rice salad. And green salad. And there's some frozen garlic bread, but we don't need to deal with that yet. I've cooked the rice; do you want to chop the things to go in it?'

'Great,' said Hilary. She could see the ingredients she was to use ranged neatly round a chopping board; she resolved quietly to forget about the tinned pineapple. 'Where's your mother? Resting?'

'Yes, she had breakfast in bed. She doesn't tend to get up for another half hour or so.'

Hilary had visited the house on a couple of occasions in the course of the week, and had been shocked by the change in Mrs Randall, but had had no opportunity to ask Claudia about it. There was no real chance now, either. The bungalow was not well sound-proofed.

'I'll wash the lettuces,' said Claudia. 'Things any better with Ellie?'

Hilary sighed. 'Absolutely not. We've hardly exchanged a dozen sentences since her outburst. Or was it my outburst? She refused to come along today, of course, because Joe will be here.'

'So what's she doing instead?'

'Learning that bloody play of yours, I expect. She's done nothing else all week, except visiting Laura in hospital. She'll know it back to front by the next rehearsal, that's one good thing.'

'The next rehearsal's tomorrow. Last day of half-term today.'

'I know – I've been counting the days. It's the first time ever that I haven't been delighted to have Ellie on holiday. But now she just lies under her duvet eating chocolate biscuits with the curtains shut. It's grim, it really is.'

'It's just late-onset adolescence, you're lucky to have avoided it this far. Most of them go through it at fourteen. We get plenty of parents of fourth-years coming to open evenings more or less in tears, saying what's happened to their loving little daughter? But they mostly come right in the end.'

'Mostly?'

'Well, we don't always know what happens in the end. But usually they turn back into beautiful, dutiful daughters, I believe.'

'Talking of dutiful daughters – and beautiful ones too of

course – how's your half-term been? It can't have been much of a rest.'

Claudia, whose ears and nerves had become finely tuned to her mother's every movement in the course of the week, grimaced to indicate that the conversation should go no further. Hilary nodded assent, and allowed the sharp edge of her knife to bite into the side of a green pepper. She loved the slight resistance followed by the tiny spurt of moisture. Claudia shook her lettuces vigorously in the colander. A moment later Naomi Randall shuffled into the room.

'I thought I heard your voice, Hilary,' she said in her new, old, voice. 'Lovely to see you, dear. I do like your hair like that.'

'Oh this is just for now. I think I'll have it down later. Do you know, I think I'm going grey? I found a couple of stragglers this morning, and pulled them out, of course.'

'About time too, you lucky girl. I was completely grey by the time I was your age. Claudia hasn't inherited that, I'm glad to say. She's got her father's hair. Very good hair, too.'

'Oh, I've got the odd streak, if you look hard enough, see?' Claudia held a handful above her head so that her roots could be inspected.

'Hardly anything, for thirty-seven. Will you colour it, Hilary, when it does happen, do you think?'

'Probably not. I quite like the idea of a wild, white frizz. In fact I quite like the idea of turning into a white witch, when I get old.'

'You've already got the little cottage in the woods. What other props does a white witch need?'

'A cat. And I'm getting one. Mr Pitchford's cat has had the sweetest kittens, and he wants me to take one.'

'Ugh! Don't bother. It'll ruin your garden.'

'That's not a very life-enhancing thing to say, Claud.'

'Are you sure white witches have them, anyway? I thought it was only the wicked sort.'

'I don't know, but this one's grey, not black, so it ought to be all right. It's adorable, Claud, you'll love it once you see it.'

'Is your daughter pleased with the idea?' put in Mrs Randall.

'Yes – at least, she was, until she stopped talking to me. Now I expect she'll just turn it into another thing to be jealous of. No, I shouldn't have said that, that's not fair to Ellie. But Naomi, do tell me what you think I should do. You were the mother of a teenager once.'

'Indeed I was, though I must say Claudia never gave us any trouble. She went her own way, but her own way was always sensible, as far as we could see. But I do think it's terribly important –' Naomi spoke even more slowly than usual, and nodded for emphasis – '*terribly* important, that you don't let this opportunity pass you by. The young can take care of themselves. But if a chance of happiness comes your way, then hold onto it, my dear. Otherwise you'll always regret it.'

The older woman sank back in her chair, fatigued by the length and intensity of her utterance. Claudia and Hilary exchanged brief glances over the top of her head.

'Hmmm,' said Claudia, '*carpe diem*. I think I tend to agree with Mother, Hil.'

'Thank you both,' said Hilary, 'for the support. Thank you very much indeed. Have you any olives I could put in this, Claudia?'

Pierre lay on his back amidst the tussocks of sharp grass that grew, rather improbably, out of the sandy hillocks at the dividing line between beach and solid land. He was exhausted with the effort of trying to get Jaques to run and gambol and behave like any normal dog. Jaques had flumped on the sand now, and was panting quietly at a respectful few inches from his master. Even his panting was slow. Pierre gazed at the bright, arching sky, now a kind of gauzy white, for as long as his eyes could stand it. He knew that today would be a turning point in his relations with Sarah Stanhope. He hadn't seen her since that time when he had kissed her in her kitchen; he'd deliberately put the thing on hold, to discover whether there was anything worth pursuing, and oddly enough it seemed that there was. Her image – slightly air-brushed and honed down, admittedly – had been at the forefront of his mind for the last couple of weeks. It would be difficult to arrange, with all those children, and yet somehow the children were part of the attraction. Strange.

Pierre wasn't in the habit of analysing his motives. He rolled over onto his stomach and let sand run through his fingers. He could see her now, as he had left her that evening, lips parted, thick hair falling over her face. He could almost hear her heart beat.

Sarah was ripe for the picking, that was certain. The next move was up to him.

Whatever his shortcomings, thought Claudia, peeling the cling-film off the salad bowls, Pierre was an excellent host. After its unsettled start the day had decided to be sunny, and the guests had spilled out onto the wide stone patio. Pierre moved gracefully from group to group, smiling, laughing, even winking; making introductions where necessary, and establishing intimacy where awkwardness might have set in. Perhaps it was because he was a doctor that he was able to remember details about people, and bring them up in a way that made them feel wanted, not embarrassed. As she spooned mayonnaise into sauce boats – the only thing that she and Hilary had forgotten it seemed – Claudia saw Pierre pat Leonie's almost imperceptible bulge and refill her glass with mineral water; Leonie beamed, and John, her husband, beamed too, almost idiotically. Claudia could tell that something Pierre had said had made John feel manly and proud. How ironic, she thought, without bitterness.

Now he'd set the Spencers up with a urologist and his wife, who had been a nurse at the local hospital until she'd stopped work to give birth. Their month-old baby dangled against its mother's still protruding stomach in its padded sling. Its face was invisible, but both couples still seemed to be getting a lot of conversational mileage out of its hands and feet. Pierre had deftly slipped away and was pouring wine for the Baldocks, the Prescotts' nearest neighbours, a rather shy couple who turned up dutifully to every social event they were asked to, although they spent most of the time talking to each other. Oh bless him! thought Claudia, as Pierre steered them towards her mother, stranded in her striped canvas chair in the sunniest corner of the patio.

Claudia did a headcount. She'd invited thirty-five; she thought twenty-eight were already here. Fine – she'd unwrap the garlic bread. She couldn't remember off-hand who the latecomers were.

Joe Coventry was here, with his two sons, products of a short-lived, far-off marriage. Matt and Spike were twenty and twenty-one respectively; she'd met them several times but she still got muddled as to which was which. They were both skinny, gangling, beardless versions of their father, she thought, both friendly and energetic and innately untidy. One was at drama school, the other an artist – conventionally unconventional. The important thing about them today was that they were meeting Hilary for the first time. Claudia craned her neck. The four of them were standing just round the corner and all she could see was Joe's bulk against the rhododendrons and the back of the boys' heads. One – Spike, she thought – had a curly black ponytail, which was bobbing up and down in an animated fashion. The other was flicking his cigarette ash into a stone urn from which dark blue lobelia flowed. All she could see of Hilary was the edge of her cobwebby skirt.

Claudia scorched her finger on the tinfoil that wrapped the garlic bread. She half-dropped the loaf, and to her intense irritation a few spots of melted butter spattered the front of her blouse. They were only tiny, but on the silky coffee-coloured fabric they were definitely noticeable. Claudia hated looking dirty more than anything. She had to change, there was an almost identical blouse in navy blue hanging in the wardrobe. As she slipped it on she heard the doorbell ring; would Pierre hear it above the hum of conversation? She hurried to fasten the buttons, but then relaxed as she heard Pierre's springy step in the hall.

Children's voices – adult apologies for late arrival – something to do with a baby's nap time. Of course – that Sarah woman and her family. Two shrill little creatures were crying 'Pierre! Pierre!' and, to judge from his laughing response, leaping all over him. They must be very forward little brats – they couldn't know him that well. Then their father's voice, scolding affectionately, 'Now come on, monsters, give Pierre a break. Come out into the garden.'

Claudia smoothed the front of her blouse and opened the bedroom door. Adrian had led the older children away; Sarah stood holding the smallest one. In the split second before he registered her presence, Claudia saw Pierre raise his hand and run his fingertips along Sarah's jawbone. Or at least she thought she saw it; that evening, after replaying the incident for the hundredth time on her mental cinema screen she no longer felt so sure.

'Look at these fantastic flowers Sarah's brought, darling,' said Pierre, holding out a bunch of white lilies.

'How lovely,' said Claudia coolly, 'I'll put them in water.' She marched into the kitchen with them, not trusting herself to say another word.

'They're not very suitable, really,' explained Sarah, jiggling Thomas. 'I did look for a proper present for you, but I didn't know what you wanted.'

Pierre bent forward, 'Let me take him,' he said loudly, grasping Thomas. Then in a murmur he said, 'Sarah. You know what I want.'

Claudia settled the lilies in a tall cut-glass vase, taking care not to let the stamens brush their staining pollen against her fresh blouse. Her face felt scalding hot – she knew she ought to get people to come and eat, but first she had to get her breathing under control. She had just finished an internal recitation of Milton's sonnet on his blindness – sonnets were good for subduing turbulent emotions, she found; short, but tricky enough not to slip by unnoticed – when Hilary dashed in.

'Oh God, I'm sorry,' she said. 'I should have given you a hand ages ago. But I've been talking to Matt and Spike.'

'I know. It's all just about ready. The garlic bread's cold, because I had to go and change my blouse. But never mind.'

'Don't you want to know what I thought of them, then?' Hilary sounded a tiny bit peeved.

'Of who? The boys? Not particularly. I'd rather know what they thought of you.'

'Why?'

'Because what you thought of them is completely predictable.'

'What is it, then?'

'Oh, that they're sweet, absolutely lovely, really good fun. And you feel you've known them for ages. Yes?'

'Hmm … I can't deny it. But they *are* sweet. They'd be so good for Ellie, if only …'

'Give it time. She'll come round in the end. We ought to get going on this food. Can you get Pierre to come in?'

'Where is he?'

'Over there. Enjoying himself.'

Hilary followed Claudia's pointing finger. Pierre stood on the lawn, deep in conversation with Sarah. In theory, Adrian was in on the discussion, too, but actually he was chasing Thomas who was delighted to find such a large sunny space in which to practice his newly acquired crawling skills. Hilary glanced at her friend's face. It was a mask of misery. She let her hand rest briefly on Claudia's. 'I'll get him,' she said, and was gone.

Trapped in her garden chair, Naomi Randall saw more than she wanted to see. For some minutes now Naomi had been half listening to the worthy, diffident Baldocks' account of their loft conversion while trying to keep her gaze from wandering to her son-in-law and that fair-haired woman. Nothing happened, of course. They were standing in the middle of the lawn in full view of everyone, including both their spouses. And yet something in the way Pierre kept his eyes on her, something in the way she ignored her baby and flicked her thick hair back from her pink, laughing face, made the old woman profoundly uneasy. Pierre was a charmer, of course, and always had been, but he'd stopped circulating, and was lingering unduly in this one spot … Then Hilary approached and tapped his arm, and he sprang to attention and darted back into the house, and Hilary embraced the fair-haired woman and greeted her poor harassed husband, and sat down on the grass to help the little girl make a daisy chain, piercing the juicy stalks with her long strong thumbnail. Naomi tried to reassure herself. If that woman was a friend of Hilary's then things must be all right – but she knew in her heart of hearts that that didn't necessarily follow. Sylvia Baldock, instantly alert to any signs that the food was ready for collection, offered to fetch a plateful for Naomi, who accepted gratefully, glad of a few free moments to collect her thoughts.

'Look, Mummy, look! I've got a necklace.' Hannah tugged at Sarah's hand to call her attention to the daisy chain Hilary had made.

'Lovely, darling! Silver and gold.'

'And what about the green bits, Mummy?'

'They can be emerald. Look, Hannah, Hilary's got eyes like emeralds. Have you ever seen anyone with such green eyes before?'

Hannah shook her head. 'Only cats,' she whispered reverently, gazing at her mother's friend. Hilary laughed and sprang to her feet, shaking out the creases from her skirt.

'So that's Joe,' said Sarah. Joe had been introduced to Leonie Spencer and was now standing on the terrace deep in animated conversation. Sarah had been surprised, at first glance, by Hilary's choice, but she liked the way he gave his full attention to whoever he was talking to, and she could see how his loose, shambolic, colourful style could have grown on one. 'He looks – really nice,' she commented lamely.

'He is – oh, he is.' Hilary was clearly reluctant to take her eyes off him. 'It's so marvellous, the way he can talk to people. Anybody. Just anybody.'

'Elinor?'

Hilary sighed. 'He never gets the chance. She's already told me she thinks I'm disgusting. Presumably she feels the same way about him.'

'But she must have had to put up with your – men friends before,' Sarah said boldly.

'Yes, it's true I've never kept anyone secret from her. Well, almost never. And although she was always pretty lukewarm she never seemed unduly fussed. But this time it's different. You see, I told her that I ... I told her that this time it was serious.'

Sarah had never seen Hilary blush before. She still hadn't taken her eyes off that shabby giant laughing and quaffing his wine on the terrace.

'But this can't be the first *ever*!' she exclaimed. 'Somebody must have been important to you before.'

Joe shambled indoors, carrying Leonie's glass. Hilary turned her level gaze on Sarah. 'You're right, of course,' she said, 'I haven't reached the age of what-ever-it-is without falling in love, more than once. But somehow I knew that none of them would be permanent. There was one – only one – who I really, really minded about.'

'But he didn't stick around?'

'No, he didn't. He was Malaysian, and very stunning. But he had – different ideas.'

'About women?'

'Yes. About women. He always told me he could never take me to meet his family. I should have known better.'

'Than to fall for him?'

'Than to try and have his baby.'

Hilary's simple words resonated in the summer air. 'Oh, I'm sorry,' Sarah gasped, 'I've been so nosy. I'm always doing this with you.'

Hilary placed her hand briefly on Sarah's arm. 'It's all right,' she said, 'I don't mind talking about it. I never did talk about it, in fact, but maybe it would have been better if I had. Then I wouldn't have made so many mistakes.'

Sarah said nothing, but cocked her head and murmured encouragement. Hilary continued, 'I did it deliberately. It was utterly crazy, but I thought Sunil would change his mind when he was confronted with the reality. But he didn't. He just disappeared.'

'And so you –'

'Yes, I had an abortion. He would have been about Gabriel's age by now. A little older.'

Both women looked at Gabriel rolling on the sunlit grass. His sky blue shorts and T-shirt intensified the brown of his slender limbs. His rich wavy hair was full of bits of twigs and leaves, and he was laughing.

'He?' asked Sarah.

'It was too early to tell, thank God, but I always thought of the baby as a boy. A beautiful black-eyed boy, like Sunil.'

'But why – I mean, you kept Elinor.'

'It was because of Elinor. We had barely enough money to keep the two of us, and I didn't want to ask Sunil for money. Not that I knew where to find him.' Hilary's tone was wistful, not bitter.

'Did she know?'

'No. She'll never know, I hope. I tried to tell her about Sunil, but she didn't want to hear. And about the baby – no. It can't ever be nice for a child to think that its mother killed its sibling, whatever the reason.'

'Killed – that's too strong. Don't be so hard on yourself, Hilary. You did what you thought was right.'

'Though I started off doing what was obviously wrong. And I went on doing wrong for some time afterwards. Losing the baby made me desperate – truly lonely, for the first time in my life. I did some wild and awful things, to fill the gap.'

'I won't ask what,' said Sarah. Though she was dying to know.

'No, don't ask,' replied Hilary, 'because I probably shouldn't tell.'

'Well, Joe seems perfect. You deserve a happy ending.'

Hilary pulled a face. 'There's still Elinor,' she said.

The wind was getting up, and with the advent of food most of the guests decided to stay indoors rather than cope with paper napkins blowing away and insects embedding themselves in the sticky sauce. Hilary, once she'd checked that everyone had everything and that Claudia was actually sitting down and eating and talking to somebody she liked, took Joe by the elbow and steered him outside again. 'I've talked to everybody I want to see,' she said quietly, 'now I just want to be with you.' They spread their plates and knives and forks and glasses out by the edge of the ornamental pond in the middle of the lawn. 'I think I've had this chicken just about every time I've been to dinner here,' remarked Joe, not unkindly.

'I did my best with the rice,' replied Hilary, 'but the chicken was a *fait accompli*, I'm afraid. It is rather slimy, isn't it? Claudia's too clever to be a good cook.'

'I'd say that was nonsense, if I didn't think it was probably true,' said Joe. 'Poor Claudia. I sometimes think she's too clever by half. She's certainly too clever for Pierre.'

'Maybe. I think he's a little afraid of her, and that might be a good thing. Keeps him on the rails,' Hilary replied.

Joe looked at her with meaning. 'What makes you so sure Pierre does keep on the rails?'

'Well maybe he doesn't literally, but he does in his heart. I hope.'

'Does it mean anything, to feel one thing, and do another?' Joe asked. 'When it comes to infidelity –'

'Joe, don't let's talk about it. It scares me. I'm worried for her. But he does love her, you know, in spite of it all.'

Joe raised his eyebrows, 'Well, I'll take your word for it. And now –' he leaned over and pulled her hair loose from its fastening. As it tumbled he ran his large hands through it, fluffing and shaping it.

'I meant to let it down earlier, and I never got a moment,' said Hilary, smiling at him. 'I know you don't like it up.'

'I do. I like it up very much. But I like it even better down. Because it's such marvellous stuff, and I can never have enough of a good thing.' He held a handful to his face and inhaled.

From the kitchen window, Spike watched. 'Hey Matt,' he said, 'what do you think of our new stepmother?'

Matt – the one without the ponytail – ripped back the ringpull on a can of beer. 'D'you reckon?'

'Yeah, I reckon. Take a look.'

Matt stood in the doorway and watched his father's hands twining in Hilary's loosened hair. He licked up the foam that spilled from the hole in the can. 'Could be worse,' he said. 'Could be a whole lot worse.'

The mood of the party was brisk and upbeat. Adrian thought he hadn't talked to so many likeable people for ages. He was very impressed by the young woman who worked at the Abbey School with Claudia, and he'd met a couple of very nice doctors, too. But by four o'clock Hannah and Gabriel were growing restless. They had prodded and poked their fill at the accommodating but unresponsive dog Jacques, and had filled the pond with floating daisy heads. They had run races at the bottom of the garden, but in Hannah's view these were largely a waste of time, as Gabriel, who didn't really understand the concept of winning and losing, was liable at any minute to lie down and roll. They hadn't been too bad, Adrian thought, but it would be doing everybody a favour if they took them away. Sarah agreed readily. She had been chatting happily to Hilary and later to her – boyfriend? escort? companion? – but she seemed a little tense. Tired, perhaps. Thomas, who was teething, had been uncharacteristically wakeful for a couple of nights.

Pierre showed them out. In the hall, hanging by the front door, Adrian noticed two framed photographs, in black and white, of saucer-eyed street urchins in some scruffy European city – Naples, perhaps. 'Did you take these, Pierre?' he asked.

'Yes – some time ago. In Palermo – we had an excellent holiday in Sicily once.'

'They're very good,' said Adrian. 'And the ones you took of our bunch, too – we're delighted with them. Do you take pictures of adults, too?'

'Absolutely. Anything human – or else a building. I'm not so good with landscapes.'

'I was wondering if you'd take some pictures of Sarah. She's never had any done, and I'd really like some for my office. Sorry, Sarah, I should have asked you first, but actually it only just occurred to me. Would you mind?'

'I'd be delighted,' Pierre cut in, before Sarah could reply. 'Do say yes, Sarah. It wouldn't take very long.'

'Oh, it's not that,' said Sarah, flustered. 'It's just – oh, all right then. I submit.'

'Excellent,' said Pierre. 'Let's fix a time right now. I have a day off on Thursday – not really a day off, but I catch up with the paperwork here and I'm not on duty. Could you manage Thursday morning?'

'I expect so. I'll give you a ring.' Sarah's efforts to sound unconcerned made her voice flutter and squeak.

Pierre shook Adrian's hand, and pecked Sarah lightly on both cheeks. He behaved with the utmost propriety, but the firmness in his voice as he said, 'Thanks for coming. Till Thursday, then,' filled Sarah with longing and dread.

CHAPTER FIFTEEN

When the Stanhopes reached home, the telephone was ringing. Adrian dashed to answer it, leaving Sarah to disentangle the children from the car. As she shepherded the two older ones in with a sleeping Thomas slung over one shoulder and the changing bag dangling from the other, Sarah was struck by the expression on Adrian's face. 'Is everything all right?' she asked.

Adrian placed a hand over the receiver. 'It's mother,' he whispered. 'Not well.' Sarah sighed, and went into the kitchen to supply Hannah and Gabriel with the apple juice they were so insistently requesting. Her mother-in-law's health had been giving cause for concern for at least a year now. Sarah considered privately that Diana made rather a drama of it – a Pinteresque drama, perhaps, with long pauses and anticlimaxes and false alarms. She laid Thomas, now comatose, on an ancient beanbag in the corner and filled the kettle.

The telephone conversation went on and on. The children were squabbling over who was to drink out of the mug with the penguin on it; what with this and the roar of the kettle and the running taps as she hurled a few odds and ends into the washing-up bowl there was too much noise for Sarah to work out the gist of Adrian's conversation.

She sorted out the quarrel by doling out juice in two identical, dull, white mugs and removing the penguin option altogether; she'd made the tea and was about to unload the washing machine when Adrian came in. She'd warned herself in advance to say something sympathetic, but now it came to it all she could manage was a fairly non-committal 'Well?'

'It sounds bad, I'm afraid. I think I'll have to go over there.'

Sarah slid a mug of tea over the table towards him. 'What kind of bad?'

'Thanks, Sal.' He took a sip. 'She blacked out this morning, she thinks for a long time. She'd been trying to ring us all day, but of course we were out.' Adrian's shoulders sagged.

'Did she call a doctor?'

'No. She's being silly about the doctor.'

Sarah knew what he meant. Since the recent retirement of the GP who had served her family since time immemorial, Diana Stanhope had adopted an inflexible attitude towards the medical profession. She dreaded being seen by a woman doctor, holding fast to the belief that they weren't given as much training as the men. 'Jumped-up nurses, with a little of the social worker thrown in,' was her verdict.

'Oh dear,' said Sarah. 'You'd have thought – what is it, Han?' Hannah had crept over and was leaning against her mother's knee.

'Is Grandma going to die?' she whispered. Sarah gave Adrian a reproachful glance. A long-standing resentment between them was that each felt the other was careless about bringing up potentially distressing subjects in front of the children

'Oh no, honey, of course not. She's just not feeling very well, that's all. Daddy's going to go and see her and make her feel better.'

'Will he give her medicine?'

'That's right, he'll give her some medicine. Some grown-ups' Calpol. Then she'll feel better.'

'But she will die one day, won't she, Mummy?'

'Well, everyone has to die one day, darling. But not yet. Grandma's not very old yet, you know.'

'Tortoises don't die for a long time, and horses don't, and cats don't,' put in Gabriel, apparently finding consolation in these ideas.

'Cats do!' exclaimed Hannah. 'Cats do. Don't they, Daddy?'

'Do what, love?'

'Cats do die soon – sooner than people.'

'Yes, sooner than people. People live a long time.'

'See, Gaby? You were wrong. Can anybody live for ever, except God? And Father Christmas?'

'And Mrs Meadows,' put in Gabriel, referring to his kindergarten teacher.

'Don't be silly, Gaby. Mrs Meadows can't live for ever –' Hannah, absorbed in the topic, hoped her brother would argue back, but he had lost interest, and was kneeling on the floor with his bottom in the air, enacting repeated crashes with model cars.

Sarah, looking at her daughter's tense little face, suggested to Adrian in French that she should go and sort out the old lady, taking Hannah with her to reassure her, and leaving Adrian to cope with supper and bathtime for the boys. Adrian willingly assented. He knew his mother needed to be helped into bed, possibly washed, and he shrank from performing such intimate actions for her. Besides, the presence of her little granddaughter might lift her spirits.

Hannah was delighted with the plan. 'I'm like little Red Riding Hood,' she exclaimed.

'Only there's no wolf,' put in Adrian hastily.

'Would you like to take some nice things for Grandma, like Red Riding Hood did?' asked Sarah.

No suitable basket could be found, but they brushed out a small trug used for gardening, and filled it with some apples, a bunch of roses, and a jar of marmalade. Marmalade was the only such thing Sarah made herself. She thought this would strike a more appropriate note than a partly-used jar of Robertson's Seedless Raspberry, which appeared to be the only jam in stock. Hannah covered the offerings with a folded tea towel and they set off.

Diana Stanhope lived in a large, handsome, square, white-fronted house that stood close to the verge of the narrow road leading from Barcombe to the neighbouring village of Leabridge. This was the house where Adrian had grown up. Most people would have said that it was a ludicrous house for an elderly woman living on her own, but Sarah couldn't imagine her mother-in-law in any other setting. She had enough money to pay for a daily woman and a gardener, and everything was immaculately kept up, from the variegated evergreens in the garden, clipped into neat overlapping, oddly pointless shapes, to the well-dusted collection of porcelain figurines in the glass-fronted cabinet in the dining room. These figurines were greatly admired by Hannah, who had been told that when she was seven she would be allowed to touch them for the first time. She couldn't decide which she would want to touch first; the old woman with a bobbly red shawl holding a bunch of balloons, or the little boy in plum-coloured knicker-bockers offering an achingly realistic biscuit to a begging spaniel. On every visit to March House she agonised over these two.

Sarah had rung just before they set out and knew that the glossy yew-green front door would be left on the latch for them. As she pushed it open the thought struck her for the first time that Adrian would inherit all this. She wondered why this obvious fact had never occurred to her before. Perhaps because Diana was so strangely dateless; like her house, she never seemed to alter, so it was hard to think of her in terms of deterioration and death. Would Adrian want to live here, in the mausoleum of his childhood, she wondered?

In some ways the house was superior to their own. It had more bedrooms, and the garden was much bigger and more interesting, but would they be able to overcome the sense of doom that lingered everywhere, a faint but recognisable odour? With a jolt Sarah realised that she still assumed she would be spending the rest of her life with Adrian. Perhaps that assumption needed to be overhauled. On Thursday she was going to see Pierre Prescott to have her photograph taken. And she was going alone.

'Sarah?' her mother-in-law's voice sounded pale and far away. 'Sarah, is that you?'

'Yes, we're here.' Sarah adopted a bright-and-breezy, invalid-visiting tone. 'And Red Riding Hood's come to visit her grandmamma.'

They opened the door of the music room, as Diana rather wistfully named the smaller of the two reception rooms. In fact the piano was little-used these days. Diana sat in an armchair by the fireplace, which was swept and dusted and filled with its summer arrangement of dried foliage. She had wrapped herself in a tartan travel rug, but despite this Sarah could see that she was trembling. She offered her cheek to be pecked in her usual formal way; the powdery skin seemed to be drawn tighter than ever, and there were yellow and grey shadows round her eyes. 'How kind of you to come,' she said. 'I've been here all day. I haven't been able to manage the stairs.'

'All day?' Sarah was worried. 'Have you had anything to eat?'

'I haven't wanted anything. But I must admit a cup of tea would be more than welcome. I didn't want to risk the kettle.'

Sarah hurried into the kitchen to oblige, while Hannah approached shyly with her trug. 'We've come to make you well, Grandma,' Sarah heard her explain.

'Why, thank you, my darling,' Diana replied, and with a pang

Sarah realised that there was a genuine wobble in the older woman's voice. She's frightened, she thought, she really is.

She made some toast, cut very thin, and spread it with a little of Diana's favourite anchovy paste. She cut it into fingers and put the plate on the tea tray. She carried it all into the music room, where Hannah sat on a little embroidered stool at her grandmother's feet, reading aloud from a volume of Hans Christian Andersen fairytales. The edition was old, certainly predating Adrian's childhood and possibly even Diana's. It was bound in dove-grey cloth and the thick creamy pages were uneven and fuzzy at the edges. As Sarah bent over to give Diana her tea and toast she inhaled the sweet, drowsy odour of the ancient paper.

Diana smiled a thank you, sipped her tea and nibbled her toast, 'Take a cup for yourself, dear.'

'Let me know if she's tiring you,' said Sarah, indicating Hannah, who was making steady progress with *The Little Mermaid*. She settled into the armchair opposite with her cup of tea and allowed her gaze to wander round the room. She noticed the pile of sheet music on top of the piano, untouched for years; the books – not many, a few rows of leather-bound classics, a few large lavishly-illustrated works about gardens; on the mantelpiece, Adrian's first shoe, cast in bronze – an uncharacteristic flash of sentiment amidst the restraint. Next to the tiny gleaming shoe was a silver-framed photograph of herself and Adrian on their wedding day. It wasn't the best photograph, really. She looked plump and very young indeed; Adrian looked frankly anxious. She remembered the touch of Pierre's fingers on her jaw bone earlier that same day, and shivered.

'I'll straighten things out for you upstairs,' she said, rising. Diana nodded, her eyes half closed. Hannah's clear little voice seemed to soothe her.

Sarah had rarely been inside her mother-in-law's bedroom; certainly never alone. She had said she would 'straighten things out', but everything was already exceedingly straight. The high, narrow bed was made up with sheets and blankets, tightly tucked in, and covered with a plain white counterpane; Sarah remembered Adrian telling her that his parents always had separate bedrooms, his father's with an attached dressing room, his mother's with a private bathroom. He had told Sarah how once, as a tiny child, he remembered waking from a nightmare and going to seek shelter from a parent, but being unable to decide which door to knock at. After hesitating in the corridor for some time he had crept back to his own chilly little bed. Sarah recalled the pang she had felt when she first heard this story. Her eyes had filled with tears for the little bewildered boy standing in his bare feet on the icy polished floor; she had longed to comfort him, to patch up the holes left by his sheltered but rather lonely childhood. Where had that feeling gone?

She walked into the adjoining bathroom and turned on the taps. She would help Diana to bathe, get her into bed, put anything she might need within easy reach, and then take Hannah home. It might be that she or Adrian would have to spend the night there; Adrian might have to take a day off work. Or more, if Diana got worse. Oh God, she thought with a shrug of realisation, not Thursday. Please, please, let her be better by Thursday.

The great charm of the bathroom was its view. There were no blinds or curtains, because it was impossible for anyone to see in, and Diana loved to sit in the windowseat wrapped in her dressing-gown gazing at the dips and hillocks and patches of woodland that undulated in all directions. To the north east lay Barcombe, but a ridge prevented you from seeing anything other than a few straggling cottages dotted here and there. Due north was the hill on the brow of which stood the Prescotts' bungalow. It must be at least a mile and a half away, but, as Sarah realised with a thrill, you could see the house and surrounding trees quite plainly. The Prescotts' view was Diana's view, seen from the other end.

Sarah stared, fascinated, at the little strip of brick that was the house. Human figures would be invisible at this distance, but the spot drew her like a magnet. The breeze had dropped and the evening of the June day was still and clear, like in a Claude landscape – dream light. All of a sudden, a light winked on in the bungalow – no, just outside it. They must have lights on the terrace, she thought. Of course he couldn't know she was watching, but it felt as if he did, as if he was flashing a message of hope and yearning.

'Oh grow up,' she told herself angrily, out loud. The rushing bathwater would muffle the sound of her voice. The bath was ready. She turned off the taps, spread a large towel on the chair next to the bath, made sure soap, flannel and sponge were ready to hand in the spotless aluminium bathrack. Diana's nightgown was folded under her pillow; Sarah shook it out, hung it over the heated towel rail, and returned to the invalid and her tireless little companion.

The last stragglers from Pierre's party drifted away about six. Claudia was happy for people to stay; she would have liked them to stay all evening. She wanted to postpone direct contact with Pierre for as long as possible. She wanted to think that she was wrong, that she hadn't seen Pierre stroke Sarah Stanhope's face, that the sense of communication passing between them had been the product of her imagination. She ran the scene through her mind over and over, until the edges were blurred and the truth impossible to ascertain, but the disquiet remained.

She kept chatting to her guests quite cheerfully; detaching the various sections of her brain from one another had always been one of her specialities. Her mother had gone to lie down; Naomi had eaten little, though she had tried to disguise the fact, and her face was a sort of ashen yellow. Claudia tried to replace worrying about her husband with worrying about her mother, but found this even more painful. It was harder to talk to people that way round.

She looked at Pierre, who was cracking open cans of beer for Matt and Spike. It was incredible how much alcohol young men could consume without it making any visible difference. It was also incredible how long they had stayed – there couldn't be much in it for them, this arty, laid back pair, at a party for assorted specimens of the middle-aged, middle class backbone of England. They seemed perfectly content, though, gnawing on hunks of bread and laughing with Pierre. Perhaps at that age free beer was enough in itself. They could have escaped if they'd wanted to.

Pierre was doing well – had done well all day, she had to admit. He had combined being seamlessly charming with a considerable amount of surreptitious tidying up, and the place didn't look too bad. Glasses had been endlessly refilled, everybody's needs had been catered for. Including her own? Pierre had acted the part of the supportive husband to perfection. Claudia tried another mental tack; if he was having an affair with Sarah Stanhope, she would simply not mind. It would hardly be the first time. She had coped in the past; why not play the waiting game once more? She felt utterly certain, as she always had, that Pierre would never leave her.

As long as I'm not confronted with the evidence, she thought, nodding and smiling at a longwinded anecdote narrated by the Baldock couple. As long as it's not pushed in my face, I can cope. I'm strong — stronger than anyone.

Diana Stanhope had managed her bath more or less unaided, to Sarah's relief. Sarah could not reconcile her sense of the older woman's dignity, held for so many years, with the exposure of her wrinkled nakedness that she had been dreading. No one, Sarah imagined, had had any part to play in connection with Diana's bodily functions, at least not since the birth of Adrian. She was immensely relieved that she had to do nothing more intimate than help her climb into bed and place the telephone and pitcher of water closer to hand.

'This bed's awfully high,' Sarah said. 'Shall I make another one up for you? I could easily bring in a divan from the blue room.'

'Thank you, dear, but I couldn't possibly sleep in any other bed. I shall be quite all right.'

'But what about the stairs?'

'I shall not need to go downstairs during the night, and Mrs Fairley arrives at eight o'clock tomorrow morning. Perhaps you would telephone her, Sarah, to let her know that I may need a little help.'

'Of course,' said Sarah, but at that moment the telephone rang. Diana waved her hand to indicate that Sarah should deal with it. She had already closed her eyes; she lay on her back, with her hands folded on her chest.

It was Adrian. He asked Sarah routine questions about his mother, but his tone was anxious and twittery. Sarah was unjustifiably aggravated. She told herself that the call was tactless and would only upset Diana, but she knew that wasn't the real reason for her snappish tone.

When she had replaced the handset she said brightly, 'That was Adrian. Just asking how you were.'

'So I assumed,' murmured Diana. She opened her eyes.

'Hannah, will you please go down and fetch my reading glasses? Thank you, dear.'

Hannah had been given Diana's costume jewellery to examine, and had been deeply absorbed. She loved running errands, though, and trotted off happily, a string of amber beads clanking against a necklace made of chunks of jet.

Diana pulled herself up a little in bed. 'Are you very tired, Sarah? Have the children been wakeful?'

'Well – Thomas is teething, but it hasn't been too bad. Why? Do I look tired?'

'I couldn't help noticing that when you spoke to Adrian your tone was a little ... weary.' Diana turned on Sarah one of her penetrating stares. 'I hope everything is quite all right at home?'

Nosy old bat, thought Sarah. She thinks I'm mistreating her precious son. Aloud she said, a little coolly, 'We're quite all right, really. It's just that Adrian is a little anxious about you.'

'Ah,' said Diana, 'your tone was one of concern. I mistook it for irritability.'

She really is the limit, Sarah said to herself. The re-entry of Hannah saved her from replying.

'I've looked for them everywhere but I can't find them.' Hannah's solemn face looked more worried than ever. She hated to fail in any task, super- or self-imposed. 'I'm sorry, Grandma.'

'Never mind, darling. Good gracious, they were here all the time!' Diana pointed to the glasses case on her dressing table. 'How silly of me.'

Not silly at all, thought Sarah grimly as she led Hannah to the car. Cunning, not silly. Illness had not dimmed Diana's habit of scrutiny. Sarah put her fingers to her face, to the spot where Pierre had touched her that morning. Her mother-in-law's inspection of the state of her marriage was something she could do without.

'Claudia,' called Naomi's faint voice, 'I wonder if you could help me pack?'

Claudia pulled off her rubber gloves. The guests had finally departed, and Pierre had immediately popped out on the – possibly genuine – pretext of taking Jaques for a walk. 'May as well dump this lot at the bottle bank at the same time,' he said, indicating the party empties, and Claudia had nodded assent.

Alone with the washing-up she felt calmer; she had even been able to think about her play instead of about her private life. Her mother's interruption was particularly unwelcome.

Naomi sat, hunched, on the edge of the bed. She had pulled her suitcase out from under the bed and was attempting to fill it, but the pain in her side made her gasp and her arms felt leaden and woolly at the same time. She didn't seem able to grasp a bundle of clothes, even, and had to let them fall.

'Mother,' said Claudia, 'what *are* you doing?'

'Would you mind giving me a hand, dear? I'm a little tired.'

Claudia sat next to her mother on the edge of the bed, and noticed that the jolt made Naomi wince.

'You're surely not thinking of going anywhere? You're simply not well enough.'

'I said I would go on Monday. I don't want to outstay my welcome.'

Claudia sighed. 'It's not a question of that. You're going to stay here until you get better. I insist.'

Naomi said, faltering, 'I don't want to be a burden.'

'Why shouldn't you be a burden for a bit? I was a burden to you once.'

'Oh, no, dear. Never.'

'Yes I was – when I was a baby. All babies are burdens. So now I'm paying you back.' Awkwardly Claudia covered her mother's puffy, brown-spotted hand with her own.

'Hard work, perhaps, but so welcome!' All week, Naomi had been plucking up courage to raise the all-important subject with her daughter, but the time never seemed right. Now, emboldened by Claudia's uncharacteristic gesture of affection, she went on. 'It's wrong to think of babies as burdens. Don't imagine that they will tie you down. It's almost a liberation, having something you can love so completely.'

Claudia stood up. 'Yes, well, I don't suppose I'll ever find out.' She started to gather up the fallen clothes. 'We need to get you back into bed, Mother. When Pierre comes in I'll get him to look at you. How do you think the party went?'

Naomi realised that the subject of grandchildren was firmly closed.

CHAPTER SIXTEEN

Hilary had offered to stay and help Claudia tidy up after the party, but her offer was refused, so she drove home with Joe late that afternoon. Their conversation veered back to where they had left off earlier. 'The great thing about Claudia,' said Hilary, 'is that I always know she's telling the truth. If she wanted help she'd have said so.'

'I know. She's a frighteningly honest person. Unlike Pierre.'

Hilary was driving, so she didn't turn her head. 'I didn't know you knew them that well,' she said.

'How long does one have to know Pierre Prescott to realise he doesn't know the truth from his elbow? About half an hour?'

'Goodness, Joe. You sound bitter. I thought you liked him.'

'Oh I do. He's fun, and friendly – genuinely, I think. He just wants a good time, and Claudia doesn't give it to him.'

'For a novelist, that's a very obtuse remark.'

'Why so, madam? Sex is what's wrong with that marriage.' Joe slid his hand under the silvery fabric of Hilary's dress and stroked her thigh.

'Stop it, I'm driving. Anyway, it's not funny – Claudia's my best friend.'

Joe withdrew his hand. 'I didn't say it was funny. It's actually very sad. They ought to have so much going for them, but it's all disappearing down the plughole. What does Claudia think about Pierre chasing other women all the time?'

'Oh look. Fox.' Hilary swerved to avoid the lithe, vivid creature. 'I'm not sure. We don't discuss it, just allude to it sometimes. She notices it, but I think she chooses not to mind.'

'Could anybody really not mind?'

'Well, she tries.'

There was a pause. Then Joe said, 'I'm surprised you don't discuss it, since you're such good friends.'

'Contrary to popular belief, women don't choose to spend *all* their time discussing their men.' Hilary's tone was snappish. Joe, surprised at her touchiness, kept his counsel.

They drew up at Petts End Cottage. Plant life rampaged everywhere, over and around the little house, so that even its walls seemed to tremble and flutter. Joe had left his own car at High House for Matt and Spike; as Hilary had driven him to the cottage it meant she wanted him to come in.

'I'm sorry I bit your head off. I just worry about Claudia. You are coming in, aren't you?'

'If I may.' Joe smiled. 'I don't feel up to a five-mile walk just yet. Is Ellie in?'

'Probably. But never mind. She's got to get used to you.'

Elinor was indeed in. She had spent the day reading and dozing and regretting not going to the Prescotts' party. She had ignored the tasty little lunch – potato salad, and a piece of smoked trout – which Hilary had left for her, much though she had longed for it, and had stuck to biscuits and bread – she couldn't even be bothered to toast it – and gallons of black coffee. Despite the fine weather she wore a baggy black sweater over her jeans, with holes at the elbows and sleeves that were far too long for her skinny arms. Her unwashed hair hung over her face. At the sound of the car her heart had lifted, only to stiffen again when she heard Joe's footsteps on the path. She had been sitting in the living room, having another go at *The Mill on the Floss*; now she scuttled back to the bedroom. Hilary and Joe entered to the sound of her door slamming.

Hilary rolled her eyes expressively at Joe. She called cheerily up the stairs, 'Hi, darling! D'you want to have a cup of tea with us?'

No reply. 'Never mind, sweetheart,' Joe said tenderly. 'I could murder a cup of tea. I'll do it.'

In her room, Elinor pressed her fingers to her eyelids to check the angry tears that threatened. Mum had been with that man all day, why did she need to bring him home as well? She'd been looking forward to seeing her mother, had even made up her mind to be nice to her – she wouldn't bother now. There was no point caring about what Mum did any more. She just acted to please herself – well, good luck to her. Elinor had half promised to visit Laura that afternoon. If she didn't go soon, the nurses would start chucking visitors out for the night. If she went now her mother and that bearded troll would have the place to themselves – fine. She would show who was the mature one, by letting them know she didn't mind. She would go into the kitchen, exchange a few pleasantries with them, and be on her way. She scraped her hair back into a ponytail for the bike ride, and groped under her bed for her trainers.

Downstairs, while Joe made the tea, Hilary moved about the kitchen, tidying it with brisk, practised movements. Crumbs were swept up, rings made by coffee mugs sponged away, the Sunday newspaper realigned and folded and placed on a clean work surface. Joe had loved to watch her strong, supple limbs moving so smoothly; he followed the graceful swaying of her body beneath its gauzy party dress. Such a rarity! A sense of her splendour overcame him, and as she splashed water into the sink to wash the dirty mugs he grabbed her by each wrist and drew her to him.

Hilary melted. She could feel his strength pounding through her, energising and relaxing at the same time. She wanted him to hold her like that for ever. Here was comfort, here was luxury, here was a promise that would banish all cares. She had struggled long enough. Now she could let herself go.

She didn't hear Elinor's light footsteps on the stairs, nor the lifting of the latch of the kitchen door. Joe's mouth was warm on hers and she had closed her eyes. When she opened them she saw a small, pale, stricken face in the doorway, and a dark figure that turned and fled.

Hilary struggled free of Joe and hurried to the door. Elinor had already run round the house and was wheeling out her bicycle. 'Ellie! Don't go! Where are you going? Don't leave me.'

Elinor said, without turning her head, 'Oh for Christ's sake don't be so melodramatic. I'm going to see Laura, of course. Where else? So you've got a couple of hours to do whatever you want to that Terry Waite lookalike. Have fun.' Hilary hardly recognised her daughter's voice in the strained vulgarity of the tone.

Joe came to the door at that moment. 'Elinor,' he said, 'won't you stay? I'll order us a takeaway and we'll all have supper together.'

Elinor turned to look at him. She could hardly bear the sight; his grizzled beard, like a cartoon pirate, his round belly filling out his checked lumberjack shirt, his broad bulk filling the door space, blocking the entrance to her home. She said slowly, 'Thank you for inviting me to supper in my own house. It's very big of you. But I'm not particularly hungry, and you look like you could do with skipping a meal or two.' She mounted her bicycle. 'Goodbye.'

'Elinor!' Hilary shouted, her voice shrill with anger. Joe put his arm round her shoulders. 'Don't bother,' he said, 'leave her. It's my fault.'

'She was bloody rude. I've got to make her apologise.'

'It's too late now. And I don't need an apology. She's just acting her age. That's mild stuff – Matt and Spike used to come out with far worse than that.'

Hilary wandered along the edge of her tiny front garden, snapping off the dead heads of the rambling yellow rose. 'I can't just ignore it. I've let her get away with it for too long. I've spoilt her. She's got to learn that other people have a right to –' she broke off, choking with sobs. 'Oh Joe, Joe, she looked so frightened.'

Joe guided her to the wooden bench by the front door. He sat her down, resting her head on his broad shoulder. 'Don't talk,' he said, 'don't talk. There's no need.'

The late afternoon sun lingered longest in this spot. The bench was bathed in a pool of golden light. Bumble bees tumbled over the lavender bushes on either side of the front door; swallows swooped low over the rutted track. In the field beyond, what seemed to be lumps of earth shook themselves and bobbed away with a flash of white – young rabbits at play. Hilary's sobs subsided. She tucked her legs up on the bench and snuggled into Joe's lap.

They stayed like that for a long time, until the sun had sunk behind the wood. Hilary shivered a little as the shadows stretched across the house front. Joe twined her hair in his fingers, then traced the strong clear outline of her nose and chin. 'Hilary,' he said, suddenly, 'Hilary, I've got to ask. I don't know how to put this, but – I wish you'd marry me.'

She looked up at his face. His bright blue eyes, set deep in their web of laughter lines, were full of kindliness and ardour and real, warm love. She could say yes, and it would all be so very, very easy. But a wan little face interposed itself in front of those generous eyes, a hurt, bewildered face that was still, after all, the face of a child.

She got up, and straightened her hair and her dress. 'How can I?' she said. 'How can I? It's not as if I was a free agent.'

Joe took her by the hand. 'Please,' he said. 'Think about it. Is it such an outrageous idea?'

She shook her head, squeezed his hand, and withdrew her own.

'I'm sorry, Joe, I'm sorry.' And she walked into the house.

'Guess what?' said Laura. 'I'm coming out tomorrow.'

'Brilliant!' replied Elinor, seating herself gingerly on the edge of the bed. The chair was piled high with Laura's belongings – night clothes, magazines, an over-stuffed make-up bag. Laura had spent much of her fortnight in hospital doing creative things to her face, and now had virtually no eyebrows. This gave her a surprised look, like a giant baby doll.

'I'll miss this place,' Laura continued, with a lordly wave at the rest of the ward. 'I'm dreading going home. Can't I come and live with you, Ellie? Then at least I could smoke in peace.'

'I thought you'd given up.'

'Only because I had to, in here. They took advantage of my immobile state. But I intend to go back to it as soon as I can hobble to the shops. I was getting quite good at it, and now I'll be out of practice.'

'Actually, Lor, I wish I could move in with you.' Elinor picked at the white candlewick bedcover.

'Why on earth – ? You've always been a bit slow on the uptake about the ghastliness of my family, haven't you?'

'Well, I wish we could get a little flat together, or something. I just don't want to go home. Mum's getting more and more involved with – with –'

'With Terry Waite? He's all right, isn't he? It's not his fault he's ugly.'

'Honestly, I don't know how she can bear to touch him.'

'You're always saying that.'

'It's always true.'

'OK, but I don't see that it matters. I mean, you're not the one who has to touch him.'

'But I might be the one who has to live with him. This

afternoon he was in the kitchen, leaning against the sink, and they were … oh you know.'

'No! Really? In the *kitchen*? In the middle of the afternoon?' Laura leaned forward, deeply interested.

'Oh no, no, no, not *that*. Just – you know – kissing or whatever. The point is he was acting like he owned the place. I couldn't stand it. I just had to get out.'

'Mmmm.' Laura seemed to be losing concentration. 'Sounds rough. Look in the bottom of my locker, would you? I think there are some Munchmallows in there.'

Elinor didn't look. 'Laura,' she said in a small voice, 'I'm really upset about this.' Her fingers tugged little white tufts out of the counterpane.

'Well,' said Laura, 'don't take it out on the innocent bedspread. Now listen to Auntie Laura's words of wisdom. Your ma is having a relationship with a man who looks like a cross between a retired Radio One DJ and an axe murderer, right? And it's making her happy, right? And that makes you *un*happy; you claim because you wish she had better taste, but really because you want her all to yourself. Let's face it, if she was going out with Hugh Grant you'd still be slagging him off. Right?' Elinor nodded, smiling weakly. 'OK. Well, you can try to drive him away by sulking and bad mouthing him and acting like a retarded two-year-old, and you might even succeed, but how good would you feel, exactly, having made your mother so miserable?'

'It's for her sake,' put in Elinor; 'she's making a mistake –'

'Oh, bollocks it's for her sake! It's for yours. She knows what she's doing; she's been hanging around for long enough. Leave her alone, Ells. It's her life.'

'And what about me?'

'Accept it. Like him, or if you can't like him, keep out of his way. But I bet he's nice, really. I'd trust your mother not to fall in love with a real wally.'

'Hmm,' said Elinor, only half convinced.

'Look, in a year's time we'll be leaving school. You can do what you want to then. You'll be going to university; you won't even be living at home any more.'

'A year's a long time.'

'Not very. Seems like no time to me since GCSEs and that was a year ago. And he hasn't moved in yet, has he? All he's done is set foot in your kitchen. It's not as if you're finding bits of his beard blocking up the bath or whatever.'

'Ugh, Laura, don't be so gross.'

'Sorry, sweetie. Just preparing you for what lies in store. Listen, if he moves in, we'll get a flat together as soon as we leave school, OK?'

'Promise?'

'Yup. As long as you let me smoke.'

Elinor stayed until the ward sister indicated that her presence was no longer welcome. As she cycled slowly back home she pondered what Laura had said. It was annoying to think that she might actually be right.

When Pierre came back from the bottle bank Claudia was standing outside their front door. His heart sank. She'd noticed something. He could see her from a few yards down the road, and the way she was standing, thin shoulders raised, arms tightly crossed over her chest, indicated a tense preoccupation. He had a few seconds to rehearse internally a couple of alternative explanations or excuses; he liked to have a few simple stories at the ready. Which one he decided to use would depend on how she broached the subject.

'Hi, darling,' he called as he swung his long legs out of the car. 'Everything all right? Come on, pooch.' He unlocked the hatchback and gave Jaques a slap on his rear end to make him move. The dog uttered an intensely human sigh and flumped onto the gravel.

Claudia came up close. 'It's Mother,' she said quietly, 'I'm really worried. She's gone a most peculiar colour. I said you would have a look at her.'

Thank God, thought Pierre. The irony of being grateful for such news didn't immediately strike him. He patted Claudia on the shoulder. 'Don't worry, darling. I'll sort it out.' This patronising, I'm-in-charge mode of Pierre's usually irritated Claudia, but this evening she was grateful for the sense of temporary security it gave her. She'd almost forgotten about Sarah Stanhope. It was quite easy to shove her on to the top mental shelf, for the time being at any rate.

She was setting out cheese and biscuits for a light post-party supper when Pierre finished examining his mother-in-law. Her stomach turned over when she saw his face, the look of worry was so obviously real. It was so rare to see a simple, unclouded emotion in him, though it was only a moment or two before he'd regained his professional composure. 'Pierre,' she said, almost in a whisper, 'you don't need to hide the truth from me.'

'I know, I know. I'm not happy. She ought to go into hospital as soon as possible – she needs proper pain control, apart from anything else. I'll ring Valerie straight away and see if I can wangle a bed.'

'What? At St Swithin's? Shouldn't she go to the one where she was before, where they did all the tests? What's it called –'

'I don't think she could travel that far. Even in an ambulance, it'd be a very uncomfortable ride. She was asking for you, Claudia – go in and see her, and I'll make that phone call. Now don't worry –' that firm hand on the shoulder again – 'it'll probably be all right. She just needs proper treatment, that's all.'

'Pierre, you must tell me, it's the cancer again, isn't it?'

Pierre held her gaze for a few seconds, nodded slightly, and moved to the telephone.

Diana Stanhope rallied considerably the next day; Sarah rang Adrian at work to tell him he needn't hurry back. Mrs Fairley, the daily, was to prepare the meals, and Diana was very insistent that no doctor was needed. Adrian said he'd call in on her straight after work, so Sarah shouldn't expect him back before nine at the earliest; was that all right? Of course, said Sarah, hoping her voice did not reveal her delight. She'd be able to ring Pierre. Hilary had mentioned in passing that there was going to be a long rehearsal of *As You Like It* that evening, so Claudia wouldn't be home till late. Pierre might be out too – doing an evening surgery, perhaps – but it was worth a try. The minute the children were in bed ... Sarah found herself glancing at the clock with increasing impatience as the day wore on.

The children seemed particularly trying that afternoon. Thomas had a nappy rash – a sure sign of a new tooth with him – and grizzled continuously, holding up his sausagey little arms to be carried whenever Sarah crossed his field of vision. Gabriel collected every single building brick he could find and laid them out in mysterious patterns all over the kitchen floor. He lay on his tummy kicking his feet in the air and muttering at the bricks in an incantatory tone, coming out of his reverie only to object querulously when the foot of a passer-by knocked a brick out of line. He's obviously going to be a druid when he grows up, thought Sarah – that is, if he isn't one already. Hannah seemed out of sorts. She objected to Gabriel's monopoly of the kitchen floor, couldn't play out of doors because it was drizzling, and for once refused to read in the bedroom. 'I'm sick of reading. I've read all the books there are.' Sarah tried to point out that this was manifestly untrue, but Hannah was set on unreasonableness.

'I know why you're so grumpy,' said Sarah.

'I'm not grumpy.'

'You most certainly are. It's because I let you stay up so late last night, when we went to Grandma's. I'd better not let you do that again.'

Hannah's eyes filled with reproachful tears. 'Oh Mummy! You said I was a great help.'

'You were, darling, but being tired has made you cross now. Never mind, don't cry – I expect you can come with me, if I go again. How about watching television now, if you're bored with reading?'

With Hannah installed in front of the television and Gabriel absorbed in his arcane ritual, Sarah saw the opportunity to make her telephone call. Of course Pierre might not be back yet; it was only about twenty to six. But it was worth a try. She dosed Thomas with Calpol and set him at her feet with a packet of crisps to rummage in. She felt slightly guilty about all that salt battering at his poor little kidneys, but she knew it would keep him happy for at least ten minutes … She closed the kitchen and living room doors and reached for the hall telephone.

He answered, after only two rings. She felt a surge of heat. 'Pierre? It's –'

'Sarah! How marvellous. I was just thinking about you.'

'Were you?' She giggled, foolishly.

'Mmm. Excellent timing too. I've got evening surgery at six, so I've got a few minutes. And Claudia's not back.'

That sounded like an unequivocal statement of intent. Sarah was emboldened.

'I'm longing to see you.'

'Not as much as I'm longing to see you. Thursday, right? Eleven o'clock? And alone?' He put a purring emphasis on the last word.

'I'll get a babysitter. I'll be there.'

'You are so sweet … I suppose I'll have to take some photographs too. Perhaps we'll need more than one sitting? I've a feeling the camera may go wrong.'

Sarah hardly recognised the sound of her own girlish laughter. His voice was so rich, so alive – she could already feel his hands on her hair, her face, her body. She wanted to say wild things to him, that she loved him and craved him and wanted him for ever … she had to end this conversation before any semblance of control was lost.

'I'd better go. The children are playing up. Thursday, then.'

'I wish it was now, Sarah. I'm ready for you any time.'

Sarah breathed a goodbye and put the telephone down. Her head was swimming. She leaned against the wall and put the palm of her hand to her chest so that she could feel the thump of her heart. She looked down at Thomas, gumming the crisps into a slimy paste; he seemed a very long way off. She had to book a babysitter for him, but she didn't trust herself to speak to anyone else right now.

'Oh, Mummy!' Hannah's voice from the living room was shrill and pained. 'Oh, Mummy! Look at this!'

Sarah stepped over Thomas and opened the living room door. The news was on. Sarah's policy was to prevent the children from watching it, it was so often so harrowing. The item was about Bosnia. Two orphans, with pinched, scabby faces and shaven heads, lay on makeshift hospital beds in what looked like an abandoned barn. Their thin white chests, rising and falling laboriously, were bare beneath a blood-stained sheet. One jerked a stump of an arm towards the camera. The voiceover spared no detail of the manner in which they had lost all the other members of their family. And Sarah had let her little girl be exposed to this horror, while she giggled on the phone to her married lover.

'Oh Mummy,' said Hannah, 'you can't see if they are boys or

girls.' She turned to her mother, her face blazing. 'Does God know about this?' she said.

CHAPTER SEVENTEEN

Joe Coventry put the telephone down, and cursed at what he thought was empty air. Then he seized two fistfuls of grizzled wiry hair and bashed his forehead against the window frame. He had not heard Spike, who padded in from the kitchen in socks and boxer shorts, looking for matches in the study, on his way back to bed with two big mugs of tea.

'What's up, Dad?'

Joe turned his head slowly and regarded his son with tragic eyes.

'She's not answering,' he replied, taken off his guard. 'Why won't she even answer the bloody phone?'

'Perhaps she's out,' offered Spike.

'Spike,' said his father, 'that was a rhetorical question. I tell you, she's not answering the telephone because she knows it's me.'

'I know she's pretty special, Dad, but she's not clairvoyant. How's she supposed to know it's you?'

Joe wagged his head from side to side, as lugubrious as a St Bernard. 'Spike,' he said, 'just go back to bed. Please.'

Spike sloped off. When he and Matt stayed with their father they still slept in sleeping bags on bunk beds, like schoolboys. Matt, on the bottom bunk, was awake, reading. 'Here's your tea,' said Spike, slipping in beside him and taking the book out of his hands. 'What's this? Poetry? You're not in love too, are you?'

'Might be,' said Matt. 'Give it back.'

Spike found a packet of cigarettes in the tangle on the floor that uncoiled like intestines from an unzipped holdall. He lit two, and inserted one in his brother's mouth. 'Dad's got it bad,' he said.

Matt sat up. 'What was that little encounter about just now?'

'He bit my head off. I found him in the study, looking like Brian Blessed rehearsing for some over the top RSC role, asked him what the matter was, and he told me to fuck off.'

'Just like that?'

'More or less.'

'And what was the matter?'

'His bird wasn't answering the telephone.'

'She's probably out. What's the big deal?'

'That's what I said.'

'Oh well,' said Matt, draining his mug and then flicking ash into it. 'It's his life.' He reached for his poetry book again. 'Rilk,' said Spike. 'Never heard of him.'

'Rilk*er*, you dork. He's German.'

Spike got up, and began gathering his scattered clothes. 'It'll be a shame, if this one goes wrong. The old man deserves a break.'

'Spike, do me a favour and keep out of it. You'll do more harm than good.'

'I reckon he needs a spot of encouragement.' Spike pulled on his baggy green jeans. 'I've never seen him so gone on anyone before, but he might let it slip through his fingers. You know what he's like – kind of careless. And fatalistic.'

'Yeah. And I know what you're like. So leave him alone, there's a good boy.'

'We'll see,' said Spike. He left the room, whistling.

'Duck!' said Elinor, sharply.

Laura looked round the high street. 'Where?' she asked.

'Oh for God's sake, I didn't mean there was a duck. I meant hide.'

'Hide? Why?'

'Because it's *him*. Over there, by the post office.'

'My God, you mean that's Terry Waite?'

'Laura, if you won't hide, at least keep your voice down.' Elinor, aware that nothing would now shift Laura from the spot, tried to give the impression of being engrossed in the florist's window display.

'He's coming this way,' hissed Laura. 'Do you think he's going to buy your mum some flowers? Who are those people with him? His sons?'

'Probably. I've never seen them. Laura, do look at these flowers. Look, aren't those purple ones gross?'

Bur Laura was not to be distracted. 'He's not that bad,' she said, 'he's not as fat as you made out. He's seen you. You're definitely going to have to say hello.'

Joe said it first. 'Ellie,' he said. 'Good to see you. You haven't met Matt and Spike, have you?'

Elinor thought angrily, he knows I haven't. She muttered a greeting without looking anybody in the eye.

'And you must be Laura,' said Joe. 'I heard about your adventure.' He indicated her plastercast. 'I had a motorbike when I was about nineteen. A Triumph Bonneville. I set off, once, with a girl I was trying to impress. I shot off too quickly. I was half way down the road before I realised I'd left her sitting in a ditch.'

Laura laughed – immoderately, Elinor thought. 'Well, it hasn't put me off,' she said. 'I'll be desperate for another ride as soon as this thing's off my leg.'

'I'm sorry we can't oblige,' put in Spike. 'Matt's a pushbike man, and I'm scared shitless of the things.'

Elinor tugged at her friend's arm. 'We'd better go,' she said. 'Come on, Laura. It's nearly the end of lunch break.'

'No it isn't,' said Laura, fixing her gaze on Matt. 'We've got over twenty minutes.'

'But you take forever because of your plaster.' Elinor said a brief goodbye, and set off. Laura grudgingly hobbled after her. 'Slow down, Ells. I've got something to tell you.'

Elinor quickened her pace. She didn't want to hear Laura's comments until they were out of earshot. At the end of the street she paused, and waited for her to catch up.

Laura, moist and red-faced from exertion, said solemnly, 'Elinor, I'm in love.'

'What? You can't be serious.'

'Yes I can.'

'But you always said men with beards –'

'Oh no, not with *him*.' Laura's tone was scornful. 'No, no, your ma's welcome to him. Though he's quite nice, actually. But no, I'm in love with – shit, what's his name?'

'Which one? Ponytail?'

'No, earring. And deep, deep eyes.'

'I think he's called Matt.'

'Matt. That's it. I'm definitely in love with Matt.'

'Oh Laura.'

The Coventry family still stood in front of the flower shop. They watched the retreating girls in amused silence.

'Well,' said Spike, 'here's a flower shop. Why don't you send some flowers, Dad? Those big white ones are nice.'

'Lilies,' said Joe. 'I'm not allowed to send her flowers. Expressly forbidden.'

'Why the hell –'

'Because it upsets Elinor.'

'Ah,' said Spike, 'the root of the problem.'

'I think so. But it's a pretty deep and complicated root.'

'Send her some anyway. Sod Elinor, she'll come round.'

Joe only shook his head.

'Oh come on, Dad. Faint heart never won fair lady. That girl will have left home in a year or two. At worst it's a question of waiting.'

To the surprise of all of them Joe said, 'I want her now.' Matt and Spike exchanged glances.

'Then go for her now. Lay siege.'

Matt said, unexpectedly, 'Spike's right, Dad. Go for it. It's her life, not her daughter's.'

Joe sighed, hugely. 'She's so sensitive,' he said, 'you've no idea –'

Spike clapped a hand on his shoulder. 'Well, if you won't send flowers, at least you can sink a pint. To drown your sorrows.'

'Or to celebrate,' said Matt, 'the day we first met our grumpy little sister.' They wheeled their father back down the high street in the direction of the King's Head and Eight Bells.

'Caroline, I still can't hear you. We need to go through that again.'

Claudia stood at the back of the Abbey School assembly hall. The space was huge; all sound seemed to float up into the vaulted roof and lose itself there. Really, the pomposity of this Victorian Gothic! But the school had no purpose-built theatre, so there was little choice. She had thought about staging *As You Like It* out of doors, but voices were even harder to project there, and even in July, evenings could get distinctly shivery.

Caroline Crouch sighed as loudly as she dared. She was Orlando, and if the truth be known Claudia had selected her as much for her long legs and flat chest as for any acting talent. It was important to avoid obvious pitfalls, and in an all-girls school play, a bosomy leading man was one of them. 'Where from?' Caroline called.

'From "My fair Rosalind —" Are you ready too, Elinor?'

Elinor nodded.

' "My fair Rosalind, I come within an hour of my promise." '

' "Break an hour's promise in love! He that will divide a minute into a hundred parts" — oh sorry, it's a thousand isn't it?' Elinor flushed. Caroline would hate her for fluffing it again. This was the fourth time they'd been through this scene that evening, and she knew Caroline was in a fever of impatience because she was meeting her boyfriend later.

Claudia stepped forward, out of the shadows at the back of the hall. 'OK, you two, sit down.' There was nothing to sit on, so they sat on the floor. Caroline folded her long legs effortlessly into a half-lotus position. She was supple, and she moved well. That was something, Claudia thought.

'Yes, it is "a thousand", Elinor, but a mistake like that doesn't really matter at this stage. Just keep going — continuity is the important thing. Without it, you're not acting, just reciting. When they were filming *Some Like It Hot*, Marilyn Monroe forgot a line forty times. They had to paste it onto the furniture in the end, so that she could just read it. And I believe she still managed to get it wrong.'

Caroline laughed. 'What was the line, Miss?'

'I think it was, "Where is the bourbon?" Not very complicated, and she was still a great star. So you two aren't doing so very badly — this is only the fourth take. Now, let's do it one more time — and if it goes wrong again we'll drop it for tonight, I promise. Let's go right from the beginning of the scene. Vicky's gone, so I'll read Jaques.'

Knowing the end was in sight encouraged the two girls. They made plenty of mistakes, but they ploughed on, even remembering to move and touch one another from time to time. Caroline had the advantage in this, being more used to touching people than Elinor. Is she imagining I'm Alex? wondered Elinor as Caroline grabbed her hand and planted a kiss in its palm, while Mrs Prescott nodded approbation. As the scene progressed Elinor felt a kind of power seeping through her. She had an inkling at last that she knew what she was doing. Rosalind was playacting, exploring her own desires through the boy's disguise; now Elinor began to sense the liberation of speaking her own mind through her part, 'No, no, Orlando; men are April when they woo, December when they wed; maids are May when they are maids, but the sky changes when they are wives." ' That seemed forceful, and true. Love was blindness; her mother couldn't possibly see what she was doing. If she married the troll she'd regret it in a year, or less. Love wasn't the only thing in the world. ' "But these are all lies: men have died from time to time, and worms have eaten them, but not for love." '

Louise Potts, who had been picking at her nails, bored, in a corner, had stepped forward to do her little bit as Celia, and put Orlando and Rosalind through their mock-marriage. This time it was Elinor's turn to take Caroline's hand – ' "Give me your hand, Orlando." ' The gesture was strong and without embarrassment; Elinor–Rosalind was asserting her new-found control. She held Caroline's hand tightly. It was large and sinewy, like a man's. Elinor remembered holding Clicker's hand, that evening on the beach. That was just about her only experience of touching a man – if that's what Clicker was. Touching Caroline felt more like that than touching Laura.

'Excellent!' Uncharacteristically, Mrs P was beaming. 'We really got somewhere that time. We've still got to work on the voice projection, but you managed to get some atmosphere going. Elinor, you really sounded as if you meant it.'

Elinor smiled shyly. 'I think it's beginning to make more sense to me,' she said equivocally.

'Well done, all of you. Next rehearsal, same time on Friday. We'll have the musicians then so we'll go through the songs.'

Caroline grumbled faintly as the girls made for the door, but Elinor could tell she was quite pleased. 'God, that was boring. At least she said a few nice things though. She even cracked a smile.'

'I'm dreading singing,' said Elinor.

'You don't have to do a solo, do you?'

'No, just join in that one at the end. But if I sing you'll hear this terrible drone. I think I'll just open and shut my mouth.'

'Mrs P won't let you get away with that. Christ, is that the time? Alex will think I stood him up.'

But when they reached the school gates, Alex was nowhere in

sight. He was a tall, aloof eighteen-year-old, head of the cricket first eleven at Frenching, the only boys' public school of any repute in the area, and was regarded as awe-inspiringly cool by most of Caroline's classmates. Caroline herself was a little uncertain of him, even though they had been together for six months and were therefore virtually married in the eyes of their contemporaries. She clutched Elinor's elbow, and asked with less poise than usual, 'Will you stick around for a few minutes, Ellie? I don't want to be stood here looking like some kind of slag.'

Elinor readily assented. She knew that what Caroline wanted was to be engaged in lively conversation so that when – if – Alex deigned to show up he would see that she had a life, that she was having a good time regardless of him. Elinor launched into a perennial mode of conversation amongst the Abbey girls, which was poking fun at Mrs Prescott. She felt disloyal, but it was a conversational context that she could easily drift in and out of and raise a few laughs. All teachers were fair game at school, she felt, whatever they might be like in private.

'God, her *shoes*!' exclaimed Caroline. 'They look like barges. People with big feet should wear heels.'

'Do you reckon she's really only got one cardigan, or did she buy three hundred and sixty-five identical ones?'

'Special knockdown price – no one else would want them. I wish Mrs Spencer taught me English. I had her for GCSE and she's really nice.'

Elinor didn't mind attacking Claudia's dress sense, but always defended her teaching. 'Mrs P's really clever though. She gets really good results.'

'Yeah, but I don't understand a word she says. Oh I know what I wanted to ask you – can I borrow your notes for that homework? You know – comparing those two unbelievably tedious poems. I was writing a letter to Alex in that lesson and I didn't take anything in.'

Elinor hated lending her work. What she wrote felt personal to her, though none of the others seemed to feel this way. She was saved from replying by hearing Caroline say 'hey!', and there was Alex, sauntering towards them with his hands in the pockets of his baggy chinos. He wore a collarless linen shirt of a deep jade green that might have laid him open to ridicule if he hadn't been so outrageously handsome, and a battered but shapely jacket of brown suede. He was not alone. Elinor was so busy admiring Alex's cheekbones and thick, wayward chestnut hair that she didn't immediately recognise the skinny red-headed figure slouching self-consciously by his side.

Alex put his arm round Caroline's shoulders; not many boys were tall enough to do that. He nodded hello to Elinor, whom he had met once or twice, but said nothing about being late. It would have been uncool to notice the time. Clicker stood proprietorially by Elinor, but he didn't touch her. 'Hi,' was all that he said, as if he met her like this every evening. Caroline shot Elinor a why-didn't-you-tell-me glance.

'We're going to the Eight Bells. There's a crowd there,' Alex announced. 'You guys coming?'

Clicker looked as if he were about to assent, but Elinor intervened. Until she knew whether she was Clicker's girlfriend or not she didn't want to hang around with him in public. ' 'Fraid not,' she said. 'We're going to my place.' She couldn't think of a reason. 'You got your bike, Clicker?'

'Nope. Needs a new clutch.'

'We'll walk, then.'

'See you.' Alex and Caroline wandered off, hand in hand.

Elinor turned to Clicker. 'My pushbike's chained up over there. But we could leave it here for now. Let's go.' She spoke quickly, amazed at her own daring.

'Back to your place, like you said?'

She pondered. 'I don't think so. Mum will be in. We could walk down to the river, and you can tell me how you found me.' To the surprise of both, she slipped her hand into his. Claudia, driving out of the school gates on her way to visit her mother in hospital, almost hit a bollard in surprise. 'Well I never! That's something to tell Hilary.' She laughed out loud. 'Good for Ellie. I didn't know she had it in her.'

'I got a letter from Nicky this morning,' said Sarah to Adrian on Wednesday night, as he came into the kitchen after kissing the children goodnight.

'A whole letter? Amazing.'

'Yes – well, one of those aerogramme things. Guess what?'

'She's engaged?'

'No; quite the opposite. She's chucking the job in and coming home.'

'Really?'

'So she says.' Sarah laid out their supper on two trays, claiming that there was a play she wanted to watch on television. On this evening, with her tryst with Pierre the next day, she wanted to avoid too much contact with her husband. Nicola's letter was a welcome diversion in a way – something on which she could base a conversation that had nothing to do with what was uppermost in her mind. Another way, though, the news was less welcome.

'But why? Has something gone wrong?' Adrian asked, pouring two glasses of red wine.

'She claims she's bored of the job, hates New York, and can't find a decent man. But knowing Nicky –'

'– there's a hidden agenda. I agree. Oh well, I don't know that England's exactly crawling with decent men. Actually she's always seemed to favour indecent ones in the past.'

'Don't be snide, Adrian. Remember she's my sister.'

'Oh come on, darling, you know I'm fond of Nicky. But her taste in men – you've commented on it yourself. I bet she's got herself into some kind of tangle – a married man, or something like that.'

Sarah bent over the cooker so that Adrian couldn't see her face. 'Would you blame her if she did?'

'Did what?'

'Go to bed with a married man?'

'Of course. It would be wrong.'

'But why should she care about someone else's wife?'

'Hey, isn't there supposed to be solidarity amongst you women? Is there any Parmesan?'

'Yes, I've already put it out. Nicola's never been a great one for solidarity.'

'No – that's where she's different to you. I really like the fact that you value women.'

Adrian put his hands on Sarah's waist and dropped a kiss on her collarbone. It took all her concentration not to wince. 'Watch out,' she said, 'I've got to drain the pasta.'

'Anyway,' said Adrian, moving off, 'this is all a bit hypothetical.

We don't know what Nicky's been up to, and I don't suppose she'll tell us. When's she coming back?'

'In a couple of weeks, apparently. And she wants to come and stay.'

'Great!'

'Absolutely.'

Clicker pushed her bike for her all the way home. She walked by his side, noticing the stars come out, silent and happy. They had scrambled down to the river; there was a spot by the foot of the old brick-built bridge which was level and comfortable to sit on; she and Laura sometimes spent their lunch break down there. Clicker had thrown pebbles and bits of stick into the water and had told her how after the night of the accident he kept thinking about her but didn't know how to get in touch with her. 'I didn't even know your name,' he said, 'I thought you were called Emma.' All he knew was that she went to the Abbey Girls. He'd been trying to pluck up courage to hang around the gates looking for her, but there'd been half-term, and in any case, he didn't want people to think he was 'some kind of weirdo'. Then he'd risked asking Baz if he knew whether Laura was all right, and Baz had said he was well out of that one, but had he, Clicker, seen Ellie again? 'So that's how I knew your name, see.' And then he'd heard Alex say he was driving to Barcombe to meet his girlfriend after cricket, and he'd asked Alex on the spur of the moment if he could cadge a lift, and Alex had said come and say hello to Caroline, and Ellie had been standing there like a fucking miracle. Overcome with the emotional effort of this explanation, Clicker lit a cigarette.

Elinor leaned against his shoulder, watching the blue smoke unravel in the still air. The surface of the water was like a skin, with insects skidding weightlessly across it. Cars rumbled across the bridge from time to time, but she and Clicker, under a tangle of elder and hazel, were almost invisible from the road. He hadn't kissed her yet, but she thought he probably would at the end of this cigarette. She nerved herself to enjoy it.

He flicked ash onto the ground.

'So how do you know Alex?' Ellie asked. Clicker shuffled round and stared at her. 'From school of course,' he said. 'He's in my maths set.'

'Oh. Right,' said Ellie sheepishly. 'I didn't connect.' So Clicker went to Frenching! So fixed had she been in her mind that he was from the other side of the tracks that she hadn't cottoned on, even when he'd said something about cricket. A public school boy! She was a tiny bit disappointed. 'And what about the others?' She asked, 'Piggy and … that lot. Do they all go to Frenching too?'

'Yeah. Baz does. And Charlie, and Piggy. Not Slash. He got chucked out after GCSEs. He went to the sixth form college but dropped out of that. Now he's drifting.' He threw his cigarette into the water, where it extinguished itself with a faint hiss. He took her face between his hands. 'Ellie,' he said. 'It's a great name.' Sure enough, he kissed her.

And now he was prepared to push her bike all the way to the cottage, which was nearly two miles. She hadn't worked out what he was going to do after that. He said he lived in St Wilfreds, which was a posh suburb of Dinsford, Elinor knew. At least six miles. Oh well; first things first. She had to work out whether she was going to invite him in before she made any further plans.

They reached the turn-off to the cottage. 'You mean this is where you live?' said Clicker, wheeling the bike up the bumpy track. 'It's amazing.'

'I like it.'

'It suits you. There should be goblins and sprites and animals that talk up here.'

Elinor laughed. 'Well, there is a troll, sometimes. This is it – our cottage.' She took the handlebars from him, uncertain how to proceed.

Clicker said, 'I'm starving. Can I – have you got –'

'Oh sure,' said Ellie, 'come in for a bit. Mum's in, by the way.'

Clicker hesitated. 'Will she mind?'

'She'll be in bed, I hope.'

Sure enough there was a note anchored under the kettle. 'Hello darling. Claudia told me you were out with a friend, so I wasn't worried. (Hint!) I'm done in. See you tomorrow. XXX Mum.' Elinor screwed it up.

'Yup, she's in bed. Shall I make you a sandwich?'

'In a minute,' said Clicker. His eyes looked glazed and intent as he stepped towards her. He put his arms right round her and pressed against her, pushing her backwards against the sink. Her neck and spine were arched uncomfortably but she didn't know how to move without seeming to reject him. And she didn't want to reject him. Though she had the feeling that the kissing was more interesting for him than it was for her, she definitely wanted to find out more about it. And now his hand was under her shirt, cold on her back, moving up and round. She didn't stop him.

He pulled back for an instant, his mouth wet and blurred. 'Christ, Ellie,' he whispered, 'this is great.' And then he plunged back into it, his mouth on her neck this time. An image flashed into her mind. This was where she'd seen her mother and the troll, against the sink like this. Uneasy, she wriggled a little, and said, 'Mum will hear us.'

'Sorry.' Clicker pushed his hair back, out of his eyes. 'I got a bit carried away. I'm sorry.'

Elinor felt a warmth spreading through her, as she had done in the rehearsal that afternoon, that seemed like an age away now. She looked at Clicker. He was embarrassed, and worried. He thought he had upset her. She put the palms of her hands flat against his chest, and kissed him lightly on the lips. 'It's OK,' she said. 'Are you still hungry? I'll make you that sandwich.' She knew what this warm feeling was. It was to do with power. She turned away to the bread bin, hiding the slow, secret smile that was creeping unbidden across her face.

She made huge cheese sandwiches, and coffee. She didn't eat any; she didn't want him to see her eating. They perched on kitchen stools, opposite each other; he ate quickly and untidily, she cradled her mug of coffee. She kept one foot on the rung of his stool, so that their ankles touched. She found she didn't want to stop touching him altogether.

'How will you get back?' she asked.

Clicker shrugged. 'Don't worry, I'll hitch a ride back. I'll manage.'

'You could take my bike,' said Ellie, 'and bring it back to me after school tomorrow.' She hoped she didn't sound too eager.

Clicker had a sheepish, lop-sided grin. 'Does that mean you want to see me again?'

'Looks like it,' said Ellie. She hopped down from her stool and stood between his legs and pulled his head against her shoulder. It was a long time before he cycled back to St Wilfreds. When he had gone, she undressed in her room with the curtains open, in the moonlight. She examined her pale, cool body and fingered the mark his mouth had made on her neck. Then she pulled her high-necked, long-sleeved nightgown over her head and brushed her hair with one hundred strokes, like a Victorian governess. She watched her actions dimly reflected in the mirror. She thought, 'And I don't even know his name.'

CHAPTER EIGHTEEN

Sarah woke at dawn on Thursday morning. She knew she wouldn't be able to sleep again. Beside her, Adrian slept, noisily because he had mild hay fever. Sarah felt irritation with him like a heat rash all over her body. It would be another couple of hours until he woke, at least. She longed to get up and get away from him, but it was imperative that he should detect nothing unusual in her behaviour that day. If he woke and found her gone, he'd be alert to any other slight irregularities. And yet to lie here beside him almost amounted to physical torture.

She tried to remember the relaxation techniques she'd learnt in preparation for childbirth. First you tensed all your muscles, and then you let them go slowly, working up from your feet ... Sarah clenched her whole body, feeling her hands curl into talons and the backs of her calves turn into flat plates. She released each toe individually as far as possible, then her insteps, her ankles ... She tried to concentrate, but by the time she'd got as far as her knees the activities of the day had come crowding in and her mind was churning with the cycle of arrangements. Adrian would leave for work at seven fifteen, by which time she'd be dressing the children. She'd just fling her own clothes on and take no trouble, she'd take Gabriel and Hannah to school at a quarter to nine, come back, plonk Thomas in his cot with a pile of toys and indulge herself in a deep scented bath. She'd wash her hair and shave her legs and put on – what? The final decision about that would come later. Mrs Crump was turning up to mind Thomas at a quarter to eleven, at which point Sarah would hop in the car and drive to Pierre Prescott's house where she would proceed to commit adultery for the first time in her life. Then – but she couldn't think coherently beyond that point. Her head swam.

Adrian rolled over and stuck out an arm. His hand brushing against her side was like a branding iron. He grunted comfortably and rolled the other way. This was intolerable. She would have to take the risk. She slid out of bed and, not daring to hunt either for slippers or dressing-gown, slipped out of the door.

She eased the bolt of the back door and lifted the latch. The garden was still in shadow, except for one sharp-edged golden triangle of sunlight. She walked towards it, the cold dew squelching between her bare toes. It was going to be a glorious day. She stood in the sunlit patch in her thin white nightgown, feeling shivers tighten her flesh. A rambling rose scrambled all over the wall at this end; its flowers were of the deepest possible crimson, velvety, almost black. She held one to her face and nuzzled its fragrant folded centre.

The morning passed in bursts. Time seemed to crawl, and then all of a sudden speed up and terrify her with its relentlessness. Adrian got off to work without noticing anything, she thought; the radio was on and Gabriel was cavorting in the kitchen in his pyjamas, and the normal domestic burble provided a screen for her absent-mindedness. She was even a little late getting the children to school, because Hannah's ballet leotard was still damp and had to be given a spin in the tumble dryer. She got home just after nine. Only a couple of hours to go. She tipped some creamy, peachy essence into the bath – a present from Nicola, ages ago – and turned the taps on as hard as they would go to make it all foam up. She laid some clothes out on the bed. She wanted to wear the blue sweater that she'd bought that morning when she'd met Pierre in the precinct because he'd noticed it, but the day was already too hot for it. She remembered she was supposed to be having her photograph taken. Better wear something quite smart then, something Adrian liked. She pulled out a dark blue linen dress, with a plain sleeveless top and a low waist. It made her hair look brighter, and was discreet and unprovocative. It didn't hide the bulge of her stomach, still there despite six weeks' steady weight loss, but Pierre would be seeing that anyway. That was the thing she was most worried about.

She put Thomas in his cot with a beaker of juice and a cardboard box full of toys that squeaked and rattled and squished. She left the doors open so that she could hear him and pulled off her clothes. She paused before getting into the bath to look at herself in the full length bathroom mirror. She ran her hands over her breasts, that had never quite recovered their elasticity after feeding three babies, over her heavy thighs, her buttocks striped with silvery stretch marks. She thought of Claudia Prescott's graceful efficient body cutting through the water as she dived into the swimming pool, and was gripped with doubt. Could it really be true that Pierre found her desirable? And if he did would he still, when all was revealed? She stepped into the bath to comfort herself. Her body always looked better lying in the water.

She was brushing her teeth furiously hard when the telephone rang. It would be bad, she knew – it would be Pierre, telling her he'd changed his mind. She spat and dashed into the bedroom, wrapped in a big pink towel. 'Oh, Sarah? It's Molly Crump here. I'm ever so sorry, dear, but I won't be able to mind Thomas this morning. You see I –'

Sarah could hardly absorb the explanation. She heard herself saying, 'No, that's quite all right, of course I understand. No, don't worry. Really.'

She replaced the receiver. It was ten to ten. There was nobody – simply nobody – whom she could ask to take Thomas at this short notice. She felt the energy drain out of her. She sat, bent-backed, on the edge of the bed, her face in her hands.

A squawk from Thomas roused her. He had thrown every toy out of the cot and had pulled himself up into a standing position from which he couldn't get down. She barely registered that this was the first time he'd ever managed to stand. She looked at him with cold indifference. She'd have to ring Pierre, and cancel.

The thought of a normal, home-based day, playing with Thomas and picking up the children and waiting for Adrian, was simply unendurable. As she crouched on her hands and knees, gathering the fallen toys, she changed her mind. She'd take Thomas with her. At least she'd see Pierre. They could talk. And perhaps Thomas might fall asleep ... She could hardly take the travel cot, but he might curl up on a pile of cushions somewhere. She just couldn't stay at home, not today.

As she drove up to High House her heart was full of misgivings. The wheels scrunched on the deep gravel: she knew Pierre would hear her arrive. She left Thomas in the car as she went to ring the doorbell. The door was opened almost immediately – Pierre stood there, lean and brown in faded blue jeans and an immaculate white shirt, open at the neck, the sleeves rolled up to his elbows. He let his eyes travel up and down her body before he said anything. He smiled slowly. 'Well,' he said, 'ready for action?'

Sarah couldn't return his smile. 'The baby's in the car,' she blurted out. 'The babysitter cancelled.'

A look of acute impatience clouded Pierre's face. He held her by the shoulder and steered her into the house. 'Let's leave him there,' he said, 'just for a little while?' And he ran the back of his hand lightly over her breast.

Sarah shook her head. 'I can't,' she said. 'I can't leave him. I'm sorry, I shouldn't have come. I'll take him home.' But she didn't move.

Pierre turned away and raked through his hair with his fingers. 'No,' he said, without enthusiasm. 'Bring him in.' Sarah still didn't move, frozen with indecision. 'Go on,' said Pierre. 'Bring him in.' He made no attempt to conceal the irritation in his voice.

Sarah opened her mouth, shut it again, and went back to the car. When she came back with Thomas, Pierre was making coffee. 'Well, well,' he said, handing her a mug. 'How are things? Gabriel and Hannah OK?'

They made stilted conversation while they sipped their coffee. How on earth had she imagined that they'd be able to talk? thought Sarah. And why should he want to talk to her, anyway? As he'd said to her at his party, he only wanted one thing. She heard herself asking him if he'd enjoyed his birthday. She could have slapped herself, it was all so fatuous.

Thomas, clingy at first, had relinquished his hold on her knees and was crawling off in pursuit of the dog. 'The dog wouldn't harm him, would he?' asked Sarah. 'I mean, he might pull his tail or something.'

Pierre let out a short laugh. 'Jaques finds it difficult to harm a dog biscuit, let alone a human being.' As the dog waddled out of the kitchen Pierre prodded his sagging belly with his foot, not kindly. His Adam's apple was very prominent. Sarah had never noticed that before. Thomas flapped off into the hall, crowing for the dog, with that odd humping crawl of his that Adrian said was like the way a seal moved. From where she stood Sarah could see that he was safe; she didn't follow him.

Pierre came up close. 'So, am I not going to have my wicked way after all?' he said softly, placing small kisses lightly on her collar bone, her bare shoulder, behind her ear. She shivered, and closed her eyes. She wanted to want him. Now his hands were on her breasts and his mouth was on hers, but she was more aware of the taste of the coffee than anything else. She grasped his hands and pushed him a little away from her, looking up into his face with mute appeal.

For an instant she caught an expression of blind frustration, then his face resolved itself into a sardonic smile. 'I'm sorry,' he purred, entwining his fingers with hers. 'I'm taking advantage. Not very gallant. Now, what about these photographs?'

Photographs! Sarah had forgotten about those. He saw that she had.

'Remember what you're here for?' he said, enjoying her embarrassment. 'Shall I show you my portfolio, and then we can discuss what would suit you.'

She picked up Thomas and followed him into a study that doubled as a spare room, judging by the single divan bed draped with a mauve batik counterpane. The room was cheerless, furnished with imitation pine like a room in a students' hall of residence. She was only just beginning to notice how strangely impersonal the whole house felt. Thomas was beginning to whine; she gave him her car keys to jingle.

Pierre spread manilla folders of different colours on the bed. 'Take a look,' he said. Sarah flipped through a pink folder containing mainly portraits of children, including some of those he'd taken of her own. She made the requisite noises of appreciation, though she found it difficult to pay much attention. A light-green folder held studies of adult heads, mainly women. There didn't seem to be any of Claudia. The women were not all good-looking, by any means, some were quite middle-aged, but Pierre had given them all a similar glamorous, almost Hollywood look, with bare shoulders, dramatic lighting, and heads tipped to one side. Coming to the end of the series, she gasped. Here with hair cascading magnificently and a sideways come-hither look, was Hilary Nightingale, looking a little younger, but unmistakable.

'Oh yes,' said Pierre, leaning over her shoulder, 'Hilary. What do you think?'

'You've made her look – stunning. But it's not very like her.'

'Funny. That's what she said. She didn't like it. I was rather proud of it myself.'

'It's lovely, but it doesn't quite suit her. It's too in-doorsy, or something.'

'Hilary has always found it hard to cope with the fact that she's a highly attractive woman,' said Pierre. 'Now look at these.' He placed a blue folder in her hands.

Sarah had felt a sharp prick of jealousy when he had made that remark about Hilary, but that feeling was soon overwhelmed by the contents of the blue folder. The picture on top was of a naked woman seen from the back. She was kneeling at an open window; her black hair hung like a bell rope down her back. Because the body was in shadow, little detail was visible; the woman's nakedness was veiled by her anonymity. But as Sarah progressed through the photographs the poses became more candid. The pictures weren't exactly pornographic. Women lay on beds, on their stomachs, or held swathes of fabric up to chests, or – in one instance – floated in a pool beneath strategically placed bunches of flowers; a blur of tasteful restraint prevented any more than the roundness of a breast or buttock from being revealed, but nonetheless the fact remained that Sarah held in her hands a dozen or more photographs, all of naked women, posed with considerable care by her would-be lover. And she was next in line.

With a shock she realised that Pierre had left the room. She raced through the photographs again. One thing they all had in common – they were faceless. Faces were shrouded by hair, or curtains, or darkness, or were simply turned away. One could find the odd chin, or ear, or cheekbone, but nothing approaching a whole face. It wasn't even possible to tell how many different sitters there were. It could have been only three or four. As she flicked through the pack again, Sarah realised that she was trying to work out if any of them was Hilary.

A noise distracted her. Thomas, bored with the car keys, was trying to pull himself up by the knobs on the drawers of the desk; a full in-tray was perilously within reach. Sarah shoved the photographs back into their folder and threw them onto the bed. She disengaged Thomas' hot little hands from the desk and draped him, protesting, over her shoulder. Her mind was made up. She wasn't going to join this Bluebeard's gallery.

She stepped out into the corridor just as Pierre emerged from wherever he had been waiting. 'Well?' he said, turning on her the full power of his deep-eyed stare. 'Are you ready?'

She shook her head, and made an awkward noise in her throat. 'They're really good,' she said politely, 'but I don't think – look Pierre, I'm sorry I came. It was foolish of me. Thomas is tired now. I'd better take him home.'

'Another time, then.' Pierre opened the door for her. 'I don't give up easily, Sarah.' He chucked her under the chin, but his look was more vulpine than affectionate. The car had been parked in the full sun and was horribly hot, but it felt like a refuge to Sarah.

'I'll see you then,' she called out cheerily, and eased out of the drive. She tried not to look back.

CHAPTER NINETEEN

Diana Stanhope seemed to recover remarkably well from her mysterious illness, so her telephone call on the Monday after Sarah's encounter with Pierre came as a great surprise. 'Oh, Sarah dear,' she said. 'No need to worry, but I'm to be admitted to hospital this afternoon. I'm in need of a few days' bed rest, it seems. I wondered if you could possibly drop in and help me pack.'

'Of course I will,' said Sarah. 'I've got a couple of hours before I need to pick the children up. I'll have to bring Thomas, I'm afraid.'

'It will be lovely to see him. I could ask Mrs Fairley to help, but one doesn't like to have someone like that investigating one's things, if you understand me.'

'Absolutely. I'll be right over.'

In the car, Sarah smiled to herself as she thought about the barrel-shaped Mrs Fairley 'investigating' Diana's possessions. Mrs Fairley had cleaned for Diana for at least thirty years; any urge to garner intimate knowledge of her employer must long ago have been satisfied. In any case, it was not possible to associate Mrs Fairley, with her swollen ankles and brown acrylic cardigans and broad, placid features, with curiosity of any kind. Mrs Fairley was a systematic and reliable cleaner, but she had always reminded Sarah of a root vegetable. Her mother-in-law was just a bit of a snob, she thought, wanting to keep the servants in their place.

She wondered about Diana's real state of health. She must have called out the doctor herself; this was unique, as far as Sarah could remember, so presumably indicated genuine anxiety. But her voice on the telephone had sounded firm and calm – stronger than it had been a few days ago. For some years the older woman had been prone to a series of ailments that had never been fully explained. Sarah couldn't help noticing how Diana's symptoms were always lady-like ones – palpitations, giddy turns, breathlessness – though she'd never pointed this out to anyone else, aware that it was a somewhat mean-spirited observation.

Diana dangled beads in front of Thomas while Sarah filled a small leather suitcase for her. 'What made you decide to call the doctor?' Sarah asked. 'We had so hoped you were getting better.'

'It's this breathlessness, dear. The stairs are a real effort, now, which shouldn't be the case at my time of life. I've changed my doctor – did I tell you? As you know I've never been satisfied with the West Street practice, so at Adrian's suggestion I've put myself on your GP's list.'

'Dr Maxwell? She's excellent – but I thought you didn't like being treated by a woman.'

'No, not Dr Maxwell. Dr Prescott. Adrian told me you knew him socially.'

Sarah bent over the little suitcase. She could feel her mother-in-law's eyes boring into the back of her skull. She didn't trust herself to say anything.

'Adrian told me you all went to his birthday party. He told me he had offered to take your photograph, Sarah.'

'That's right. What about a hand towel?'

'I think so, yes. Not one of the best, in case it gets mislaid in the hospital laundry. You'll find a pale blue one in the airing cupboard.'

Sarah escaped to the corridor where the airing cupboard was. She pulled out the towel and pressed its warm, fluffy surface against her flaming cheeks. Somehow, Diana had guessed about Pierre. She never made idle conversation. All these comments had a purpose behind them. Ironic, since in a sense nothing had happened. She returned to the bedroom.

'Has he done it, dear?'

'Has he – ?'

'Has Dr Prescott taken your photograph yet?'

'Not yet. My appointment was on Thursday, but the light wasn't right, so it's been postponed.'

'It was a very sunny day on Thursday.'

'Yes, I think it was too bright or something.'

'How peculiar. I thought that these modern cameras could cope with anything.'

Sarah was seething. 'Apparently not. What about your sponge-bag?'

'It's packed and ready, next to the bath. Dr Prescott called on me last night, Sarah. He told me that the reason he had failed to take the photographs was because his camera was broken.'

Sarah paused, sponge-bag in hand. She decided to take the bull by the horns.

'If you already knew about the photography business from Dr Prescott, then why did you ask me?'

Diana didn't even attempt to answer. Her calm effrontery was just incredible, thought Sarah.

'Here, dear, I think you'd better take Thomas. He may have filled his nappy. Thank you so much for helping me. The hospital car is calling for me at three, so there's no need for you to stay.'

'Fine.' Sarah scooped up the malodorous Thomas. 'I'll put the suitcase by the door and one or other of us will call on you this evening.'

Sarah was brimful of impotent fury. She couldn't trust herself to drive. Once out of sight she pulled into a lay-by and wiped the hot tears from her cheeks. 'Damn her!' she whispered, smacking the steering wheel with the flat of her hand. 'Oh, damn and blast her to hell!' That woman was such an enigma. Was it possible she'd have said anything to Adrian?

Sarah rang Adrian at the office and he made a brief visit to the hospital, St Swithin's, on his way back from work.

'She's given me a message for you,' he told Sarah later. 'Wants you to pick up some more things for her.' Anticipating Sarah's annoyance, he added, 'I offered to do it, but she made out they were articles not fit for masculine eyes. You know what she's like.'

Sarah managed a natural-sounding laugh. 'I'll go over there after supper, then, shall I? Then I can drop them in tomorrow morning. If I've got to rummage around I'd rather do it tonight, without Thomas' help.'

'Sure, whatever you like. Here's the key, and here's the note she wrote.'

It would not have been difficult to carry out Diana's orders the following morning, Thomas or no Thomas, but Sarah seized at the chance of being alone. She had spent the whole weekend trying to be unaffectedly nice to Adrian, and she was beginning to feel the strain. She made a simple supper – grilled chops and salad. She bolted it quickly. 'Don't clear the dishes,' Adrian said, 'I'll do that.'

The evening was very, very still. Letting herself into March House was exciting; she could almost hear her heart beating. Despite the legitimacy of her purpose, Sarah felt like an intruder. 'Mrs Fairley?' she called out, to make sure, but as she expected she was alone.

She stood in the hall for a few moments, breathing in the characteristic aroma of lavender and floor polish and wood smoke – faintly there, even in June. She decided to poke her nose into each of the downstairs rooms before going up to the bedroom, but each door was locked. Locked against me, thought Sarah; she can read my mind. On the wall in the front hall, above a barometer, hung the mask of a fox, mounted on dark wood. Adrian's father had been a sportsman. In the twilight its grin unnerved her. She consulted her note, and climbed the stairs.

'Dear Sarah,' the note read. 'I have foolishly forgotten my tissues and my cold cream. It would be so sweet of you to pick them up. They are in the left-hand drawer of my dressing table. No hurry – I can manage without until Tuesday. With love, Diana.' No one else, thought Sarah, would regard going without tissues and cold cream for one night as anything of a sacrifice.

On an impulse, she tried the upstairs doors as well. Every single one was locked, except the door to Diana's own bedroom. She's controlling me, thought Sarah, fascinated as well as horrified. There's more to this than tissues and cold cream. The heavy bedroom door clicked behind her and made her jump.

She pulled out the drawer of the dressing table, as requested. The required articles were not there. There was nothing in the drawer at all except a thick leatherbound notebook. Sarah picked it up. On the first page was written 'Diana Constance Stanhope. Household notes.' Then nothing for a couple of pages, and then the narrative began.

'September 16th. So sad to take little Adrian back to school! He tried to hide his distress, brave little chap. So glad I had David with me, to help me bear up.'

So far, so predictable. Sarah was irritated by the superficiality of the writer's reaction to her little boy's grief, but at least she had registered some response. She read on.

'September 21st. Caught the 8.26 to Charing Cross. David met me at the station. Water colour exhibition at the Royal Academy, then lunch in Fortnum's. Five blissful hours.'

Sarah was surprised. This expression of rapture at a day out with her husband didn't tally with what little she knew of Diana's marriage. Then the truth came to her with a jolt that made her gasp out loud. Adrian's father hadn't been David. He had been Robert. Robert Thomas Stanhope. She was reading about an extra-marital affair.

'October 1st. My birthday. An enormous bouquet arrived, from David of course. All in the most marvellous autumnal hints. Robert was at the office when it came, thank heavens, but I took the precaution of dividing it into four or five smaller bunches and placing them at intervals throughout the house. If R. notices them at all he'll think they came from the garden. He knows nothing about flowers. But I really must ask D. to be more discreet.

'October 20th. I threw away the last of my birthday flowers today. They have lasted wonderfully well. I have to confess I have pressed one or two of the loveliest between the pages of my prayer book.

'The weather is cold and wet, and there is no prospect of seeing D. for at least another week. Robert is out of sorts, complaining of pains in his chest and arms. He is growing old before his time. I feel as trapped and restless as a caged tigress, but what can I do?

'November 11th. I slipped away to London, on the pretext that I wanted to watch the Armistice Day ceremony in memory of my father. I told R. that I needed to go alone, to grieve in private, but I do not think his health would have allowed him to go in any case. Of course, the Armistice had nothing to do with anything. David whisked me off to a little hotel in Bloomsbury and ... well, I'm still shaking like a leaf. I never felt this way about Robert, not even when we were first engaged.

'D. says he loves me. He says he'll leave Clarissa if I'll leave Robert, but how can I, with Adrian to consider? David, being childless, doesn't understand the difficulty.

'I have asked myself, do I feel guilty, using my dead father's memory as a kind of alibi, but I have to say no, I do not. Love overcomes all such considerations, it would seem.'

Sarah paused in her reading. She felt guilt, shame, disgust, excitement, and the mixture made her feel physically sick. She closed her eyes and felt the blood spinning in her head. Her mother-in-law was holding a mirror up to her, to force her to observe her own behaviour, and she didn't like what she saw. Still, she knew she must carry on to the end.

'November 23rd. R. has seen the heart specialist. He is not to think of returning to work until the New Year at the earliest. In the meantime he is to rest as much as possible. My feelings of despair at this news are hard to describe. I will be confined to the house for six weeks or more with Robert. Seeing David will be virtually impossible.

'3rd December. A letter! Like a shaft of light breaking through the gloom that shrouds my life. David suggests visiting me here on the 6th. I am to tell Robert that he was passing through Barcombe and dropped in on the off-chance. We will not be alone for long, but anything is better than nothing.

'R. is far from well. He is a patient invalid, I must admit – and I am a very impatient nurse.

'6th December. He came. R. was resting upstairs. Mrs Fairley was in the kitchen. I ordered coffee, and until it arrived we chatted about this and that. Then I told Mrs F. that she could go early – I don't care what she surmises – and as soon as we heard the door shut we fell into each other's arms. Now he is gone I do feel some guilt, but when he is with me I am as weak as water.

'26th December. Christmas was a torment. I put on a brave face, for the sake of Adrian, but the effort was tremendous. We ate lunch on trays by the fire; R. is too weak to sit at table for long. I have to face the fact that he might not recover. Moreover, I have to accept that part of me desires his death. What kind of monster have I become?

'Adrian was excited about his presents, of course. I, too, was excited about one of mine – a tiny heart-shaped locket, beautifully wrought on a silver filigree chain, that arrived from David. He had packed it with a Christmas pudding, and marked the parcel "Urgent – perishable," so that R., if he saw it, would think it was something I had ordered. So clever! I cannot wear it, of course, but I look at it and touch it almost hourly.

'2nd January. I can stand it no longer. I have asked Mrs Fairley to spend the whole day here tomorrow, to look after Adrian and Robert while I go shopping in the Sales. Ironically, Clarissa really *is* going to the Sales, so I can meet David at their flat. I know I'm sailing close to the wind, but I don't seem to be able to help myself. And I always prided myself on my self control!'

Yes indeed, thought Sarah. She could hardly reconcile the passionate risk-taker revealed in these pages with the reserved, judgmental eccentric Diana had become.

'4th January. It is all over — everything. The plan went like clockwork. I met D. at the flat — we walked in the frozen park, lunched early and spent the afternoon in a hotel — Claridges, of all places! And I caught the five-fifteen train, to be in time for Adrian's bedtime, and my heart was dancing. And when I reached home I saw that Mrs Fairley had closed all the shutters, and I was seized by a terrible premonition. Mrs Fairley met me at the door, and told me that Robert was dead. She had not been able to contact me of course. It had happened at three o'clock, at the very time when … Adrian had not been told. Mrs F. had managed very well, keeping him playing quietly in his bedroom.

'Why am I writing all this? I spent the night sitting next to Robert, holding his cold hand.'

Sarah found tears running down her cheeks. She laid the notebook aside and wiped her face, anxious that no drops should fall and smudge Diana's narrative, of which little more remained.

'January 23rd. I am still consumed with grief and shame. I had resolved to let David know that I would no longer see him, but as it turns out there was no need. Once he heard of R.'s death that was that. He has melted away as if he had never been. This afternoon I took the locket he gave me and flung it into the centre of the pond. From now on, Adrian is my life. I shall have nothing more to do with men.'

And there the story ended. Diana had scored a line in thick black ink after the final entry, and had placed her initials, D.C.S., beneath. But below that, in green, were the letters P.T.O. Sarah turned the page.

'Sarah,' the message read, 'the tissues and cold cream are on the bathroom shelf. If you bring them to me, I shall know that all is well.'

Sarah walked over to the window, notebook in hand. She gazed out at the sleeping garden, at the dark pond, verged by rhododendrons now at the height of their glory. As she watched, one of the trumpet-like blossoms, of the richest possible magenta, detached itself and fell onto the viscous surface of the water. It described a circle slowly and then came to rest; there was no breeze, and it was too light to sink. Somewhere in that pond Diana's locket must still lie, thought Sarah. She tried to imagine its cold glitter in the shifting shadows, and wondered if Diana ever stood and stared at the spot as she, Sarah, was staring now.

She felt in her cardigan pocket and found a stumpy red crayon, picked up off the kitchen floor that afternoon. She opened Diana's notebook, and beneath Diana's message to her she wrote 'Adrian is out of danger. Thank you. S.' Then she replaced the notebook, closed the drawer, and went into the bathroom to fetch the tissues and the cold cream.

She drove home in a daze. When she reached the house on Maiden's Hill Adrian opened the door to her. 'At last!' he cried. 'I was beginning to worry.' Sarah smiled weakly and allowed him to embrace her. 'It's such a beautiful evening,' she replied, 'I walked in the garden for a bit. Children all right?'

'Not a peep. Come and have a drink.'

'I'll take it upstairs. I'm longing for a bath and an early bed.' She pecked him on the cheek.

Sarah didn't want or need a bath, she needed and wanted a locked door. As she lay in the hot water, sipping the whiskey Adrian had poured for her, she found tears scalding her cheeks. She knew she could no longer betray her husband.

'Oh thank you, nurse. I'm sorry to be so much trouble.' Naomi Randall sipped at the cup of tea the nurse held steady for her. It was maddening, but sometimes she didn't feel strong enough to lift the cup without slopping it everywhere, and she did so hate to make a mess. It came and went, this feeling. For an hour at a time, or sometimes even longer, she'd feel like her old self, and even think about asking to go home. Then the pain would return with renewed vigour, and fighting it would take every scrap of her strength, and afterwards she'd lie under the blanket panting and limp like a newborn rabbit.

She lowered herself back down onto the pillow, and smiled a refusal at the plump young nurse who was offering her a Rich Tea biscuit. She had no appetite at all any more. Drinking was easier than eating, so she made efforts with Ovaltine and a kind of protein-enriched fruit juice that came in one of those fiddly little cartons; she could manage that, though it left a metallic taste in her mouth. But with main meals all she could do was stir the food up a little to make it look as though she'd had some. She hoped the nurses weren't offended.

Lying back on the huge pillows now, feeling as comfortable as she was ever likely to, she ran her mind back over food from the past, hoping to stir some faint desire for it. In her early childhood, everything was white – white bread and butter, white sauce cloaking repulsive grey fish skin, white boiled potatoes. Mugs of milk. And on special days, hundreds and thousands sprinkled on the bread, some sticking in the butter, spreading tiny rings of colour, others bouncing off onto the white china plate. Herself licking a finger so as to scoop up the fallen ones, and an adult voice telling her that Mr Manners would never do a thing like that. Then the war – butter disappearing, and endless bottled fruit, and beef dripping from Australia sent in silvery tins. They wouldn't bother to do that now, she thought. Importing dripping just wouldn't be a priority. Like all those powdered eggs – we'd just do without, now. Funny how things change.

She'd never been more than a middling cook, herself. She thought about the early years of her marriage, in the fifties, and the efforts she'd made at first to provide Harold with something tasty and nourishing every evening; how she'd pored over the recipe book and laid out all the utensils hours in advance to make sure nothing would go wrong, and then how one day the cooker had broken down and she hadn't been able to get it fixed in time so she'd bought a Walls pork pie and served it up with a quartered tomato and many apologies to Harold, and he'd tucked into it with delight and eaten every scrap, even the pale jelly in the corners. Then he'd beamed at her and said, 'What a treat,' and she'd never taken quite so much trouble over cooking after that, certainly never bothered with anything like choux pastry or clear soup, anyway. Food had never meant very much to her personally, but if she'd had a growing boy to cook for ... she'd daydreamed about it often. How the Peter of her imagination would come home from school and fling the door open. 'I'm starving, Mum,' he'd say, dumping his muddy games kit on the floor, and putting his arms round her waist and his head against her chest. And she'd reprimand him gently and tell him to sit at the table and she'd ladle out a giant helping of meaty stew and dumplings … but in reality little Peter had never taken any nourishment at all. He had been too weak to suck. She thought of her breasts in the days that followed, rock hard and burning to the touch, until the pills began to work that made the milk go away. Tears slid from under her tired lids. That was all right; tears eased the pain.

Claudia moved quietly through the ward. Her mother was often dozing when she visited, and she always brought a book with her, so that she could sit and read until she woke. She often thought of her own infancy, and her mother sitting patiently by the side of her cot in those warm, blank, unremembered days, much as she would sit now. But today though the eyes were shut the breathing was not even, and tracks of moisture were clearly visible on the folded, faded cheeks. Claudia stood motionless for a few seconds, looking down, swallowing hard. 'Mother,' she said, 'I'm here.'

Naomi opened her eyes. 'Claudia,' she said, 'you're a good girl.' She struggled to raise herself, but Claudia held her lightly by the shoulders and settled her back down. It felt like holding a metal bedstead, or the back of a chair. There just wasn't any flesh left.

Claudia sat on the chair next to the bed. She smoothed her mother's pillows and straightened the blankets. Naomi's hooked hand scrabbled for hers; the touch of it was horrible, but she tried not to flinch. The eyes that were like black holes sought to hold and arrest her own; she was glad of the slight barrier her spectacles provided. She knew, instinctively, that everything had changed, that her mother had to tell her something, that a lifetime's habit of reticence had to be broken.

'Claudia,' said the pale whispering voice, 'I need to talk to you about something.' I could lay this ghost, thought Claudia, I could lay it to rest while it is still living. She pressed the tiny, terrible hand. 'Don't tell me yet,' she said softly, 'because I've got some news for you, Mum. I might be – we're going to – I think I'm – yes I am. You're going to be a grandmother.' With one last gentle squeeze, she withdrew her hand, and tweaked at the flowers on the bedside stand, pulling out a couple that had withered. 'Next

February,' she said, her voice matter-of-fact. 'Early February. What do you think of that?'

The sound from the bed was like the release of a long held breath. Claudia couldn't look. 'Oh darling,' she heard her mother say. 'Oh my darling.'

'I'll pop in tomorrow,' said Claudia, 'in the evening. I can't stay now – I'm only on a double free period. Pierre'll come by later, I expect. See you, Mum.'

Outside the hospital, Sarah saw Claudia out of the corner of her eye. She had Thomas on her hip, and her car keys in her mouth; she ducked her head slightly so that Claudia wouldn't think she'd noticed her. But such a precaution was unnecessary; when Sarah, just inside the glass door of the hospital, sneaked a look back, she saw Claudia break into a stumbling run. Various explanations popped into Sarah's head, but she dismissed them all for now. She had to concentrate on her interview with Diana.

The older Mrs Stanhope sat bolt upright in bed, doing nothing but watching. She was three beds along from Naomi Randall and on the opposite side of the ward, but even from that distance she could see that that unfortunate woman would not be there for long. Diana rather resented being in the same ward with people who were dying. Her bed was next to the wall, which pleased her; she had only one neighbour, a whiskery old woman who could spend, it seemed, a whole morning on a single copy of the *TV Times*. The bed opposite was empty; she had a view of the hospital garden, strangely flowerless even in June. People would be wheeled out there, sometimes, looking small and exposed in their night-clothes. She was glad she had a decent bedjacket; not many people did.

She saw her daughter-in-law at the end of the ward. Sarah was holding a plastic carrier bag as well as the baby. Diana knew what was in the bag, and was pleased. She liked to know things in advance, so she could prepare accordingly. She set her face into a smile that was meant to be both knowing and welcoming, and waited.

Sarah walked the length of the ward slowly, feeling like a fish on the end of a line being reeled in. Every step she took felt like a step away from Pierre. She imagined him as a figure on a station platform, growing smaller every second as the train gathered speed. Her throat was choked with self-pity. She avoided looking at Diana as she sat down next to the bed, trying to contain the wriggling Thomas in her lap.

'How are you?' she said. 'You're looking well.' Indeed, compared to the apathetic bundles in the other beds, Diana looked the picture of health.

'Much rested, thank you, dear,' replied Diana. 'Various tests have to be carried out, it seems – I'm not to eat anything for the next few hours, but hospital food being what it is the deprivation is not enormous.' She held out her hand to Thomas, who loved to practise his pincer movement with the prominent diamond on her engagement ring. She said nothing more. She wants me to make the running, thought Sarah bitterly. The feelings of admiration, even gratitude, she had had for her mother-in-law the night before had hardened in the light of day to a sulky resentment of the older woman's perspicacity and cunning.

'Well,' she said, 'I can't stay long. I just popped in to bring you your things. I brought them, you see.' She glanced at Diana's face, and was almost alarmed by the sharp enquiry in the bright old eyes. 'Where would you like me to put them?'

'In that little drawer in the locker, please, Sarah. The handkerchiefs to the left, and the cold cream to the right, within easy reach. Did you find them without any – trouble?'

'I found them,' said Sarah, grimly. 'I found them.' But Diana just held her head to one side. That look of enquiry would not go away. She tried again. 'I found them. But it took me a long time. All evening, in fact.' She drew a deep breath. 'It's Adrian's birthday in a couple of weeks, isn't it? I want to get him something really nice. What do you think he would like?'

The birdlike head relaxed a little, the expression softened. 'You're the best judge of that, my dear. I have already ordered him an ornithologist's encyclopaedia. You know how he has always been interested in birds.'

Or was when he was twelve, thought Sarah. She suppressed a smile. 'I think I'll get him something a little more romantic. I'd better go now, Thomas is getting restless. He needs a nap.' She rose to her feet.

'Come closer, Sarah,' Diana said, unexpectedly. 'Bend your head.' She held Sarah's face between her hands and with slow deliberation planted a kiss on her forehead. 'How lucky you are,' she said, 'to have such a marvellous complexion. Thank you for bringing my things.'

Naomi Randall, fully awake now, had been watching the encounter with interest. She could overhear nothing of the conversation, and wasn't trying to. What she was trying to do was to establish whether the girl with the thick light-coloured hair was the same as the one who had aroused her anxiety at Pierre's birthday – an anxiety now well and truly assuaged. The baby was the right age, but she hadn't felt certain until she had seen the girl run her fingers through her hair to stop it from hanging in her eyes, a gesture that struck her as wholly characteristic. It wasn't in Naomi's nature to address a stranger, but Claudia's news had given her new courage. 'Excuse me,' she said, as loudly as she could, when Sarah passed the foot of her bed, 'excuse me.'

Sarah looked up, her face a mask of preoccupation. She didn't recognise the tiny, simian creature propped on the stiff white pillow.

'Excuse me, but don't you know my daughter, Claudia Prescott?'

Sarah reddened, as she acknowledged the fact, but Naomi was too intent to notice.

'I wonder whether you would mind doing me a favour?' the old woman continued. 'It's a terrible imposition, but I need something, and I don't know who to ask.'

Sarah came closer. She thought the request might be something intimate and embarrassing, and the poor old woman wouldn't want the whole ward to know. It was possible Claudia's mother was senile. She smiled as kindly as she could.

'Could you possibly buy me six balls of white wool and a pair of knitting needles? It may seem a very odd request but – the thing is I'm going to be a grandmother, and I just don't know who else to ask.'

'Of course I will!' Sarah cried. 'What wonderful news. I'll be visiting the hospital every day while my mother-in-law's here, so it won't be any trouble at all.'

'Thank you so much, you are too kind.' Naomi's voice trembled. 'You'll find my purse in the drawer –'

'Don't worry about the money,' said Sarah, and then realising that not being allowed to pay would only increase the anxiety she added, 'I'll keep the receipt, and we can sort it out then.'

Naomi's smile was beatific. 'It really is so sweet of you. I've always considered that Claudia is blessed in her friends.'

'Six balls, you said? I'll bring it all tomorrow.' Sarah hurried from the ward, consumed with guilt and shame. Naomi slipped a little down the pillow and turned to one side. She felt peace descend on her like a soft blanket. Curled up like that, the old woman looked hardly bigger than a sleeping baby.

Sarah walked automatically towards her car, but when she reached it the idea of clambering into its sealed stuffiness was intolerable. She hoicked the push-chair out of the boot and belted Thomas in; he could have his nap just as easily like that. She wheeled him out of the car park and turned left; she didn't know where she was going but to go right would lead eventually to Dinsford town centre, which seemed undesirable. She saw a patch of greenery about a hundred yards ahead. Perhaps she could sit there for a while and sort out the untidy rummage of emotions inside her head.

The patch turned out to be an overgrown churchyard. The smart new hospital, on the outskirts of Dinsford, had sliced in half a neighbourhood that had been an ancient village, and which still liked to think of itself as something other than just a part of Dinsford's suburban sprawl. Little remained beside a few cottages of crumbling rosy brick sandwiched between the newer stuccoed villas, and the White Hart Inn, which retained its thick walls and tiny windows at the front, but which had had a bunker-like structure grafted onto its back to accommodate a pool table and family dining area. Just beyond the pub, set back from the road, was the tiny mediaeval church, a shy huddle of grey stone, squatting in the rush of mid-June luxuriance. Sarah pushed the buggy up the bumpy path into the churchyard. Thomas' eyelids drooped.

She parked him in a shady corner, kicking on the brakes after giving a few more gentle rocks to make sure that he was properly asleep. She looked round for somewhere to sit. Grey tombstones streaked green with damp or rosetted with lichen the colour of egg-yolk leaned at odd angles; some had fallen flat, and no attempt had been made to right them. The long grass filled with dogdaisies and purple vetch provided the only ornament for most graves but one or two were kept up, ornamented with green glass domes, rusty chrysanthemums and brown-tinged carnations stuck into their little holes. Sarah saw a wooden bench against the ivy-covered wall. A little metal plate stated by whose generosity it had been provided. 'Thank you, Muriel Steadman,' thought Sarah, sweeping leaves and ants and dried bird droppings from it so that she could sit down.

It was noon now, and the sun drained the colours from the flowers and simplified everything to a pattern of light and dark patches. Sarah, elbows on knees, propped her face between her hands and stared unseeing at the mossy brick path at her feet. I've done it now, she thought. No more adulterous dabblings. Back to the straight and narrow; if my children come to any harm, no one will be able to say it's because of me.

So Claudia was pregnant after all! The old woman's request could only mean one thing. Sarah knew, somehow – from Hilary presumably – that Mrs Randall had no other children. That meant that relations between Pierre and his wife could not have been as frosty as Sarah had supposed, or hoped. She had no real basis for making such assumptions; she certainly had no right to this painful new feeling of being let down by Pierre.

An ant, shouldering something pale, crawled over the toe of Sarah's sandal. Suddenly noticing it, she looked more closely. That was a grain of rice it was carrying. Where on earth could it have found a grain of rice? Behind this first ant crept another similarly burdened. And another, and another. Intrigued, Sarah got up and followed the trail to its source, in front of the church porch. Here a few discs of coloured paper lay on the flagstones, with more grains of rice scattered between them. Of course! A wedding! Sarah bent down to look at the caravan of insects, dragging the heavy grains to some distant larder. She was at once moved and depressed by their single-minded determination.

The sound of a sob aroused her. She looked quickly at Thomas, even though it didn't sound like him – and sure enough, he slumbered on, in the shade of the antique yew tree in the corner of the graveyard. The sound came again; a kind of coughing cry, strained and painful. Sarah moved cautiously into the porch, and there, on the wooden-slatted seat where the bellrope hung, sat Claudia Prescott, her hands over her face.

Sarah's first instinct was to slip away unnoticed, but at that very moment Claudia raised her blotched face, saw Sarah and said, 'Oh.' Her spectacles lay beside her on the seat. She wiped her eyes with the back of her hand and put them on.

'I'm terribly sorry,' faltered Sarah, 'I didn't know you were here. I saw you coming out of the hospital, but –' Claudia stared at her, struggling to regain composure. She looked tiny, somehow, in the shadowy porch; shrunken and lost and old. 'Look,' said Sarah, 'I'm not going to say "Is anything the matter?" because obviously quite a lot is. And you've nothing to lose by telling me about it.' Amazed at her own daring, she sat down next to Claudia and put an arm firmly round the narrow shoulders.

Claudia stiffened momentarily, as if to reject the comfort, and then collapsed, leaning against Sarah and weeping bitterly. 'I can't – I can't –' was all she could say. Sarah soothed her and sshhed her as if she were a frightened child.

When the rasping sobs had quieted a little, Sarah started to talk. 'I'm going to tell you what I think's the matter,' she said, 'and then you can tell me if I'm totally wrong. OK? You went to see your mother in hospital this morning. I know it's your mother because she recognised me. And you told her you were going to have a baby. And you're frightened that she won't live until it's born. That's it, isn't it? And it's awfully, awfully sad about your mother, but it's brilliant news about the baby.' She gave Claudia a tighter squeeze.

Claudia shifted her position and looked at Sarah for the first time. She had almost regained her composure. 'You're nearly right,' she said. 'My mother is dying, yes, but I'm not pregnant. I'm never likely to be.'

'Oh God,' said Sarah, 'I've said so much the wrong thing. I thought – you see your mother told me –'

'I know, I know. No, she's not senile. I told her I was. I wanted her to die happy. It was stupid, wasn't it? Now I'll be living a lie.'

Sarah moved back a little, and looked at the upright, resolute figure beside her in silence for a little while. Then she said slowly, 'It wasn't stupid. It was heroic. It was entirely the right thing to do.'

'Thank you,' said Claudia. Her voice was firm and clear again. 'Thank you, Sarah. That makes me feel better.' She smiled wanly. 'I'm glad you found me,' she said.

Sarah awkwardly patted the pale long-fingered hand, unadorned except for a smooth gold wedding ring. 'It's difficult for someone like me to understand,' she said. 'I mean, I never had any trouble getting pregnant. But I have tried to imagine what it must be like. A friend of mine in London had all that IVF treatment, she said it was horrendous. I suppose you've been through all that.'

Claudia shook her head. 'No, no, I haven't.'

'Oh – but couldn't you? I mean, I know it's very expensive, but – oh dear, I'm getting this all wrong.'

'Don't worry. I know what you're trying to say. But IVF treatment wouldn't help us. You see, it's not me that's infertile.' Claudia twisted the dull gold band round and round her finger. 'I've never told anyone that before. I wonder why I'm telling you now.'

Sarah said nothing. It took a little while to assimilate this information, and all its implications. From where had she gained her certainty that Pierre had sacrificed his chance of fatherhood for the sake of his barren, sour-tempered wife? From those old women at the swimming pool, from Hilary, from Pierre himself. And now she had to replace her treasured image of a handsome, generous, uncomplaining hero looking elsewhere for the love and understanding which he lacked at home, with a new idea of an insecure philanderer with a folder of dirty pictures who was happy to allow the world in general to hold Claudia responsible for their miserable childlessness.

'You mean,' she said carefully, 'that you could have children with someone else?'

'Presumably,' replied Claudia. 'We had all the tests years ago. I was clear, as far as they could tell, but with Pierre there wasn't a sperm in sight. And there's nothing they can do about that.' Her tone was matter-of-fact, with no trace of rancour.

'But,' said Sarah, 'why does everyone think it's you who can't – I mean, even Hilary –' she stopped. 'Oh Christ, I shouldn't have said that.'

Claudia gave a crooked smile. 'It's not news to me. I know what everyone thinks, and I'm happy for them to think that way.

Pierre's very insecure you know, and he couldn't stand it if people knew. You know what men are like when it comes to their precious manhood.'

'What about donor sperm – what's it called, AI?' asked Sarah, scrabbling for practicalities. 'Or adoption. I know it's difficult these days, but we know a couple who –'

Claudia shook her head. 'Pierre wouldn't consider raising a child who wasn't genetically his,' she said sadly. 'He's got a thing about his bloody genes. He won't even discuss other options. It's a closed subject.'

'But what about you and your precious womanhood?' Sarah was angry now. 'Don't you have a right?'

'What kind of right would that be?'

'Oh I don't know – the right not to be misjudged.'

Claudia pondered for a moment. 'I suppose truth isn't always the most important thing.'

'You're so strong. Doing it all to protect his ego. I couldn't manage.'

'Don't think of me as some sort of martyr,' said Claudia. 'Yes, I am strong, but I'm arrogant about my strength too. And I patronise Pierre. It's a sin of pride, I think. And after all, it's not Pierre's fault.'

Above their heads, they heard the wheeze of rusty machinery, and the church clock struck the hour. A pair of doves fluttered out of the spire, alarmed, blindingly white against the sapphire sky. Claudia sprang to her feet. 'Is that the time? I have to be back at school. I'm teaching again straight after lunch.'

'I could ring up and make an excuse for you,' suggested Sarah. 'I shouldn't think you feel like teaching now.'

'Thanks, it's kind of you, but I'll be fine. I'm always fine when I'm at work. It keeps the lid on things.'

Sarah rose too. She had been agonising as to whether to tell Claudia the truth about Pierre. There was the danger of having her motives misinterpreted, but if Claudia was intending to waste the rest of her life with this monster of hypocrisy, then she ought to know the facts. She had to say it now, seize the moment. Claudia was about to slip away, and she knew she'd never find the courage again.

'Claudia,' she said, looking straight at the older woman, her cheeks burning, 'there's something I ought to tell you.' Her mouth twitched, and she couldn't go on.

Claudia gave her a level, appraising stare. 'Just now,' she said, 'you did the talking for me, because I couldn't. Well, now I'll do the talking for you, because I know what you want to tell me. Pierre's tried it on with you, hasn't he?'

Sarah nodded, dumbfounded.

'But it hasn't happened yet, has it? It rarely does, you see. The journey not the arrival matters for Pierre.'

'Actually,' said Sarah, a little nettled, 'it was me who called it off, not him.'

'Oh really?' Claudia's tone was almost indulgent. 'He must like you quite a lot, then. I can see why, too.'

'But don't you care?' burst out Sarah. 'It's not *funny*. I mean, don't you care about anything he does? How can you be so – detached?' Her anger had switched from Pierre to Claudia, almost.

'On one level, I care very much,' said Claudia, 'but on another, I can't afford to. It would wear me out. I know what Pierre gets up to, but I know why he does it too. *Tout comprendre, c'est tout pardonner.* Isn't that right?'

'But why should you forgive him?'

'Because I love him.'

'But love isn't the answer to everything.'

'No, it's not, but it'll have to do.' Claudia smoothed the wrinkles out of her skirt and hoisted up her shoulder bag which had lain unnoticed in the shadows. 'I have to go now. But thank you for telling me, Sarah. I really appreciate what you were trying to do but the fact is, no one ever knows what's going on inside a marriage except the couple themselves.'

'Please forgive me,' said Sarah. 'I wouldn't have done it if I'd known you properly. Not that I really did much –'

Claudia let out a distinct chuckle. 'Stop it, stop it,' she cried. 'Don't embarrass yourself with details that I don't need to know. Whatever it was, or wasn't, it's over now. Hang on – haven't you forgotten something?' She pointed to the corner of the church-yard where Thomas still obligingly slept.

'Oh my God!' Sarah exclaimed. 'I almost had forgotten, you know. My memory started to go after Hannah was born, and after three of them it's totally shot to pieces.' She stopped herself. 'I'm so sorry. It's inexcusable to talk about babies to you.'

'It would be artificial not to talk about them, seeing as they're there. And I'm training myself not to mind.' Claudia walked over to the buggy and peered short-sightedly at its small occupant. 'He's quite sweet, isn't he? I like their veiny eyelids.' She put out a forefinger and stroked the back of his curled fist. Sarah pushed off the brakes and the two women walked down the sunlit path together.

By the time Claudia got back to the Abbey School all traces of her tears had disappeared and her face had resumed its normal even pallor. She had only five minutes left before the end of lunch break; just time to dash to the Ladies, put a comb through her hair, gather up her pile of worksheets and arrive, as usual, precisely on time for her class of first years. She put them swiftly through some grammar exercises, set them a comprehension passage for prep, then moved on to the lower sixth class and quizzed them on *Paradise Lost* with a relentlessness that left no room for discussion or distraction. It was only during the last period of the day, when Claudia was pacing the cool, hushed hall invigilating an A-level exam, that she remembered that Pierre would certainly visit her mother before long. She would have to tell him about her deception.

She had a rehearsal after school. But Pierre wouldn't be home until half past six anyway. She remembered their brief conversation at breakfast, when Pierre had offered to cook supper, since she was so busy. She'd accepted, ungraciously, as usual. Breakfast-time was like a twenty-year-old memory now; she seemed to have entered another life.

She completed her circuit of the hall and propped herself against the raised platform at the front, a few feet away from the front row of examinees. The heads were bent low over the desks, pens whispered across the papers, hay fever sufferers gasped into tissues, mints were unwrapped and sucked. The little noises seemed to weave together and create their own kind of silence, intensified by the foggy beat of the clock. A girl very near her raised her head, scraped back her fine, dull brown hair, and stared at Claudia with blind, blurred eyes. Then she let her hair flop back again and resumed her writing. And Claudia felt her throat constrict as she understood how deeply she longed for a daughter, how she wished, some day, to have her own stake in some distant examination hall, how she wanted, when she was shrunken and old, slipping down the pillows in some future hospital, to have someone of her own to sit by her bedside and touch her hand, however awkwardly, however reluctantly.

An arm was waving at the back of the hall. Somebody wanted more paper. Claudia swallowed and blinked, and moved with her quick soundless steps to provide what was needed, the image of detachment and composure.

Pierre had been plagued all day by a feeling of restlessness, a sense of unfinished business. Patients had come and gone; he'd given them their seven minutes each, and as far as he was aware he hadn't seriously misdiagnosed anything or dished out inappropriate treatment, but he'd been operating on about 45% capacity, that was certain. This business with Sarah Stanhope was most unsatisfactory. Clearly, it wasn't worth pursuing. She was hung about with children, she was dangerously friendly with Hilary Nightingale – the idea of women comparing notes about him always put Pierre off his stride – and moreover, she almost certainly wanted something more emotionally meaningful than anything within his repertoire ... and yet, the itch still needed scratching. Then there was the problem of his mother-in-law. In Pierre's professional judgment, she wouldn't last more than another month. And while some adventuring was, in Pierre's opinion, just about acceptable before her death, even his elastic morality took into account the need to support and comfort Claudia in the weeks – months, even – following her bereavement. So he had to act now or not at all.

It wasn't until he had tidied his desk and bidden his usual jaunty goodbye to the receptionists that he remembered his promise to cook supper. Damn – most shops would be shut now, and he'd meant to take some trouble over it. Claudia was under a hell of a lot of strain, she deserved some spoiling. He drove slowly down Barcombe High Street, peering at the shop fronts to see if any of them were still open. He could get a takeaway at worst, but it looked lazy, and Claudia always complained about the smell. One small, expensive, poorly stocked supermarket boasted that it was open '8 till late'. That would have to do.

As he filled the wire basket, Pierre mused briefly on his dying mother-in-law. He had nothing against the old lady – indeed, he had always got on quite well with her, and had respected her for not interfering in their lives – and yet he found he could feel very little for her now, as she shrivelled and slipped from sight. Perhaps it was because, as a doctor, death had become commonplace to him, he thought. But the explanation was not satisfactory. The fact that he could think of his wife's many visits to the hospital as potential occasions for playing around with other people's wives should shock him, but didn't. It was probably the way most people thought, it was just that they were too timid or hypocritical to admit it.

It wasn't the way Claudia thought, though. Whatever the murkiness of his own behaviour, he always thought of his wife's crystalline integrity with pride. She'd been enough for him for years and years – more than enough. And she'd be enough for him now if only this baby thing hadn't got in the way. Since they'd had the tests, she'd always made him feel that sleeping with her was a bit pointless. And the way she seemed to draw strength from his weakness! He hated that. But he still yearned for her – not for her as she was now, but for the way they used to be. But that time could never come again.

He pushed his purchases through the checkout. The checkout girl was one of his patients. Girl wasn't quite the right word, actually. About thirty-five with four eczematic children, and frizzy hair dyed the colour of a new copper coin. 'Ooh, Dr Prescott!' she squealed. 'Steak and a bottle of wine! Why don't you get 'er some flowers as well?' She indicated a plastic bucket by the door in which a few dusty bouquets lolled.

'D'you know, Mrs Atkins, that's not at all a bad idea!' Pierre smiled his slow, wolfish smile and winked. 'Those pink ones are nice. I'll have a couple of bunches of those.'

'Spray carnations? Lovely. Last a long time, too. That should tickle her fancy.' Mrs Atkins screeched with laughter. 'Special occasion is it?'

'Hope so, Mrs A.' With another wink Pierre gathered it all up and was gone.

He reached home before Claudia. That was good. He put the flowers in the utility room, on top of the washing machine, to surprise her with later, and turned his attention to the steak. Two brick-coloured slabs, squashed onto babyblue polystyrene and covered with clingfilm. They looked dreadful. He peeled back the clingfilm and with distaste removed the damp paper pads, stained pink, that stuck to their backs, looking like surgical waste. The steaks smelled even worse than they looked. He dropped them into a dish, opened the wine, and tipped a little over them. At least that should mask the smell, he thought.

He turned his attention to the rest of his shopping. A limp lettuce, a dusty pepper, a fibrous avocado … he would make a good strong dressing to mask the deficiencies of the salad. Salad dressing was something Pierre was good at. He hesitated over laying the table, considering candles. If he could get his wife to warm up a bit then he wouldn't need to bother with this Stanhope woman. Perhaps.

He'd just put the candlesticks out when he heard Claudia's key in the latch. He could hear her sigh as she patted Jaques; without seeing her, he could sense the weariness in the accustomed movements as she took off her jacket, hung it carefully on a coathanger, unpacked her schoolbag and picked up her post. He could guess at the pallor of the small face behind the big glasses, could envisage the deepening furrow between the eyes. His heart contracted with pity. He turned on the grill.

'You're tired,' he said gently, as she entered the kitchen. 'Sit down, I'll get you a drink.' He poured them each a glass of wine. She gave him the tiniest twitch of a smile as he slid it across the table to her. 'How are things?' he asked. 'How's –'

Claudia shook her head.

'Worse,' she said, 'worse. She's going, I think. I'll go back there after supper. Did you get any, by the way?'

'I'll put it on now. Steak. OK?'

Claudia raised her head and noticed the candlesticks. She didn't know whether she was touched or annoyed.

'Oh dear,' she said, touching them. 'Oh dear.'

'Never mind those.' Pierre turned the steaks. 'It doesn't matter.'

Claudia noticed that he hadn't put any foil in the grill pan.

'You haven't –' she began, but scrapped it. 'Pierre,' she blurted,

'I told her I was pregnant.' Then she covered her face with her hands and wept, silently, painfully.

Pierre looked at the small, hunched figure. He turned to the window and stared at the neat lawn, the snipped shrubs, the row of conifers at the end of the garden beneath which nothing would grow. And he looked beyond at the long and rolling landscape. 'Well,' he said in a squeaky voice unlike his own, 'maybe you will be.'

Claudia's quiet sobs shuddered to a halt. She uncovered her face. 'How can I?'

'What I mean,' said Pierre, 'is that I'm not going to be the one to stop you.'

Her face was piebald and lined with crying, but across it spread a tentative, crooked, hoping smile.

'I'll try,' he said. 'It won't be easy, but we'll look into it. Artificial insemination, adoption – let's see what we can do.' His voice wobbled. 'You deserve a baby.'

She was on her feet, and in his arms. She clung to him, hiding her face. 'Come on, now,' he said, gently disentangling himself, 'let's eat, and then I'll come with you to the hospital. I'm glad she knows she's going to be a grandma.' He switched off the grill and grimaced.

'I hope you fancied your steak assassiné, old thing, because I'm afraid that's what you're getting.'

That night, Claudia woke violently, hurled into consciousness by the horror of her dream. Her mother had become an inert, smiling, outsize baby slipping off a rickety camp bed suspended over a gaping break in the floorboards. Claudia knew, with a dreamer's certainty, that the hole was bottomless; with equal conviction she knew that she alone had to carry her mother to safety. But when she tried to lift the humped, foetal shape, she found it heavy and slippery, immobile and yet fluid. The harder Claudia tried to lift her, the louder grew the mother-baby's uncomprehending chuckles; the shape squirmed away, delighted as a child in a tickling game. Then the bed tipped up and the hole loomed near and Claudia jerked herself awake. She lay motionless, paralysed with fear and disgust, still feeling the boneless, cloying weight of the coiled dream-mother. Then she rolled over, crept into the circle of Pierre's arms, nestled in their cocoon, and slept.

CHAPTER TWENTY

Sarah dreaded the sound of the telephone now. In the days following her churchyard encounter with Claudia, her passion for Pierre had rapidly evaporated, leaving nothing but a murky puddle of embarrassment and self reproach at the bottom of her mind. She kept indoors a lot, anxious to avoid a chance encounter with him – anxious, indeed, to avoid another encounter with almost anyone she knew. She tried to concentrate on Thomas, to make up to him for what she now saw as weeks of neglect, but Thomas had always been a stimulus-resistant child. Picture books, nursery rhymes, clapping games, infant gymnastics, all soon palled; he simply liked doing his own thing. Sarah turned to household tasks. She would finally get rid of the last vestiges of their house move, she decided. There would be no more cardboard boxes full of odds and ends in the cupboard under the stairs. And their books would be rearranged in some kind of order – they'd just been shoved on the shelves any old how. So while Thomas practised his new-found standing skills on the edge of the living-room sofa, Sarah pushed up her sleeves and set to work.

But the contents of the boxes didn't seem to belong anywhere else. A few things could be thrown away, a few others given to charity. Most of it – camping equipment, spare fan heaters, lilos – went straight back into the cardboard boxes. And sorting the books created new problems. Should she arrange them alphabetically? In which case, should she go by the first letter of the title, or the author's name? So often she could remember a book but not its author. Should they be arranged according to subject, or type, or size? Or colour, even? Those orange-backed Penguins really looked hideous against the peachy wallpaper of their living room. All the time she was pondering these things, Sarah was bracing herself for the sound of the telephone. The last words Pierre had spoken to her repeated themselves endlessly in her head; 'I don't give up easily, Sarah.' Claudia had said … Sarah just prayed Claudia was right.

Adrian had a big case on, and was working extra hard, even bringing documents home at the weekend. That was a relief. Sarah skimmed past her husband during these days, unobtrusively avoiding contact, putting children, or talk of the children, between herself and him. Co-existing like well-disposed acquaintances was the best she could manage right now. Renouncing your lover was the easy bit, Sarah thought. Breathing new life into your marriage was quite another matter. 'To have and to hold.' How resonant, how reassuring, those words had once sounded! It seemed that only now did she grasp their sinister implications.

The telephone did ring, eventually. But it wasn't Pierre. 'Hello, darl,' said Louise's voice. 'I've got the office to myself for once, so I thought I'd take advantage. Is this an all right moment? You sound a bit –'

'Oh no, it's fine. I was day-dreaming, that's all. Sorry if I sound vague.'

'Day-dreaming! My God, I *day-dream* about day-dreaming. In the forty-five seconds of any day when no one's making demands on me. But anyway, how are you, Sal? Still married?'

Sarah couldn't help but laugh. 'We're fine,' she said, 'really fine. I'm sorry we were so crabby when you came.'

'Don't apologise, I enjoyed myself. So you've forgiven Adrian for his reckless extra-marital romp with the handsome Henry over a half of bitter at the King's Wotsits, have you?'

'Lou, if you carry on I'll hang up. It's not fair –'

Louise carried on regardless. 'And what's happened with you and the doctor?'

'That's all finished,' said Sarah firmly. Then she gasped. 'Louise, what are you on about? I didn't tell you about the doctor.'

'I don't need to be told in words, it was obvious.'

'Obvious? Do you think Adrian –'

'Oh no, no. Obvious to me – that's not at all the same thing as obvious to Adrian. Anyway, it's finished you say?'

'It never even started.'

'And how are you feeling?'

Sarah paused before replying. 'Bored and ashamed.'

'Hmm. You need some fun. That's what I was ringing about, actually. Can't think how I got side-tracked onto daft subjects like extra-marital affairs. Listen, it's Ade's birthday around now, isn't it? Jack and I want to take you both out, somewhere really nice. Let's make a night of it, like we used to.'

'That would be brilliant. Ade's got a big case on right now, but when it's over, I'll get back to you, shall I? Thanks, Lou. Oh and –'

'Yes?'

'You won't – say anything, will you? To anyone? Not even to Jack?'

'Sarah, you don't have to ask me that question. And I won't pester you again about it, either. Like you said, nothing happened. It would just be great to see you both. Ah –' Louise's tone changed. Someone had evidently come into the office. 'So you'll ring to confirm arrangements. Thank you, goodbye.'

Sarah put the phone down and wandered into the kitchen. Hearing Louise's voice had the same effect on her as having the first drink of the evening. She'd discuss a suitable date with Adrian, organise babysitting, and they'd go and have fun, the four of them. Just like they used to.

As she reached to unhook a coffee mug from the dresser, a brown envelope caught her eye, sticking out between two little-used milk jugs. She drew it down. Inside was the photograph Diana Stanhope had given her. Adrian as a little boy.

She looked intently at the shadowy little face, at the high cheekbones, the tufty hair, the skinny knees between the cuffs of baggy shorts and high, ribbed socks – the kind held up by elastic garters. Judging from the little boy's age, it was probably taken before his father's death. His father was so soon to slip out of his grasp. Poor little chap. He had no inkling of the precariousness of his family life. And yet even at this stage there seemed to be anxiety mixed in with the childish excitement.

Sarah pressed her lips to the little face, quickly, once. He really was very like Gabriel.

The telephone rang again. Sarah stepped out into the garden and waited for it to stop. She didn't want to answer it right now, whoever it was.

The nursery finished, Hilary had set to work on the Stanhopes' bathroom. She'd painted the walls a creamy yellow and was half way through a frieze of fantastical dolphins, porpoises and seahorses in a slatey blue, curving and twisting their way along the top where the walls met the ceiling. The dull green seventies bath had already been replaced by an enamelled Victorian one, satisfyingly deep; its dolphin-shaped feet had been the inspiration for the frieze.

On this particular Monday, Elinor was off school because the lower sixth were given a few days study leave before their end of term exams. She hadn't wanted to be left alone and, to Hilary's immense but concealed delight, she'd volunteered to accompany her mother to the house on Maiden's Hill. Now she was lying in the garden with her copy of *As You Like It*, which in its limp and grimy state was beginning to remind Hilary of the woolly blanket that had dominated their lives for the first three years of Elinor's existence. Hilary, in indigo dungarees and with a red gingham scarf to protect her hair, was filling in dolphins on top of a stepladder. Sarah, soothed by the fine weather and confident in her ability to put Pierre out of her mind, was pottering contentedly, clearing out the kitchen cupboards with one hand while balancing Thomas on her hip.

Hilary was worried. Life, she realised, didn't often present her with obvious moral dilemmas, but there was no evading this one. She had been convinced for some time that Sarah was heading for an affair with Pierre Prescott, if indeed she hadn't already embarked on one, and she, Hilary, was the only person with power to do anything about it. Hilary had never intervened before. She knew that Claudia had her own private ways of dealing with Pierre's serial infidelity. But this time it was different. Sarah was no flighty young thing, peripheral to Pierre and Claudia and the world in which they moved. She was a mature woman, deeply embedded in responsibilities; she was a neighbour, and she was well on the way to being a real friend. And Claudia's mother was dying. There was so much to damage, so much to lose. Hilary wiped down her dolphin stencil, paused, and sighed. She had delayed long enough. Sarah would probably go her own way whatever was said to her – people usually did, and quite right too. But if Hilary didn't at least try, could she call herself a true friend of Claudia's? She had let Claudia down badly once before. Once was more than enough.

Sarah had found some old plastic pastry cutters, which interested Thomas enough for her to be able to set him down. She surveyed her large kitchen cupboard with satisfaction. On the top shelf, out of reach of little fingers, stood jars of honey and marmalade and chutney, freshly wiped, and next to them sugar and flour and raisins, no longer lolling in collapsing bags but efficiently decanted into airtight glass jars. On the second shelf were pasta and rice and tins of tuna fish and beans – an unexciting selection, but no longer muddled up with odds and ends of plastic pots containing three glacé cherries and dried yeast that had long outlived its usefulness. Such things, along with burned stumps of candles and half empty tins of treacle with the lid stuck down, she had placed firmly in the bin. On the bottom shelf, cake tins and measuring jugs, whisks and patty pans, were now neatly ranged, like stacked with like. 'Good' said Sarah, aloud. That was stage one. The next stage was to go out to the organic food shop in Joy Street and buy interesting pulses and pastes and spices. And the stage after that was actually to use them. She caught sight of her reflection in the silver meat cover, hanging from the dresser. 'This is it, girl,' she told herself, smiling. 'It's called setting your house in order.'

Eleven o'clock. Time to take Hilary a cup of coffee. Often, she'd mooched about all morning, dying for an excuse to interrupt Hilary, pretending to be busy but achieving nothing. How much better it felt to be purposeful! The back door was propped open to let in the sweet midsummer air. Sarah could see Elinor, in black jeans and huge grey sweatshirt despite the heat, lying half in and half out of the shade of the cherry tree, twiddling the grass. *As You Like It* lay forlornly by her side. She didn't look exactly overworked.

'Elinor,' Sarah called, 'would you like some coffee, or fruit juice or something?'

Elinor sat up with a start. Thomas abandoned the pastry cutters and set off for the garden with his soft splatting crawl. 'Coffee would be great,' said Elinor. 'Can I play with him, please? I mean, will he mind?'

'He'd be delighted. He loves long hair.' Sure enough, by the time the coffee was ready, Thomas had pulled himself up by gripping fistfuls of it, like a fat pink version of the prince in Rapunzel. Sarah, smiling indulgently, went back for Thomas' sun-hat, then took a mug up to Hilary.

'Fantastic,' said Hilary. 'I'm dying for a break.' She looked out into the garden. 'Goodness, Ellie and Thomas seem to be getting on like a house on fire. She's not usually keen on babies.'

'She asked if she could play with him.'

'Did she now? That's great. She's loosening up a little.' Hilary looked wistful. 'At least, to everyone except me.'

'She's come with you today,' Sarah pointed out.

'Yes, I think that's a good sign. But she may just be keeping tabs on me.'

'So she's still being difficult about – about –'

'About Joe, yes. In fact I haven't seen him since Pierre's party, so I don't really know if she's changing her attitude or not. His name has not been mentioned.'

'Your choice, or his? Not to see him, I mean.'

'Mine.' Hilary's generous mouth was set in a tight line. Sarah didn't dare ask questions. She approached the subject from an oblique angle instead.

'That's a pity, because I was going to ask you both to dinner on Saturday night … My sister Nicola is coming to stay, and we're inviting Adrian's friend Henry to meet her. Adrian got to know him on the train. He's about the most glamorous thing Barcombe has to offer.'

'Ah! matchmaking! He's the single handsome, blond one, isn't he? You told me about him before. Sounds too good to be true. Are you sure he's not gay?'

'Oh no, he's not gay. The reason he's living in Barcombe is because he and his girlfriend bought a house here as a kind of escape-from-the-city-and-leave-your-worries-behind idea. But it didn't work, of course.'

'What happened?'

'She upped and left him. And now he's all alone in his empty love nest and doesn't know what to do. He's dauntingly handsome, but he's a big softie really. Or that's what Adrian says.'

'And your sister's going to mend his broken heart?'

'Well, I think hers may be a little the worse for wear as well. The dream job didn't live up to expectations, and I think she's ready for a bit of cocooning. That's what the Americans call it, apparently.'

Hilary chuckled. 'They have to have a brand name for everything, don't they? Even for states of mind.'

'Oh, and Claudia and Pierre are coming.' Sarah threw that in as nonchalantly as she could, and turned back to the window. 'Ellie's still doing fine with Thomas. I'll go and rescue her in a moment.'

Hilary swallowed, and said in a tight voice that she hardly recognised as her own, 'Sarah. About Pierre.'

'Mmm?' Sarah didn't turn round.

'Oh God,' said Hilary, 'oh God, oh God. I've started so I'll finish. The Magnus Magnusson principle. Look, Sarah, I don't know what's happening between you and Pierre, but I ought to warn you – he's not – he's not what you think he is.' She stumbled to a halt.

'It's all right, Hilary.' Sarah still gazed out of the window. 'I know what you're talking about, but you've no need to worry. I saw the photographs.' She picked up the empty coffee mugs and rinsed them under the washbasin tap. 'You've done it, haven't you? You've slept with him. Well, I didn't even get that far. Thank goodness.'

'Well,' said Hilary, 'you've taken the wind out of my sails. Yes, I did sleep with him – more than once. We all went on holiday together – to France – a few years ago now. It was just after ... just after it all finished with Sunil. Claudia wasn't getting on particularly well with Pierre. She was reading all the time, and I – I pretended I was interested in photography. Pierre and I used to slip away ...' she ground to a halt.

'The details don't matter,' said Sarah gently. 'You don't need to tell me all this.'

'I want to,' said Hilary. 'I want to tell. I've never told anyone, ever. I felt so terribly, terribly empty. I was trying to fill that space, I suppose – and I told myself that if Claudia never found out it wouldn't affect her, so it wouldn't matter. Which of course is utter rubbish.' She paused again. 'It was disgusting,' she said with venom. 'The worst thing I've ever done.'

'I'm no better than you. I'd have done it, except that I couldn't get rid of Thomas.' She put her arms round Hilary. 'Thank you for trying to warn me. I need warnings. I've been a fool – worse than a fool.'

Through the open window a wail from Thomas floated up to them. Sarah disengaged herself from Hilary's embrace. 'Sounds like he's getting tired. I'll put him down, and leave you to get on with your dolphins.' From the doorway, she gave Hilary a sheepish smile. 'So, will you come to dinner on Saturday, with or without Joe, and help to defend me from the big bad wolf?'

That evening, as she sat on the back doorstep shelling broad beans while the children ate a picnic supper under the cherry tree, Sarah's heart was light within her. For the first time in months, she was truly looking forward to the scratch of Adrian's key in the lock. She had tested Elinor on her lines earlier, and Rosalind's words to Phoebe still ran through her head.

> 'Mistress, know thyself. Down on your knees,
> And thank heaven fasting for a good man's love.'

A good man's love. Why had it taken so long for her to notice? She'd had it, all along.

Hannah abandoned her peanut butter sandwiches and sidled over to share the doorstep with her mother. She prised open a bean pod and ran her little fingers ruminatively over the five beans and their soft white setting. 'It's all snug and nice,' she said. 'It's lovely for beans to live in a pod, isn't it, Mummy? It's cosy for the beans.'

Sarah stretched out an arm and squeezed the small figure in the pink smocked sundress. 'That's right,' she said. 'It's their cosy little house.' Then before Hannah could dwell on the beans' imminent rude eviction into the hard, cold colander, she stood up. 'Bathtime, I think. Unless anyone would like a chocolate mini-roll first.'

Once the sound of even breathing could be heard from all three children, Sarah set about preparing for her husband's return. She pulled out the drawer of her dressing table, looking for the grand scent that Adrian had bought her duty free once, and that she always forgot to wear. Right at the back of the drawer was a piece of folded paper. It looked important, somehow, but she couldn't think why.

She unfolded it. A telephone number – a local one. No name. Of course! The number she'd found in Adrian's briefcase, what felt like years ago. She'd meant to ring it, and had completely forgotten. That shows, she thought, that I wasn't as worried as all that.

She hesitated now. Perhaps she should just throw it away. After all, in her heart she loved and trusted her husband. She knew that, now. But on the other hand, there was no harm in ringing it. If she didn't there might remain a little fertile patch for suspicion to take root in, in future.

She checked the time. Not long now before Adrian got home. This evening had to go well for them; she had to get any other considerations out of the way. She picked up the telephone, swallowed twice and braced herself.

'Hello,' said Henry's voice, sounding deeper than usual on the answerphone, 'you know how to use this thing. Leave your message after the silly music.'

Sarah replaced the handset. She tore the scrap of paper into dozens of tiny fragments. She faced herself in the mirror, and burst out laughing. 'Sarah Stanhope,' she said aloud, 'it really is time you grew up.'

When Adrian got home at eight, Sarah greeted him in her bathrobe.

'What's this?' he asked, laughing as she held herself against him. 'An early night?'

'I hope so. An early birthday present, too.' Sarah took his hand and slid it under the robe so that he could feel the satiny edges of her black basque. She tugged at her loosely knotted belt and let the gown fall open. There she stood, in stockings, silk top – the lot.

'Hey!' murmured Adrian. 'So that stuff fits after all.'

'It does now.'

He pushed her back a little. 'Let's have a look.' His gaze travelled up and down, then he gathered her to him. 'Marvellous,' he breathed, 'absolutely marvellous.'

Later – quite a long time later – he ran a deep bath for the two of them and fetched a bottle of wine from the kitchen while Sarah stretched out and luxuriated. 'Adrian,' she said, as he climbed in with her, balancing two long-stemmed glasses precariously on the bath rack, 'one thing.'

'As many things as you want, my love.'

'Why did you get out of bringing Henry back to the house for such a long time?'

Without his spectacles, Adrian looked bewildered, comical. Like a fledgling, Sarah thought fondly. He handed her one of the glasses before replying.

'I suppose,' he said, 'I suppose I was a little frightened.'

'Frightened? Is Henry frightening?'

'He's very good-looking, and – young, and unattached, and – not bald. Not bald at all.'

'And you thought – oh Ade, did you really think I'd run off with him?'

'No, not run off, but I thought he might make you – well, make you restless, I suppose. But then I decided that was silly, and tried to put it out of my mind. Was I right?'

'You were. It was silly. Very.' Sarah leaned forward to kiss her husband's nose – the easiest bit to reach. She chinked her glass against his.

'You know what the first thing I thought was, when I saw him?'

'What was it?'

'That he'd be ideal for Nicky.'

Adrian laughed. 'We'll find out on Saturday, won't we. Have you asked Pierre What's-his-name and wife, by the way? We ought to really, because of their party.'

'Oh yes,' said Sarah. 'That's all under control. And Hilary's coming too, on her own. I thought I'd go to Dinsford and see if I can get fresh crabs – or would Henry not like that? The others are all hard-hearted enough. Could you turn on the hot again, Ade? Thanks. Oh and could you get some decent cheese in London on Friday? The only thing wrong with Barcombe is that you can't get decent cheese.'

CHAPTER TWENTY-ONE

Nicola Anderson crossed one silky leg over the other and tweaked at her long, sheer split skirt so that it fell like a bronze waterfall over the wickerwork garden chair she sat in. She'd lit her cigarette from one of the candle flames and now leaned back, languidly.

Six months in New York had added whole new dimensions to her already extensive wardrobe, and removed a pound or two from her long, spare frame. There was a sense of controlled neurosis, as if her graceful feline movements indicated a feral self only barely contained. This is new, thought Sarah, pouring coffee. New York has troubled her – but that suits her somehow. Trust Nicky to turn anxiety into a style feature.

'I do apologise,' said Nicola, dispersing the thin blue smoke with a wave of her manicured hand. 'I gave up years ago – until I went to the States. Then I needed a prop. Everybody does.'

Henry pulled a crumpled packet of Gauloise out of his shirt pocket. 'I'm delighted you've given me the excuse. Do you mind?' He leaned forward and, quite unnecessarily, lit his cigarette from hers. Adrian and Sarah exchanged a tiny smile.

Hilary was talking to Pierre about mutual friends, but his eyes kept darting, lizard-like, to that slender arrangement of bronze and blond in the wicker chair. The fluidity of her hair, her limbs, her garments, the gleam of her eyes and shins and earrings worked upon his senses and threatened to knock down his new-formed resolutions like a row of skittles. He didn't dare look at Claudia.

Sarah handed round the tiny cups, turquoise with a gold rim. Wedding presents – seven years old, and none cracked yet. She liked using them tonight, liked administering to everybody, even liked the sight of her own busy hands, slightly pudgy and with the veins beginning to stand out, the nails irregular and unpolished. The tubs on the patio were full of madonna lilies, pouring fragrance out into the night. The jasmine was just beginning to offer up its pure white stars. Sarah looked at Hilary, at the lived-in, earthy beauty of her freckled face, colourful and domestic like a wallflower, the antithesis, almost, of Nicola's cool elegance. Her heart swelled with pride in them both. *Her* garden, *her* husband, *her* sister, *her* friend. Her hands at the centre, making and giving.

Her gaze fell on Pierre, so obviously transfixed by Nicola's splendour. Next to Henry's easy, rumpled charm, Pierre seemed like an also-ran, a little tired, a bit of a sham. He'd politely avoided Sarah all evening, which was just as it should be. It was now firmly established that the Stanhopes and Prescotts were cordial members of the same social network. How could she ever have wanted more?

Adrian had gone in to fetch brandy and glasses, leaving Claudia temporarily with no one to talk to. Sarah shuffled her chair closer. 'I was hearing Ellie's lines the other day,' she said. 'I'd forgotten what *As You Like It* was all about, if I ever knew. But it seemed to me that Rosalind has the clearest idea of what's good for her because she can't get it. And Phoebe doesn't recognise what's right under her nose.'

Claudia smiled her small, tight smile. 'I think I agree with you. The whole thing's about people chasing round after other people, often the wrong ones. But they all get it right in the end.' She sipped her coffee. 'One thing's certain, no one wants to be alone. Elinor's shaping up nicely as Rosalind. She's just beginning to realise what the whole thing's about.'

'I'd love to see it. May I?'

'Of course. It's on in a couple of weeks. I'll send you an invitation.' Claudia lowered her voice. 'Honestly, look at Pierre. Like an old dog with its tongue hanging out. I can't say I blame him. Your sister's rather wonderful.'

Sarah looked at her in amazement. There was no trace of rancour in her tone. Claudia gave a low laugh.

'Don't worry, Sarah. It happens all the time. He can't help himself, poor love. Looks like he's met his match this time, though.' She bobbed her head at Henry, nodding and laughing at something Nicola had said. 'He's rather divine, too. Looks like something out of a Merchant Ivory film. I bet he's got the most marvellous underwear.'

Adrian re-emerged from the house empty-handed. His face was grave. 'Claudia,' he said, 'telephone. It's the hospital.'

The group fell silent. Looking at no one, Claudia rose and

walked into the house with steady, measured tread. Hilary shot a look at Pierre, who seemed to shake himself awake. He bounded to his wife's side. Sarah touched Adrian's arm – 'Is she –?'

He shook his head. 'I didn't ask much, of course, but no, she's not – she's still alive.'

Hilary rose, and gathered up glasses and coffee cups. 'Thank you, you two,' she said, 'for an excellent evening. If only it didn't have to end this way. Poor, poor Claud.'

Nicola and Henry had also risen. In the darkness, Henry thought that no one could see that his hand had found the small of Nicola's back. They stood close together, feeling the warm current pass between them.

'Lunch tomorrow then?' said Henry, *sotto voce*. 'I'll call for you at one.'

When Claudia replaced the receiver, Pierre folded her in his arms. 'We'll go over there right away,' he said, his voice firm. 'I only drank a glass and a half all evening, just in case.' He sounded like a child, boasting shyly. Claudia buried her face on his shoulder. Sarah, entering with a loaded tray, saw them in silhouette in the front hall. Other people's marriages, she thought. Claudia was right. You never know what they're really made of.

Hilary insisted on helping with the washing-up; it was nearly one by the time she reached home. The night that had been almost oppressive in its stillness, had changed; a cool wind, like a whirling genie, shook the trees awake, heralding thunder right over head. Hilary remembered how Elinor had been so frightened of storms when she was little; she'd got them muddled up with *Jack and the Beanstalk*, and had thought that the thunder meant giants would crash down on her through the sky. Perhaps she was still frightened of them now. Hilary realised that she no longer knew. After a certain age, one simply didn't know some things about one's own child. It was sad, but it had to be so.

As lightning ripped repeatedly through the sky, Hilary tapped softly on her daughter's door. No reply. She raised the latch and tiptoed in. The narrow white bed was empty, but at her feet, sprawled over a bean bag Hilary had made for a long-distant birthday present, were two sleeping figures. Elinor's fine dark hair covered her face; one thin, pale arm poked out of the eternal grey T-shirt and draped itself over the chest of her angular companion.

The mysterious young man! Hilary had glimpsed him, but had not even been told his name. The curtains were open; a lightning flash showed blue-white skin and deep red hair, like in that painting of the death of Chatterton she thought. He had on a black vest with some sort of skull emblem on the front, jeans, and heavy boots, done up with purple laces. His long arms were almost as thin as Elinor's; one was flung behind his head, the other encircled her little girl's shoulders. Hilary bent down to remove a full ashtray. Her presence seemed to disturb the young man, who stirred, and pulled Elinor closer to him. Hilary moved back quickly, but he didn't wake. Her heart contracted, but the pang she felt was soon blunted by the sight of such innocent vulnerability. Smiling, she let the latch fall.

In her own room, she undressed slowly, putting her jewellery away in the right places and brushing her hair with loving deliberation. Outside, the rain had begun; the wood roared and swayed like a ship tossed at sea. The ache of being alone on a night like this! Hilary remembered a poem Joe had showed her.

> *'Wild nights, wild nights! Were I with thee*
> *Wild nights should be our luxury,'*

she whispered to her face in the mirror.

The raindrops and the leaves of the clematis spattered the window panes with a shower of sound, and it was some time before Hilary noticed a different, sharper, brittle noise. She paused in her brushing – no, she wasn't imagining it. Someone was throwing stones against her window. She flung it open.

'It's midsummer night,' said a voice below. 'Oh Titania, let me in. Don't shut me out on midsummer night.'

She hurried barefoot down the stairs and ran out into the rain. Joe caught her in his huge embrace. His hair and beard were dripping; his flesh glowed warm through his drenched shirt.

'Oh Joe,' she said, laughing and crying. 'How could you be such an idiot?' She pushed her hands up under his shirt, peeling it away from his skin.

'I couldn't sleep,' he said. 'I couldn't read, I couldn't even think, So I'm here. Can I come in?'

'Of course,' she said. 'Of course, of course. Come in out of the storm.'

CHAPTER TWENTY-TWO

'So, how's she taken it?'

Sarah, sitting on the wooden bench outside Petts End Cottage, pushed the buggy to and fro with her foot, hoping that Thomas would fall asleep.

'Badly, I'm afraid. When I went to see her she was lying, curled up, on the bed in their spare room, where Naomi had slept. She didn't want to talk, so I just left her a note and some flowers. I'll try again tomorrow.'

'And Pierre?'

'I rather think he's come into his own. Very proprietorial about Claud and efficient about funeral arrangements. He said Claud hadn't eaten anything at all for the first two days. He was bustling about making nourishing little soups. Quite sweet, really.' There was only a hint of derision in Hilary's voice.

Sarah checked the contents of the buggy. 'Almost there,' she said, resuming her rocking. From behind the cottage came squeals of terrified delight as Hannah and Gabriel, supervised and encouraged by Laura and Elinor, took it in turns to roll down the steep grassy bank, while round them frolicked the tiny grey kitten, recently acquired from Mr Pitchford.

Hilary drew her legs up onto the bench and embraced her knees. 'You know,' she said, scrutinising her toes, 'one thing really bothered me.'

'About Claudia?'

'Yes. She was lying on that bed clutching something – a paper bag full of knitting. White fluffy knitting. I've never known Claudia knit in my life. And I saw – or thought I saw – what it was. There was a tiny white sleeve sticking out. It was a cardigan for a new-born baby, I'm pretty sure.'

Sarah said nothing for a moment. Hilary looked up, her forehead furrowed. 'She was clutching it, as if it were a teddy bear,' she went on. 'I've always thought of Claudia as the sanest person in the world, but what with putting up with Pierre, and her mother dying, and being infertile – the strain of it all – could it have tipped her over the edge? I mean, the way she was just lying there –'

Sarah said quickly, 'She's not infertile.'

'What do you mean, Sarah. You mean she's pregnant?' Hilary stared at Sarah with tremendous concentration. 'That's incredible. But how on earth do you know?'

Sarah took her foot off the buggy. 'Oh dear,' she said, 'I've broken a confidence now. No, she's not pregnant – unfortunately. But I can explain it all – the white wool, and everything. It'll take a while though.'

Hilary's leaf-green eyes scanned Sarah's face. 'That's all right,' she said, 'I've got a while.'

At the back of the cottage it had become too hot for rolling. Elinor brought out cans of Coke for herself and Laura and juice boxes with bendy straws for the children, and a couple of felt tip pens so that they could draw on Laura's plaster cast. 'If you can find a space,' said Laura, for the cast was already amply graffittied with hearts and initials and skulls-and-cross-bones. Hannah touched it with deep respect. 'Are you allowed to wear it for ever and ever?' she asked. Gabriel said he was going to write 'Lots of love from Gabriel' on it. 'He thinks all writing says that,' explained Hannah. 'You shouldn't worry that he'll take up too much space, because he can only do Gs.'

Gabriel's Gs did in fact take up an awful lot of space, and they threatened to obliterate many of the humorous messages inscribed by Laura's contemporaries. 'That's enough now,' put in Elinor. 'Gabriel, give me back that pen, and I'll give you a sip of my Coke.'

'You're a born nanny,' said Laura, 'or else a school teacher. How's poor old Mrs P, by the way? Didn't your ma go and see her yesterday?'

'She's in a bad way, apparently. Mum said she wouldn't talk much. She doesn't think she'll be back at school for ages.'

'I wonder why. She can't have been surprised. She must have known her mum was going to die.'

'Laura! You're so heartless. Of course it's still bad when it happens.'

'I suppose so. But she was old and –'

'Yes, but old people never realise how old they are.'

'Eh?'

'I mean people don't think I'm about forty so my mother's about seventy so she's going to die soon so I don't mind. It's still a shock to them.'

Laura tugged at some yellow stonecrop growing in the garden path. 'I don't know,' she said, 'sometimes I can't wait to be shot of mine.'

'You don't really mean that. You'd be devastated. Hey, leave that flower, it's pretty.'

'You've become exceedingly bossy lately, Miss Nightingale. Must be love. I thought flowers were supposed to grow in flower-beds, anyway. I thought you were meant to dig things up that grew in the path.'

'That depends if they're pretty or not.'

'Well, Dad always does. Or puts Pathclear on them. You're right, I would miss the crumblies. It would be scary, knowing that you were the next in line.'

Hannah's round grey eyes had been moving from one face to the other.

'I love my mummy,' she said suddenly, in a strained high-pitched voice.

'Oh Hannah.' Elinor took her hand. 'I know you do. We all love our mummies. Don't pay any attention to Laura and me – we're only joking.'

'Thomas loves Badger,' Gabriel volunteered. He had chewed his straw until it was completely flat and was now waving it underneath the kitten's nose, hoping to make him pounce.

'And who do you love, Gabriel?'

'Oh don't ask him!' said Hannah with scorn. 'He only loves himself.'

Gabriel lay on his back, laughing. He made pedalling movements in the air. 'I love Gaby, I love Gaby, I love me, I love me,' he sang to the tune of *Frère Jacques*.

'See?' sniffed Hannah. 'I told you so.'

Elinor fetched a bag of crisps for them to share. Laura looked at it longingly. 'Sorry, Lor,' said Elinor, 'I forgot it was at least half an hour since you'd eaten. I'll get you one.'

'Cow,' grunted Laura. 'This love nonsense has made you too cocky by half.'

'It isn't.'

'What isn't what?'

'It isn't love.'

'What is it then?'

'It's like. And lust.'

'Lust? Coo-er.'

Elinor smiled enigmatically. 'It's good. You should try it some time.'

'Just wait till this thing's off my leg, and then try and stop me. Matt Coventry won't know what's hit him.'

'Try and stop you from what?' asked Hannah.

Laura tweaked her ponytail. 'Never you mind,' she said. 'Ellie, what's going to happen about the play?'

'I don't know. It'll be called off, I guess. We can't do it without Mrs P.'

'But that's terrible! It's got to happen.'

'You did your best to get out of it, when you were in it. No, Gaby, I don't think Cobweb will eat crisps. I'll bring some milk in a minute.'

'Yeah, but I was crap.'

'How do you know I won't be?'

'It's obvious. You're really into it. And Caro Crouch is looking forward to showing off her legs in those knickerbockers. It's got to go on.'

'I don't see how.'

'What about a joint effort? Mrs Spencer would help, and we could ask your mum if she'll do a bit with the costumes and the programme and everything. It shouldn't be too difficult – only two weeks to go.'

'Ten days, actually. Maybe it's worth a try.'

'I'll go and ask Hilary now.' Laura heaved herself up and stomped off along the little brick path that ran all round the cottage. Hilary and Sarah heard her coming, and stirred themselves. Sarah had come to the end of her narrative, and Hilary, amazed, was adjusting the focus on her long-unaltered assessment of the Prescott marriage.

'Listen,' said Laura, with no further introduction, 'Hilary, you've got to help. It's really important that the play doesn't fold just because Mrs P's not there, so I thought –'

'Yes,' said Hilary, smiling at Laura's florid, ungainly form, 'I'd already thought about the play, and I was going to ask you what we should do. How about if we discuss it over lunch? A picnic in the wood, I thought – if you can hobble that far, Laura.'

'Sure can. Brilliant. I'll tell Ellie.'

'That child,' remarked Hilary, looking at Laura's broad retreating back, 'is less shy than any other I've ever known.'

They took rugs and baskets to the edge of Petts Wood, where some fallen logs made neat little seats, and a hollow tree provided a good vantage point for Hannah's rag doll Mopsy and Gabriel's plastic stegosaurus. They ate slices of cold pizza and carrot sticks and cherry tomatoes, then the grown ups had slightly squishy peaches and the most delicious Roquefort, while Hannah and Gabriel finished off with Penguin biscuits. By the end of the meal the problem of the play was solved, depending on Leonie Spencer's consent. Leonie was to oversee the last few rehearsals; Hilary and Sarah were to take over the management of props and costumes, and Hilary was to design posters and a programme. Laura was to be front of house; she would round up three or four other girls to distribute programmes and usher people to their seats, and make sure everything was tidied up afterwards.

'Which will be ideal,' Laura pointed out, 'because I'll be able to tell everyone what to do but I won't have to do any of it myself. For once in my life.'

The air in the wood was thick with insect life, and Sarah worried about the still-sleeping Thomas. 'They'll make a meal of him,' she said, 'and who can blame them? Such a plump little morsel. I'd better push him back to the house. Han, Gaby, are you coming?'

'Can we stay here with the big girls, please?'

'Well, "big girls", it's up to you. Have you had enough of my little pests?'

'Oh no, let them stay here. We could dam the stream,' replied Elinor. 'I've longed to dam the stream ever since we've lived here, but I've never had any excuse.'

Hilary gathered up the remains of the lunch, and she and Sarah walked back to the cottage.

'Gabriel and Hannah have really taken a shine to Elinor,' Sarah remarked. 'It's very unusual for Gabriel. Normally he ignores people until he's known them for months and months.'

'Maybe he recognises a kindred spirit.'

'What, bloody-minded, you mean? Quite possibly. She's very natural with him, isn't she?'

'It's an amazing transformation. She always used to say children made her nervous. It'll do wonders for her confidence if you tell her he likes her.'

'I'd be delighted.'

'I think it's important that the play does happen,' Hilary went on, 'for Claudia's sake as much as for Ellie's. I'm sure Leonie Spencer will help. I'll ring her tonight – I can get her number from Pierre.'

'From Pierre? She's not another one of his –'

'One of his what?' asked Hilary, laughing. 'Victims? Is that the right word?'

'No, that's too flattering.'

'To the victims, or to Pierre?'

'To Pierre. How about short-term interests?'

'Sounds about right. Is Leonie one of his short-term interests then? Well, it had never occurred to me, I just thought that the number would be in the Prescott address book – but anything's possible. We're all as bad as each other, it seems.'

'Except Claudia.'

'Except Claudia, of course.'

They reached the door of the cottage. 'Talking of such matters,' said Hilary, 'did anything come of your spot of match-making last Saturday?'

'You could say that. She's seen him every evening since, and today they're going for a romantic cliff top walk at Eastings Head. You'd hardly know Nicky was staying with us, except that no one else can ever get into the bathroom.'

'Good for her. Good for them.'

'But a little irritating for the rest of us. Only about the bathroom, I mean. I'm definitely in favour of Henry.'

'So,' said Clicker, setting two sloppy beer glasses down on the table in the garden of the Rose and Crown, 'I've met your mum at last. When do I get to meet your dad?'

Elinor looked up, startled. She took her own fatherless state so much for granted that she tended to forget that other people found it unusual. She sipped at her glass; she was training herself to like beer, half a pint at a time.

'It would be a bit weird,' she replied, 'if you got to meet him, seeing as I've never met him myself.'

'You've never met your old man?' said Clicker. 'Jesus!' It occurred to him that this might be a cause for distress. He shuffled closer to her on the wooden-slatted bench, and encircled her with his arm.

His misplaced concern made Elinor smile, but she couldn't help being touched as well. 'At least you haven't bombarded me with questions about who he is,' she said, 'that's what Laura always does.'

Clicker chuckled. 'Laura would.' He lit a cigarette. 'I won't ask you no questions, Ellie. I reckon you'd tell me if you wanted to.'

'You're brilliant.' Elinor rubbed her head against his shoulder. 'It's no big deal, actually. It's never bothered me, until recently. Laura thinks I'm crazy, but I never wanted to ask Mum about it much. But then suddenly the other night I just did.'

Clicker, not wishing to fall into the Laura category, merely grunted encouragingly.

'It was like I thought,' continued Elinor, 'it was a one night stand, more or less. Mum never even told him about me. She said she'd tell me his name if I wanted, and more about him, but I said no, it's OK.'

'Yeah,' said Clicker, 'you did the right thing. I mean, if he doesn't even know you exist, then him being your dad doesn't mean much. And it might muck up his life, knowing about you.'

'That's what I thought,' said Elinor. 'I can always find out more later, if I change my mind. But I'm glad it isn't someone I know.'

'Did you think it was?'

'Well, I had my moments. But I'm not that interested in what Mum does any more.' Elinor ran her fingers up and down the edge of Clicker's leather jacket. 'And anyway, I respect her privacy.'

'Yeah,' said Clicker. 'That's right.' He stubbed out his cigarette, and kissed her.

'Telephone for you, Sarah. It's Hilary.'

'Oh good. Nicks, could you just watch Thomas while I answer it? Don't let Gaby throw sand over him.'

'OK, but are you going to be long? I'm expecting a call.'

'You don't say. No, not very long. Hello, Hilary?'

'Hello, my duck. Did you manage to get hold of anything for Hymen's robe?'

'Yes, I had a brainwave. Sari material! Purple shot through with gold.'

'How wonderful. Where on earth –'

'I got Ade to look in the Mile End Road for me, in his lunch break.'

'How clever of him to get the right thing.'

'He is quite clever, really.'

'Pierre just rang. He said Claudia's back on her feet and definitely coming to see the show.'

'Brilliant!'

'And he's booked that bistro in Crown Street for the cast party.'

'Cast party? What, for all of them?'

'Well, not for the younger ones perhaps, but for all the adults involved, and for the main parts. He's very insistent. Says it's his treat.'

'It'll cost him a fortune.'

'Yup. But I think he thinks it'll show Claudia he cares.'

'He's been doing quite a bit of that lately, hasn't he? Oh well, fine.'

'My sentiments exactly. Does Adrian want to come? And what about Love's Young Dream?'

'Youngish. Are you sure? It'll be an awful lot of people.'

'Pierre said, the more the merrier. And Nicola helped sew on all that Velcro.'

'True. OK, I'll ask. She's in agonies now because I'm taking up valuable telephone time.'

'Sod that. It's your phone.'

'Sometimes I wonder. Is Joe coming?'

'Definitely.'

'Does Ellie know that?'

'Nope. I'm still too cowardly to tell her. But I will, I will. Here she comes now, back from school.'

'I'd better go and rescue Nicky from Thomas – or perhaps it should be the other way round. Can you come over tomorrow, to help me cut out that robe?'

CHAPTER TWENTY-THREE

'Just keep by me,' Elinor had said to Clicker as they entered the dark bistro with its warm smell of garlic and coffee and candle wax, but somehow they got separated and she found herself with Dr Prescott on one side and Joe Coventry, of all people, on the other. She cast an anxious glance at Clicker, but he was all right, in a little huddle at the end of the long, long table with Laura and Caro Crouch and her boyfriend Alex. It was she who would have to endure an entire evening with bloody boring adults. Still, her success as Rosalind was glowing like wine in her veins and she was, all of a sudden, amazingly hungry. She could concentrate on the food and relive the best bits of the play and more or less ignore her companions. They wouldn't be interested in talking to her, anyway.

It wasn't one long table, in fact, but several small ones placed in a row, covered with claret-coloured tablecloths and decorated with fat green candles and cushiony bunches of sweet williams. Elinor was handed a menu at least two feet long; yet more offerings were chalked up on a blackboard. Plenty of reading matter; no need to talk yet. Her stomach rumbled as she pulled little bits off her bread roll and squidged them into pellets.

Mrs Prescott sat opposite, more gaunt and pale than ever. The girls had made a collection for her; some people had been quite generous, and they'd managed to amass a fairly impressive sum. There'd been the question of what to get with it. Most people had said a huge bouquet and a bottle of champagne, but Elinor had spoken up and said no, Mrs P would want something more permanent, flowers were too sentimental for someone whose mother had just died, and what about a book? The others had objected, saying that she must have thousands already, but Elinor had pointed out that every book is unique, and that they could all sign their names in it. So on Saturday afternoon Elinor had scoured the secondhand bookshops in Dinsford, alone. Caroline and Kelly had offered to come along too, but she'd made some feeble excuse and got rid of them. She knew she wouldn't be able to concentrate with anyone else around.

In the section of Dinsford Old Town known as Arcadia – where junk shops and antique emporia of every description abounded – Elinor had worked her way systematically through four or five bookshops before she found something that seemed right. It was a collection of folk tales from the British Isles, in two volumes, bound in yellow cloth with a black flame-shaped pattern, and beautifully illustrated with strong simple woodcuts in black and white – Elinor remembered Mrs P saying that myth and folklore provided the foundation for all great literature, and though she hadn't fully understood what this meant, the books had seemed to cry out to be bought. And *en route* to them she'd picked up several bargains for herself – the poetry of George Herbert, Keats' letters, and Mrs Gaskell's life of Charlotte Brontë – the purchase of which had confirmed her resolution to tackle Oxford entrance in the autumn. She had emerged, dazzled by the sunlight after the dim basement of the bookshop, to realise that she had been so absorbed that three hours had passed and she'd hardly noticed.

Now the folk tale volumes were neatly wrapped and labelled, by Laura, who was good at that sort of thing. They were lying in a bag by Elinor's feet, waiting to be presented whenever the moment seemed right, and there'd been enough money left over for a bottle of champagne as well. There were no spaces left at any of the tables, the waiters were dishing out the starters, and down at Clicker's end of the table they were already asking for more wine.

Hilary had deliberately seated herself between Sarah and Nicola, realising that they would know few people, and not wishing to impose herself on the young cast who would far rather gossip amongst themselves than make polite conversation with the parental generation. Hilary had never been a great respecter of the convention that places men and women alternately round a table, and she commented on this to Sarah as she stirred chopped cucumber and croutons into her gazpacho. 'Nine times out of ten I'd rather talk to women, in any case,' she remarked, 'with Joe as the miraculous exception. The first time I ever met him I knew that we'd actually be able to *talk*.'

'And he's not doing so badly with Elinor, either,' replied Sarah.

They both looked across the table to where the great grizzled head was bent towards the small dark one. 'Beauty and the Beast,' Sarah commented. Then she clapped her hand over her mouth. 'Oh my God! I wish I hadn't said that.'

Hilary guffawed. 'I know exactly what you mean. But as it happens the Beast has always been rather a hero of mine.'

As they watched, Elinor's face opened in sudden laughter, till she caught her mother's eye and became grave again. Hilary sighed.

'She saw me looking. Now she's shut down again. And Joe was doing so well.'

'Don't worry.' Sarah refilled Hilary's glass from one of the carafes that had been placed at intervals along the table. 'It's only a matter of time. She's getting there. Which one's her boyfriend?'

'The one with red hair and – well, spots. Down the end there. That's Clicker.'

'What's his real name?'

'I haven't been able to find out. I haven't ever had a conversation with him yet.'

'By the look of him I shouldn't think many people have. What does she see in him?'

'Well, he seems very gentle. And he's desperate about her, judging from the number of phone calls. But who can say what anyone sees in anyone else? What's that line that Touchstone says about Audrey in the play – "A poor thing, sir, but mine own." I suppose that's what it's all about.'

Nicola had been inwardly dismayed to find herself separated from Henry, but he had managed to wedge himself in more or less opposite her, and she had shaken off her thonged sandal and was caressing his bare ankle with her toe. She loved the way Henry eschewed socks; his brown bony ankles rose straight from his scuffed brown loafers. He wore a slate grey shirt that accentuated his storm cloud eyes; she allowed herself to imagine the undulations of his smooth golden torso beneath the heavy coarsely-woven fabric. The received wisdom was that you couldn't judge a book by its cover, but Nicola had never been able to understand why not. With such an image projected onto the back of her brain she could converse with her neighbours, Hilary Nightingale and Claudia Prescott, with perfect equanimity.

'Forgive me for asking the question everyone must have asked you,' Claudia was saying, 'but have you any regrets about leaving New York?'

Nicola glanced at Henry then turned to Claudia and changed her small smile of secret intimacy into a charming social one. 'Not at all,' she replied. 'It's strange. I was so excited about going. I thought I wouldn't miss England at all. But I found myself thinking more and more about – well, about Mum and Sarah and Ade and the kids. There wasn't one person in that entire city who cared whether I lived or died, and that spooked me. So I came back. Silly, really.'

'It makes perfect sense to me,' said Claudia. 'People are what attaches us to places, after all. You can't enjoy the one without the other.'

Nicola's foot had reached Henry's knee. She admired the way he could stroke it surreptitiously with one hand while forking up spirals of *linguine alle vongole* with the other, chatting to the awkward teenager on his right all the while. She nodded her blonde head in emphatic agreement with Claudia's statement.

'You're so right,' she said. 'The crunch came one Sunday morning when I was standing in the middle of a Matisse exhibition. I thought he was one of my favourite painters, but I was staring at these great big pictures and seeing – nothing. And that's when I realised that to see something properly I need someone to see it with.' She slid her foot back down Henry's shin and slipped her sandal back on. Any more of that and her concentration would be shot to pieces. She speared an artichoke heart from her plate of mixed hors d'oeuvres and began asking Claudia polite but intelligent questions about the play.

Two down from Henry on the other side, Pierre watched her. He watched her honey-coloured shoulders shift slightly under her sleeveless black silk top. He watched the way her wrist bent gracefully as she brought her wineglass to her lips. He watched the way she sipped, carefully, so as to leave no smudge of coral lipstick on the rim of the glass. He watched the way she conversed with his tired edgy wife, all courteous attention. And then he saw her glance across at Henry and flash him a private smile, quick as a dragonfly darting across a sunlit pool. Only looking, thought Pierre. I'm still allowed to look. He gave himself a little shake, rose to his feet and chinked the side of his glass with his fork. The roar of conversation subsided.

'I'd like to thank you all for coming here tonight,' he began, 'and I'd like you to make sure your glasses are full, because there are so many people here tonight to whom I'm going to propose a toast.'

Amidst approving murmurs, Joe Coventry topped up glasses all round. Pierre spoke with ease and confidence. He thanked everybody who'd stepped in at the last moment to help. He thanked all the cast and made humorously flattering remarks about the main performances, singling out Elinor's for especial commendation. 'And lastly,' he said, changing the note in his voice and looking straight at Claudia, 'and above all, let's drink a toast to my supremely talented wife. The show was her baby, and I know she'd like me to thank you on her behalf for taking such very good care of it.'

Sarah suppressed a gasp when Pierre made that remark about 'her baby'. She looked at Hilary, to register her reaction, and widened her eyes to express her own dismay. But Hilary winked at her, and with the tiniest movement of her head directed Sarah's attention to Claudia herself. Claudia's eyes swam behind her spectacles, but as Pierre sat down amidst thunderous applause she beamed at him, and her wide, uncomplicated smile was echoed in her husband's face. 'I think,' Hilary murmured to Sarah, 'that there's something going on that we don't know about.'

Caroline Crouch, as the show's male lead, thanked Dr Prescott for the wonderful meal (lots of clapping and foot drumming) and thanked Mrs Prescott on behalf of the cast. Then Elinor fished the folk tales out from under the table. She'd meant to make a little speech but now it came to it she couldn't think of a thing to say, so she just muttered, 'They're from all of us,' and thrust the parcels at Mrs P, who fiddled with her spectacles and gave Elinor a dry peck on the cheek and the moment passed. The waiters brought in bowls of caramelised oranges and *tiramisù* and the general chat began again.

Joe said to Elinor, 'Is there a play you can get involved in next term? You really were superb, you know,' and Elinor replied she couldn't get involved in anything next term because she'd definitely decided to do Oxford entrance. So Joe started asking her lots of questions about what she was going to be reading and Elinor began to feel quite lucky that she had access to a genuine published novelist. Laura leaned over and started asking Leonie Spencer daring questions about her pregnancy and Clicker plucked up courage to ask the waiter for a lager.

Nicola said to Hilary, 'Sorry to be a bore, but could you tell me what it's like being self-employed? I'm thinking of going freelance.' Hilary told her how she'd really bitten off more than she could chew. Commissions were coming thick and fast and she hated turning things down, but doing her own accounts was a nightmare …

'Why don't you set up a business properly?' asked Nicola. 'With a partner. That way you could offload some of the stuff you're not so keen on. If you worked with someone with a bit of business sense –'

'Yes, but who?' replied Hilary. 'I've thought about it. But I don't generate enough money to make it worth anyone's while.'

'What about Sarah?' said Nicola, levelly.

'Sarah?'

'Why not? She's not looking for money – not much, anyway – but she's bored out of her skull unloading the dishwasher and ironing little T-shirts all day long. I always thought she was crazy to give up work altogether. You worked well together on this show, didn't you? She enjoyed that. She hasn't been so full of bounce for years.'

Hilary looked at Sarah, who did not appear to have overheard this truthful but unflattering account of her life. 'It's a marvellous idea,' she said slowly, twisting her wine glass between her hands, 'but Sarah's never said she's looking for anything.'

'Well, she wouldn't, would she? People don't often admit that their life's not perfect. Ask her. She'll say she can't because of Thomas, but it could be just part-time at first. They could easily afford a nanny, and just a few hours a day wouldn't hurt him. I'll do it myself, until I've sorted out where I'm going to live.' Nicola cast another furtive glance at Henry.

Hilary decided to keep Nicola's nannying offer to herself, but the rest of the plan seemed flawless. By the time Adrian arrived at midnight it was a *fait accompli*.

Adrian had been working late. Mrs Crump didn't really like

babysitting after midnight, so he'd arranged with Sarah to pick her up at that time. Coffee was coming to an end, and Joe and Henry were trying to force Pierre to accept contributions towards the bill. The younger generation, unused to the dinner party format, were growing restless. Adrian stood behind Sarah and put his hands on her shoulders. Sarah tilted backwards, nuzzling the back of her head into his stomach. 'Ade,' she said, 'I've got something to talk to you about.'

'No,' put in Hilary, 'let me.' And she unfolded their plan.

'My God!' said Adrian, 'you women move fast. At the beginning of this evening I was married to a full-time mother; a couple of hours later she's a fully-fledged career woman. What'll it be next?'

Sarah said in an undertone, 'Ade, I want you to decide. I won't do it if you think it'll be bad for the children, or – or bad for … us.'

Adrian was taken aback by the note of seriousness in her voice. 'My gut reaction,' he replied, 'is that it could be very good for us. And what's good for us must be good for the children. But it's not for me to decide, Sal – it's for both of us. How about if we go out to dinner at the weekend and discuss it properly. Do you realise, we haven't been out together since we moved down here?'

Sarah nodded. 'If Nicky will babysit.'

'I'm sure she will, if she's got Henry to help her.'

Sarah picked up Adrian's hand and held it with both of hers. 'I want to say something,' she muttered, 'but I'm not sure what it is.'

With his free hand Adrian squeezed her shoulder. 'I don't mind what it is,' he said, 'as long as it's not "Sorry." '

Outside in the street, Pierre kept his arm round Claudia as they waited for an ordered minicab. Hilary and Joe, Elinor and Clicker, left the restaurant together. As they made their farewells, Pierre said to Clicker, 'We haven't actually been introduced. I'm Pierre Prescott. And you are –'

'Russell,' said Clicker. 'Thanks for the meal.'

Russell! Elinor decided to stick to Clicker. She put her arm through his.

'We're all going back to Kelly's place,' she said. 'You don't mind do you, Mum? It's the last day of term tomorrow, we can sleep –'

'Of course I don't mind, darling. Do you mind if Joe comes back with me?'

Elinor blushed. ''Sup to you,' she grunted, and with a grudging smile at Joe she said to him, 'Tell Mum she doesn't need to ask.'

Hilary stood and watched the cast and their acolytes as they meandered up Crown Street and turned into the High Street. The cool night air felt marvellous on her face after the heat and smoke of the bistro.

'Goodbye, partner,' she said, kissing Sarah. 'I'll ring you tomorrow, yes?'

She turned to Joe. 'I've got a confession to make.' She leaned against his broad bulk, sweaty beneath his corduroy shirt. 'I'm far too drunk to drive.'

Joe was temporarily carless; he had lent his to Matt and Spike for the Glastonbury festival.

'Minicab, then?'

'No, I fancy a walk.'

It didn't take long to leave the little town behind. They walked hand in hand, Hilary's long legs keeping pace easily with Joe's loose stride. They said almost nothing, listening to the sounds of the night. When they reached the little hollow just before the turn to Petts End cottage, a mother stoat rippled across the lane in front of them, her five young following in her wake.

Hilary clutched Joe's arm. 'The things we see!' she whispered. 'And look at that moon. Have you ever seen anything so beautiful?'

'At the risk of sounding unforgivably corny,' he said, 'I must admit I have seen something more beautiful, yes.' He stopped walking and pulled Hilary towards him.

Hilary giggled. 'If I wasn't so drunk, that would really make me cringe. As it is, I rather like it.'

They walked on. Joe cleared his throat. 'Is it my imagination,' he asked, 'or is the cause or just impediment, why these two persons et cetera, beginning to soften up a little?'

Hilary's voice was small and cautious. 'You could be right.'

'And are any other impediments about to loom up on the horizon?'

'I can't think of any.'

'So perhaps the old holy matrimony bit could go ahead some time. If that's all right with you, Ms Nightingale.'

'I don't know much about holiness,' said Hilary, 'and "matrimony" always reminds me of a sensible financial arrangement, for some reason. It sounds like stuffing money into a mattress. But if you'd really like to know, Joe, then yes, I'd love to marry you.'

Joe picked her up and whirled her round. 'When? I'm not putting you down until you say when. Commit, damn you, woman!'

'Put me down and I'll tell you. After Elinor's A-levels. I promise.'

'In a year's time then? A year from today?'

'How about "a year and a day"?' replied Hilary. 'Let's give ourselves a bit of a fairy tale ending. I'm just beginning to think we deserve it.'